Lynda La Plante was born in Liverpool. She trained for the stage at RADA and worked with the National Theatre and RSC before becoming a television actress. She then turned to writing and made her breakthrough with the phenomenally successful TV series *Widows*. She has written over thirty international novels, all of which have been bestsellers, and is the creator of the Anna Travis, Lorraine Page and *Trial and Retribution* series. Her original script for the much-acclaimed *Prime Suspect* won awards from BAFTA, Emmy, British Broadcasting and Royal Television Society, as well as the 1993 Edgar Allan Poe Award.

Lynda is one of only three screenwriters to have been made an honorary fellow of the British Film Institute and was awarded the BAFTA Dennis Potter Best Writer Award in 2000. In 2008, she was awarded a CBE in the Queen's Birthday Honours List for services to Literature, Drama and Charity.

✉Join the Lynda La Plante Readers' Club at
www.bit.ly/LyndaLaPlanteClub
www.lyndalaplante.com
🇫Facebook @LyndaLaPlanteCBE
🇹Twitter @LaPlanteLynda

VANISHED

Lynda La Plante

VANISHED

ZAFFRE

First published in the UK in 2022 by
ZAFFRE
An imprint of Bonnier Books UK
4th Floor, Victoria House, Bloomsbury Square, London, WC1B 4DA
Owned by Bonnier Books
Sveavägen 56, Stockholm, Sweden

A CIP catalogue record for this book is
available from the British Library.

Hardback ISBN: 978-1-83877-871-2
Trade paperback ISBN: 978-1-83877-874-3

Also available as an ebook and an audiobook

1 3 5 7 9 10 8 6 4 2

Typeset by IDSUK (Data Connection) Ltd
Printed and bound in Great Britain by Clays Ltd, Elcograf S.p.A.

Zaffre is an imprint of Bonnier Books UK
www.bonnierbooks.co.uk

Max, my faithful writing companion, you are greatly missed.
Hugo, a new companion and a new chapter begins.

CHAPTER 1

Avril Jenkins was in her early 70s, but, tucked beneath an old heavy duvet in her king-size four-poster bed, she could easily have been mistaken for a child. Avril's messy grey hair was piled up into a top-knot and held in place with a pink ribbon, then tucked beneath a hairnet. A frilly eye-mask finished her night-time look. She wasn't snoring, but she was breathing loudly as the air escaped through her slightly blocked nose.

The thin hairs on Avril's exposed arm suddenly stood on end, gently stirring in a new breeze – a window, or a door, had been opened. Avril lifted her eye-mask, held her breath and listened. Her eyes involuntarily flicked from left to right, as though it might help her to hear better.

The second she heard a landing floorboard creak, she flung back the duvet and sat bolt upright. Her toes landed in her fur-trimmed slippers. She bent quickly, put one finger behind each heel and pushed her feet home. As she stood, her hand slipped beneath her pillow and by the time she was upright she was armed with a fire poker.

Avril wore cream pyjama bottoms adorned with butterflies, and a pink vest top that was far too baggy for her old cleavage. Rather than being fearful, Avril was furious. She did not leave her bedroom with any degree of caution, rather she raced out, flicking on every light switch as she moved. She bolted along the landing towards a set of billowing curtains and slammed the sash window closed. For a second, Avril's head spun as she tried to visualise her evening routine of checking all the doors and windows. Had she missed this one? Truth was, she couldn't be certain of anything anymore. Floor-to-ceiling rosewood wall panels kept this landing dark, and even with the lights on, the heavy shadows taunted Avril's imagination with the prospect of her intruder being close . . .

. . . and then the distinctive noise from the sticky door handle linking the hallway to the kitchen told her that he was one floor below. Her left hand grabbed the balustrade whilst her right hand wheeled the poker above her head.

'Get out! Get out! Get out!' she screamed. 'I know it's you!'

Avril tackled the wide imposing staircase as quickly as she could, shouting all the way. Each deep step down made her old knees click with a sharp pain and, by the time she was in the hallway, her right arm had dropped to her side with the weight of the heavy poker. Avril's body could no longer keep up with her brave and fearless spirit, but at the bottom of the stairs, fuelled by rage, Avril summoned a second wind.

She headed along the hallway towards the kitchen, flicking every light switch on as she went. One of the switches lit a series of six antique brass picture lights which illuminated the extensive art collection adorning the hallway walls. Avril shuffled and shouted her way towards the kitchen door, which moved and creaked in the night wind from the open back door that the intruder must have used as their exit just seconds earlier.

As she burst into the kitchen, she could see the first twenty feet of back lawn lit by a semi-circle of light. Beyond that, the remaining five acres of land stretched out into the pitch-black night. By the time Avril reached the back door, she could hear someone running through dried leaves, which she knew were piled up against the east wall because she'd put them there earlier that day. Then she heard the scrabbling of feet on brickwork as he dragged himself up and over the ten-foot-high perimeter wall.

'I'm not scared of you, Adam! You hear! This is my bloody home. MINE!'

Avril scurried back into her kitchen, slammed the back door shut and slid the top and bottom bolts into place. She stood with her back to the heavy wooden door and panted until her breathing returned to normal. All the while she listened in case he had a mind to come back.

Avril moved towards the dining room, leaning heavily on the large island in the centre of the kitchen. She flicked the light on and glanced around to see if there was anything obviously missing. Her display crystal was where it should be, as was her Royal Crown Derby dinner set. Avril looked at the poker in her hand – her cold white knuckles were frozen in place and, as she slowly uncurled her arthritic fingers, her joints felt like they might snap. Now much calmer and certain that she was, once again, the only person in the house, she walked through to the living room, constantly looking and checking for what he'd stolen this time. He'd have taken something. He always did.

Avril opened the large, ornate globe that stood next to the fireplace, to reveal an extensive array of half-full bottles of spirits, wines and those drinks that only came out at Christmas, such as Advocaat, Baileys and Cinzano. As she poured herself a large brandy, Rossetti's Venus Verticordia looked down on her from above the white marble Georgian mantelpiece. It was only when she closed the lid of the globe that she noticed the space on the mantel where a silver-framed picture had once stood. Although her face gave away no trace of emotion, Avril's eyes filled with tears. A precious wedding photo was no longer where it should be. It wasn't the best picture of Avril and her late husband, Frederick, but it was her favourite. It captured one of those moments in time, in between the obligatory posing, when they had glanced into each other's eyes and laughed at how deliriously happy they were. It was an impromptu snapshot of pure, honest, soulful love. And Adam had taken it from her.

It was another twenty minutes before the solo police car arrived, driven by a weary young officer who had drawn the short straw. He diligently took Avril's statement and added it to the other thirteen which all claimed exactly the same thing: that Mrs Avril Jenkins' ex-lodger, Adam Border, was on a mission to slowly drive her insane. And when he finally got bored of doing that, Adam would put an end to her torment by murdering her in her own home.

* * *

Maggie looked at her reflection in the black screen of the monitor. Operating theatre 1 was so high-tech, Maggie thought it could probably fix Mr Thornton's heart all by itself. With its perfect, sterile steel lines, it looked like it had come from the imagination of a sci-fi writer. Four screens, two robot arms, numerous computers and seven people were about to come together to save the life of a 47-year-old man; it was a fabulous and terrifying feeling to be part of something so special. This was the first week of Maggie's surgical rotation, but she knew exactly what she was doing and so really had nothing to be nervous about – except for the fact that the lead surgeon was none other than the great Mr Elliot Wetlock. And he made her blush like a schoolgirl.

Wetlock's reputation preceded him, and the very mention of his name brought on palpitations in male medical staff as well as female. He wasn't a tall man, possibly the same height as her husband-to-be Jack, and he was slightly overweight, but he had a velvety voice and pale blue eyes framed by a perfect pattern of crow's feet. His beautiful eyes, above a black surgical face mask, was a vision made for a global pandemic! In fact, Maggie thought that he looked better in a face mask, because he also sported a rather outdated goatee, which was the only bit of his appearance that didn't make her go weak at the knees. She imagined that his 60-odd-year-old body probably left a lot to be desired, too, but it looked magnificent inside a grey waistcoat and a silk shirt with sleeves rolled up high until they were tight around his biceps.

The black monitor blinked into life, and the operating table in front of Maggie appeared on the screen. Soon, the screen would show Mr Thornton's chest cavity being penetrated by numerous needles and tubes, making him look like a cyborg. It never ceased to amaze Maggie what the human body could endure, and still keep going.

Mr Wetlock entered the operating theatre and the male scrub nurse behind Maggie audibly swallowed at the sight of him. 'Good morning, Mr Wetlock. It's an honour to be working alongside you. I'm grateful for the opportunity.' Maggie had been practising speaking out loud in his presence, so she didn't stutter, or run out of breath, or do that inexplicable thing of choking on her own spit. Maggie beamed with childlike pride at her ability to open a conversation with the greatest heart surgeon in London.

Wetlock, however, was not impressed. 'It's 1.30. Morning has been and gone.'

* * *

Surgery took seven hours. Wetlock didn't take a break, so neither did anybody else. By the time they were ready to scrub out, Maggie's pale blue scrubs were patterned with sweat patches around her neck, under her armpits, down her spine and, most embarrassingly, beneath one breast where the material had become trapped. Wetlock's scrubs, being dark blue, didn't look sweaty at all. He still looked angelic.

As they stripped off their PPE and binned it, Wetlock spoke to Maggie for the first time about something other than heart surgery. 'Your husband's a policeman, isn't he?'

Maggie hid her disappointment. She'd just done seven hours in an operating theatre, in the cardiac field, which was not her speciality, and she'd not put a foot wrong . . . and Wetlock was more interested in whether or not Jack was a policeman.

'Can I rely on your discretion, please, Maggie?'

Maggie's attitude shifted from offended to serious. Wetlock sounded troubled. He perched on the large windowsill of the scrub room, folded his arms and considered how to start. 'My daughter has potentially got herself into a little trouble. She's 17 and has her heart set on being a movie star. Not a television actress, you understand, an actual movie star.' Wetlock smiled and his perfect crow's feet appeared. 'There's been this talent scout on the scene for the past few months. He's promised her the world and, because she's so young, she believes he can deliver it.' Wetlock dropped his gaze and rubbed his forehead as he prepared himself to open up further. 'She has her own flat as well as a bedroom in my home. I'm a little closer to town, so she stays over sometimes.' When he looked up again, he had two new lines in between his eyes that Maggie had never noticed before which instantly made him look his age. 'I hardly see or hear from her anymore and, when our paths do cross, we don't speak. Not properly. I feel like I'm losing her. Bit by bit. And I'm concerned that I might be losing her to a man who hasn't got her best interests at heart.'

'If you know the man's name, I can ask Jack to check into him for you.'

As soon as Maggie had spoken, the two deep furrows vanished, and the crow's feet returned.

* * *

During her run home, Maggie felt a mixture of emotions. Wetlock had been embarrassed not to know the name of the so-called talent scout, so she would not only have to ask Jack to look into something that was currently not a crime, she'd also have to ask him to try and persuade Tania Wetlock to give up the name of a man she clearly cared for and trusted. But Maggie's overriding emotion was one of contentment at the last thing Wetlock had said to her before they parted company: 'Thank you, Maggie. I realise it's an imposition. And well done on your performance in theatre today. I'd like you to consider a six-month rotation onto my surgical team. Let me know by the end of the week.'

Maggie didn't need until the end of the week to decide – it would mean she would be learning from one of the most brilliant cardiac surgeons in the country. It was an easy 'yes'. But she decided to take at least three days to tell Wetlock that. As for persuading Jack to help her new mentor with his wayward daughter, Maggie was certain he'd say 'yes', too.

* * *

'No! Of course, no. What were you thinking?!' Jack wasn't angry. It was worse. He was laughing. 'Every time I log into HOLMES, it's recorded. So, it has to relate to something.' Jack quickly spoke again before Maggie could interrupt and argue her case. 'Something other than your boss not liking his daughter's new boyfriend. And why doesn't he know the bloke's name anyway? I'll make it my business to know everything about everyone Hannah meets.' Maggie tried to be indignant, but Jack was right. And when her look changed to self-pity, he knew exactly what she'd done. 'You've already said "yes", haven't you?'

Jack was in the middle of making a chicken curry with leftover meat from the Sunday roast. He'd thrown in a pack of sausages to bulk it out and was now at the stage of measuring the rice. He did this in silence. Maggie knew she'd annoyed him and so, whilst she waited for him to be ready to speak again, she opened the most expensive bottle of red wine they had, a San Martino Toscana.

As the rice began to simmer, Jack turned down the flame and refocussed on Maggie. 'How worried is he?'

'I think he's out of his depth. He's a single dad with a teenage girl. Imagine working the hours you do and having no one else to constantly reassure Hannah of how loved she is. I think their relationship is severely damaged and Mr Wetlock's only just seeing it. He's terrified he may have lost her already.'

'I could ask Laura to go and speak to . . . what's her name?' Maggie smiled in relief as she reminded Jack that Wetlock's daughter was called Tania. 'Laura used to work in Juvie and, way back, she also did a stint in Victim Support. It'll have to be logged as something, though, Mags. And of course, when Laura turns up to talk to Tania, she'll immediately know it's her dad who's sent us. There'll be domestic fallout for him.'

Maggie said she was sure it was a risk that Wetlock was willing to take, because the alternative was far worse: the thought that his daughter was being groomed by an older man.

Jack let out a long, heavy sigh. 'I'm dreading Hannah growing up.'

* * *

Jack stood by the overworked, knackered old coffee machine in the corner of the squad room, listening to it make a noise like someone dragging phlegm from the back of their throat. Then he watched it dribble out a flat white as he re-tuned his ears to Laura, who had finally started speaking again. She was on the phone to Wetlock and, for the past five minutes, had been silent apart from the odd 'mmm' and 'I see'.

'I can promise discretion for now, Mr Wetlock, but if it turns out that your daughter is in any danger, this will escalate beyond me . . . OK . . . yes, sir. You have a good day too.'

DS Laura Wade hung up the phone and looked at Jack, eyes wide, mouth open. 'He sounds gorgeous!' Jack handed his partner the flat white and broke the news that Wetlock was, in fact, short, fat and old. Laura grinned. 'Maggie tell you that, did she? I've got his home address. Today, he's expecting Tania to be there at five, 'cos at six she's having her hair bleached by a mobile hairdresser friend and she hates her small flat stinking of ammonia. She likes to look like Marilyn Monroe.' Laura rolled her eyes. 'The silly kid can't even know who Monroe is. Anyway, I'll get there for a quarter past six. Once she's got the bleach on her hair, she'll be going nowhere for a good forty-five minutes, so she'll have to speak to me, won't she?' Laura asked Jack what his afternoon looked like.

'I'm off to see an elderly lady who claims she's being threatened by her ex-lodger. Kingston nick has had fourteen reports in total, with insufficient evidence to support any of her claims. But she's just made an official complaint about them, so her case has come to us. They want it closed one way or the other.'

* * *

Jack parked outside the large wood-and-iron gates and pressed the buzzer which was set into the brickwork. Nothing happened. No noise sounded and no light came on. The thick wooden parts of the gate were embossed with studs which made the front of this property look like a prison. Even the main private road that the narrow lane to Mrs Jenkins' house veered off had a red-and-white striped barrier, clearly telling passers-by that this area was access only. Jack had had to flash his badge at the private security detail pacing the end of the street looking bored out of his wits.

Through a thin gap in between the heavy wooden gates, Jack could see a wide gravel driveway and a parallel flagstone footpath that cut through a substantial garden of at least two acres. The driveway curved round to the right, so the house itself was obscured from the roadside. After waiting for another minute, Jack pushed the wooden gate to see if it was even locked. It wasn't. He wondered if it had been left unlocked specifically for him because the buzzer didn't work.

The garden to either side of the flagstone footpath was overgrown and untamed, but somehow managed to look as though it was meant to be that way. Jack noted that the main gravel driveway looked like it had been battered by heavy vehicles with wide tyres – goods lorries? Grocery deliveries?

By the time Jack reached the house, the front door was open, and Avril was waiting for him. She wore a knee-length frilly dress with puff sleeves, white buckled shoes and white ankle socks with a double frill around the top. Her hair was in a high bun and adorned with a flowered scrunchy that matched the dress. She had her hands on her hips and, as she looked him up and down, Jack could tell that she was already disappointed. 'I know they told you I'm mad, but I'm not.' She sounded as gruff as a forty-a-day smoker. 'So, are you going to believe them or me?'

Jack walked up the three wide stone steps leading to Avril's front door. 'I thought I'd make up my own mind, Mrs Jenkins. How about you? Are you going to assume that my visit is nothing more than a placatory paperwork exercise, or do you want to tell me about Adam Border?'

The inside of Avril's house made the back of Jack's eyes hurt. There was so much information to take in, with an array of different patterns, textures, styles and colours. Avril led Jack through the house and out of the back door, into a sprawling wild garden contained by a crumbling, high brick wall.

'He knows my home is full of antiques and collectables, the best of which are slowly going missing. I made a list. You have it on file. He knows my routine, although he also follows me. You see, he's playing games and trying to scare me.' Avril picked up a pair of shears from an old wooden bench with broken slats and randomly snipped at something that looked like a white aster. Avril threw the daisy-like flowers into an already full wheelbarrow, then headed away from the house along a stepping-stone path and disappeared behind a row of fruit trees. 'Bring that, would you?' Jack grinned as he obediently followed with the wheelbarrow. He liked Avril already.

As Jack emerged out of the trees, the garden opened up again. To his left, still about twenty yards ahead of him, was an extensive greenhouse with filthy, cracked windows, some of which had been whitewashed on the inside. To the left of that was a solid wooden gate leading God-knows-where, and next to that was a sprawling compost heap which was where Avril waited for him. 'His intention isn't purely to rob me, you see, otherwise he'd bring a van and get it over with . . . it's to torment me. The biggest torment being that sometimes when he breaks in, he walks past a £5,000 painting, and steals a £5 ornament just because he knows it's full of sentiment. It makes me sound mad when I report that!'

'Avril . . .' Jack couldn't think of a subtle way to ask his next question. 'How secure is your property? I ask because . . .'

'I lock up! I have my routine and I stick to it.' Avril sounded like a petulant child. 'And, yes, I have changed the locks since he left. But maybe he can pick locks? How do burglars normally get into places?'

In the second it took Avril to inhale ready to continue her rant, Jack spoke. 'Why is Adam Border trying to scare you, Mrs Jenkins?' His polite, caring tone stopped her in her tracks. She breathed a heavy sigh and her body visibly relaxed. 'That's the first time anyone's asked me that. Everyone else said, "Why *would* he try to scare you?" not "Why *is* he?" Them at Kingston station may as well have called me a liar straight to my face.'

Avril paused to lop the head off a sunflower and throw it onto the compost heap. By the time she turned back to Jack, her façade of ballsy old woman had returned, and she set about taking her frustrations out on a bed of perfectly good plants at the base of an ornate pillar. By the time she'd finished, she'd chopped everything into pieces and was left with a big ugly hole in the ground. 'He's scaring me because I kicked him out. And I kicked him out because he was scaring me.'

Avril's large eyes suddenly locked with Jack's and he got the distinct impression that she was about to say something that meant his report would make her sound just as potty as the previous fourteen.

'I'm a single woman, DS Warr. I think Adam Border wants to destroy what he can't have. Have you heard of gerontophilia? It's when a younger man has a sexual preference for much older women.'

Jack quickly promised Avril that he'd find her list of stolen items, check out Adam Border and discuss home security with her on his next visit. He then left her with his card and retreated before she could accuse him of being sexually attracted to her too.

Back in the safety of his car, Jack read a grammatically perfect text message from DCI Simon Ridley:

Did Kingston station just waste an hour of your time? Or is Avril Jenkins the victim of a targeted terror campaign?

Jack didn't mention her theory about gerontophilia in his reply. Instead, he said that he'd start by doing his own background check on Adam Border and see where that took him.

* * *

Laura stood by the open window of Elliot Wetlock's living room, as the stench of peroxide was making her eyes water. Tania's hairdresser friend had left the room to give them privacy, with the promise of returning in exactly twenty-eight minutes, otherwise Tania's scalp would start to burn.

Tania was a beautiful seventeen-year-old who could easily have passed for mid-twenties, especially in her low-cut white dress. She was petite, very pale-skinned with stunning aqua-blue eyes, and she spoke with a Monroe-esque breathiness. She also had a beauty spot above and to the left of her upper lip, just like her idol. On the mantelpiece, pride of place, Elliot Wetlock had one framed photo of his daughter, aged about fifteen, and she looked like a different girl. Back then, she had a far more natural appeal, with long red hair, no beauty spot and a far healthier weight to her. Laura felt saddened by the fact that this lone photo seemed to represent a daughter long gone. There were no photos of this new version of Tania Wetlock, who was not a daughter to be proud of, it seemed.

Laura had been right to turn up during the bleaching phase of Tania's hair appointment, because if she'd been able to flounce out, slam the door and totter off down the road on her too-high heels, she certainly would have done. Not that talking was getting Laura very far at all. Tania used the word 'fuck' as a verb, adjective and noun whilst flatly refusing to betray the confidence of her beloved talent scout. 'I'm not stupid, Miss Police Lady. I tell you his name, and my dad pays you to scare him away. This is my life, and I can spend time with whoever the hell I like.' She was also convinced that with his help she was on her way to Hollywood. Laura didn't stay the full twenty-eight minutes. She stayed ten, leaving before she lost her temper.

Laura's handover to Jack had been littered with expletives, which he omitted when he reported back to Maggie that night at home. As he spoke, Jack loaded the dishwasher whilst, by his side, Maggie visually quality controlled his work and, when necessary, took a dish or a plate back out and rinsed it properly.

'There's no doubt Tania's vulnerable,' Jack clarified, 'but Laura doesn't think it's a police matter. A therapist matter, maybe.' Jack could see Maggie was disappointed. He knew that the last thing she'd want to do was go back to her new mentor with no solution to his problem. 'She's almost eighteen, Mags. We can't make her cooperate if she doesn't want to. And she doesn't appear to be a danger to herself or others, so any therapy would have to be voluntary. And it would have to be suggested by Wetlock. Not us.'

Maggie grabbed a bottle of red from the wine rack, plus three glasses.

'Please tell Laura I'm grateful.' She smiled. 'I think Mr Wetlock's attempted to persuade Tania into therapy already, but she was having none of it.' She stepped close to Jack and kissed him. 'Thank you for trying. Forget about them for tonight. We've got a wedding to arrange!' Jack raised one eyebrow. 'OK,' Maggie corrected. 'Me and your mum have got a wedding to arrange. You just nod in all the right places.'

CHAPTER 2

The following morning, Jack was in and at his desk by 7 a.m. Between lying awake thinking about the price tag of the wedding his mother, Penny, and his fiancée had in mind, and a bad patch in Hannah's teething, he'd had a fairly disturbed night. By 5 a.m., he'd given up trying to sleep and headed downstairs to make himself a cup of tea. As he looked out of the darkened kitchen window, all he could see was the tired reflection of himself . . . until the moment the security light reacted to movement by their small shed. As Jack watched the next-door neighbour's cat dig a hole in Penny's beautifully planted border, he thought about how frightened Avril Jenkins must be if she was actually telling the truth. His gut was still leaning towards it being a waste of time, but what if it wasn't?

Jack had called Kingston station on his way into work so, by the time he arrived, he'd been sent all fourteen of Avril's previous statements, together with the list of alleged stolen items: a twenty-four-piece set of hallmarked silver cutlery, a Rossetti painting, a fur coat, two statues, a set of silver napkin rings, a wedding photo, £500 and a double duvet cover with two matching pillowcases patterned with fairies. The Rossetti had captured the attention of Kingston police but, as it wasn't listed on the latest insurance document, they soon questioned its existence. And the two statues had subsequently been found in the dishwasher, lending further credence to the theory that Avril was nothing more than a confused old eccentric. But that theory was now making no sense to Jack.

Regardless of her eccentricities and awkward personality, all of her statements were consistent and included personal details that were strangely vivid if the incidents were figments of her imagination. Like the night her fairy duvet set went missing: this was the set she used to put on Adam Border's bed, and it was stored in the airing cupboard just outside the master bathroom. In her statement, she said she used to tuck the duvet cover and pillowcases behind the central heating pipes so that when she made his bed it was nice and warm. The duvet and pillows were not stolen along with the duvet set; they were left on the floor outside the airing cupboard. Which is exactly how the police found them when they arrived at four in the morning. Jack would admit Avril did seem like the sort of woman who lived with one foot in cloud-cuckoo-land, but she did not seem like the sort of woman who would go to the trouble of actually creating a crime scene.

The thing that troubled Jack the most was the same thing that Kingston was using against her: she'd reported fourteen break-ins, yet only eight items had been reported stolen. Kingston station had asserted that Avril was simply losing track of the lies she'd told, but Jack speculated that it could just as easily mean that the mysterious Adam Border was sometimes breaking in and taking nothing. So maybe his main aim was to frighten her, just as she claimed.

At 7.15 a.m., Ridley arrived with his morning coffee in a tall, reusable cup. 'Don't tell me . . .' Ridley could see the subject heading on the paperwork scattered across Jack's desk. 'You want to keep the case for a while longer because you've seen something that the whole of Kingston station has missed.' Ridley, not needing or wanting a reply, continued into his office. 'Do what you have to today, Jack. By end of play, I'd like you to either know for sure that Avril Jenkins is being stalked by her former lodger and get the case officially transferred, or sign it back to Kingston.'

Ridley had been uncharacteristically detached of late, in terms of how closely he monitored his team. Normally, he'd insist on knowing each case as well as the officer running it but, over the past couple of months, he'd shifted the bulk of the responsibility down a level. This brought him in line with how most divisional bosses worked, so he wasn't doing less than a normal DCI should; he was just doing less than *he* should. Ridley was no longer an anally retentive, micro-manager; he'd become ordinary.

Anik who, after three years as a detective constable, remained the baby of the squad not due to age but to attitude, presumed that only the love of a good woman could have distracted a man like Ridley from his job, which silently broke Laura's heart. 'The bags under his eyes . . . he's defo getting his end away,' Anik said. 'You'd think he'd finally have a smile on his miserable face as well, though.' Jack wanted Anik to be right. He was concerned that Ridley had decided to put in for retirement: he didn't know how old Ridley was but assumed that he must be close to having done his thirty-year stint on the force. Most officers worked till they secured their full pension, then called it a day. If Ridley was in love, Laura would lose. If Ridley was retiring, everyone would lose.

* * *

When Jack arrived at Avril Jenkins' home, the large wooden gates were already open, so he drove up the gravel driveway to the house and parked in front of the double garage. By the time he was out of the driver's seat, she was on the doorstep. His opening comment was to ask why the gates were open when she so clearly had an issue with security and this immediately got them off on the wrong foot.

'He doesn't drive up to the front door in broad daylight, DS Warr,' she said. 'He creeps in through the back garden in the dead of night like the monster he is.' She then sharply enquired why he'd come back. When Jack said that he'd come for the purchase prices and insurance documents connected to the stolen items, Avril's mood plummeted further and she barked at him about already having been accused of insurance fraud, so if that was his train of thought, he might as well get back into his car and eff off!

Jack assured Avril that he wasn't accusing her of anything and she stomped back into the house leaving the front door open, which Jack took as an invitation for him to follow.

In the drawing room-cum-office, Avril was rifling through an antique bureau, whilst muttering about the ineptitude of every police officer she'd ever met. 'The stolen items are secondary! He's *stalking* me. You *do* know that stalkers invariably escalate to murder, don't you? That'll no doubt make you happy. When I'm found dead in my bed.' Avril whipped round, with a scrap of paper in her outstretched hand. 'These are the only prices I can remember. And no, I don't have receipts. I'll try again to find the paperwork for the items listed on my insurance, but I'm not good with record-keeping.' Avril then turned back to the bureau and began searching again.

The handwritten list, headed 'The stolen property of Avril Jenkins', stated that the Rossetti painting was the most valuable item taken, at around the £2.2 million mark. And the duvet set was the least expensive, at £32.99. Jack asked if Adam Border would have been aware what the Rossetti was worth. 'I told him,' she said. 'He also knew that it wasn't the most expensive item in the house. He stole it because my dead husband bought it for me thirty years ago. I *told* you this already. He knows how to upset me.'

Avril slammed one drawer shut, forced out a long, whisky-scented sigh and opened up another drawer. In the second drawer, Jack could see several leaflets for the purchase and installation of burglar alarms and security lights. Avril saw him looking. 'I'm updating. Everything's old and temperamental.' A tiny smirk crept across Jack's face. 'Yes, yes,' she said, catching his expression. 'Just like me!'

He offered to help her choose the best security for her size of property and even supervise its installation by the end of the day, which immediately put her on the defensive again. 'I'm more than capable of choosing my own security, thank you. The gate was left open because I have a delivery coming, not because I'm stupid. The downstairs doors and windows are alarmed. And I have security lights outside. And to save you asking, yes, I *do* turn them off when the sodding spring fox cubs start bounding about on the lawn. It's like a bloody disco! Lights flashing on and off.'

'Mrs Jenkins?' Jack said with a sigh. 'I'd like you to imagine that we're starting again. So, please direct me to Adam's bedroom. Then, if you don't mind, I'd love a cup of tea.'

Adam Border's bedroom was at the very top of the house, little more than a white box containing a queen-sized bed and small wardrobe with matching chest of drawers. There were no pictures or personal documents, although a Dior jacket still hung in the wardrobe and a neatly folded Bolongaro Trevor jumper was in the bottom drawer. The way these pricey items had been left behind made Jack think that Avril was right to suggest money was not the primary reason for the numerous alleged thefts. On top of the wardrobe was a leather carry-on flight case and, on the handle, was an old luggage label.

As Jack jotted down the flight details, he could hear shouting from outside.

A bald man wearing a blue uniform and a paper face mask was standing with his hands in his pockets, looking despondently at his feet, whilst Avril rifled through the box of groceries on her front doorstep, shouting about broken celery stems, out-of-date avocados, and various missing items. 'You think old people will accept any old shit, well, we won't . . . what's this? A bloody replacement item that's nothing like the thing I ordered. Take it back. And the bruised fruit. I'll pay you when you come back with everything that's missing.' The bald man didn't bother to reply. Her outburst was clearly nothing new to him.

'Don't worry, mate,' Jack said. 'You can go.' The delivery man didn't need telling twice, quickly heading back to his van. Jack picked up the box of groceries and took it into Avril's kitchen before she could say anything to the contrary.

To Jack's surprise, on the kitchen island, a pot of tea was brewing beneath a knitted tea cosy, sitting next to two mismatched cups and saucers. He placed the box of groceries on the island and poured two cups of tea. The second Avril entered the kitchen, Jack started talking so that she couldn't have a go at him for sending the delivery man away. 'Tell me how you met Adam Border. I know he was your odd-job man, but where did you find him?'

Whilst she replied, Avril put her groceries away – even the items she claimed not to want. 'I heard about him from someone. Can't recall who. I started him in the garden, which he did a good enough job of, so I moved him inside the house, fixing door handles and doing bits of tiling. He came one day to fix an outside tap and, my God, he stank! I told him as much. He apologised and that's when he told me that for the past two weeks he'd been homeless and washing in the sink of the public toilet on the high street. So, I offered him the attic room.' Avril glanced at Jack, pre-empting what he was about to say. 'I'd known him long enough by then. I figure people quickly, DS Warr.' Avril sipped her tea to indicate that she had nothing more to say on the subject. Clearly, she had been very wrong about Adam Border.

* * *

Jack drove the thirty minutes from Avril Jenkins' house in Kingston to a potential wedding venue in Fulham. Maggie and Penny had whittled the list of possibilities down from around twenty to just three, so he was now being brought into the final part of the selection process. He had Laura on hands-free and she'd just told him that the details off the luggage tag belonged to a 10-year-old flight. British Airways couldn't tell her much, other than the destination was Colombia and the address of the person who booked it, which she'd just texted to him. Jack asked if she'd mind checking it out.

'When I get back, I'm probably going to request the Jenkins case is officially transferred from Kingston to us but, right now – and don't tell Ridley – I've really got to go and see this wedding venue. Mags and Mum have done everything so far. If I'm a no show, there'll both leave me!'

For a good ten seconds, Laura said nothing. For some reason, old feelings she once had for Jack were suddenly rekindled at the thought of Maggie actually leaving him. The feelings vanished just as quickly but, for a moment, Laura felt her skin heat and the hairs on her arms stand up, just as they used to each time Jack was close. When she did speak, she agreed to go and visit Adam Border's old address.

'Take Anik with you, Laura. Let's play it safe until we know who we're dealing with.'

Laura made a wry comment about being safer if she took Sheila from the canteen as backup, then put the phone down.

The venue in Fulham was a large pub with an extensive top floor, which could be hired out in part or in full. Location wise, it was perfectly situated in relation to the Chelsea Register Office. However, the manager, Mrs Kasabian, was really already getting on Jack's nerves, directing her entire pitch, mostly aimed at guiding them towards the five-course rather than the three-course menu, at Maggie. After half an hour of rehearsed waffle, she finally looked at Jack and said, 'I haven't forgotten you, Mr Warr. You're going to make the most important decision of all . . . to free bar or

not to free-bar? I know that's all you grooms care about!' To stop
Jack from walking out, Maggie quickly asked Mrs Kasabian to give
them ten minutes to explore on their own.

Maggie led Jack by the hand back through the rooms they could
be hiring. Finally, she sat down at one of the dining tables in order
to get a feel for the space.

'I like the place,' Jack said. 'I don't like her, but I like the venue.'
When Maggie asked if he thought it might be a bit small, he sat
down opposite her, and laid his hands on her thighs. 'We only need
three seats and a highchair, Mags.' As he watched the tears well up,
he knew that with nine perfect words, he'd convinced her that this
was the wedding venue for them.

* * *

Laura and Anik had parked one street away from Tetcott Street in
Chelsea and were now walking back towards the address connected
to the 10-year-old luggage label found on Adam Border's suitcase.

The beautiful four-storey terraced house was currently owned
by Mrs Flora Garner and, with no landline listed, they'd had no
option but to attend the property in person. Anik was dragging
his feet, whinging about being sent on an out-of-date wild goose
chase, whilst Laura, pleasantly immune to his usual moaning, was
fantasy house hunting.

Mrs Garner was an attractive forty-something with two teenage
sons, as evidenced by the gallery of professional-looking framed
family photos lining the hallway walls. There was also a man in
all of the pictures, who Anik quietly pointed out was definitely
punching above his weight. Mrs Garner explained that she'd
bought the property eighteen years ago from a lady called Hester
Mancroft who'd rented the top two floors out as student flats. On

moving in, they'd immediately converted the property back into one big family home. Mrs Garner remembered that Hester had joked about being able to buy the house after fleecing her husband in their divorce. She'd lived with her son, Julian, who had attended Harrow, but he'd turned out to be rather useless and certainly not the businessman Hester had hoped he would be. The name of Adam Border meant nothing to Mrs Garner at all.

*　*　*

Back at the station, Laura set about trying to trace Hester Mancroft, whilst Jack was at his desk contacting antique dealers to see if he could trace any of the alleged stolen items from Avril Jenkins' house. This rather arduous job had been attempted a couple of times before with no success because Avril hadn't noticed some of the thefts straightaway, didn't immediately report the ones she had noticed and had no photos of some items as they weren't insured.

Ridley was just about to step from his office and comment on how much time was being put into this probable non-case, when Jack got a phone call from Avril. Her voice was whispered and panicked. 'He's following me. Right now! I'm in Borough Market, the Green Market section. I have to keep moving or he'll catch me.' She sounded more and more out of breath with every word. 'Please come quickly, DS Warr. I'm not making it up!'

Ridley quickly drove with Jack to Borough Market, where they split up and entered through opposite entrances. They did a loop of the market, before meeting back by the drinking fountain just inside the Borough High Street entrance. Avril was nowhere to be found. After a second, more urgent loop of Green Market, they quickly moved into Borough Market Kitchen to see if Avril had been forced further afield. Jack was constantly calling Avril's mobile but there was no answer. They were getting worried. If this turned out to be the decisive moment when Avril's stalker upped the ante and actually made physical contact, the result could be life-threatening for her and the fallout would be disastrous for Ridley's team.

As they raced around Borough Market Kitchen down parallel aisles, it was Ridley who spotted Avril Jenkins first from Jack's description. She was perched on a stool outside Mei Mei's Singaporean Street Food stall. Within seconds, Jack was by his side.

'Take her home.' Ridley pushed the words out through gritted teeth. 'Sign the case back to Kingston. I don't want to hear the name Avril Jenkins in my station again.' Then he walked away. In their desperation to save her from potential harm, they'd both jumped into Ridley's car, meaning that Jack would have to take Avril home in a taxi, but that was a problem he thought it wise not to share with Ridley right now.

Jack walked slowly to Avril's side, hoping to have calmed his temper by the time he reached her. Avril gave him no more than a fleeting glance as she tucked into an ox cheek rendang curry. 'Too slow.' She spat rice as she spoke. 'You missed him.'

From the street, Jack watched Avril walk up her driveway, her huge home looming ahead of her. He couldn't tell whether she was deluded, ill, actually being stalked or, possibly, and worst of all, whether she was just a lonely old woman who wanted his attention.

* * *

In the garden next door, a man was up a tall ladder trimming his boundary hedge into a wave pattern. Jack introduced himself and the man returned the favour – Bernard Warton was a retired banker in his mid-seventies and was only too happy to tell Jack what a pain in the arse Avril Jenkins was. Noisy, rude and cantankerous were the words he kept coming back to. He said she complained about everything: his hedge was too high, so he trimmed it down only to be told that his trimmers were too noisy. His fountain was too noisy. His cherry blossom blew onto her gravel. His driveway wasn't weeded to her liking. His bird feeders attracted squirrels.

When asked, Mr Warton said that he did recall seeing a young man in Avril's garden, on and off, over the years. He knew the man was called Adam because they'd spoken on a couple of occasions. He was mid-thirties, pleasant, well-spoken and drove a silver Porsche. Once, he'd even given Mr Warton some petrol from Avril's shed, to refill his lawn mower – this had been their secret as both men feared Avril's wrath if she ever found out.

'I sometimes didn't see him for weeks, even months at a time. He could have come and gone, I suppose, or he could simply have been working in the rear garden or the west section over the other side. Her property's huge, as I'm sure you know. Often, I don't even see Avril for months! She can be quite the hermit. As time went by and the silver Porsche was a more regular sight driving up and down our private street, speculation then became rife about him becoming her toy boy! Her husband had passed a couple of years after I saw Adam for the first time, so no one was judging her: it had just been amusing gossip for a while.'

Mr Warton couldn't recall the last time he'd seen Adam, but several months ago the small section of Avril's front garden that he could see from his property had started to look neglected, so perhaps Adam had gone by then. 'I can only see ten or fifteen yards into the east side of her front garden, from mine. Her driveway is too far away for me to see who comes and goes, and her house is set too far back to be visible from my comparatively modest bungalow. There's a public footpath running between her and the golf course, round the back somewhere. I can't see that from my garden at all, so I couldn't tell you about any comings and goings there.'

Jack ended by enquiring whether Mr Warton had any CCTV.

'I've got a Ring doorbell. That any good to you?'

The two most interesting things Jack learnt from his chat with Mr Warton were that when her husband was alive Avril used to be charming. Her eccentricities came on slowly over the subsequent years. She turned into a woman who no longer cared how she behaved or cared what people thought of her. And the second was that no one had seen Adam Border, or his distinctive silver Porsche, for months. There was no physical evidence that Avril was being stalked at all – but there was evidence that she had declined, physically and mentally, since her husband died. Jack was coming to the same conclusions as Kingston station – that Avril was perhaps lonely, perhaps a fantasist, perhaps unwell. But probably not in danger. He thanked Mr Warton for his time and retraced his footsteps back towards Avril's house. Taking another look at the proximity of Warton's bungalow, Jack was certain that very little of Avril's property could be seen from his home. Neighbours in this street were so far apart, that they made for very bad witnesses.

As Jack headed back down the winding driveway towards the waiting taxi that had brought them from Borough Market, his mobile rang. He turned to see Avril standing on her doorstep, mobile in one hand and a red notebook in the other. 'Have you spoken to Adam's girlfriend?' Jack's weary sigh could be heard at the other end of the phone. 'Rude bitch. She used to call and, if I answered, she'd hang up. I dialled 1471 and got her number. Do you want it? I don't know her name, but she stole from me as well, so that's another crime for you to look into.'

Jack was considering how to reply when she added, 'Jewellery. She stole jewellery.' When Jack pointed out that there was no jewellery on the list of stolen items given to the police, Avril insisted that she wasn't sure exactly what had been taken, but something definitely had because her jewellery box wasn't as full as it used to be. Then she said, 'I'll make a pot.'

With no option but to follow this potential new lead, Jack reluctantly went and paid the taxi and walked back up the driveway.

CHAPTER 3

Avril Jenkins was growing on Jack. The couple of hours he spent with her was very revealing – not particularly in regard to the case, but certainly in regard to why she was this odd mix of old and young, past and present, strong and vulnerable.

He got the sense that Avril had willingly taken on quite a traditional role in the marriage which, after the death of her husband ten years ago, became redundant. She went from being 'looked after', to being solely responsible for an enormous property. She regressed, so as not to feel weighed down by the responsibility of adulthood. She hoarded, in order to keep hold of everything that made her feel safe, and she developed masculine traits, so as not to come across as a pushover to anyone who might be out to take advantage of an old widow. The result was this mishmash of contradictory characteristics, wrapped up in a woman who dressed like a child. But he could tell that at one time she must have been a very attractive and seductive woman.

* * *

Maggie listened as Jack described Avril, then quickly came to her own conclusions. 'She reminds me of that woman you went to see on the Isle of Wight that time. Less dominatrixy, but just as eccentric in her own way. It's a defence mechanism to be odd. Keeps people on their toes.' Jack loved talking to Maggie about the strange people he came across in his job. She had a wonderfully generous way of assessing a person's quirks and she understood that there was almost always a valid reason behind them.

'She's still a non-case,' Jack said, as he toiled over fixing a small toy fire engine that Hannah had become particularly attached to. It was a pull-back-and-go vehicle, but something had broken inside, so now it just reversed without the satisfaction of then whizzing off forwards. 'Sometimes, Mags, this job is one step forwards, two back. I mean, it wasn't that long ago I was in the Cotswolds chasing down a gang of international mercenaries. And today? Today I drank tea with a seventy-something-year-old woman dressed like a teenager, who's being stalked by the invisible man.'

Jack fell silent. Maggie could see that he had more to say, so she waited. Like a therapist waiting for their patient to reveal a deep-seated fear.

'I think Ridley might be retiring,' he said finally. Maggie was openly shocked. Not just because she genuinely liked Ridley, but because she knew how much Jack respected him. That mattered. Jack didn't respect people easily and her fear was that, without Ridley, Jack might regress to being the apathetic policeman he was when they first moved from Totnes to London. Jack pulled the toy fire engine back across the coffee table and let go. It didn't move. 'Fuck it,' Jack muttered and went to the kitchen to get two beers.

When he came back into the lounge, Maggie changed the subject. 'Mr Wetlock's daughter is taking drugs. He's very worried about—'

'You know what, Mags,' Jack interrupted. 'She's chosen a dodgy path because she's lacking something from him. Security, guidance, I don't know. But he's in the privileged position of being able to sort this himself. She's a young adult. A troubled one, sure, but still. He doesn't need the police to get her back onto the right path – *he* needs to do it.' Jack gulped at his beer and gathered his thoughts. 'I'm sorry. But it's not a police matter.' Jack leant forwards and kissed Maggie firmly on the lips. 'I love you. You know I'm not just being an arsehole, right?' The gentle kiss that Maggie returned, told Jack that she knew he was right. 'How's your wedding dress coming along?'

A childlike smile crept over Maggie's face. Her excitement was getting harder to contain as their wedding day got closer. Tomorrow evening, she was going to the home of the seamstress sister of Barbara – who worked in the hospital pharmacy – to do the first fitting. Penny was her wingman, the champagne was on ice, and Jack was babysitting.

'Maggie Warr.' Her words brimmed with pride. 'I'm going to be Maggie Warr.'

*　*　*

By eleven the next morning, Laura was sitting on a bench looking out across a long stretch of sandy beach, polishing off a large portion of fish and chips. She wiped her greasy fingers on her jeans, so that her mobile screen would respond to her touch, and called Jack, back in the squad room.

Her interview with Hester Mancroft had filled in some of the blanks from Adam's past – when he lodged with her and her son, Julian: Adam was an eighteen-year-old student at Chelsea Art College. He'd rented one of the rooms in her B&B for about six months but, once her business began to fail, she'd had to ask him to leave. Hester described Adam as a very handsome, clever and articulate young man. He and Julian were close friends and, although she wasn't certain, she thought they'd lived together for a short time in London.

'I asked her for Julian's contact details, but he died of a heroin OD five years ago. "Oops" moment or what!' Laura tucked her mobile between her ear and shoulder, so she could screw up her chip paper. 'He had a record for possession and supplying, but it wasn't big-time. Three prison sentences for distribution. Cocaine, cannabis and heroin. Last conviction was seven years ago, after which he travelled to the US to attend an elite drug rehab course. Then back to the UK, to pick up where he left off. Rented a few places, did a bit of sofa-surfing and was found dead in a disused warehouse in early 2017. Anyway, her description of Adam is the same as the neighbour's – he's a nice, normal man.'

Jack decided they were probably at a dead end. The elusive Adam Border remained elusive; but seeing as there was no evidence that he'd done anything wrong, they had no justification for continuing to try and track him down.

Whilst Jack had been liaising with Laura, he'd finished his final report, which concluded that the Avril Jenkins case should be referred back to Kingston as 'no further action'. 'I've got one more thing to do, and that's try a phone number, which I don't expect actually belongs to anyone. Then I'm going to sign this off. Cheers for your help, Laura.'

Jack dialled the phone number belonging to Adam Border's girl-friend. As expected, no one answered, and no answerphone service kicked in. Jack signed the back page of the report and Avril Jenkins was officially back to being the responsibility of Kingston.

'Hello?' The tiny voice on the other end of the phone made Jack stop dead. He formally introduced himself and asked the name of the person he was speaking to. 'Jessica Chi . . .' Her voice began to tremble. 'Have you found him? Have you found Adam?'

CHAPTER 4

Jessica, Jack learnt, was a model and wannabe actress, and she lived in a small flat off the King's Road. She'd not seen or heard from Adam in more than two months, regardless of the fact that she'd called his mobile daily. Jessica shared Adam's mobile number with Jack, along with numerous photos, which he then sent to Anik, asking him to run the information through every database he could.

Jack then asked Jessica if she knew Avril Jenkins.

'She's a freak. A sad, horrible snob of a woman, who's living in some sort of deluded time warp. She wanted Adam all to herself – and genuinely thought that he might want her. After he moved in, she started to get more aggressive with me – not physically, just words. Adam thought it was funny until she started accusing him of theft and – you'll never believe this – sexual impropriety! That's what she called it. But when a woman claims something like that, the police have to believe her, don't they? She scared Adam away with the threat of that.' Jessica began to sob. 'God, I hope that's all she did to him.'

Jessica now seemed to be insinuating that Avril was the aggressor, and Adam was the victim. Jack encouraged her to keep talking.

'Her husband died of a heart attack . . . supposedly. Don't trust her little-girl-lost routine. It's fake. Avril Jenkins is a hard, crafty old bitch, who thinks she can hide in that mansion of hers, protected by all the money her husband left behind. Avril plays the naive housewife card when you ask her about business, but she did his books. I know she did 'cos Adam told me.' The tears came again. 'Maybe he got to know too much, living under the same roof as her? Maybe . . .'

Jessica had brought to light two clear possibilities: either Adam had been scared away by the accusations of theft and sexual impropriety and decided to run, leaving his bereft girlfriend behind; or he'd been murdered by a pensioner and was buried in the overgrown mess of a garden he used to get paid to tend. Jack knew which one of those possibilities was more likely. But then, nothing about this case was straightforward. The main thing Jack couldn't get his head round was why a good-looking, well educated, Porsche-driving young man ended up being a gardener and odd-job man for a batty old eccentric in the first place. The relationship between Avril and Adam simply didn't make sense. Annoyingly, Jack was back to being intrigued.

Later that afternoon, Jack, Anik and Laura talked through everything they knew – which was a lot less than everything they didn't know. How and why had Adam gone completely off grid? This could be the trait of a man who didn't want to be found, so was there more to him than met the eye? Or had something happened to him, just as Jessica feared? On the other hand, if Avril had done something illegal, such as murdering her ex-lodger, why would she get the police involved by claiming he was stalking her?

'I've just got an email back from Avril's insurance company,' Laura said. 'Items of jewellery reported stolen . . . diamond stud earrings, gold necklace, an emerald and diamond ring, three silver bangles . . . total value, around the £40k mark. Reported stolen on a series of different dates between, let's see . . . three and seven months ago.' Laura frowned. 'So Adam and Jessica were randomly nicking off the old girl?'

Anik piped up. 'My guess is that he's a chancer. He wheedled his way in, thinking he'd con the old girl out of some stuff, but met his match. He'll be playing the gigolo with someone else now. And the stalking's all in her head. The neighbours say so. Even you and the boss say so.'

'OK . . .' The reluctance in Jack's voice was clear. 'Check Chelsea College about Adam's next of kin, then we'll call it a day. Laura, the paperwork's on my desk, already signed off. But don't give it to Ridley till tomorrow morning. I want to mull everything over one final time this evening.'

As Jack headed home for his pre-arranged babysitting duties, something deep in his gut was telling him that this wasn't finished.

* * *

The moment Jack stepped through the door, Maggie and Penny rushed past him, giving him a kiss on the cheek and an assurance that Hannah was sleeping soundly upstairs as they hurried off to their appointment.

In the centre of the kitchen table was an open bottle of Malbec and a white paper bag which Jack knew from years of experience would contain two random cakes from the hospital canteen. Their home bakes were phenomenal, and Jack loved them all.

In the microwave was a bowl of chilli on a bed of cooked rice. Jack set it to reheat and poured himself a glass of wine.

He then slumped onto the sofa. He opened the nursery camera app on his mobile, propped it against the wine bottle, put his feet up on the coffee table and tucked into his chilli whilst scrolling through Netflix. Hannah had started sleeping through, but Jack still liked to watch her when he was babysitting alone. The first time, he had the sound on the app turned up high so that, through the distorted static, he could hear her breathing. If she skipped a breath, or sighed, or coughed, he'd race upstairs and watch her from the bedroom door until he was satisfied that there was nothing wrong. He was calmer about it now – but still liked to keep her in sight.

At half past ten, the doorbell rang. Jack opened the door and was stunned to see a young Marilyn Monroe lookalike, wearing a skin-tight dress, and carrying a bottle of champagne. She swayed on her stilettos and had to cling on to the wall just to stay upright. From Laura's description, Jack guessed this had to be Tania Wetlock. But why the hell was she on his doorstep? He didn't want to let her in, but she was clearly drunk and therefore vulnerable, so he didn't want to leave her outside either. As soon as she stepped through the front door, giggling and waving the champagne bottle in the air, Jack could see her pinpoint pupils – not only was she pissed, she was also as high as a kite.

'I want to speak with . . . Maggie.' She was hard to understand because, as well as slurring, she was also pouting and doing an exaggerated Monroe impression. Jack was trying to imagine a scenario in which Maggie would have told Tania where she lived. He eventually asked her outright. 'Daddy has the CV of everyone on his team.' Tania shook her head and tutted playfully. 'I think Maggie's been playing detective.'

Jack told Tania that Maggie was out, but she wasn't deterred. She stumbled uninvited into the lounge, kicked off her shoes and, with both legs tucked beneath her tiny body, she made herself comfort-able on the sofa. 'Call the police if you like. I'm not leaving until I speak to her.'

Tania held the bottle of champagne out to Jack with a flirtatious look, but with her smudged make-up and pupils the size of a grain of rice, she just looked like a vulnerable little girl. Jack picked up his mobile and called Maggie. Her phone wasn't even on, so he was sent straight to voicemail.

Tania waggled the champagne bottle at Jack, but he wasn't playing. 'I am the police. And you're 17.'

A wry smile crept across her enhanced red lips, and she faintly breathed the amended words to a familiar tune. '. . . going on 18.'

Jack said that he was going to call her a taxi. She asked his name and he saw no reason not to tell her. 'I'm seconds from stardom, Jack. It's just around the corner. But if Daddy Dearest continues to cause trouble, I could lose it all.' She pouted. 'I'm going all the way. As the great lady once said, "A wise girl knows her limits, a smart girl knows she has none."'

Tania untucked her leg, reached out her perfectly manicured red toes and touched the inside of Jack's thigh. He wasn't expecting it and he instinctively jumped back. 'Oh, don't be scared, Mr Policeman.' She slowly and seductively looked him up and down. 'I was just thinking, maybe you could put Daddy back in his box for me? So that I can follow my destiny and be a star. Is that too much for a girl to ask?'

Tania spotted Jack's glass of wine on the coffee table. She leapt up, snatched the glass and scooted around the other side of the sofa, out of his reach. Then she kept the sofa between them as she polished off the contents.

'Who's making you a star, Tania?' Jack hated being a man in the company of such a volatile, yet vulnerable young girl. But with his policeman's head on, he also knew that this could be the perfect time to question her about the currently nameless talent scout. He forced himself to smile. 'Whoever he is, he's doing a great job.'

'We're not ready to go public yet,' she whispered, putting a finger to her lips. Tania started to move back around the sofa. 'Will you help me, Jack? I can be very grateful . . . if you'd like me to be.' Tania put her hands on her thighs and slid them upwards, taking her skin-tight dress with them. Jack gently grabbed her wrists and moved them away from her legs before she exposed her underwear. Jessica Chi's words came back to him, about the police always having to listen to a woman who claimed 'sexual impropriety' against a man – here was Tania, with a face and figure that would sexually arouse any red-blooded male, offering herself to him. Fortunately for Tania, Jack was not only a decent man, he was also a father. And all he saw when he looked at her was a child.

'Don't you want me, Jack?' Tears welled quickly in Tania's eyes. 'Am I ugly?'

'You're beautiful, Tania. But I don't like this version of you. And I don't think you do either.' As Jack's words hit a nerve, she began to struggle. Jack didn't want to hold on to her wrists, but she was pulling away so hard that he feared if he let go, she'd fall. He steered her towards the sofa and dropped her onto the cushions. Tania curled up into a ball and started sobbing.

In her small black leather shoulder bag, Jack found a provisional driving licence with her home address. He ordered an Uber to come and collect her, then perched on the coffee table. 'Tania, I'll help you with your dad, if you tell me about the man who's promising you the world.'

When Tania spoke, the Marilyn Monroe impression had gone, and her natural upper crust accent had taken over. 'He takes care of me. He loves me.' Tania struggled to sit up. Her hair was a mess, her make-up was smudged, and her tear-streaked cheeks and neck were blotchy.

But just as it seemed she was about to open up, Tania vanished, and Marilyn Monroe returned. She leapt up, collecting her shoes and the bottle of champagne. 'I make mistakes . . .' the breathy, whispered voice was back, 'but if you can't handle me at my worst, then you sure as hell don't deserve me at my best.'

Tania moved to the front door, taking small, careful steps, so she could dial and walk at the same time. 'Where am I? I need to tell my lift where I am.' Jack reminded her there was an Uber on the way, which was already paid for. Tania struggled to open the front door, dropping her shoes, then the champagne. Jack handed her champagne bottle back to her then helped her get out into the street where, thankfully, the Uber was already parked up waiting. As Tania climbed into the front of the car, Jack caught part of what she said before she slammed the passenger door shut. 'I didn't think he was going to let me out . . .' Jack got a long, disgusted look from the driver as he turned the car round and drove off .

Jack sat on the sofa, poured himself a fresh glass of wine, and waited for Maggie and Penny to come home. It was 11 p.m. when they finally staggered in, so excited about the wedding dress fitting that he chose not to mention his visit from Tania Wetlock. Penny went straight to bed, but Maggie was in the mood for talking.

*　　*　　*

When Jack next glanced at the time on his mobile, it was 2 a.m.

At 7 a.m., Jack woke on the sofa beneath a blanket. Maggie was now sitting in the armchair, swiping through her mobile, checking out novelty ideas for homemade wedding favours. She'd covered him up around 2.30 a.m. and gone to bed. Jack sat up, massaging his stiff neck. Maggie smiled across at him. 'Whose red lipstick is on your wine glass?'

Maggie sat on the closed toilet seat listening to Jack rant about bloody Tania Wetlock as he showered for work. 'She came on to me, I'll tell you that up front. If I'd been a shitter person, I could have done anything I wanted.'

'I am sorry, Jack. I'll talk to him again.'

'She needs help. But that's on her dad's shoulders, Mags, not mine. And not yours. If I had the name and address of her talent scout, I could check him out, but until then . . .' Jack let out a heavy sigh. He dropped his head, closed his eyes and let the water cascade through his hair and down his face. 'You should have seen the look the Uber guy gave me.'

Maggie stepped into the shower and wrapped her arms around him. 'I'll tell Mr Wetlock that you've done all you can.'

Jack looked thoughtful and slightly sulky. 'Is he really short and fat?'

Maggie laughed, putting her hands around his waist and kissing him whilst confirming that Wetlock could look like Gerard Butler, and she still wouldn't notice him.

'Gerard Butler! Really?' Jack laughed. 'Should I grow a beard? Would you like that?' Their playfulness soon turned to spontaneous passion, and they made quick, intense love in the shower before both having to race to work.

* * *

Jack expected to be last in but, in fact, Ridley crept in five minutes behind him, fuelling Anik's immature speculation that he'd got himself a sexually demanding girlfriend. Ridley, with his mobile to his ear, didn't acknowledge anyone, heading straight to his office as he listened intently to whoever was on the other end of the phone. Whoever it was, they were putting him in a visibly bad mood.

Eventually, he stepped back out of his office looking very serious, even for him. 'In the early hours of this morning, Mr Bernard Warton, the next-door neighbour of Avril Jenkins, was woken by the sound of breaking glass. He saw smoke coming from her back garden, so called the fire brigade. The greenhouse and its contents were pretty much gone by the time they arrived. The fire service immediately put on face masks to protect themselves from the toxic fumes coming from the hundreds of cannabis plants that had been growing inside.'

Laura and Anik, open-mouthed, turned to Jack in stunned slow motion. He'd been to her house twice! How the hell didn't he know she was growing enough weed to supply the whole of Kingston? Anik brought his hand to his mouth in a half-hearted attempt to hide his giggling – he was going to enjoy making sure this monumental cock-up followed Jack around for years.

Ridley continued. 'A gas canister exploded, injuring one fire officer, but they eventually made the area safe. The sub officer called Kingston nick to check the house for occupants. In the en suite to the master bedroom, they found the body of Avril Jenkins. It wasn't pretty.'

In that moment, all eyes turned to Anik as he desperately tried to rewind the last twenty seconds of his life. Ridley dropped the Jenkins file into the bin. 'Needless to say, the Avril Jenkins case stays with us.'

CHAPTER 5

The remains of the burnt-out greenhouse were taped off by an inner cordon which started around eight feet away from the blackened brickwork. Just inside this cordon, two men in blue boiler suits and face masks were exploring every inch of the scorched garden whilst waiting to be told by the fire brigade's sub officer that it was safe to step inside the greenhouse walls, where a knee-deep mess of rubble, ash and water awaited them. On the back of their boiler suits was DRUG SQUAD in white lettering.

Jack and Anik stood just outside the inner cordon, wearing white paper suits and face masks complete with carbon filters and air vents to protect them from the stagnant air, still heavy with the smell of cannabis. The outer perimeter for this particular crime scene was further out than normal as an extra precaution, and the immediate neighbours had been temporarily evacuated.

A familiar voice came from behind Jack. 'It's a pro set-up.' Mal Kaminski's Polish accent immediately told Jack that this case was in good hands. Malomir had come to the Met less than a year ago. He'd learnt fast and quickly surpassed other, far more experienced members of his team. He was now invaluable in trying to keep a lid on the various London drugs gangs. As well as being the world's self-proclaimed expert in inappropriate Polish sayings, he was also an encyclopaedia of drug-growing and local dealing knowledge. 'Drainage, water pumps, heating lamps, infrareds; all top of the range. Looks like most of it was concealed in the glass apex under tarpaulins. This was done with care. Not like the temporary units we see in the lofts of gang houses: they're makeshift, so they can be torn down, moved or disposed of in minutes. This was set up like a permanent business premises.'

Jack asked Mal to confirm the size of this cannabis farm. 'We found the remains of approximately four hundred plants in pots, some pots stacked ready for the next crop, and some boxes already packed for distribution.'

For the life of him, Jack couldn't imagine that Avril Jenkins was the mastermind behind such a huge drugs haul.

To Jack's left, a paper-suited CSI was taking a footprint cast from the soil beneath the back garden wall, and another was taking fingerprints from the handle of Avril Jenkins' wheelbarrow, which had been propped up against the brickwork, handles upwards, in a position that suggested it had been used as a ladder. Jack gave a heavy sigh, making the vents in his mask click as they allowed his excess breath to escape. Jack toyed with the idea of whispering quietly to the CSI, but the truth was that good gossip shot round the station like a dose of the clap so, instead he decided to own his mistake – loud and proud.

'That will have my prints on it.' Anik, the CSI and Mal all looked at Jack, waiting for clarification. 'I moved the wheelbarrow when I was here interviewing Avril Jenkins.'

'You interviewed the victim in this garden?' Mal asked in a neu-tral tone, containing his amusement as best he could. 'Next to a greenhouse containing four hundred cannabis plants?'

'Seems that way.' Jack quickly turned and headed for the house. He could hear their muffled sniggers as he walked away.

At the open back door, Jack added protective shoe covers to his outfit before entering. He could tell by the CSI's evidence markers where they'd been and where they were heading – their meticulous, inch-by-inch route through the crime scene was carefully plotted to collect and preserve as much evidence as possible from the most likely path taken by the killer or killers. Jack stood still, assessing the area, before moving carefully forwards. He didn't want to disturb or contaminate anything. The CSI taking prints from all the internal door handles, nodded him towards the stairs.

On the first floor, Jack paused sharply outside the master bedroom and Anik almost walked into the back of him. With reluctant steps, Jack moved inside the bedroom and paused again. To their right, the en suite was curtained off by plastic sheeting and, beyond that, paper-suited bodies milled around. Jack could just make out the body on the floor, framed in a pool of red. Anik looked impatient to get to the heart of the investigation, but Jack was in no rush to see Avril again. He told Anik to go ahead if he really wanted to.

The luxurious master bedroom was as eye-wateringly fussy, cluttered and eclectic as the rest of the house. The four-poster bed was made of solid oak and adorned with heavy embroidered drapes, like something from the 1700s. The carpet was deep blue and so thick that it twisted beneath Jack's weight. The wall-to-wall, floor-to-ceiling wardrobe was modern, with mirrored sliding doors; but the rest of the bedroom furniture was antique or at least looked as though it was. The walls were scattered with artwork, from Lowry to Erte – although Jack had no idea if they were real or copies – and right in the middle of all that culture was a seventy-five-inch flatscreen TV. The bedside table was stacked high with modern design and décor magazines. Inside was a cut-glass whisky decanter and tumbler, a calculator, a landline phone and an intercom for the gate buzzer that he doubted even worked.

Jack slid open one of the large, mirrored wardrobe doors to reveal a vast collection of elegant clothes, expensive-looking shoes and furs. On a high shelf inside the wardrobe, were several wigs displayed on polystyrene heads.

Jack took his time to absorb everything. Whilst he was getting inside Avril's complex mind, Anik had rushed to get to the monstrous spectacle that they knew was waiting beyond the makeshift plastic doorway into the bathroom. This was the main differences between the two of them: patience. Patience brought detail, which brought knowledge, which brought clarity. Anik would never learn to see clearly because he either moved too fast or didn't move at all, depending on how excited a case made him feel.

Jack left the master bedroom and headed upstairs to the attic room which he knew once belonged to Adam Border. It was now even more sparse than the last time he'd seen it: the coat, jumper and suitcase had all gone, which was disturbing. Had Adam come back or had Avril thrown it all away? And if Adam had come back, was he their killer? Jack closed his eyes and recalled Avril's prophetic words from their previous meeting. '*You* do *know that stalkers invariably escalate to murder, don't you?'*

Jack couldn't put it off any longer. He walked back downstairs and re-entered the master bedroom.

Anik now stood by the open sash window, trying to hold in his breakfast as he inhaled the heady mix of corpse secretions from indoors and cannabis smoke from outdoors. His greying skin was speckled with goosebumps from the cold and he was already deeply regretting his eagerness to see the murder scene. Jack gave him a nod, meaning, 'You do what you need to. I've got this,' and Anik grabbed the opportunity to scurry downstairs and put a decent distance between himself and the house.

Jack made his presence known to the paper-suited bodies assessing the crime scene behind the plastic sheeting, and all but one of them made way for him to enter. The CSI who remained by Jack's side was Angelica Blenkinsopp; a woman with the most inappropriate given name Jack could imagine. Angel was from Northumberland, with a thick North-East accent and a sick sense of humour.

The blood pool on the floor had spread swiftly across the white-and-grey chequered tiles, until it had congealed, leaving little room for manoeuvre as Jack entered the en suite.

Avril Jenkins was not in one piece. As Angel described what she believed had happened, Jack pulled up his paper hood and secured his face mask, swallowing repeatedly to counteract the natural over-salivation that comes just before being sick. But it wasn't the gruesomeness of what he was seeing that made him nauseous, it was the failure he felt in the pit of his stomach as he looked down at the naked body of the murdered woman who had insisted she was being stalked and who had asked Jack for help.

Angel got straight to the point. 'Let's start with the good news, ay Jacky. She died quick. One massive blow to the top of the skull killed her outright.' Angel looked directly at the poker in the corner of the en suite. 'It's the right width and weight to have caused the wound, but I'll confirm back at base, of course. The blood up the walls and on the ceiling is cast-off from swinging the weapon back and forth. Whoever was wielding it carried on hitting her around the head and face ten, twelve times at least.' Angel looked at Jack's eyes, which watered slightly. 'Step out if you like. I'll wait.'

'I don't need to step out, thanks, Angel. I knew her, that's all.'

'Right you are. So, they kill her – I say *they* speculatively for now, although I can't see one person doing all this – then dismember her body. Exsanguination, as you can see, occurred where she fell. Never use white grout on floor tiles – I can't even get the stain of cat shit out of my white grout, so there'll be no saving these.'

Angel went on to explain that, during dismemberment, they used the joints as natural points of weakness. Her lower legs and one lower arm were in the bathtub, and her head was partly severed but still in place. Just. The rest of Avril was on the en suite floor.

'Your killer or killers would have been covered in her blood, and I mean head to toe.'

Jack looked around the en suite. There were blood-soaked towels piled high at the non-tap end of the bathtub and a red watery stain ran from them to the plughole. Blood smears covered the walls and bath rim, where a vain attempt to clean up had been made. The CSI team would be here for days.

'How did they get out?' Jack asked. 'I didn't see any blood on the way up here. So, how did they get out through the house and leave no trace of what happened in here?'

Angel tapped Jack on the shoulder. 'Well, Jacky, I'd wear one of these paper suits. Take it off before you leave the room, pop it into a plastic bag and Bob's your auntie, £4.99 on Amazon.'

Anik was in the front garden, away from the stench of the greenhouse and the sight of the en suite slaughterhouse. He was instructing a couple of uniformed PCs to round up all CCTV from the area, including the one belonging to Mr Warton next door. Through the large bay window of the front drawing room, Anik could now see Jack rifling through the drawers of an oversized antique bureau.

Jack was looking for the red notebook he'd seen Avril with on the day she gave him Jessica Chi's phone number. The scrappy list of stolen items she'd given him was written on a page torn from a notebook of that size, so Jack suspected that it was Avril's go-to place for all of the things she wanted to remember. Perhaps she'd written something important in it. Jack moved from the drawing room, into the lounge, picking up Anik on his way through the hall. 'She had a notebook. A5. Red. Help me look for it.' In the lounge, Anik searched one side of the room and Jack searched the other.

Anik pulled his mask down and tucked it under his chin. 'CSI have moved up into Adam Border's old bedroom, till the green-house is safe for them to go into. And the body can be removed whenever.' Jack was just about to have a go at him by pointing out that 'the body' was a person with a name, then quickly thought better of it. Every murder victim sometimes gets referred to as 'the body'. Jack knew he only found it disrespectful today because of his own feelings of guilt.

Jack opened an ottoman that doubled as a footstool. Inside there were more brochures for various security systems. Again, Jack's guilt rushed to the surface: he should have helped Avril choose the best system and he should have insisted that she get it installed right away. Why the hell hadn't he? But Jack knew why: it was because he'd pre-judged her as an eccentric who was probably exaggerating or even lying. And because she was annoying, he'd just wanted to get out of her house.

Every drawer Jack searched was crammed with old receipts, mainly for food shopping or from the garden centre. From a cursory flick through, Jack could see that they supported the timeline suggested by the neighbour, Mr Warton: during the time Adam Border worked as Avril's gardener, there was an abundance of garden centre purchases, but these stopped when he moved out. Also, her grocery receipts showed the moment she went from shopping for two people to shopping for one. Everything Jack found was rubbish that most people wouldn't bother keeping; there was nothing remotely important, such as a passport, birth certificate or bank documents.

There was a knock on the open lounge door. 'Give us another half hour . . .' the sub officer had sweat streaks down his face from wearing his tight mask, 'then the greenhouse is all yours. There's no chance of the fire reigniting now, but we have to remove the remaining glass, 'cos that's all at risk of falling. Your Drug Squad boys are eager to get inside too.'

Jack continued to search inside the house and Anik opted to search outside.

From one of the grocery purchases, where Avril had used contactless payment, Jack noticed that she'd mistakenly been given the merchant's receipt which had her entire bank card details on it, rather than the customer copy which only displays the final four digits. He made a short call back to the squad room and set Morgan the task of trying to gain access to Avril's finances. Jack was intrigued to know just how much money she'd been left by her husband. If she was loaded, as Jessica Chi suggested, then why was she taking the monumental risk of growing cannabis? Especially on such a large scale.

DC Morgan still spent his days sitting in the corner of the room, defying medical science. He injected insulin twice daily, ate enough calories to keep an elephant alive and existed on a blood glucose level of 25 millimoles per litre. He generally moved at the speed of a snail but give him a computer-based task and he was a blur. Morgan said that he'd get the correct permissions to dig into Avril's bank accounts and get back to Jack as soon as he was in.

Jack moved methodically from room to room, searching for . . . he didn't know what.

Avril's kitchen was surprisingly new and high-tech, something he hadn't really noticed on his previous visit, and her food tastes were as eclectic as her décor. She had herbs and spices he'd never heard of and ingredients he'd never tried and equipment he couldn't work out the purpose of. He found himself smiling . . . Avril could be obnoxious, but at least she was an interesting woman.

Jack wasn't expecting Ridley to attend the crime scene until the preliminary investigation had been done, especially not in light of his recent shift towards arm's-length supervision, so it was a surprise when he appeared. 'Raeburn wants me on the ground with this one. PR and marcomms have painted a worst-case scenario, and she wants to deliver something to the press before they invent their own headlines about police incompetence.'

Ridley and Jack walked together through the overgrown front garden. 'Raeburn's only concern is that we've done everything right up until this point. But I know that she's also thinking that dismemberment could mean gangs.' Jack shared his opinion that it was highly unlikely to be gang related. Ridley wasn't reassured. 'So, she's a bloody drug-dealing pensioner who's run rings round all of us then, is she?' Ridley couldn't hide the concern in his voice. 'Or maybe she's a frightened old woman who's consistently cried "stalker" in fourteen official police statements, all of which we filed and did nothing about? Which one of those horrific options should I tell Raeburn to give to the press?' Ridley sat down heavily on a low wall.

'She was scared.' Jack plucked a leaf from the tree above their heads and picked it apart as he spoke. 'We didn't know if it was real or imagined, but—'

'I'd say we know now,' Ridley interrupted.

'Yes, sir, we do. But whilst figuring it out, Laura, Anik and I did everything right. We took the piss a bit behind closed doors, and we got frustrated with Avril for being an awkward and confusing person to deal with, but procedurally acted correctly. We followed every lead, considered every possibility. We just didn't do it fast enough.' Jack thought Ridley looked troubled and tired and, God forbid, he also looked apathetic. Ridley eventually broke his silence, instantly proving Jack's assumptions wrong.

'Sounds like she was crying out for help, in her own annoying way. So, probably not gangs. Right . . .' Ridley paused for a moment to order his thoughts. 'Jack, you stay here and work with Mal. I want you to be the one to process the greenhouse. Anik can come back to the station with me. I'll get him and Laura to carry on tracing Adam Border. And I'm going to speak with Arnold Hutchinson, Avril's family lawyer. He's acted as liaison between her and some of the jewellers after she started reporting stuff going missing. One or two refused to deal with her directly, so he stepped in. Arnold knew her late husband too. I'll see what light he might be able to shed on things.' Ridley put his hands on his knees and pushed himself to his feet. He looked old. If he did have a new woman in his life, she was either wearing him out or dragging him down. Jack was now more certain than ever that Ridley was heading for retirement.

Jack had finally been allowed into the greenhouse around 4 p.m. and, since then, had been sifting through the debris with Mal. They'd been told that they had to confine themselves to the front half of the greenhouse, due to most of the debris falling towards the back. This had not yet been checked by CSI and it was their hope that whoever installed the vents, heaters and filter system might have left usable prints behind on items currently buried.

Mal had asked CSI to bag several stacks of plant pots which had melted together in groups of twelve. His hope was that one of them might have a branded label or barcode on the bottom which, due to being stacked, might have been protected from the flames. The rest of the greenhouse was an unsalvageable mess in terms of evidence. Mal confirmed that the plants themselves gave them nothing unique to go on. 'There's a metal shell from one of the heat lamps with forensics which could have prints, and I've written down the serial number. The water pump had a serial number too. You can get all of this stuff online or from garden centres but, once we know the shop, we might get lucky with CCTV.' Jack asked Mal to keep in close contact as their separate investigations progressed. 'I'll call you every day, Jack, even if it's just to say that there's nothing to say. This looks like gangs to me, but you have doubts?'

A voice came from the back door. 'Sir, she's coming out.' Jack acknowledged the uniformed officer with a wave before returning his attention to Mal.

'No, I get it, Mal. The volume of drugs says gangs. And callous dismemberment says gangs. But the victim . . . where does she fit in? How does someone like Avril Jenkins get involved with gangs?'

Jack thanked Mal for his usual meticulous attention to detail and walked round the outside of the property to the front driveway where the black mortuary van was parked close to overhanging bushes, away from prying eyes. A trolley with a black body bag on it bumped down the three steps which led from the front door. Angel followed it out. Once outside, she removed her face mask.

'I did a walk through, Jack, and you're right about there being no visible blood drops anywhere else in the property. I think your killer or killers must have worn paper suits.' Angel headed for her car. 'Right, I'm knackered. I'm going before you ask me to do anything else. We processed the attic room like you asked – results from everything will start filtering through from tomorrow afternoon. Send me a priority running order if you've got one, otherwise I'll start with the en suite and work my way out. 'Night, pet.'

Jack walked slowly down the driveway, surveying the vast, multi-faceted crime scene. Above a lowest part of the partitioning hedge, Bernard Warton was watching vehicles leaving. He looked deeply shocked and made no attempt to hold back the tears. 'Find whoever did this, won't you, Detective Warr? I know I said some horrible things about Avril, and I'm not going to be a hypocrite by taking any of them back, but I don't think she did any harm.' Warton managed a crooked smile, even though his lower lip was trembling. 'She kept me on my toes. I don't know what I'm going to do without her.'

'I'll find who did this, Mr Warton. And when I do, I'll knock on your door. Then me and you can have a drink to Avril Jenkins.' Warton nodded in tearful agreement, then disappeared below his immaculate hedge.

Jack looked back and watched the mortuary van doors slam shut. Avril had been her own worst enemy by being so challenging, defensive and untrusting. But she'd not always been like that. Mr Warton had known a better woman than the one Jack met. That was the woman Warton cried for now. And that was the woman Jack would get justice for.

CHAPTER 6

Arnold Hutchinson was a man in his early 70s, wearing a three-piece pinstriped suit and with a mane of grey hair that might not have been his own.

A smartly dressed young lady entered his large, opulent office with a tray of tea. 'That's May. She'll be my boss before I know it. Very smart girl, but serious as hell.' Arnold stirred the pot. 'I can't believe Avril's been murdered, DCI Ridley. I mean, why would anyone do such a thing? I've looked after their legal, business and financial matters for going on forty years. When her husband Frederick died she inherited everything. In truth, that house has been beyond her means for the best part of a decade. It's mortgaged to the hilt. Freddie had some high- and low-risk investments, but the Iceland Bank crash lost him a great deal of money. Lost some of his clients' money too. Clients can hold grudges if the losses are big enough. Maybe one of them . . .?'

'I don't think it's likely . . .' Ridley said. He couldn't imagine vengeful investors resorting to the dismemberment of a spouse, ten years after the husband had died. 'But we'll not dismiss anything without checking into it.'

Arnold shook his head. 'I can't believe she's gone. She was an extraordinary lady. Didn't suffer fools – and why should she? But she was always charming to me. After Freddie died, she became very careful with money. The house cost her far more than she got in, so she sold a few paintings to keep the wolf from the door. She'd have been ripped off, no doubt, but she was a proud woman who struggled with asking for help, regardless of it being freely offered.'

'Did you know Adam Border?' Ridley could tell by the blank expression on Arnold's face that the name didn't even ring the vaguest of bells. 'He was her gardener and odd-job man.'

Arnold explained that he never saw Avril at the house, she always came to his office, so he hadn't met any workmen. When Ridley asked if Avril and Frederick Jenkins had any family, Arnold mentioned that Freddie had a brother in California, who lived with his partner. Other than that, it was his understanding that there was no extended family on either side. Arnold became more disturbed when Ridley asked about the cannabis in the greenhouse.

'You're bloody joking! Drugs? Well, she didn't know they were there, I can tell you that much. Where was the greenhouse? Miles away from the house, I bet.' Arnold took a moment to calm himself. 'She can't have known, DCI Ridley. She was eccentric in recent years, but she was good. Fundamentally good.'

Ridley reminded Arnold that he had only just finished explaining how Avril had been known to sell the odd painting to – in his words – 'keep the wolf from the door'.

'I did say that, yes . . . which is exactly why I don't believe she'd need to sell drugs for financial reasons.'

Arnold confirmed that he'd last seen Avril ten months ago. They'd spent the hour exchanging pleasantries and drinking tea, just as they always did. The only business they discussed was why her utility bill was so high when she'd not changed her habits. They'd concluded that it was a mistake and she'd left saying that she'd call the utility company with an accurate meter reading. Arnold couldn't seem to get his head round the idea that he'd never see Avril again.

'After Freddie died, it felt like my duty to look after Avril for him. She didn't make it easy, but I called her monthly. Not that she always answered. Each time I spoke with her, I asked if she was OK and if there was anything she needed. She always said she was fine. I'm so sorry if I let her down. I tried my best.'

* * *

By 8 p.m., Jack was alone inside Avril's property. Outside, two uniformed officers stood on sentry duty by the front gates, whilst others were still doing door-to-door around the neighbouring houses, and one SOCO van was still parked on the driveway.

Jack had explored every room in the house and was about ready to call it a day, when he noticed the double garage. He'd parked outside it on his second visit, but he now wondered if it had been searched yet.

Jack stood on his tiptoes and peered in through the filthy window. He tried to clean away the grime with his coat sleeve, but it was as much on the inside as the outside. He could, however, make out two vehicles under tarpaulins – one large, one smaller. As he was still wearing his protective paper suit, Jack pulled on a fresh pair of nitrile gloves and turned the unlocked Yale. Jack pulled at the wooden door which dug into the gravel where it had dropped over the years, but not too deeply for it to open.

Jack lifted the edge of the nearest tarp to reveal the bumper of a black Range Rover. Then he lifted the smaller tarp and Jack's skin went cold. The smaller vehicle was a silver Porsche. As he looked at the long, sleek headlight poking out from beneath the tarp, Jack could hear the stick he was going to get if this turned out to be the same silver Porsche that allegedly belonged to the elusive Adam Border. Not only did he not spot a greenhouse full of cannabis when he was standing virtually right next to it, but he'd also parked next to a garage containing a car that was currently being tracked by half the Met!

Jack leant heavily against the cobwebbed wall. If Adam Border had been stalking Avril Jenkins and escaping into the night before anyone set eyes on him, he'd either been doing it on foot or he'd had another vehicle. And in the even more unlikely event that Avril Jenkins was a drug dealer, she'd been expertly hiding all of the evidence such as transactions, suppliers, distributors and earnings.

'You, OK?' Jack looked up to see Laura standing just outside the garage. 'Fuck me, is that the missing Porsche?' Laura couldn't help but laugh. Jack pushed the wooden door back through the gravel, closed the garage and told one of the uniformed officers to ask CSI to make it a priority.

Laura offered to take Jack for a pint before they headed home, but he was too distracted to hear her. 'There's got to be a safe. You wouldn't expect to find proof of illegal earnings from drug sales in plain sight, but there's no normal paperwork either. No passport, no driving licence – assuming the Range Rover is hers – no bank statements, utility bills, nothing.' Laura patiently listened. Jack often did this, voicing all of his thoughts out loud to make sure they sounded feasible. All he wanted her to do was listen and challenge him when he said something that didn't stand up to scrutiny. 'Someone cleared the attic room, Laura. There was a jacket, a jumper and a suitcase. All gone.'

'How do you know Avril didn't get rid of them?'

'I don't. But they'd been there for months, so why would she suddenly decide to get rid of them in the last few days?' Laura added the thought that if Adam had finally returned for his clothes and suitcase, why not collect his car at the same time? Jack had no answers.

'OK, Jack, look, CSI will process the cars and garage tonight. Tomorrow, we'll come back and go through the whole place again to see if we can find a safe. But right now, come to the pub. We can talk more stuff through if you need to, or we can just chill. But don't stay here.'

Jack thanked Laura for being his level-headed sounding board. Then he declined her offer of the pub and headed home to be with Maggie.

CHAPTER 7

The streetlight outside Jack's bedroom window part lit Maggie through a thin crack in the curtains as she reached behind her back to fasten her bra.

Jack watched her every move from beneath the duvet.

Next he looked at the bedside clock, sitting next to a newly brewed cup of tea. Half past six. He sat up and sipped his tea.

'I took an early shift.' Maggie whispered her explanation so as not to wake Hannah. 'Your mum's looking after Hannah till one. I should be home by then.' Now dressed, she turned to Jack as she pulled her hair up into a ponytail. 'We need to do something really special for her birthday, Jack. Your mum's a live-in nanny, cleaner, cook, agony aunt. I don't know what we'd do if she wasn't here.'

'She's always wanted to deliver a lamb.' The memory had come from nowhere. Jack suddenly recalled how, during summer months in Totnes, he and Penny would walk to the shops past fields of newly born lambs, tottering on their new legs. It was her fantasy to be responsible for that much joy. Before she left, Maggie suggested that perhaps some nice smellies, posh gin and a party might be easier to arrange.

* * *

Jack got himself a coffee as the squad room filled, and everyone settled at their desks. Ridley began by relaying the information he'd learnt from Arnold Hutchinson. Then he got down to business. 'Why haven't we found Adam Border?' The room erupted with the sound of feet shuffling, throat clearing and deep sighing as everyone looked around in the hope that someone else had an answer.

'That's not a rhetorical question. All we know about him is that he was her handyman and lived in her spare room. Avril swore blind that he was her stalker, but none of her neighbours have seen him in months. His girlfriend thought he'd moved on, but his car is in Avril's garage. And now Avril's dead. Is he her killer, or is he potentially another victim and we should be looking for someone entirely different? Again, not rhetorical. And who the bloody hell is responsible for the ton of cannabis in her greenhouse?'

Jack thought it was unhelpful of Ridley to ask questions that he knew were currently impossible to answer, so he tried to change the subject. 'Laura and I are looking into the possibility of a hidden safe at the property, sir. My feelings is that—'

'Laura's going to interview Jessica Chi.'

Ridley never interrupted! He considered it to be disrespectful and, as a do-as-you-would-be-done-by sort of man, interrupting Jack now was very out of character. Jack stared at Ridley as he continued, nodding to Laura. 'Get a recent photograph of Adam Border from Jessica and learn everything you can about him. Anik, the cars?'

Anik told him that both cars found in Avril's garage were registered to her. 'I'm expecting her phone records in by 10 a.m. Nothing came from the door-to-door, sir. None of her neighbours can see Avril's property from theirs, 'cos of the high wall and overgrown hedges. And none of them ever really attempted to be friendly with her 'cos it was never reciprocated. Oh, and I've tracked her brother-in-law, Terence Jenkins, in California. I'll call him as soon as I can to inform him of her death.'

Ridley asked the room in general if any forensic reports had come in.

'Prints are still being processed, sir.' Laura was jotting down contact details for Jessica Chi as she spoke. 'But due to the lack of blood or unexplained DNA anywhere else in the house, Angel thinks that Avril was either taken into the bathroom to be murdered or was already in there when she was attacked. They found no bloodstained clothes or night clothes, so whatever she was wearing before the murder could have been removed. Foxy's doing the post-mortem this morning.'

'Fine. I'll catch up with Foxy later. You all know what you're doing?'

The room started to move, which Ridley took to mean 'yes'. He headed for his office and shut the door.

As he opened his desktop computer to go through Avril's phone records, Anik shared his latest theory around Ridley's mood swings: his new lover had dumped him.

Laura and Jack exchanged a look. 'Have a word, eh, Jack? He listens to you.'

Jack knocked on Ridley's office door and entered without being invited. Ridley answered a call on his mobile, listening intently for a good thirty seconds. Then his eyes flicked to Jack. 'Jack's on his way to the property now. You want to meet him there? Of course. Full disclosure.' Ridley hung up. Jack had entered the office to ask if Ridley was OK, but, in truth, he was relieved that something else had come up. 'That was Mal. Behind the greenhouse there were stacks of partly burnt packing crates, probably used to distribute the cannabis plants. Forensics found traces of a second drug. fentanyl.'

Jack frowned as he acknowledged the seriousness of what Ridley was saying. Jack knew that fentanyl was used as a post-operative pain medication, because Maggie had mentioned it in their numerous evening chats. He also knew that being fifty to one hundred times more potent than morphine, it was a lethal street drug.

'Mal will meet you at the property. He wants to know everything you know about Avril Jenkins. Voluntarily or not, she was into something far bigger than we realised.'

* * *

On his way to Kingston, Jack called Arnold Hutchinson and asked if he was aware of a safe at the Jenkins' property. 'How big are you thinking, DS Warr?' Jack realised that he'd not thought about size at all. 'I have other clients in properties like Avril's who have walk-in safes. The metal door is frequently hidden by a discreet wood-panel door, so it looks like another room when closed. I'm not aware of Freddie or Avril commissioning anything like that. Nor a wall safe if that's more what you're thinking. Not that they'd have had to tell me of, course. I do know that some of the big safes, or ones that require structural changes, often need planning permission, though.'

Arnold's speculation was enough for Jack to put in a call to Kingston Council, eventually getting through to the building application manager, who promised to check into safes of any size being requested by either Frederick or Avril Jenkins at any point during their ownership of 27 Woodridge Place.

* * *

As Jack pulled into Avril's garden through the open gates, he was met by a large white trailer with no windows and one centre door at the top of two shallow steps. From his car, Jack could see two members of the Drug Squad sitting inside the trailer drinking coffee

He got out and asked where he could find Mal.

Jack walked round the outside of Avril's house towards the greenhouse, when his mobile rang. Kevin, the building application manager. 'In answer to your initial enquiry, I'm now authorised to tell you that I have no record of either Frederick or Avril Jenkins requesting planning permission for a safe room inside the property.' Jack was about to thank him and end the call when he added, 'However, Mrs Jenkins did go on to make numerous applications throughout 2017 for external changes. A brick building towards the rear of the property to be used for the storage of garden equipment, namely a ride-on mower. And a second, similar structure beyond the garage. There's extensive paperwork, including design plans, connected to each application if you'd like copies sent out—'

'Kevin, you've been a great help, thank you. Are the design plans and paperwork digital? . . . Good, please email them to me straight away. Thank you again.'

Jack was suddenly eager to find and explore the recently added outbuilding.

'Jack!' Mal stood outside the burnt-out greenhouse. 'I take it Ridley told you what we found?'

'Fentanyl. Nasty stuff. Fill me in, Mal.' Jack's mobile pinged as an email from Kevin appeared in his inbox. 'I'm checking out some building plans . . . but I'm listening. Go on.'

'Pure fentanyl is one of our biggest problems right now. It's relatively cheap to make, so suppliers mix it with poor quality heroin and cocaine to boost their profits. It gives a huge bang for your buck, the flipside of that being that it's lethal in the wrong hands. Low level street dealers don't know what they're buying, some even go on to cut it again with counterfeit oxycodone and Xanax, so by the time it gets to the user, it's poison. Which is why we've brought in our secret weapon.'

Jack glanced up from his mobile where he'd been double tapping the blueprints of the new outbuildings and expanding them so he could see every detail. 'What secret weapon?'

In the kitchen, a large man in a blue Drug Squad boiler suit that fitted snugly on his muscular frame and a blue woollen beanie hat leant over the table picking through several evidence bags from around the greenhouse. A fancy-looking blue hearing aid sat behind his right ear attached to a thin wire disappearing beneath his hat, suggesting that he had a cochlear implant. As Jack and Mal entered the kitchen, the large man turned and Mal introduced him as Josh Logan, a DEA officer on loan from New York who, for several months, had been doing the rounds with numerous UK drug squads. He had years of experience studying how gangs moved drugs across the States, similar to the UK's county lines problem. Josh was originally from Alabama and spoke with a deep accent. Jack smiled as they shook hands: he knew that Laura would fall in love with his voice the second she heard it.

Jack asked if Josh knew where this fentanyl had come from and where it might be heading. Josh took the sugar bowl from the kitchen worktop and spilled a tiny amount onto the table. He separated three grains from the pile. 'That amount'll kill ya. Mal's boys only found traces, so we don't know how much we're dealing with yet. What I can tell you is that it's pure – so my guess is that it's come from Germany or China. And those guys don't move small amounts. As for where it's heading, some will continue on to another country, and some will end up on your streets.'

Jack nodded sombrely. 'I've just received blueprints for two outbuildings we may not have found yet. One near the greenhouse, I think, and a second behind the garage.'

Mal told him they'd already opened the one behind the greenhouse, which contained gardening equipment and old garden furniture. It was by no means conspicuous or easy to access through the undergrowth, which made him suspicious about its real purpose. Why make storage so inaccessible? Or had the garden naturally just taken over and hidden the building from sight?

The outbuilding a hundred yards behind the greenhouse was a square-brick, flat-roofed structure with no windows, which didn't look unlike an old coal store. And, just as Mal said, it was filled with discarded tools and junk such as broken garden furniture. The

mower was parked to the side of the building. Jack got an odd feeling from the space: the broken furniture and messily stored tools
just didn't feel like something that Avril would allow. And why
was the mower parked outside when this building was specifically
built for it? It was pointlessly chaotic. In fact, it felt staged. Jack
stepped into the centre of the eight-foot-square space. He thought
for a moment then stamped his foot down. The sound told him
that what he was stamping on was not concrete.

The men cleared out the building and, beneath a tool bench on
wheels, they found a trap door held shut by a chain and padlock.
Josh grabbed a pair of bolt cutters from the tool bench and with
one gargantuan effort, he cut the chain.

* * *

Beneath the outbuilding was an unlit space. Jack took out his
mobile, flicked on the torch and looked down into the darkness.
He could see that the floor below seemed to be clear of obstacles,
so he dropped down. Within a few seconds of searching, Jack had
found a pull cord and turned on the light, then he re-appeared
beneath the trapdoor.

'We've got shelves full of gas canisters, heaters, strip lights, hose
pipes; basically, loads of replacement kit for the cannabis farm in
the greenhouse.'

'Your dead old lady's got an impressive outfit in her backyard,
Jack.' Josh seemed excited by their find. 'She doesn't happen to
have a mixing lab down there, does she?'

'No.' Jack looked up at their expectant faces. 'But she does have
a second outbuilding.'

The outbuilding behind the garage, which was exactly the same
in structure as the one near the greenhouse, was so well hidden

in the treeline that it hadn't yet been searched by the police or by SOCO. Josh, who had brought the bolt cutters with him, broke the padlock off the external door. Inside were more tools and broken garden furniture, and it was now clear that all of this junk had been purposefully collected to make each outbuilding look like a perfectly normal household junk space. Sure enough, beneath a broken picnic table was another trap door complete with chain and padlock. Josh cut the chain and Jack dropped into the darkness. This time, when the light came on, Josh took one peek into the concealed room and immediately knew what he was looking at.

'Don't breathe. Don't touch anything.' Josh dangled a vented mask down to Jack and shouted an urgent instruction: 'Mask on, Jack. I'm coming down.' Josh took a second vented mask from his pocket and jumped down by Jack's side.

There were two trestle tables covered in plastic sheeting running the length of two of the walls. Beneath the sheeting were Bunsen burners, plastic bags, bowls, wooden spoons, masks, gloves ... everything needed to mix pretty much any drug with any other drug. And against a third wall was a floor-to-ceiling shelf stocked high with fentanyl. Josh laughed from beneath his mask as his excitement and anticipation rose.

'Holy moley. We're looking at a street value of three, maybe four million. This is one smart operation, Jack. I've seen labs and stores before, but this ... this is a careful set-up. This could have been down here for years, mixing and manufacturing streets drugs and, from the surface, you'd never know.' Josh put his hands on his hips. 'Well, Jack, looks like we're partners from here on in, 'cos murder and drugs go hand in hand. You know, I've seen some sights back home, but this is the first time I've seen such a pro set-up hidden beneath a suburban backyard, owned by a dismembered pensioner. How very English!'

CHAPTER 8

Although the two outbuildings and their contents were hugely significant, Jack was still looking for a safe which was, he assumed, where Avril Jenkins kept all of her personal information, because it sure as hell wasn't anywhere in her house or in the wine cellar. He decided to do one final sweep of the entire property, looking behind every picture frame and tapping on every wall, looking for a false panel. But there was nothing.

He was feeling despondent when Laura called.

She'd been to visit Jessica Chi again, as Ridley had instructed. She wasn't home, but her live-in landlady, Mrs Ashton, had told her that Jessica had only recently moved in and always paid the rent in cash. Mrs Ashton rarely saw Jessica, who seemed to be a very quiet, private girl who didn't have many friends. Mrs Ashton had gone on to describe the only person who had visited Jessica in the past week: 'A shortish man. Fit-looking, quite young, with black hair and black eyes with thick eyebrows.' She said he looked like a 'wrong'un'.

Jack was indignant. 'What does she mean, "shortish"?'

'Oh, *that's* the bit that upsets you!' Laura giggled down the phone. 'Not the fact that she called you a wrong'un?'

'Listen, Laura, could you or Anik try to find something – anything – on Avril Jenkins? There's nothing here. No passport, no birth certificate, nothing. She was a married woman who ran a business and a house. There has to be paperwork.'

Laura said that she'd task Anik with the job, because she'd been told to get back to tracking Adam Border. 'Ridley's got a meeting with Steve Lewis, Mal's boss, seeing as this is a joint op now. Who's this Josh guy, by the way?'

'Josh Logan. He was working with the Manchester Drug Squad, but now we've found fentanyl he's going to work with us for a while. It's already rife in the States, so he's helping us to get ahead of it in the UK.' As he spoke, Jack made his way out into the back garden. Laura asked if Josh was fit. Jack hung up on her.

As he watched Mal lead the methodical search inside the greenhouse, Jack felt frustrated. Every case had moments where the pace slowed right down, whilst another team picked up the baton and ran with it for a while. But this murder case had only just started, and Jack felt like he was treading water whilst watching the Drug Squad have first-dibs. He decided to go to the Drug Squad van to make himself a hot drink.

Jack was sipping an extra-strong cup of coffee when Josh asked if he could join him. 'So, Jack, how do you think our cases connect?'

'In all honesty, I feel like I know less now than I did when I first met Avril Jenkins,' Jack said wearily.

Josh's deep laugh resonated around the inside of the van.

'She's the piece that doesn't fit, right enough. It's common for gangs to target houses like this for their secluded, private grounds. And they normally target vulnerable people on their own. Maybe she truly had no idea what was going on in her own backyard. I've seen it happen. And you can't see any outbuildings from the house. Maybe she discovered what was going on and became a problem they had to get rid of?'

'Dismemberment's overkill, don't you think?'

'And slow. Maybe they're not connected at all. Maybe your killer has nothing to do with our drugs.' Josh got up and filled the kettle to make himself a cup of tea. 'You want a refill?' Jack drained his mug and handed it to Josh. 'You know what confuses me, Jack? No professional security. I mean, yes, there's an old guy in a hut at the end of the main street only letting residents through. And the grounds are secluded. But, once you're in, there's nothing. Close to three million in drugs, street value, stashed beneath a lawn . . . and not even a security light or camera. I don't know, Jack; some of this says professional, some of it says amateur.' Josh beamed a huge smile. 'Intriguing, right!'

As Jack headed back inside the house, his attention was drawn to the keypad used for opening the gate – the gate that he knew wasn't locked on his first visit and wasn't even closed on his second visit. This keypad had numerous, unmarked buttons on its display, and Jack noted down the maker's name before continuing through into the kitchen.

From there, he looked out of the window and watched Josh walk beyond the trees, back towards the greenhouse. Jack followed. As he walked through the extensive garden, taking the same route as he'd done on his first visit, his mind floated back to following Avril with the wheelbarrow.

The hole she'd made when she was manically dead-heading was now filled in, but nothing had yet been planted in the space. Jack snatched a pair of gardening gloves from a wall and knelt down.

Mal was feeling his age as he continually bent down and stood upright throughout the process of meticulously sifting through the contents of the greenhouse. Now he stood, pushed his fists into the small of his back and clenched his shoulder blades together to cope with the sharp pain in his lower spine. Once the pain had passed, he relaxed his entire upper body in relief, looked out across the garden, and saw Jack kneeling in the soil, digging a hole with his hands.

Josh's heavy tan work boots stepped into Jack's eyeline, together with a second set of black boots which Jack instinctively knew must belong to Mal. Mal knew Jack well enough to simply wait for the explanation to present itself, and Josh followed Mal's lead.

Sure enough, Jack's hands soon hit something harder than soil. He found the edges of the object and lifted out a plastic bag. Jack had no inkling of what to expect inside the bag, but he certainly didn't expect to find items of jewellery. Jack stared at the gold and diamond treasures in his muddy gloves. Josh spoke first: 'Do you still know less than you did in the beginning, Jack? Or does that hoard shine any light on anything?'

'I think this is the jewellery that Avril Jenkins claimed was stolen by Jessica Chi.' Jack sat on his heels, confused and frustrated. Mal asked why she would pretend to be the victim of theft and stalking. 'The only thing she gained was police attention,' Jack said. 'I think she was scared. But right now I have no idea what else is true and what's a lie.'

*　　*　　*

Ridley, Steve Lewis and Superintendent Maxine Raeburn sat in Ridley's office going over everything that each of their teams could bring to the table at this early stage of the investigation – and Steve was doing all of the talking. The Drug Squad had so much evidence to work with that they'd drafted in extra officers in order to work round the clock. Ridley was not best pleased. He had to beg for extra officers and even then rarely got them.

Steve Lewis was the same rank as Ridley but whenever he worked in tandem with a second team, he invariably took the lead. The problem with that was that Steve had tunnel vision: he didn't care about Ridley's case or whether Ridley got a result. The last time their paths had crossed, Ridley had taken Steve to one side and asked him to be more of a team player, and in response, Steve had had Ridley removed from the investigation, resulting in the only complaint against him in his otherwise blemish-free file.

Right now, Ridley's day was about as bad as it could get. He hated to admit just how little his team knew. They knew Avril Jenkins' name but nothing much else; they knew where Adam Border had come from, but not where he'd gone; they'd managed to lose track of a key witness, Jessica Chi; and, worst of all, the only two things they *had* found, a drugs farm and a missing silver Porsche, had both been sitting right under the nose of Ridley's 'best man' for nearly a week.

As Raeburn silently listened, she too was visibly frustrated. At some stage, she'd have to justify why Kingston had to all intents and purposes ignored a woman who was now in four pieces in her mortuary. And why Ridley's team couldn't get a foothold in the subsequent murder investigation.

Ridley stood up from behind his desk and moved to his office window, where he looked out across the city. 'Arnold Hutchinson shared with me that Terence Jenkins, the brother-in-law in California, is the main beneficiary of Avril Jenkins' will. He's coming over as soon as he can get a flight. We'll see what his input brings.'

Raeburn was watching Ridley carefully as he talked, noticing how his shoulders hung down and his back was bent. She brought the meeting to an end, thanked Steve for attending and said that she wanted daily updates.

Once Steve had gone, Raeburn's expression turned stern. 'Good God, Simon, snap out of it. You've not gone yet.' Ridley turned and perched on his windowsill. 'You don't have to tell your team, of course, but perhaps you should. Put them out of their misery and stop all of the speculation.'

Ridley shook his head. 'I'll tell them when this case is closed. They don't need to know yet.'

* * *

By early evening, Mal and Josh were packing up, ready to leave. They'd retrieved everything they needed from the greenhouse and from the two outbuildings in the back garden. The extensive supply of pure fentanyl had been removed from the second outbuilding, and both were now secure as they still needed to be fully processed by SOCO. An excavator puttered its way towards the greenhouse, to take down the remaining structure before it fell down.

Josh shook Jack's hand. 'Great to meet you, Jack. And by the way, I'm baking tomorrow! Any requests?' Jack laughed at the thought of Josh baking, but said he'd eat anything in the cake line and was happy to be surprised. Josh then handed Jack a bin bag full of rubbish from the Drug Squad van and asked if he wouldn't mind throwing it away as he passed the bins next to the house.

To the side of the house was a brick structure about four feet tall, split into four sections, each with its own wooden door. Inside each section was a different coloured wheelie bin and on top of each section was a lid through which you could access the bins without having to take them out. Unfortunately for Jack, the lids were all padlocked shut so when he found the black bin, he had to pull it out of its pen in order to discard the impressive amount of junk accrued by the Drug Squad in just one day.

The bin stank. Remnants of food clung to soggy cardboard that had become wedged in the bottom. As Jack pulled the bin out far enough to fully open the lid, he could see discarded cigarette butts on the ground behind it. Being fairly certain that Avril wasn't a smoker, he got a latex glove from his pocket and crouched to pick them up. He then turned the glove inside out, trapping the butts inside. He'd transfer them to an evidence bag once he got back to the station. He jotted down a note, giving his name and time he had used the bin, as it was more than likely the bins would be searched for evidence. From this new position near the ground,

Jack could now see that this bin store had been built over air bricks that led into the cellar.

The cellar had been gone over with a fine-tooth comb, just like the rest of the house. Jack knew this for a fact because he was one of the people who'd explored it; but now, as he looked in through the air bricks, he could see that the internal back wall of the cellar stopped short of the external back wall of the house. This discrepancy was something he hadn't noticed when he'd been inside but, from the outside, the size difference was obvious. Jack jumped to his feet, pocketing the latex glove containing the cigarette butts. He paced the outside wall of the building from front to back, heel to toe, then raced indoors, through the kitchen and down into the cellar. Jack measured the internal wall in the same way. It was six feet narrower than the depth of the house.

Through the air bricks, Jack could hear people running towards the back garden, and he could hear Mal shouting for everyone to stay back. Next to the greenhouse, a Wacker Neuson mini excavator had been stood down. Mal and Josh stood in front of it, looking at the pile of charred wood, collapsed metal shelving and general fire debris that used to form the back half of Avril Jenkins' greenhouse. Hearing their shouts, Jack now ran to their side and followed their gaze into the centre of the debris where he saw a tangled mass of singed, jet-black hair entwined around slender fingers.

CHAPTER 9

Jack, Anik and Laura were once again forbidden from entering the greenhouse as it had immediately returned to being an unprocessed crime scene. Kitted out in paper suits and masks, they stood next to Mal and Josh, watching Angel tiptoe her way towards the body. The dismemberment of Avril Jenkins had made Angel extra cautious: from the position of the exposed hair and fingers she, of course, knew where the rest of the body *should* be lying in order to avoid standing on it; but that was only if it was still in one piece. It was hard to watch Angel move painstakingly through the debris, trying not to disturb a single piece of potential evidence along the way. When she was close enough, she leant forwards and gently moved the tangled hair away from the face beneath.

Her mouth, chin and neck were badly burnt, and her visible clothes were melted onto her skin. Her hair had been singed away from one side of her head, leaving raw, blistered scalp beneath.

'It's Jessica Chi,' Jack said.

Mal asked what the link was between the two dead women. 'Adam Border,' Jack replied. 'Adam Border's the link.'

As night drew in, spotlights were erected in the garden to aid the tireless work of Angel's CSI team. Foxy had been called in to assess the victim in situ, in case the body didn't come away clean from the various surrounding materials. Foxy was thirty minutes from the scene, and Ridley was just pulling into the driveway.

He looked stern as he strode around the outside of the house to the new crime scene. He pulled Jack to one side and asked him the question he'd already asked himself a hundred times: 'How come two women, both recently interviewed by you, have now been murdered?'

Then Ridley added something that really got Jack's back up. 'What did you miss?' Of course, Jack had also asked himself that question, but he didn't expect his senior officer to ask it too.

'Kingston are the ones who missed things, sir! The second they dismissed Avril as a waste of time, they set this mess in motion. They assumed Adam didn't exist, and they hadn't even heard the name of Jessica Chi. I picked up this shambles of a case and have been trying to make sense of it ever since. And it might have helped if you'd stepped closer to the case as soon as it was transferred to us, and certainly after Avril's murder!' Jack held his ground, waiting for the upcoming bollocking. But it never came. Ridley absorbed the accusation thrown at him. He didn't agree or disagree; he just looked . . . disconnected. The man Jack respected more than anyone else in the world was letting him down but – worse than that – he didn't seem to care. 'Are you retiring, sir?' he asked.

Ridley didn't answer, just silently moved away towards the remnants of the greenhouse. Their conversation was over.

The sight of Jessica's body, however, brought a visible intensity to Ridley's face; something his team had missed over the past few months. 'Mal, have the Drug Squad finished with the scene?' he asked.

'The outbuildings are still ours, sir. The greenhouse is all yours.'

'OK. Steve wants to see you and Josh before you knock off, for a full review. Laura, you search Jessica's home address. Anik, continue to prioritise Adam Border. And Jack, you wait for Foxy. I didn't get the chance to speak to him this morning about Avril Jenkins' post-mortem, so get the report on that whilst you're there, as well. I'll be with the Super.' And with that, Ridley headed back to his car.

As everyone dispersed, leaving Jack alone with Angel and her team, he couldn't help but feel isolated. Jack hadn't realised how much he relied on Ridley: he was Jack's sounding board; his calm, guiding voice of reason during stressful times; and he was the man who always challenged Jack and pushed him beyond what he thought himself capable of.

Jack watched Ridley drive away. Then his eyes moved to the brick bin store which made him remember the gloved cigarette butts he had in his pocket. He was juggling so many potential lines of enquiry, yet all Ridley could tell him to do was 'wait'.

Fuck him, Jack thought to himself.

* * *

The task of removing the body of Jessica Chi from the greenhouse was like an archaeological dig, as Foxy supervised the slow and methodical clearing of debris layer by layer. As each obstruction was moved from her body, Foxy would check to make sure they hadn't caused her damage or potentially destroyed evidence. Eventually, she was lifted out and onto a stretcher. Jessica's body was blackened and charred, except where the skin had burnt off completely; in these areas, her red flesh and muscle structure showed through. Jack hoped to God she was dead before the fire started.

'This house is keeping us busy, Jack.' Foxy was cheerful, regardless of the late hour. 'Once I've got this one settled, I'll complete my report on Avril Jenkins ready for tomorrow morning's briefing.' Jack asked if Foxy had any headlines from Avril's post-mortem. 'Yes. Apart from being in four pieces, she was in rude health.'

Jack didn't smile.

'Are you OK?' Foxy asked.

Jack sighed. 'We've got all the wrong pieces of this jigsaw, Foxy. Nothing fits together.'

Jack instructed the two uniformed officers on the front gate to organise themselves a couple of replacements and, between them, maintain a 24-hour vigil on the property. 'There's also a back lane that cuts between the house and the golf course. Get that covered, too, please. No one's to go inside the house or inside the two out-buildings. They're only part-processed.' He gave the cigarette butts wrapped inside a latex glove to Angel, so she could arrange for them to be checked for DNA, then he headed home.

* * *

The next morning Jack stood by the kitchen window, staring at the birds in the back garden. Penny had been very careful with the flowers she'd planted in the borders – they were wild enough to need little tending, attractive to birds but not to bees, and safe to be handled by curious little hands. It really was a beautiful space and, this morning in particular, Jack felt very lucky to have it. It was the size of a shoe box compared to Avril Jenkins' garden, but at least his was an idyllic, picturesque haven – while hers had turned out to be a secret drugs den. He still wondered how she could have been oblivious to the fact that there was several million pounds' worth of drugs and drug paraphernalia right under her nose.

Maggie's arms crept round Jack's waist and she kissed the back of his neck. 'You showered when you got home last night. You only do that when you've been at a grubby crime scene . . . bad day?' Jack gently stroked the backs of her hands but said nothing, so she didn't push the topic. 'I'm doing a double today because Mr Wetlock is taking time off with his daughter.'

'Tell me about fentanyl,' Jack said. Maggie quickly moved away, making him turn. She looked put out. 'Sorry . . .' Jack knew exactly what he'd done wrong. 'Do you need to talk about Wetlock and his daughter?' Maggie, with a petulant undertone, said that the moment had passed and that she should no doubt just walk away from the whole Wetlock thing anyway. 'I think you're right,' Jack continued. 'So, tell me about fentanyl.'

Maggie wanted to be mad at him for being so dismissive of her problems in favour of his, but she knew she'd invited it. A smile crept over her face, and she set about treating them both to poached eggs on toast. It would be a rare event for them to sit down to breakfast together, even if they were talking about street drugs.

'Fentanyl's an opioid analgesic,' she explained. 'Mainly post-op or post-trauma. It can be administered IM or IV, via skin patches, orally with tablets or lozenges, or via nasal spray. It's incredibly strong. In hospital, it's a controlled drug, so no one can access it without someone else knowing. We caught a porter stealing used patches from a clinical waste bin once. He was selling them to his friends.'

Jack was just about to ask what an OD of fentanyl does to a person when Penny walked in with Hannah in her arms. Both of them were beaming with such joy at nothing more than the prospect of a brand-new day, that they brought Jack and Maggie's conversation to an abrupt halt. Instead, they started talking about *Paw Patrol* and Penny's plans to take Hannah to the National Maritime Museum.

All four members of the Warr family sat down to breakfast together, devouring seven eggs and half a loaf of bread between them. Maggie and Jack then left the house at the same time, and as Jack headed for the Underground and Maggie for the car, she got an envelope from her pocket.

'Give this to Simon when you see him.' Jack could tell from the dove-embossed envelope that this was Ridley's wedding invitation. And Maggie could tell from Jack's frown that something had happened between the two men. 'Don't alienate Simon as well, for God's sake. Honestly, Jack, you really need to learn how to play nicely with your senior officers. It's just because he's disagreed with you on something, right?'

Although Maggie was laughing as she said it, her words still stung because she'd instinctively assumed that Jack was the one at fault, though history definitely suggested this was likely to be the case. Jack wanted to shout, 'He's not Mr Perfect, you know! In fact, he's completely forgotten how to be a good copper because he's retiring!' But instead he kissed Maggie goodbye and carried on towards the Underground.

As promised, Foxy was at the early morning briefing ready to give the team a full handover relating to Avril Jenkins' post-mortem. He was flirting with Laura when Ridley finally emerged from his office, but quickly snapped into action when he heard himself being introduced for anyone who didn't already know him by sight. Strangely, Foxy was one man Laura never once looked at with any degree of interest. He was handsome, fit, suave and amusing – but he just didn't do it for her. The truth was, he seemed too easy. And Laura tended to go for men she was unlikely to actually get. In fact, it was her built-in self-defence mechanism.

'Avril Jenkins suffered numerous catastrophic injuries.' Foxy referenced his notes as he began to relay the details. 'She was attacked fiercely and repeatedly with a poker, suffering perimortem injuries of a fractured skull, jaw, left cheekbone and left orbital socket. Multiple stab wounds were inflicted, post-mortem, to the chest and abdomen. The blade was ten to twelve inches long. Dismemberment started with her lower legs and was done with a small-toothed hand saw. Then the left arm was removed at the elbow joint. Then they began to remove her head but didn't complete this act. In total, three different weapons were used: a poker, a knife, and a hand saw. All of which were left at the crime scene. Due to the lack of defence wounds on her hands and forearms, I'd speculate that she was either caught unawares or was held still whilst the first blow was struck. You're looking for between one and three assailants.'

Foxy closed the file and looked at the sea of faces in front of him. The silence and lack of eye contact told him that everyone in the room was as physically appalled by the details of this murder as he was.

'Avril Jenkins was in remarkable physical shape for a woman of 72. She had no significant arthritis, she had all her own teeth, her hair and nails were strong and healthy. She'd looked after herself. I found no DNA beneath her nails and no defensive wounds, but I did find restraint marks around her wrists and ankles. She may also have been drugged – but we'll have to wait for toxicology to be sure.'

Foxy invited questions, but there were none. He said that he'd be available to anyone at any time if questions did come up, because he was very much looking forward to doing the post-mortem on the sick individual or individuals who got off on mutilating pensioners. As he left to begin the post-mortem on Jessica Chi, Ridley stepped up.

'Avril Jenkins' house is worth around the £10 million mark. It became solely owned by her in late 2011 when her husband, Frederick Jenkins, passed away of natural causes. The Jenkins' family solicitor, Arnold Hutchinson, has given us reasonable access to her finances, bearing in mind he has to do right by Frederick's brother, Terence Jenkins. He is the sole beneficiary. Hutchinson has little personal information on Avril. He wasn't aware of her being harassed by Adam Border, nor has he ever met Adam, but that doesn't necessarily mean anything. She was a very private lady. He says that if Avril had been worried or scared, he certainly wouldn't have expected her to ask him for help. So, in her own way, it seems she asked us.'

Ridley scanned the room, making eye contact with each person in turn.

'What was dismissed as a cry for attention was, in fact, a cry for help. That's on us. As we progress with this joint operation, do me a favour and never lose sight of that. Avril Jenkins and Jessica Chi are unlikely participants in what is turning out to be one of the biggest drugs hauls of this kind in recent years. Mal Kaminski and Josh Logan are exceptional Drug Squad officers with extensive international experience. Work closely with them, because not only do we want in on that drug gang bust when the time comes, but their investigation will more than likely be the quickest route to our killer as well.'

Ridley paused and the room waited. This was the most comprehensive briefing he'd given in a very long time and the attentiveness from his team was tangible. Jack presumed that his confrontation with Ridley, although verging on insubordination, had also struck a nerve. But whatever the reason, it was nice to have him back.

Ridley looked across the room at Jack, and silently gave him the nod to now add whatever he considered important. Jack made his way forwards to stand in front of the whiteboards.

'Yesterday, two new things were discovered. In addition to the body of Jessica Chi, I mean. The items of jewellery Avril alleged were stolen from her by Jessica were found buried in the back garden. I checked the items found against the reported list of items missing, and they match. They're with Angel in forensics. And the second thing discovered was that the cellar seems to have a partitioned section to it that we've not yet accessed.'

This was the first Ridley had heard of it. 'A third hidden room?'

'Potentially, sir. All I know for sure is that the outside of the cellar has a bigger footprint than the inside. This wasn't flagged by the council because, rather than adding extra space, it seems that space has been taken from the existing cellar. If there's nothing else you need me for this morning, I'll head back to the house and find out what's down there.'

Ridley agreed that this should be Jack's priority. Perhaps this hidden room and its contents were what the elusive Adam Border was looking for all along?

* * *

The front and back gardens of Avril Jenkins' property were now at the fingertip search stage. Some uniformed officers swept sticks around the undergrowth, while others were on their hands and knees, checking under bushes, and the unluckiest officers were elbow deep in the drainage system.

The greenhouse, now devoid of any contents pertinent to the case, was slowly being demolished and loaded onto lorries. Burnt cannabis plants were amongst the rubble and debris, so needed to be destroyed safely and in a controlled environment. The two outbuildings were being processed by SOCO and the Drug Squad: the integrity of prints and DNA was vital to maintain, along with collecting and protecting the gas canisters, heaters, lamps, lab equipment and mixing chemicals. All of this would be a mine of information once it could be got into the safe, sterile environment of the forensic labs.

Jack walked the outside of the cellar again, and then the inside, marking exactly where he believed the missing space to be located. Against the back wall of the cellar was an extensive wine rack, twelve sections high and at least twenty feet wide. Jack's knowledge of wine was as scant as Maggie's, but the dust on the bottles and the dates on the labels suggested that this was an actual collection – for investment and not for drinking.

The wine rack was bolted to the wall with several heavy brackets, each fixed with four screws. This was the wall Jack needed to get behind.

He removed a random bottle of wine from the outer column, reached his arm into the space and knocked on the wall behind. Bricks. He then replaced this bottle, moved along one column and did the same again. By the fourth column, Jack was no longer knocking on brickwork at the back of the wine rack, but on what felt and sounded like hardboard. Jack stood this bottle against the wall of the cellar out of the way. The space it came from now marked the outer edge of what could be a hidden doorway. Jack continued to remove bottles and knock on the wall behind; when he knocked on bricks, he replaced the bottle and when he knocked on hardboard, he put the bottle to one side. Ten minutes later, the empty spaces in the wine rack marked out an area of hardboard that was around one and a half metres square. Now all he had to do was work out how to get in.

After examining the wine rack from top to bottom and left to right, Jack resigned himself to the task of having to first of all remove the numerous brackets. He started to search for a toolbox.

The cellar looked like a junk shop, with mismatched furniture, collectable ornaments, pieces of cut-glass and trunks overflowing with hundreds of items of old clothing. There were stacks of picture frames, some very ornate, others old and worn, and in various sizes.

Avril's extensive hoarding was making life very difficult and, fifteen minutes later, Jack was no closer to locating a toolbox. He was just about to give up and go back upstairs to get a butter knife to use to remove the bracket screws, when he came across a switch on the wall, hidden behind an ornate, Victorian-style bedroom mirror.

This switch was about shoulder height and wasn't connected to the lights: they were operated from just inside the kitchen. Jack flicked the switch. What happened next happened slowly. At first, all Jack could hear was a low whirring sound; then there was a click, followed by a thud. Then the wine rack began to move directly forwards – the numerous brackets were not attached to the wall at all, and the screws were nothing more than screw heads.

Jack's heart pounded as he watched the wine rack slowly and steadily move outwards, towards him. He veered out of its way, peered round the side and there, behind the hardboard, was a sliding double door surrounded by a steel frame. The wine rack stopped moving. Jack paused to find his mobile phone and turn on the torch, before reaching for the door handle. Then he paused again: if this hidden room was filled with more drugs, should he be wearing a mask? Jack quickly found the air bricks he'd identified yesterday, and which he knew opened up into the bin store. Beyond them was a pair of black boots.

Jack shouted, 'Hey!' and the boots turned on the spot, searching for the owner of the voice. 'It's DS Warr. I'm in the cellar. Find Mal Kaminsky and send him down here. It's through the kitchen. Tell him it's important and I need him now.'

Less than a minute later, Mal raced to Jack's side.

'I was getting the rubbish bins sent over to the lab, but this sounded way more exciting!'

Both men shone their phone torches towards the handle of the sliding door. Jack reached out and pulled it open.

Their two small beams of light lit the first four stone steps leading downwards, but were then swallowed up in the darkness. Jack tentatively stepped forward and felt the inside wall for a light switch.

'Look out for snakes!' Jack quickly pulled his hand back before realising it was a joke. 'Secret rooms are always protected by snakes,' Mal continued through his boyish smirk. He handed Jack a vented mask with a wink. 'Go ahead, Jack. I'm right behind you.'

* * *

Jack moved down onto the first step, using his torch to scan the wall until he found the light switch. When the lights finally came on, they were stunned to see – at the bottom of the staircase – a cavernous underground bunker that extended way beyond the cellar. 'Fuck me,' Mal whispered.

Jack and Mal followed the small bulbs that lined the top of the walls like Christmas lights. To their left were trestle tables buckling under the weight of computers and laptops, digital scales, bottles of chemicals, and dozens of sealed boxes. One shelf had hundreds of rolled canvases, and lined up on another table were boxes of oil paints and other artists' paraphernalia. The wall at the far end of the underground bunker was lined with steel filing cabinets. Mal moved to open one of the sealed boxes.

'No,' Jack instructed, 'don't touch anything. I want DCI Ridley to see this place as is.' Mal respectfully backed down. 'If there's any evidence of Avril in here, then . . . well, I'm not sure what the hell that means. But Ridley and I need to go through everything first.'

'No worries,' Mal said as he tightened his vented mask. 'I'll do a visual sweep to make sure there's nothing dangerous, then it's over to you.'

* * *

Ridley strode down the centre of the corridor with such purpose that everyone coming in the opposite direction had no option but to jump out of his way. His eyes were wide and excited as he listened to Jack relay over the phone what he'd found beneath Avril Jenkins' house. Jack said that he'd be waiting in the kitchen, then he'd take Ridley down into the cellar.

'I'll be with you in twenty.' Ridley let out a brief, breathy laugh as he negotiated the stairs down to the station car park. 'Well done, Jack. If anyone was going to find a drug dealer's subterranean mothership, it's you. We'll get them, you know. The truth with this case is, we've always had more evidence than we know what to do with. We just need to understand how to decipher it.'

This little speech, which Jack also took as an apology, was a welcome return to the old version of Ridley: the steady motivator who led from the front.

But the renewed confidence and support that Jack now felt was offset by the sadness of knowing that if Ridley was indeed retiring this would be their last case together.

CHAPTER 10

Jack checked his watch. It had been fifteen minutes since Ridley had said he was twenty minutes away and Jack knew that this ETA would be accurate almost to the second. Jack paced Avril Jenkins' kitchen, peering down into the dark cellar every now and then, in anticipation of getting back down there and beginning to process this brand new, deeply intriguing space. Mal paced outside, chomping at the bit for it to be his turn to venture down into the Aladdin's cave.

When Jack's mobile pinged to say that he had a new email, he was expecting a routine update in connection with the progress of the case. What he wasn't expecting, was an email plus attachment from Kevin, the building applications manager at Kingston Council:

I know you only asked for new information, but thought I'd send this anyway. FYI.

The attachment was a PDF showing the existing five-acre plot of land owned by Avril, with the layout of the house and garden being exactly as expected. However, beyond the wall at the rear of the garden, was an expanse of woodland, perhaps three acres in size, that was also part of the property.

Jack immediately called Kevin and asked him to confirm that this was correct. Kevin explained that, according to the notes, Frederick Jenkins had purchased the woodland back in 2009 because his neighbour wanted to buy it and build a second house for his elderly parents. To prevent this from happening, Frederick had outbid the neighbour in order to maintain the privacy of his own back garden. Jack couldn't believe it: the house and garden that they *did* know about had already provided so much information, so what the hell would three acres of woodland reveal? It was at this moment that Ridley walked in, raring to go.

Once Jack had brought him up to speed about the woodland, he organised the day ahead. 'OK. So the cellar has had the preliminary once-over from Mal and it's safe and secure, right? Then let's do the same with the woodland and, in the meantime, I'll let SOCO do their preliminary on the cellar. I'll get twenty or so uniforms, you get Anik and Laura.'

Within ten minutes, Ridley had secured fourteen uniformed officers and half an hour after that they turned up in a police van, kitted out with police tape, wellies, long search-sticks and several metal detectors.

*　*　*

The woodland area was wild and untended. It wasn't a through-way to anywhere, and it was protected on all sides by either a tall wooden fence or high chicken-wire secured against intermittent concrete posts. However, they could now also see the narrow foot-path mentioned by Mr Warton, which cut between Avril's property and the golf course. In a couple of places, the chicken-wire fence had been damaged, allowing curious walkers to stray onto Avril's property. Collecting forensic evidence from public spaces was a hellish job and this security breach would make their lives far more difficult. Jack was hoping that if this woodland had anything to reveal, it would be underground.

The uniformed officers worked in a line, maintaining a set distance from each other of around half a metre. They moved in unison, constantly looking at where they were about to place their front foot, so as not to stand on any evidence. Every now and then, one of them would find, collect and bag a discarded piece of litter and mark the spot with a flag. One officer found a small pink mitten, which they sincerely hoped belonged to a clumsy trespasser. The thought of finding another body, especially a child's, filled everyone with dread.

Eventually, the woodland began to thin out and they arrived at a large pond covered in green algae. Ferns and willow trees dipped their branches into the water – making it look quite beautiful, in an eerie, long-forgotten kind of way.

About twenty yards to Jack's left, an officer was prodding his search-stick into the pond, assessing the depth. As he did this, the water came to life – huge koi carp and the biggest goldfish any of them had ever seen, darted and splashed, dragging the algae below the surface and churning up dark silt from the bottom until visibility alongside the bank was non-existent. The koi headed into the centre of the pond where the water remained clear.

'It's much deeper in the middle,' Anik said. 'Five or more feet, I reckon. You can tell by the clarity of the water.' Anik hadn't said much since arriving, apart from moaning about how cold and muddy the woodland was. 'Those koi shouldn't be in a wild pond, really. It's good they've got hornwort for oxygen, but it's a bit too mucky and crowded for them in there.'

'Quick, call the RSPCA!' Laura said sarcastically, while Ridley instructed one of the uniformed officers to make a call for a boat, and to put divers on standby.

'Or we could just use that boat, sir,' Anik said, pointing to a small, weathered rowing boat beneath the branches of a low-reaching willow tree.

Five minutes later, Anik was seated in the rowing boat, holding the longest search-stick he could find and wishing he'd never noticed the rickety old death-trap. As he was rowed out to the centre of the pond by a young PC, Ridley couldn't stop himself from smirking.

When the PC stopped rowing, Anik lowered his search-stick over the side of the boat to see how deep the pond actually was. The stick, which was taller than Anik, hit the bottom with several inches to spare.

'Five feet was about right, then. Come back in, Anik. Good job.'

As the PC started to row back to the edge of the pond, Anik tried to pull the search-stick out, but it had caught on something. With one final yank, Anik pulled it free. He slowly raised the stick, allowing the cold, smelly pond water to run down the pole, onto his hands, down his sleeves and into his armpits. His obvious discomfort brought ironic cheers from the watchers on the bank.

On the end of the pole, just breaking the surface of the water, was a duffel bag. The laughter stopped. Anik, now oblivious to how wet he was getting, jiggled the shoulder strap further onto the stick and lifted it clear of the water. He looked back at Ridley and beamed.

Ridley moved round the edge of the pond to the spot where Anik's rowing boat would hit the bank, pulling on nitrile gloves as he went. When they were close enough, Anik swung the search-stick round, allowing Ridley to slide the duffel bag off the end. By the time Ridley had turned back towards dry land, Laura had laid a plastic sheet on the ground. He placed the bag in the centre of the plastic and glanced at Jack with the intention of asking him to film the opening of the duffel bag – only to see that Jack, mobile in hand, was one step ahead of him. The two men nodded 'ready' and Ridley carefully unclipped the two front plastic clasps. One clasp shattered between Ridley's fingers, the plastic shards dropping onto the sheeting beneath to be collected for forensics at a later time. Ridley unzipped the bag, pushed the main section open with one finger and peered inside.

It seemed to be packed like an overnight bag. Ridley reached inside and – one soaking wet item at a time – pulled out a pair of jeans, two T-shirts, a make-up bag, a toiletries bag, one pair of trainers, one bra, four pairs of knickers and four balled pairs of socks. Once the main compartment was empty, he unzipped an inside pocket and found a woman's black leather purse. Inside this, was £100 in £20 notes, some loose change, an Oyster card and a student travel card complete with a passport-size photograph of Jessica Chi.

Ridley stood up, leaving all of the contents on the plastic sheet. 'Laura, bag all of this and get it to forensics. Anik, Jessica's home address is on the King's Road. I want to know if she made her own way here on public transport, so get every inch of CCTV between here and there.'

Anik took a quick photograph of the reference numbers on Jessica's Oyster card and student travel card, then walked away to a quieter spot, announcing that he'd start by calling Jessica's landlady to find out what time her journey began.

'And Laura, we still need divers, please.'

As Laura gloved-up in order to bag the contents of the duffel bag, Ridley and Jack headed back towards the house. After an unexpectedly productive hour or so in the newly discovered woodland, it was finally time to head down into the cellar.

* * *

Ridley's initial reaction to seeing the cellar was very much the same as Jack and Mal's had been: silent shock as he took it all in. When Ridley eventually snapped on a fresh pair of nitrile gloves and began opening boxes, Jack followed his lead. As each box was opened, each man told the other what was inside, so that they built a joint picture of what this cellar was being used for.

One box contained fifteen burner phones, giving them some indication of the number of people potentially involved. Several boxes were filled with replacement parts for computers, chemical equipment, heaters and drainage pumps: clearly, if any aspect of this drugs operation broke down, they'd have it back up and running within seconds without ever having to leave the grounds.

The next box that Jack opened, made him reel. He was now looking at four Beretta 9000 handguns, two M16 rifles and two sawn-off shotguns. Jack's silence caught Ridley's attention. 'Well, we knew weapons were likely with an operation of this size.' As Ridley spoke, Jack opened an identical box to reveal a row of eight tear gas canisters packed tightly into a black foam mould. And the depth of the box suggested a second identical row would be hiding underneath.

As they systematically opened and moved each box in turn, they slowly revealed a row of five old dented and rusty four-drawer filing cabinets against the back wall. There were no labels to indicate what each drawer might contain and all of them were locked . . . except one. The bottom drawer in the fifth filing cabinet was labelled AVRIL and contained all of the personal documents Jack had been searching for: diaries, photo albums, bank statements, old cheque books and a small red notebook.

'So, if this drawer was hers . . .' Jack scanned his eyes across the other nineteen locked drawers. 'Who do *they* belong to?'

Ridley broke open the top drawer in the first filing cabinet and was stunned to find a monitor showing him the master bedroom. What the hell had they uncovered now? He then broke open the second drawer down, revealing another monitor. It showed the lounge.

'I thought you checked for security cameras?' Ridley's question wasn't accusatory. They both knew how small hidden cameras could be and so missing a complex set-up like this was definitely nothing for Jack to be ashamed of.

Twenty minutes later, all nineteen drawers were open and in their extended position, forming a tiered bank of monitors showing every room in the house, except the main cellar and the hidden cellar they were currently in. The rear garden was not covered, but there were two external cameras showing the front of the house. The Drug Squad van wasn't visible on either camera, but all their collaborative manpower milling about outside the property could intermittently be seen.

Ridley breathed the words they were both thinking: 'They're watching us.'

Ridley and Jack sat in the hidden cellar desperately trying to work out what the hell they were going to do next. If the gang were watching, what would they have seen? The fire brigade responding to a blaze beyond the range of the cameras; police and Drug Squad swarming the property, inside and out; Avril's body being removed. They would know their operation was completely compromised, and they'd know that evidence was now being collected in connection to the drugs, a murder and another potential one.

'But what they won't know,' Jack speculated, 'is that we've found this cellar. And that we know about their hidden CCTV.'

'We have to presume that these cameras are being watched,' Ridley said. 'Maybe even recording. So, we have to walk back into the kitchen from the main cellar like nothing's happened. Then we gather the main players in the Drug Squad van, which we know isn't visible on the outside cameras . . . and we work out our next move.' Ridley stood. But Jack remained seated, deep in thought.

'She told me she was in the process of updating her home security system. Why, when this place is kitted out like Fort Knox?'

'You're suggesting that this is something else she didn't know was right under her nose?'

Jack groaned as he pushed himself to his feet. 'I don't know.' He moved to the drawer containing all of Avril's personal documents.

'You can't take anything out, Jack. If they are watching, we can't be seen removing anything from this cellar.' Jack looked down into the open drawer. The elusive red notebook lay on top of an old photo of Avril, looking young and happy.

Jack agreed, bending to close the drawer. When he stood upright, his hand was in his jacket pocket.

* * *

The Drug Squad van wasn't designed for five people. Ridley, Mal and Steve Lewis sat in the only three seats. Jack perched on the desk and Josh stood in the narrow doorway blocking out most of the natural light. All of these key players were now up to speed. Steve bristled as Ridley relayed the order in which things were now going to happen, clearly feeling he should have been part of the decision making before they then *both* relayed orders down the ranks. But their joint crime scene had just got more complicated than anyone could have foreseen so, for now, Ridley was determined to keep control.

'We need to find out if there's an external feed to this CCTV before SOCO goes in, because they could be watching our every move,' Ridley said.

Steve disagreed. 'If they are watching, then the case is already compromised, so speed is of the essence.'

Ridley played to Steve's need to feel superior. 'Having seen the technical complexity of the set-up down there, let me make a suggestion, Steve. I think we should send one tech guy down there to establish who exactly has the upper hand – us or them. And the best tech guy in the Met is yours.' Steve softened as he once again began to feel like his team were the ones in control. 'Let's send Moley in. Wearing unmarked overalls. No Drug Squad logos.'

* * *

Mark Sinclair looked like a teenager. It wasn't so much his facial features, but the fact that he was very tall and slender, like he'd just gone through a growth spurt and was waiting for adulthood to broaden him out. He seemed incapable of growing facial hair and also moved like a teenager, taking long, slow strides, and with each step his lazy heels clipped the floor. All of these features and quirks had earned him the nickname of Moley, after Adrian Mole.

Ridley and Steve sat in the Drug Squad van waiting for Moley to do his stuff while Jack and Josh paced the driveway just outside. They had been waiting for almost an hour.

Steve was about to start a conversation about rank, cross-discipline working and the fact that he wasn't told about the cellar before his team was, when Moley appeared in the doorway.

'There's no external feed. I mean there can be, but it's off. I can't tell yet if it's capable of recording or storing but the monitors feed most of the house, even the en suite in the master bedroom. So this is definitely the central hub. Crackin' set-up, guv. I can't wait to start taking it apart!' Then he wandered away, noisily kicking gravel with his heels.

Steve jumped in before Ridley could. 'SOCO can go in first. Then it's ours.'

Ridley ignored Steve's bolshy tone for the sake of a smooth working relationship at this crucial moment in the case. 'I'm sorry not to have consulted you earlier, Steve, but there was no time. We could have been compromised. Anyway, yes, the cellar's yours. As are the outbuildings. We can assume they're more connected to the drugs operation than the murders. I'd like Anik to stay with Moley and act as a two-way interface to keep both sides of the investigation linked throughout. And there's one filing cabinet drawer in the cellar containing personal items belonging to Avril Jenkins. I'm going to ask SOCO to bring those directly to me.' Ridley stood, ready for action. 'My team will focus on the house, the woodland and the pond area.'

'That's fine by me, Simon.' Steve was now content that Ridley was showing him the respect that his rank afforded. 'The press will want to know about the homeowner and the fire. But we must keep them in the dark about the body underneath our cannabis farm.'

'Jessica Chi.' Jack's pacing deliberately took him past the doorway of the van, as he wanted to be able to overhear the conversation inside. 'The body under the cannabis farm, sir. Her name is Jessica Chi.'

Steve didn't care what her name was. Random victims were of no interest to him; he just wanted the dealers, the distributors and the people at the top. 'If you don't mind giving us a bit of privacy, DS Warr. We need to get our press stories straight. We'll let you know when we need you again.'

Jack wasn't angered or even offended by the way he was being spoken to. The man standing next to Steve was the DCI he answered to. 'Certainly, sir.' Jack's tone was light, with a hint of sarcasm. He then addressed Ridley in a noticeably more respectful way. 'I'll head back to the station and wait for Avril's personal documents, sir.'

Jack left the two DCIs, said goodbye to Josh and headed down the driveway away from the house. As he walked, he could feel the red notebook in his jacket pocket. He couldn't wait to see what secrets it held.

CHAPTER 11

Maggie sat at the kitchen table flanked by a stack of unwritten wedding invitations in their open envelopes on her left, and a stack of neatly addressed sealed envelopes on her right. This was one of the jobs Jack felt to be an utterly pointless waste of valuable time, pointing out that half of the people on the guest list lived within walking distance of their house or worked at the hospital, so he couldn't for the life of him fathom why Maggie was insisting that they got their invitations by post.

But she'd explained that having a wedding invitation drop through your front door felt lovely and special, and that wasn't something Jack was able to argue with.

Maggie's hair was wet from her usual after-shift shower and she'd climbed straight into her pyjamas, regardless of the fact that it was only five o'clock. In front of her was an ever-expanding list, which she added to every time something popped into her busy mind. The kitchen was silent, apart from the tinny sound made by the lid on the slow cooker as it was lifted then dropped by the building steam beneath. With no Hannah, Penny or Jack, Maggie was being very productive.

As she sealed an envelope with one hand, she jotted an addition to her list with the other: *2nd dress fitting on Tue. Me, Pen & Han (ask Jack)*. Two minutes later, she did the same thing again: *Best man? (ask Jack)*. Maggie gave a heavy sigh. When jobs were dependent on Jack doing something, she always worried about them getting done at all.

* * *

Jack and Laura were huddled together over the contents of Jessica Chi's duffel bag, which sat on a plastic sheet on a large white table in Angel's SOCO lab. Their gloved hands carefully opened the sodden make-up bag and the toiletries bag, as these were the only two items yet to be fully examined and their contents logged. At the same time, Laura was on hold with Jessica's college and they were both trying hard to ignore the godawful music playing in the background when Laura found a bottle of CBD oil in Jessica's make-up bag. 'Hemp oil. Not exactly drugs but . . . was she ill, do you think? Anxiety maybe? I can't get my head round CBD. Once the THC has been removed, what's the point? With no active cannabinoids, it can't actually work, can it?'

'We'll get it tested. Just because the bottle says CBD, doesn't mean it is. Jessica was certainly anxious when I spoke to her, but that was because she was worried about Adam. I didn't get the impression she was a drug user.'

'Certainly not to our knowledge!' The high-pitched, indignant voice came from Laura's mobile. The music had stopped, and the college receptionist was back on the line without either of them realising.

'Apologies.' Laura picked up their conversation from where they had left off. 'Did you manage to find someone authorised to talk to us about Jessica?'

'I've been given the authority to answer your questions within certain boundaries. You ask me what you need, and I'll answer what I can.'

Laura thanked the receptionist, whose name she'd forgotten, and asked her to initially confirm that Jessica was indeed a student with them. 'She was registered on our Business and Economics course. Started last year. She was on a student visa. I can let you have her home address if you need that.' Laura confirmed that they already knew it, but double-checked that it was the same address the college had on file. Laura then said that she was interested in any family Jessica may have had.

'I don't have any record of next of kin. Sorry. Is she in trouble? Drugs, did you say?' Laura ignored the receptionist's questions, instead asking what Jessica was like, who she hung around with and whether she had a boyfriend. 'I never met her. I work in the offices. I have her file details, which I've now shared with you. I can ask her tutor to contact you when she returns from maternity leave?'

Without giving anything away, Laura emphasised the urgency of the situation and requested that Jessica's tutor should be contacted at home and given Laura's mobile number to call at her earliest convenience.

Jack left Laura to process the CBD oil, whilst he headed back to the station to go through Avril's little red notebook in private.

* * *

By the time Jack returned to the squad room, there was a large evidence bag sitting in the middle of his desk, containing the rest of Avril's personal property from the cellar.

His mobile screen silently lit up:

If you'll be back by 7 – I'll wait. If not – beef stew in slow cooker. Let me know x.

Jack didn't reply, which he knew Maggie would interpret as meaning that he was going to be home later than seven. He tipped out the contents of the evidence bag, picking up an oversized photograph, which seemed to be a soft-focus image of Avril and Frederick on their wedding day. She was beautiful and elegant, with her straw-berry blonde hair held high on her head by numerous butterfly clasps which cleverly left just two slender ringlets free to frame her lovely face. She wore a chic satin gown that subtly showed off her athletic figure. She looked nothing at all like the quirky woman he'd met, dressed in clothes more suited to a child and with her grey hair held in a scruffy bun by a scrap of floral fabric. Frederick was older, taller and he reminded Jack of the late Duke of Windsor: with his tailored suit, slender hands and immaculate shirt cuffs with heavy gold cufflinks, he looked quite aristocratic and effeminate. Not inter-esting, not exciting, perhaps – but trustworthy.

The second larger photograph that caught Jack's eye was of Avril as a much younger woman, standing with a small boy at a coastal fairground. Behind them was a long pier with some kind of building at the far end which Jack assumed to be a theatre or restaurant. Avril wore a low-cut summer blouse that tied in a knot between her breasts. Her hair was long and flowing, and it tousled in the strong coastal breeze around her bare shoulders and neck.

Next, Jack sifted through an extensive pile of smaller photos, some from a 35 mm camera, some from an instant Polaroid. Most didn't particularly draw his attention until he got to one of the same small boy, this time standing alone, dressed in a school uni-form. Jack picked up his mobile and took a photo of the badge on the boy's blazer, then he zoomed in to try and see the name of the school. He couldn't see any wording, but the picture on the badge was of a bird seated on an open book. The final photo that caught Jack's eye was of Avril standing next to a tall suntanned man out-side the Bowler Hat restaurant in California.

Jack put these four photographs to one side, then moved on to a small, leatherbound photo album. It was packed with hundreds of overlapping black-and-white photographs, mainly showing a rundown estate with children playing football in the road and having picnics on front doorsteps. Two girls were skipping – with one end of a washing line tied to a lamppost. A sparse playground beyond back garden fences was overrun with excited children and dogs being watched over by smoking parents. Avril, at various ages in her late teens, was in every photograph – and somewhere in the background there was always a thin blond boy, wearing a frown far too sombre for his young face.

Trying to create a visual timeline of Avril's childhood, Jack began pinning all of the photos to one of the evidence boards.

Avril seemed to be a confident, free-spirited child, always playing outside with other children, mainly boys, and mostly older than herself. She wore a variety of clothes, some quite tomboyish, which Jack assumed to be hand-me-downs from older males in the family. Most of the photographs were not posed: they were just random snapshots of life. The ones that were posed showed Avril to be less at ease, and the most intriguing were a series of images showing her standing next to another young man in military uniform.

Jack's mind kept drifting back to the crime scene. He wondered what was happening in his absence, what Ridley and Steve were deciding to tell the press, what Moley had found on the security system, and what Mal and Josh had unearthed in the various drugs dens found at the property. Everyone seemed to be actively involved in something far more exciting than him right now. Even Anik was at the heart of the operation, as he was shadowing Moley with the Drug Squad.

Jack took a second to refocus on the task at hand and remind himself how important it was to learn about and understand the victim. And this was his forte. He had an intuition for spotting important details amongst a mess of background noise that surpassed anyone else on Ridley's team. *That* was why Jack had chosen to be back at the station sifting through the personal property of their murder victim.

*   *   *

Laura returned from forensics with a wad of paper in her hand. 'Did you know . . .' She then read in her head for a good fifteen seconds, leaving Jack hanging on the silence, 'that in the past four months, Avril Jenkins received two calls to her landline from California and three calls from an unidentified mobile. Apart from that, nothing. No one calls her. I think that's sad. And most of the outgoing calls she made from her landline were to Kingston nick and food shops. The woman had no friends.'

'The calls from California could be Terence, Frederick's brother.' Jack pointed to the photo on the board of Avril and a tall man outside the Bowler Hat restaurant. 'This could be him. And the mobile could be Jessica Chi? She used to call the house to speak to Adam Border and allegedly Avril would hurl abuse and then hang up on her.'

'Well . . .' Again, Laura started a sentence and left Jack hanging. She had numerous annoying little habits, but this was one of her worst. It forced Jack to remain silent, flicking through one of Avril's personal files collected from the cellar, until Laura snapped back into life: '. . . each call from the mobile did last less than twenty seconds – is that long enough to slag someone off and accuse them of stealing jewellery you've actually buried in your own back garden? There was no mobile in Jessica's duffel bag to compare it to, unfortunately.'

Jack had found Avril's marriage certificate. 'Twentieth of June 1998. Frederick Jenkins marries Avril Summers. Can you look into her life before this, please, Laura, now we know her maiden name?

We know she had no kids with Frederick, but . . .' Jack turned to the timeline of images he'd created on the board and pointed to the small boy dressed in his school uniform. 'Who's this? I'll send you a close-up of the badge on his blazer.'

'You think it could be Adam Border?' Jack had believed Avril when she said she'd only met Adam recently, but then again, she was hiding a cannabis farm in her greenhouse and she did get herself embroiled in something that resulted in her being dismembered in her own bathroom, so perhaps she was an accomplished liar.

'You think she went on holidays to Brighton with her stalker when he was a kid?' Laura was standing next to the photo of the pier on the whiteboard. She was momentarily bemused by the blank expression on Jack's face in response to her question. 'Oh my God, Jack! You didn't know that was Brighton Pier? How long have you been living over this way? It's literally just down the road. Never mind that, there's somewhere else that's just down the road: Hove. And who lives in Hove? Hester Mancroft, the lady who once owned the to-die-for property in Tetcott Street, where Adam Border was a . . . boarder.' Laura sniggered at her feeble joke for a second before carrying on. 'Hester's son, Julian, was done for drugs several times and died of an OD. Remember?'

'Yeah, yeah, I remember.' Jack was troubled by all of these old connections. 'God, I hope Avril wasn't some bloody drugs empire mastermind dating back to the seventies. I liked her when she was just an eccentric old woman who could start an argument in an empty room.'

* * *

It was half past nine when Jack slid his key in the front door as quietly as possible. Coming down the stairs, wearing his dressing gown, was

Penny. 'Maggie's asleep. Hannah's just gone back down, although I don't think she's in the mood for sleeping.' Penny passed Jack and headed for the kitchen. 'And I'm wearing your dressing gown because Hannah was sick on mine.' Penny flicked the kettle on, then went to the fridge and got out a clingfilm-covered plate of beef stew with a dauphinoise potato top. She put it into the microwave, set it to heat for three minutes, then began making two cups of tea.

She pointed to the stack of wedding invitations on the kitchen table, sealed, stamped and ready to go. 'Maggie asked if you could post those on your way to work in the morning. And she said, remember you still need to sort out your best man.' Penny smiled at Jack. He looked exhausted. 'I'm sure Simon will say yes, dear.' Penny's assumption that he'd ask Ridley to be his best man was a sound guess, seeing as he was the man Jack had entrusted his little girl's guardianship to. But her words stung, nonetheless. Because who else would Jack ask? Who else *could* he ask? He didn't know anyone. His only friend in London was his boss and he'd never been to Brighton. Jack needed to get a life!

Penny picked up her tea and put a gentle hand on Jack's shoulder. 'Make sure your dinner's hot in the middle.' She then went onto her tiptoes, kissed him on the cheek and headed back upstairs. 'If madam wakes, leave her to me, darling. You get some sleep.' Jack left his cup of tea and beef stew in the kitchen, took a glass of wine into the lounge, sat down on the sofa and took out the one piece of evidence that, so far, he'd chosen not to share with anyone else.

The red A5 notebook was worn and tatty, with age-old greasy fingerprints ingrained into the leather. It was partly used as an address book and partly as a notebook, with no real semblance of order to it. Jack imagined that whenever Avril needed to write something down, she simply wrote on the nearest blank page to where the book fell open. Some addresses and phone numbers had been scribbled out over the years; some had worn away because they were only written in pencil; and the odd page had even been torn out. One phone number had the unfamiliar area code of 0113. Jack did a quick online search: Leeds.

He then began working his way through, starting with the most thumbed pages.

Towards the middle, scribbled across both pages, was a list of schools, all with the Leeds area code. He also found Hester Mancroft's old address in Tetcott Street, her new address in Hove and both associated phone numbers. There was also Terence Jenkins' address in California.

The last few pages were taken up by a list of bottle companies, complete with dimensions, delivery prices and phone numbers. Underneath a strip of yellowing sellotape was a picture from a magazine of a small brown bottle and, next to that, the words 'corks extra'. Finally, on the same page, was the name MedGlobal and a phone number.

Deep in thought, Jack lifted his glass of wine to his lips – just as someone rapped on the living-room window. He jumped, spilling his wine on the notebook and leapt up, shaking the excess liquid from the pages and resisting the temptation to wipe them on his trouser leg in case the ink smudged and he lost vital evidence. He had no time to dab the pages dry, so he slid the open notebook underneath the sofa and went to the front door. At this time of night it would either be a scantily dressed, pissed and stoned teenager offering sex, or it would be Ridley.

'Sorry it's late.' Ridley jumped in with his apology before the front door was fully open. 'I knocked on the window because I didn't want to wake Hannah.' The troubled look on Ridley's face said that something had gone wrong since Jack left the crime scene earlier in the day. Jack led the way into the lounge, poured Ridley a glass of wine without asking, then sat ready to listen.

'Steve Lewis has been handed the operation. I'm not just playing second-fiddle now, he can actually pause our investigation if it's getting in the way of his.' Ridley savoured his wine as though it was the first alcoholic drink he'd had in weeks. 'It's the fentanyl, that's what swung it. International intelligence from Josh says, together with cocaine and heroin, it's coming in from China or the US. Steve thinks the marijuana's just a cover ... there to be found. Then, whilst the police are patting themselves on the back over that, the bigger deals are going on underground. Literally, in this case. I've got a meeting with Steve and Raeburn in the morning, when I can voice any objections.'

Jack asked Ridley what he intended to do.

'I'm going to let Steve have it.'

Jack swirled the last of his wine round his glass as a distraction to try and hide his disappointment in Ridley's newly resurfaced passivity. Ridley could see it as clearly as if Jack had called him a coward to his face and was determined to explain himself.

'Two things: first, with a drug-smuggling operation of this size, it'd be catastrophic if we let it reach the streets. Hundreds could die. It'd be churlish not to use the expertise of Steve, Mal and Josh. Second, Avril and Jessica weren't even mentioned in the meeting I've just had.' Jack looked up and met Ridley's stare. 'I'm not having that, Jack. Foxy's only halfway through Jessica's post-mortem, but he called me this evening to let me know that she died of smoke inhalation. She was alive in that fire.'

The tiny muscles in Jack's lower eyelids flinched, as the horror of what Jessica must have gone through flashed through his mind.

'*That's* the reaction I wanted from Steve when I told him. But you know what he said? "Who's Jessica Chi?" He'd already forgotten the name of the victim in the greenhouse.' Ridley drained his glass. 'So, he can lead on the investigation. He can have his international drugs gang and all of the kudos that goes along with that, and we'll help him when he needs it. But we will go after the people who killed Avril Jenkins and Jessica Chi.'

CHAPTER 12

One and a half bottles of wine later, Ridley was still there, passing on random information as it came to him. Josh had shared intel from the national operation he'd been heading up for the past several months. Although they still had no leads on who the main players were, they had learnt about some of the methods of transportation, the latest being a small fleet of light aircraft, the closest of which they suspected flew out of Farnham. It was already under surveillance, together with the pilot and the aircraft's owner. It had displayed no suspicious activity in over three months, but Josh insisted on remaining focussed because this level of overcautious downtime among drug gangs was common in the States.

'Josh isn't sure that they'll try and come back for their stuff – the volume of drugs and weaponry we found is all relative, and Josh thinks it's probably not worth it for them. But, regardless of that, the last order Steve gave was that a plainclothes undercover surveillance team from his squad must be in and around Avril's home, 24/7.'

'That team should be yours, sir.'

'We've got visible uniforms there as a matter of course, doing door-to-door, searching the immediate area and woodland, checking car plates – looking the way a murder investigation should. As we thin out, Steve's men will stay in place. And Steve's issuing a press release tomorrow morning. It'll mention the cannabis, but nothing about the rest of the drugs haul. The police presence will be explained as a standard response to a reported break-in, resulting in the discovery of Avril Jenkins' body. No details of how she died will be shared and Jessica Chi will be kept out of the papers altogether.'

'Well, if this smuggling operation goes as far and wide as Josh suggests, then I bet he's right when he says they can afford to write Avril's house off as a loss. I can't see them coming back,' Jack said.

Ridley firmly disagreed, but Jack knew that was only because he'd put all his bloody eggs in Steve's basket, so he *had* to believe that Steve's surveillance strategy would work.

'And you're attending the Drug Squad briefing in the morning, Jack. I need to know if they – we – have CCTV footage of Avril's murder due to the discovery of the set-up in the cellar. In the afternoon I'm meeting Terence Jenkins off his flight from California.'

Jack wanted to ask Ridley straight up why he was really splitting him from the rest of the team, but then a floorboard creaked from upstairs making both men freeze. Jack looked at the clock on the wall: 12.15 a.m. 'I'll get off now,' Ridley whispered. But it was too late. As he reached for the lounge door handle in an endeavour to sneak out, Maggie walked in, almost bumping into him. She walked straight up to Jack, took his half-full wine glass and gulped it back.

'We *were* whispering.' As soon as Jack said the words, he realised it made it sound like he was blaming Maggie for being awake.

'Well, I'd hate to hear you shouting.' Maggie took the empty glass into the kitchen. 'Thank God Penny's on the top floor.'

Ridley stood perfectly still, making no noise whatsoever, in the hope that Maggie wouldn't even notice he was there. She returned to the lounge, eating a cold dauphinoise potato, sipping on a fresh glass of wine and smiling in Ridley's direction. 'You said yes, then, Simon?' Ridley raised his eyebrows quizzically, as though he should know what Maggie was talking about. 'To being best man. Is that not why you boys are making your way through the wine rack?'

Jack wished to God that Maggie hadn't woken up. He wasn't at all sure if he wanted Ridley as his best man, seeing how fragile their relationship had been of late. Not that he had a plan B; Penny was right about that. 'I was about to ask you, sir . . . if you want to . . . no pressure.' Ridley's still-confused expression made Maggie ask Jack whether he'd even given Ridley his invitation. 'We've been busy, Mags. I meant to . . . it's in my desk, sir. I think. Or my bag. I'll check tomorrow. The wedding's on the twenty-seventh of this—'

'Twenty-fifth.' Maggie gulped more wine.

'Twenty-fifth of this month.' Then Jack said the words he should have said about three days ago. 'We'd all love it if you were there as my best man.'

Ridley gracefully accepted, saying that it would be his honour to be such an integral part of their big day. He then moved towards the front door, ordering an Uber as he went.

The frustration Maggie felt at being woken quickly disappeared. 'Just because the job is losing Ridley, doesn't mean you are,' she said softly.

Jack snatched up a clean glass and poured himself some wine. 'Jesus, Maggie, you make me sound like some lovestruck fucking girl.' He immediately regretted his words. 'I'm sorry. He could go out on a high, you know. He's exceptional. But instead of giving this case everything he's got left to give, he's handed it to the Drug Squad. Sometimes there's a spark of the old Ridley, but it doesn't last long.' Jack looked like a child who'd just realised that Superman wasn't real. 'I don't want to remember him like this. I want to be proud to have worked alongside him.'

Maggie rested her cheek on his chest and wrapped her arms around his waist. 'Do you want to hear about my day instead?'

Jack kissed the top of her head and said that he'd be happy to listen to her troubles instead of thinking about his own.

In a nutshell, Maggie was exhausted. Since the pandemic, nothing had been remotely normal. They were all working back on their own wards and in their own specialities, instead of making up the numbers in ICU; but their workload was now triple what it should be due to all of the postponed operations from the years in lockdown. Hundreds of people were now so much closer to death than they should be, and every day was filled with new horrors. Just last week, Maggie had to tell one man that his tumour had grown significantly during lockdown and was now too big to remove. His lifesaving operation was no longer an option; so, she sent him home to die with his wife and three children.

Maggie slumped down on the sofa, then slid forwards so that her backside was hanging off the front of the cushion and her chin was folded into her chest. She sat her wine glass on her stomach, tipped it until the rim hit her bottom lip, then poured wine into her mouth.

Maggie's anecdote made Jack ask about their friends Regina and Mario whose baby girl had a life-threatening illness.

'Money's their biggest problem – no surprise there,' Maggie told him. 'Regina's nursing post at the hospital couldn't be kept open because she was taking far too much time off with little Princess. Not her fault, but with the extra staffing pressures caused by the pandemic, it had to be filled. Mario's still decorating and he's taken on some odd jobs to help keep their heads above water. Princess is doing well on the new treatment from the US . . . all being paid for by their "mystery benefactor".'

Since the day Maggie told Jack that she knew the £100,000 donation to Princess's medical care had come from him – money he should have handed over as evidence, but decided to put to better use – she'd never mentioned it again. On the rare occasion that Regina's family came up in conversation, Maggie always used the words 'mystery benefactor' – it seemed to make her feel more comfortable.

'Whenever Regina and Princess go to the States for treatment, Mario stays here and works. He's always sad. He's missing so much of his little girl's life, which is doubly awful seeing as they don't know how long her life might be.'

Jack couldn't imagine how painful it must be for Mario not to be with his little girl for every second of her medical treatment. He was certain he couldn't be away from Hannah. 'It'd be good to catch up with them. Are they coming to the wedding?' Jack had been hit by a wave of guilt. 'I should call him. Do you think?'

Maggie placated him by saying that Mario had a wonderful family who looked after him. He was rarely on his own. And yes, they were coming to the wedding. 'It'll be lovely to see little Princess.' Tired tears appeared in Maggie's eyes. 'Apparently, she's getting some good movement back into her left arm.'

Jack sat next to Maggie and adopted the same slovenly position she'd chosen. 'Makes you realise that most parents have nothing at all to complain about.' But his gentle words quickly turned to sarcasm. 'Talking of prima donna parents who can't cope with their perfectly healthy kids . . . how's Wetlock?'

Maggie deftly dragged herself upright, without spilling a drop of her wine. 'Well, Jack, you'll be thrilled to hear that he's not coping. Tania continues to disappear and take drugs at every opportunity, and he continues to be out of his depth. For a man capable of understanding the intricate workings of the cardiovascular system, he's shit at understanding his little girl. He just throws money at the problem – like getting her that flat – but that just makes things worse by distancing them more, but he has no idea how to be around her. He's embarrassed by her, actually, that's the problem. She's not the daughter he wanted, and he hates the idea of others knowing he's failed.' Maggie paused for Jack to offer some consoling words, but they didn't come. She glanced to her right, about to tear a strip off him for being silently smug, but Jack was fast asleep by her side.

*   *   *

By 6 a.m, Jack had given up on any kind of proper sleep.

Maggie had covered him up and left him on the sofa, but he'd woken with a crick in his neck just twenty minutes later and headed upstairs to bed. Since then, they'd both been awake on and off throughout the night, taking it in turns to see to Hannah. She'd had a cough and a slight temperature for the past two days, and at night, she became an over-dramatic coughing and sobbing machine, who just needed to be in somebody's arms. Calpol helped to send her back to sleep, but only for an hour at a time and then they were stuck until she could have another dose. Between them, Maggie and Jack walked miles up and down the landing, squeezing Hannah against their chests as she stared at the ceiling, wide awake but content because she was being held.

Maggie appeared in the kitchen doorway as Jack was attempting to make porridge in the microwave for the first time ever. She took over as this was easier than teaching him how to do it properly. 'Maybe Princess could be a bridesmaid with Hannah?' Maggie could see how much their conversation from last night had been playing on Jack's mind. 'Is that a terrible idea?' Maggie planted one long, firm kiss on Jack's lips. She loved how things played on his mind until a lovely, heartfelt solution came to him.

'It's not a terrible idea, Jack, it's an amazing idea. But the truth is, she may not be well enough to come. She has good days and bad days. And she can't walk, of course.'

'She can be in her pushchair. Ooh, Hannah can push her down the aisle!' Maggie returned to making the porridge as Jack's enthusiasm ran away with him. 'Princess could sit in that little red car of Hannah's and Hannah could push her!'

A giggly scream came from the doorway. Hannah was bouncing about on Penny's hip, waving her arms in the air and laughing with her mouth wide open. Maggie and Jack glared at her through furrowed brows. How dare she look so fresh after the night they'd had? Jack broke first. He took Hannah in his arms and told her what a good girl she was for laughing at his idea about Princess and the red car. 'Hannah loves the idea of pushing Princess down the aisle, don't you, lovely girl, so it's two against one now, Mummy.'

Maggie smiled, but it wasn't real. Her medical knowledge was a gift, but sometimes she wished she didn't always know the horrible truth. She'd love to believe the dream of Hannah pushing Princess down the aisle in her little red car. But it would never happen.

After his shower, Jack was buttoning his shirt in front of the mirror when he remembered that he wasn't going to Ridley's briefing this morning, he was going to Steve Lewis's at the Drug Squad offices across in Staines. And the Drug Squad 'uniform' was more casual than Ridley's team's. Jack reassessed his attire and changed into jeans, a plain T-shirt and his leather jacket. He also wore the sturdy work boots he'd treated himself to when he was in the Cotswolds, not least because they made him half an inch taller.

Maggie had left the car as she'd decided to run off her bad night's sleep. Jack used to wish that he had her motivation to keep fit, but not anymore; now, he was happy to sit back in the warm blast of the car's heaters.

Jack had been to the Drug Squad offices in Staines once before, many years earlier, and it hadn't changed at all. The building still looked like nondescript offices, with only the high fence and security gate suggesting it was anything more. As Jack pulled up at the gates, a female voice spoke to him through a speaker mounted on a metal pole, asking for his name and the name of the person he was here to see. She then asked Jack to hold up his ID to the camera set on top of the speaker, before opening the gate and instructing him to drive round to the second set of double white doors, where someone would meet him.

As Jack followed the single road around the building, he saw a man in a hoody standing halfway up a set of steps. The man lifted his arm, signalled towards the parking area, then waited for Jack to join him. 'You're thirty minutes early, Jack. DCI Lewis isn't here yet. Come on up – you can sneak into the back of Josh's briefing whilst I make a cuppa.'

Jack followed the man in the hoody – whose name he hadn't been told and didn't ask for – along a bright, freshly painted second-floor corridor. To their right, a wall of waist-high windows overlooked the car park and to their left, evenly spaced posters instructed passing officers to ensure their weapons were secured and locked away at the end of each shift. The Drug Squad had never appealed to Jack – far too much testosterone was required to make the grade.

The man in the hoody paused outside a communal kitchen. 'Blue door at the end. I'll catch you up. Tea or coffee?'

Jack requested a white coffee with no sugar, then continued down the corridor as instructed.

Beyond the blue door, Josh stood at the front of a full briefing room. Jack slid in and leant against the back wall. Josh was wearing black combat trousers and a black T-shirt which was almost splitting at the seams where it stretched across his biceps. He still wore his beanie hat concealing a thin wire that stretched upwards from his blue hearing aid. The rest of the room was filled with carbon-copy men in jeans, hoodies, tight T-shirts, several ponytails, lots of three-day stubble and the odd tattoo. It was a uniform by any other name and one that Jack was only halfway to achieving, but at least he didn't stand out too embarrassingly.

'You've all read the latest report in the front of the file.' Josh glanced up and his eyes immediately found Jack standing at the back of the room. Josh handed a file to a guy on the front row. 'For DS Warr at the back.' Without looking, the guy passed the file over his head to whoever was behind him. As Josh continued, the file made its way into Jack's hands. 'A short recap . . .' Josh smiled and nodded in Jack's direction, indicating that this was for him. 'To date, we have 2,500 crimes linked to this gang, from speeding fines to murder. Twenty-nine people, all linked to this operation, are now dead . . . not including your two ladies, Jack. Three hundred and seventy-two robberies, 108 assaults, over 300 weapons offences. The guys at the top are smart and we'll only catch them by turning the guys at the bottom. DS Warr's team is investigating the murder of a lady whose property had been taken over by this gang or one on a par with it. This was an active hub until a fire brought the emergency services in and her body was found. Now . . .'

Josh paused to emphasise the importance of what he was about to say. 'Millions of pounds' worth of equipment is still on site. So, we're conspicuously retreating in the hope that they come back to collect. I'll get into why that's so important in a minute. During lockdown, this gang forcibly took over empty hotels, B&Bs, restaurants and cafés. With empty streets there was nowhere to hide, so they have laid low and used wherever they could as temporary dealing hubs. Things have opened up again now and so they're back on the streets, peddling their gear and spreading the word. This isn't just London I'm talking about, this is national. The regional figures are in the file. An operation of this size is complex and, just like in the US, many of the dealers we come across first, those on the front line doing the selling, are themselves victims.'

Josh scanned the room, looking every man in turn in the eye. 'I'll repeat that. They're kids. Or users. We help them. We turn them. We use them . . . which brings us back to DS Warr's crime scene. An undercover team is watching. If they come back to collect their equipment and their drugs, we'll be waiting.'

Jack loved Josh's decisiveness. He dealt in facts based on first-hand experience, and that gave him an unequalled authority.

'In the US, we're focussing on the big telecom companies. Tracking pay-as-you-go cell phones that are racking up hundreds of calls per day as dealers communicate with supply on the one hand and demand on the other. We know London is talking to Norfolk in a big way, 'cos we've intercepted more than 700 calls from hundreds of different cell phones. Heroin, cocaine and fentanyl shipments have been seized to the tune of around £20 million, but there's more. And it's getting worse by the day. Fentanyl, as you all know, is a hundred times more dangerous than morphine. Well, get this . . . we just got word of another drug that's a hundred times more dangerous than fentanyl. Carfentanyl is used to tranquillize elephants. And it's on your streets, killing your children.' Josh clicked his fingers. 'Like that. Emergency responders cannot save people from these new drugs.'

He took a few seconds out, to pace the small area at the front of the room in silence.

'The codename for one of the mixers is Scramble. We caught two of the main men up in Manchester with the intention of turning them. Both OD'd in police custody.' A murmur went around the room like a Mexican wave, as every officer tutted at how incompetent the Manchester custody sergeant must have been to allow that to happen. *Twice!* 'One guy,' Josh continued, 'had taped five milligrams of fentanyl to the inside of his wedding ring. The cops never did find where the second guy hid his little suicide dose. So, we start with the little people. The people who are *not* willing to die for this cause. They're our way in.'

Jack was gripped by how passionately Josh spoke. In fact, Jack was listening so intently that he physically jumped when a hand landed on his shoulder. It was the nameless guy in the hoody, carrying two mugs of coffee.

Jack was led back along the windowed corridor, then up two flights of stairs. The higher they went, the grubbier the building got. Visitors clearly never came up this far. The floors were scuffed, the walls were scratched, and the doorframes were chipped.

As they approached the final set of double doors at end of the last corridor, the young man in the hoody turned to Jack and smiled for the first time, showing off a missing canine tooth. 'They keep us up here, out of the way.' He then pressed the intercom button on the wall next to the double doors and they were buzzed in.

Beyond the double doors was a small reception area with desk, sofas and a kitchen tucked away in the corner. There were four doors, three with glass in them, so Jack could see that the rooms were empty. But the fourth door was blacked out, and this was the room the young man in the hoody headed for. The large room had blackout blinds on every window and was lit with strip lights that were just bright enough to see with, but not bright enough to give you a headache. There were six monitors, set out in twos, with each pair angled slightly inwards to surround the user. And there was a huge amount of electronic surveillance equipment. One man sat with his back to Jack, working two screens and two keyboards at once. Moley sat at another pair of screens with Anik by his side attentively watching his every move.

Steve Lewis dashed across to Jack, shook his hand and thanked him for making the trip to their HQ. He pointed to the man who had his back to the room. 'Edgar Matthews, tech wizard. And you know Mark Sinclair, aka Moley. They're civilians. You'll only ever see the backs of their heads whilst you're here. No one actually knows what Edgar looks like.' Steve gave a silent laugh at his own joke, 'And the guy who brought you up here is Sergeant Mike Tulley.'

Mike grabbed Jack's hand and began furiously shaking it. 'Oh shit! Did I not say that? I did. Didn't I? Sorry, Jack.'

'So, Jack,' Steve continued, 'in the interest of sharing, this room and everyone in it is at your disposal for the rest of today. But first, you're going to tell Mike, Mal and I everything you know about your dead woman.'

Jack bristled at the fact that Steve *still* didn't know the names of the murder victims. 'Which dead woman are you referring to, sir?'

Steve wasn't making a joke when he replied, 'The chopped-up one.'

In that moment, Jack decided that he hated Steve Lewis. A murder victim to him meant a druggie, or a dealer, or some other waste of space. Not a human being. He clearly put Avril and Jessica into one of those categories and that made them forgettable. Ignorable.

Jack now realised Ridley had been spot on to hand the lead to Steve, so that his own team could focus completely on getting justice for the two women who had died so brutally at the hands of men who would also not have cared less what they were called.

CHAPTER 13

Across London, Ridley was giving his morning briefing to a skeleton squad of seven officers. Despite their efforts, no one had any news on the whereabouts of Adam Border. It was hugely frustrating.

The photograph of Avril as a young woman standing next to a small boy in school uniform had been left in the hands of Laura. Using a blow-up of the badge on the boy's blazer, she'd tracked the school to Leeds and was now explaining to Ridley that the current school principal had only been there for a couple of years and so wasn't able to recognise the boy.

'They have copies of all school year photos going back decades, so he'll do some digging for us. And he's going to ask the geography teacher if she can help, because she's just hit seventy and has been there all her working life, so might know the boy by sight.'

'Let's hope it's Adam Border.' Ridley hadn't broken a smile yet this morning. His face looked tight, almost pained. On her way into work, Laura had called Jack to relay everything that she knew he'd miss in this morning's briefing, so Laura knew that Ridley had been drinking with Jack until the early hours. She put his dour look down to this and hoped that his mood would become more positive as the morning progressed and he got more caffeine inside him.

Ridley asked whether Laura had located Jessica Chi's family yet.

'Not yet, sir, no. Her flat just off the King's Road gives us nothing useful. The modelling agency she was registered with had her next of kin down as her mum, but the phone number in China doesn't exist. The college gave us a previous address for Jessica in the Netherlands, which we're looking in to now. Both Avril and Jessica have only got sketchy backgrounds, sir. We're moving as

fast as the evidence will let us.' Laura sounded like she was defending herself against an accusation of tardiness that Ridley hadn't
even made, but she felt it had been insinuated.

Ridley moved the briefing on. 'We've been given a report from
Josh Logan on the pilot who works out of Farnham. He's one of
several under observation, but he's the most potentially relevant to
us due to geography. This file is for information only, he's not to be
approached. If he crops up as pertinent to our side of the investigation, tell me before you do anything. Archie Calder-Blythe is an
ex-British Airways pilot. No criminal record. He used to work privately for a music producer out in Henley, ferrying his wife and two
kids back and forth to the South of France. Archie was loaned out
to various friends and family over the years, and we've got details
of all his known journeys – short jaunts to Eastern Europe mainly.
Also Belgium and the Netherlands. Morgan will filter information
on him through to us, as it comes in from Josh's end.'

Ridley put his hands on his hips and, although he tried to hide
it, inhaled sharply. Laura gave a slight shake of her head as it was
clear to her that Ridley was fighting off a sudden wave of nau-
sea. She thought it served him right for boozing on a worknight.
He exhaled, relaxed his shoulders and brought the briefing to an
abrupt end.

* * *

Mal and Mike sat silently listening to everything Jack had to relay
about Avril Jenkins, from his meetings with her and from the personal documents he'd found in the filing cabinet in her cellar. The
only thing he didn't tell them was that he'd found the red notebook: he still wanted to take a little more time to get to grips with
its contents first. Mal and Mike were giving him their undivided

attention, whereas Steve never looked up from his iPad. Once Jack had finished speaking, Mal flicked off the tape recorder, smiled and thanked him for his time.

'Steve and Mike are going to leave us now, and I'm going to talk you through some footage from the hidden cameras in Avril's home. You OK for time?' Jack said that he was, then, whilst Steve was still in the room, clarified that he'd be able to take a copy of whatever he was about to watch. Steve confirmed that Mal would sort all of that out, then he and Mike left. Mal stood up. 'Come with me, Jack. We'll get a refill on the coffee, then head to a viewing room.'

Back in the main squad room, Mal grabbed a laptop from his desk and handed it to Jack. He then went to make two coffees just as Anik finally noticed that Jack was there. 'Hey, Jack, this is Moley. He's a genius. I don't just mean he's a smart guy, I mean he's an actual genius.'

Moley let out a short and rather gormless-sounding laugh. He sat at least six inches out from his desk due to the length of his arms and legs, while next to him, Anik bounced around on his seat like an excited child. Jack felt a smile spread across his face: he didn't like Anik, but he liked that Anik was finally excited about the job in front of him. He normally spent his days looking into space, waiting for inspiration. But here he was with Moley, the tallest kid in the world, riveted by his ability to manipulate any technology and get it to reveal all of its secrets.

Jack heard a 'ready?' from over his shoulder. He told Anik to keep up the good work, then headed off towards the private viewing room with Mal.

'So . . .' Mal started, 'Moley went over the hidden CCTV system inside the Jenkins home. He knows it's not being monitored live from outside the property, but that doesn't mean it can't be logged into from a remote hub or even turned on and off. He's put all the cameras on a loop now, so if anyone does turn it on and log in, they'll see an empty house. We know the system hasn't been on since the fire.'

'Really?' Jack questioned the probability of this. 'If I'd just murdered one person and then set fire to a second inside a cannabis farm, I'd want to watch the house to see what we did when we turned up.' Mal speculated that perhaps the gang had bigger things on their minds. 'This case, Mal,' Jack continued. 'Should me and you keep in touch? Your boss seems to have a lot distracting him and, to be honest, so does mine right now. I'd hate for any key information to get lost.'

Mal grinned. 'Subtle as ever, eh, Jack. We can talk whenever you like, for sure. And no one else needs to know. As my grandfather would say, *Nie wywołuj wilka z lasu.*'

'Oh, I've been waiting for some impromptu Polish wisdom! Go on then. What does it mean?'

'It means, *Don't call the wolf from the forest.*'

'Ah. Don't invite trouble, right?'

'You are my brother from another mother, Jack Warr. You sure you're not Polish? You're too smart to be English.'

This friendship didn't go back far, but it was strong. Jack and Mal had met on a self-defence refresher course and spent seven days being thrown about on blue rubber mats whilst learning how to take a knife or a gun off an attacker. During lessons, they'd often paired up as they were roughly the same height and build. And during lunch breaks, they'd talked.

Mal stopped halfway down the corridor, opened the nearest door and slid the sign from VACANT to OCCUPIED. 'What was I saying, Jack, before you changed the subject to wolves?' Jack reminded Mal that he said the cameras have now been put on a loop. 'Yeah, that's right. So, if anyone from the outside turns the system on, they see a recording of no activity. Today, the house will be handed from your uniformed officers to our undercover officers. If the gang sees the house empty on their cameras, they could decide to come back. But you want to hear the exciting part? We're not watching the loop. We're watching live.'

The viewing room was small with two bare white walls, one wall of closed window blinds and one wall of windows facing the corridor they'd just walked down. Mal set the two coffees down on a low table in front of two small sofas positioned side by side. Then he flicked on the strip lights and closed the blinds on the corridor windows. Jack sat on one of sofas and opened the laptop. As he looked at the locked log-in page waiting for its password, Jack sipped his coffee and wondered what horrors he was about to be shown.

Mal sat down next to Jack, took the laptop from his knee and placed it on the low table. Jack listened to Mal tapping the keys before leaning back to reveal a screen filled with three videos ready to play. Each video was labelled with the name of the room it was taken from.

'What we've got, Jack, is a recording from the night Avril died. But we've only got the kitchen. No other cameras were recording. It's like this throughout. Some cameras record, some don't. And none record all the time. There's plenty for us to play with – hundreds of hours, in fact – but there are huge gaps. And, before you ask, there's no footage of your mystery man, Border, breaking in and stealing random stuff. But Edgar's ploughing through it and we'll show you anything we do find that relates to your murder investigation. The main problem we have to sort out is the timeframe. There is no timeline or date, so again Edgar will be attempting to put what we've got in some kind of order, so we can only presume that this was on the day of the murder.'

Jack leant forwards and Mal clicked 'kitchen'. Instantly they could see the view from a high-vantage camera taking in the whole of the kitchen including, beyond the open door, the hallway and the bottom two stairs of the staircase . . .

Avril walked down the stairs and past the open kitchen door carrying two small white bin bags. She headed for the front door. After a pause of perhaps twenty seconds, Avril came into the kitchen, now empty-handed, and headed for the bin. As she struggled to pull the tight-fitting bin bag out of the slender pedal bin, three men, wearing full face masks and black leather gloves rushed in. They were all average in build, but clearly muscular beneath their black clothes. One of the men took the lead – he grabbed Avril around the waist, pinning her arms to her sides, and covered her mouth with his free hand. A second man put his arms behind her knees and swept her legs from the floor, into the crook of his elbow. Her frail body was then carried with ease from the kitchen, out into the hallway where they disappeared from sight. Once they'd gone, the third man calmly cleared the contents of the split binbag from the kitchen floor . . .

Mal stopped the video. 'We don't know where they went.' Jack stared at the frozen image of the third man with the bin bag in his hand. He was so calm. So cold. 'We named the guy who grabbed her Alpha. The man who picked up her legs Beta. And the guy with the bin bag Gamma. Ready?' Jack nodded.

. . . for three minutes and twelve seconds, Gamma emptied the fridge of all ready-to-eat food, such as bread, butter, cold meats, cheese, cooked chicken legs and boiled potatoes. Whilst he made sandwiches and peeled ready-boiled eggs, the footage blanked out.

Mal paused the video again. 'We took a long time finding the hidden cameras in every room, master bedroom, bathroom, kitchen, drawing room and dining room. Very professional set-up, hidden in bookshelves, light fixtures, ceiling lights – a number even looked like part of painting frames. Next, we have footage from the exterior of the house, again no timeframe, but judging by the light it looks like afternoon. So this could have been filmed before the footage you just watched in the kitchen.' He started the video again.

'OK, so this guy arrived in a Jag with blacked-out windows. We have this from the external camera footage covering the front of the property and hidden up near the arch of the entrance. Edgar's working on it at the moment, so this is a copy.'

The footage showed the empty pathway leading to the house, and the gravel section beyond to the gates.

'Here we go, and before you ask, the licence plate has been covered in mud. Edgar's trying to clear it digitally, but as you can see it's obliterated. But the Jag is this year's four-door model, so that's another lead we can check out.'

Jack leant forward to watch the Jag driving up from the gravel section to the paved drive that led to the garages. The Jaguar pulled up not far from the greenhouse, and the outbuildings. The driver's door opened, and then the front and rear passenger doors.

Mal zoomed in on the sharp-suited man and froze the picture. 'He's wearing a black baseball cap pulled low over his face, and his collar's turned up, hiding all distinguishable facial features. There's nothing to run through facial recognition. We estimate his height to be over five eleven, he's well-built and that suit is expensive, he's also wearing black leather gloves.'

Jack stared intently as the three passengers got out of the Jaguar, sighing with frustration as all three pulled on balaclavas before slamming the doors shut.

'We are certain these are the three men in the earlier footage from Mrs Jenkins' kitchen, but again their faces are hidden and they're gloved up.'

He pressed continue as the man in the baseball cap opened the boot and handed out packages to each of the men. With the boot open, the three men leaning in all had their backs to the camera.

'We think these contained the paper suits. We are enlarging this section to make sure, and to see if there are any labels we can trace.'

The footage continued with the man wearing the baseball cap seemingly giving orders to the other three, he then got into the Jag slamming the door. He revved up the engine and did a fast U-turn before driving out of the grounds. The three men headed into the house . . . and the footage blanked out.

'OK, Jack, the next section is presumed to be a continuation of the footage we have from the kitchen. As I said we have not as yet had time to piece what we have in running order. OK here we go again.'

. . . through the open door of the kitchen, Alpha and Beta carried a struggling, clearly terrified Avril out towards the stairs. Gamma continued with his picnic preparations by searching cupboards and finding plates and cutlery. Four minutes later, Alpha and Beta came back downstairs, joined Gamma in the kitchen and they all tucked in . . .

Mal stopped the kitchen video. 'Again, we have no footage of where Alpha and Beta went. I'm sorry, Jack. I mean, I'm guessing they went to the master bedroom as that's where she was found. But they were not missing for long enough to have committed the murder and sliced her up.'

Jack didn't speak. There was nothing to say. 'You want me to carry on?' Again, Jack nodded and Mal fast forwarded. 'They each come and go from the cellar several times, bringing out all of the equipment they need for a mammoth cooking session. OK, here's where they have everything they need, and they are still wearing their balaclavas, possibly as protective masks over their mouths.'

. . . Alpha took a flick knife from his pocket and cut a small hole in one of several plastic bags on the kitchen island. He slid the tip of the blade into the hole and lifted out a small amount of white powder. By the time he'd done this, Beta had laid out a piece of greaseproof paper onto which the white powder was tipped. Alpha then filled a glass half full of water and folded the greaseproof paper into a funnel so the white powder could slide neatly into the glass. He then shook the glass, mixing the powder and water together. They all watched expectantly as the powder dispersed . . .

Mal commented on the action on screen: 'If there's any colouration, they know the MDMA's not pure. What they do next is attach a specially made heavy iron press to the kitchen table and bang out a couple of thousand MDMA tablets. It compresses the powder into that.' Mal handed Jack a small triangular tablet, with each side measuring 5mm in length. 'We used the same machine to press that out of soft rubber, so we know exactly what we're looking for. Watch these guys work, Jack. Alpha punches the tabs, Beta counts them into piles of ten and Gamma slides them into two-inch plastic zip-lock bags and boxes them up. It's almost beautiful. For five hours, they do this. Then they break for more ham and cheese sandwiches.'

Jack watched the men lifting their balaclavas and masks just enough to take bites of food and sips of drink. Their chins were fleetingly visible each time, showing that all three men were white. This seemed clumsy and stupid, so perhaps they weren't the smartest people in the world? Or perhaps they hadn't been told about the cameras?

'Mal, do you think the guy driving the Jag knew about the CCTV on the exterior of the house? I mean, he made sure his face was obscured, and so did the three passengers.'

'Maybe, I dunno.' Mal paused the video. 'The next four hours are spent mixing cocaine with boric acid powder and splitting it into half-kilo bags. You wanna watch? I'm going to send this footage to you anyway.'

'Hang on, is this it? I mean, you said there were cameras in almost every room in the house – the master bedroom, the bathroom where she was murdered . . . do you have any footage of that?'

'No, but we are still scrolling through hours of footage. There are big gaps, when the cameras were turned off or the footage deleted. Like I said before we are doing our best to find every second that was recorded.'

Jack had had enough. The missing footage was infuriating: not knowing exactly what had happened to Avril. He didn't relish the idea of watching her murder on video, but he needed to watch it in order to get the men responsible.

* * *

When Jack and Mal returned to the small reception area, Josh was seated in the middle of a double sofa, legs spread wide, taking up the entire space. He had his beanie hat in his hands and was pulling at a small thread that had come loose. He noticed Jack looking at his cochlear implant. 'Stops me doing field work. So, I consult and lecture and teach.' Jack apologised for staring. "S'OK. My nephew thinks I'm bionic. Every cloud, as they say.'

Jack thanked Mal for his time. 'If you get to these three guys before we do, Mal, don't let them take the easy route out of this by licking the inside of their wedding ring. They have to pay for what they did.'

'Deal. The external footage shows that the three men arrived in a black Jaguar on this occasion, but we also have footage of them in a Range Rover. Unlike the Jag, we have that licence plate. It's false, obviously, tracing back to a motorhome owned by a retired couple in Dorset. But we'll get them, Jack. We'll get them all. And we'll save those three for you.'

'It's the driver of the Jaguar I want.'

'We'll find him. Alive and kicking,' Josh added. He stood and asked if Jack needed anything further from them today. Jack explained that Terence Jenkins, Avril's brother-in-law, was arriving from California shortly, so he was going to head back across town and hopefully fill in some more blanks. Josh offered to walk Jack down and swipe him through the key-card doors to get out of the building.

Once in the car park, Jack paused. 'Avril had a connection to Leeds. What does your drug intel say about that part of the country?'

'Same as any bigger city. There's high-end and low-end supply and demand, sales and distribution. It makes me laugh how the middle-of-the-road-masses never see the drug dealing that goes on around them. I'll dig out some specifics if you give me a lead.'

'All I know is that Avril was connected to the place. I'll see what I can find out from Terence and let you know.' Jack paused. 'They were wearing masks and gloves. Would that be because of the chemicals? You gave me a vented mask when I dropped down into the outbuildings in Avril's back garden.'

'They'd know that fentanyl can be absorbed through the airways and skin, sure. But the men who killed her, Jack, they're small-fry. The guy in the Jag is the one we want to know more about. You know, compared to the US, this is all early days. They'll be selling mostly at festivals, concerts, raves, you know. They're using kids and druggies as runners. They got no idea of the shit they're selling, nor do the dealers. But with junk like fentanyl and carfentanyl being mixed with boric acid, cocaine, heroin . . . it's fucking Russian roulette out there. When this crap flooded the US, we were playing catch-up right from the start. People were dropping dead in the streets, literally. Like stones. Fentanyl certainly lived up to its name: the drop-dead drug. But here . . . here we can see what's coming, we know how to stop it. I mean, we still got to get ahead of them instead of just about keeping up, but we will. Your lady's house is such a good opportunity for us, being an active base.'

'I want to know what you know, Josh. I need to know how they work.' Jack knew that it was a huge request to ask Josh to share years of painstakingly acquired knowledge, but he also knew that it was impossible to chase a criminal whose behaviour you couldn't predict. 'How about dinner?' The sudden and unexpected suggestion took Josh by surprise. 'Penny's food is addictive. It's not imaginative, but if you want something heart-warming, she's your woman.'

Josh looked puzzled. 'Anik said your wife was called Maggie.'

'She is. Well, she'll be my wife soon. Penny's my mum.' Jack suddenly thought how lame Josh might think it was for a grown man to be living with his mum. He was just about to explain how she recently became a widower when Josh leapt in.

'Mamma's cooking! Oh my God, Jack, I miss my mamma's cooking like you wouldn't believe.' Josh's laugh boomed and his deep Alabama accent bubbled to the surface. 'Heart-warming! I know that kinda food. And you guys really know how to make gravy. I'd love to come. Thank you. And, yes we can talk shop, but not at the table and not in front of your mamma.'

CHAPTER 14

Jack got back to the station shortly after 3 p.m. and headed straight to Ridley to relay the details of his morning and to see if he could sit in on the interview with Terence Jenkins.

Ridley was in his office with the door shut, something he only usually did when he was on the phone or in a meeting. Today, he was seated at his desk just staring at his mobile phone. Jack knocked, opened the door and asked if now was a good time. Ridley put his mobile in his jacket pocket and looked up. He took a moment to find the arms of his chair with his elbows and then said that he was eager to hear how Jack's morning had gone. He didn't *look eager*, but Jack took him at his word.

Jack explained about the three masked men, the nine hours of drugs production, the fact that they had tracked the number plate of the Range Rover but as yet they had nothing on the mysterious suited man who arrived in the Jag. 'Mal's sending all of the footage across later and then more daily as it's sifted through.' Ridley questioned whether Anik was the right man to be sitting across town with the Drug Squad. Was he capable of making sure that Steve's team shared everything relevant? 'No, sir, he's not. But Mal is. And, from what I've seen, so is Josh. I trust them.'

'Oh, well, if you trust them . . .' Ridley stood and moved to the window. Jack didn't like the sarcasm in his voice. But rather than be annoyed by it, he was simply concerned. Jack waited for Ridley to elaborate on how he was feeling, but he didn't. Instead, he changed the subject. 'Terence Jenkins is at his hotel, freshening up. There's a police car waiting to bring him here by . . .' Ridley checked his watch. 'They should be here now, in fact.' Ridley took his jacket from the back of his chair and slowly put it on. He looked tired. When he spoke again, his voice was apologetic. 'Mal's a good man, you're right. And if you trust Josh, then so do I.'

*　*　*

Terence Jenkins was a tall, suntanned, elegant-looking man in his sixties. His full head of hair was suspiciously dark and the skin on his face was suspiciously taut compared to that on his neck. But he was from California, where every other building belonged to a plastic surgeon . . . or so Jack had heard.

Terence sat on a sofa in the soft interview room, opposite Ridley and Jack. They all nursed mugs of proper tea, made from the machine in Ridley's office.

'One doesn't fully value people until one loses them.' Terence had not picked up any American twang at all during his years in California. 'Avril could be ghastly. Did you meet her?' Jack confirmed that he had spoken to Avril on a number of occasions. 'Then you know what I mean. I think I would have found her amusing if she had been some other poor sod's sister-in-law.'

Terence was given time to speak freely about Avril, saying whatever came to mind. Eventually, Ridley began guiding the conversation by asking about their upbringing.

'Freddie and I grew up in Surrey. We never wanted for anything but were taught the value of everything. That's what happens when your father's an investment banker. When he died, Freddie, being older, inherited, lock, stock and barrel. No reason other than tradition and yet it was the beginning of the end of us, I'm afraid. Freddie stepped into our father's rather large shoes, and they were far too big. I told him as much and . . . money does cause such problems. Anyway, I moved to California. Within five years, I was married with my first child on the way and had a jolly good managerial position in real estate. From that moment on, dear Freddie was always rather angry with me for surviving without him. And he was a shit businessman as it turned out – I'm sure you know more about his investment crash than I do, so I doubt I'm betraying any confidences.'

Terence blew on his tea, then took a sip. 'Ahh, lovely. American tea is truly offensive.'

Ridley had now got the measure of Terence and the fact that he was not a man to use ten words when he could use fifty. Ridley asked if he could speak more specifically about Avril.

'When Freddie called to tell me he was marrying, I couldn't believe he'd found someone who'd have him . . . such a mean-spirited old bastard he'd grown into. He knew I was in London visiting old friends so, when he suggested meeting up, I agreed. Avril was . . . common. I, of course, presumed she was after his money. Especially when my brother bragged to me that they'd met in a Soho pub, after he'd been mugged one evening and gone in to use the phone. She bought him a drink whilst he waited for the police to arrive and they . . . fucked . . . his word . . . that very same night. I'm not a prude, but he was an old man! Avril gibbered on about her family: her father was a truck driver and her mother was a housewife. As I understand it, Avril flew their Leeds council nest at a very early age. Anyway, the next time we met was at their wedding.' A wry smile crept across Terence's lips. 'She got inexcusably drunk, and during a slow dance, she cupped my scrotum. I think that's my fondest memory of dear Avril.' Jack turned his head away in an endeavour to hide a snigger. Terence saw it and his smile broadened. 'That's what I mean when I say I could have liked her if she were some other poor sod's relative. Anyway, beyond the wedding, it was several years until we all met again. I don't suppose I could trouble you for another cup of tea, could I?'

The ten-minute comfort break turned into a half-hour phone call between Terence and his wife back in California. Although Ridley and Jack couldn't hear the other half of the conversation, it was obvious that Terence's wife was sending him her love and asking for presents from England: she wanted branded bags from all the top London shops, so that she could show off to her friends. She didn't need anything in the bags.

*　　*　　*

Back in the soft interview room Terence began again, unprompted, from exactly where he'd left off.

'There was a time before we lost Freddie – can't recall the year – when I invited Avril to use my place in California whilst the family and I were on holiday in Florida. To be honest, I didn't want to leave it empty. Rather surprisingly, she said yes. When we returned from Florida, something told me to send the family out for lunch, whilst I nipped back home ahead of them. Thank goodness for gut instinct! Avril was on my daughter's lilo in the pool, smoking marijuana with some very unsavoury characters from Santa Monica ... as was advertised by their tattoos. I asked everyone to leave, including Avril, but she wouldn't go. Six months, she stayed. To be honest, she was on her best behaviour the entire time and the kids thought her highly amusing, but ... six months!' Terence's tone barely concealed hid an undertone of regret.

'She didn't want to come home. I think her relationship with my brother had soured. She inferred he had become paranoid – as I said before, he was always a bit twisted – but she said he had been very difficult due to some insurance about a painting. Our father was a consummate art collector, and in reality poor old Freddie would have preferred becoming an artist to running the company. As it turned out he was pretty useless and lost a fortune. I suppose I wish Avril had been an easier woman, then perhaps I would have asked her why she had married him in the first place, but then my own wife pointed out that my brother was very wealthy.'

Ridley asked if Terence had been aware of Avril's drug use prior to the swimming-pool incident.

'It was medicinal. I don't know what for and I didn't ask. I allowed it in the summer house at the far end of the garden. My wife wasn't happy because of the children, but she turned a blind eye. For me.'

Jack leant forwards. 'Terence, do you know if Avril had a child? Before her marriage to your brother.'

'She insinuated it once. When she was squatting in my house in California. She mentioned that her new life in London was cut short by a "mistake" – she said she'd returned home to Leeds to fix said "mistake". Actually, when Arnold Hutchinson called to tell me of Freddie's death, he asked a similar question. He asked if I knew whether Avril had ever been married before. I neither knew nor cared, but apparently Freddie had grown to suspect that there had been a marriage and family in Avril's past. I never discovered if there had been, and to be honest my brother never bothered to call or write, so I sort of let it go. I most certainly never wanted Avril to visit again.'

Terence quickly stood and brought the interview to an abrupt end. 'Got to go. I'm Skyping the kids shortly and I want to do it from the top of the Gherkin. My daughter will be green with envy.' He seemed to suddenly become aware that his demeanour was not that of a man who'd just lost a family member. 'Avril and I . . . Avril and anyone really . . . often clashed. She could be cruel. When

Freddie passed, I asked her, through Arnold, if I could collect a few sentimental items. Things from our childhood, collections of paintings dating back to our grandfather's days. Granted they were of value, but that wasn't why I wanted them. She never replied and eventually I stopped asking. Anyway, I get it all now, don't I?'

* * *

On the way back to Ridley's office, he and Jack speculated about the timeframe and the order of events leading up to the establishment of the multi-faceted drugs factory at Avril's home. The start of the cannabis farm in her greenhouse no doubt aligned with the date of the high utility bill brought to their attention by Arnold Hutchinson. But was it her set-up initially, started to feed her own cannabis habit, or was it the work of the drugs gang? There were too many questions and nowhere near enough answers.

'Go back to the beginning, Jack. One of the very first questions we asked was who's Adam Border? Why the hell haven't we been able to find him? Ordinary people don't hide like this. Ordinary people have histories, use credit cards, leave paper trails. Therefore, Adam Border isn't ordinary. So find him.'

CHAPTER 15

As Jack walked in the front door, the smell of baking told him which room to head for first. Maggie and Penny had been multitasking. There was evidence of homemade pastry, several cakes, ironing, and another stack of wedding invitations, almost as big as the first, sat on the kitchen table, all sealed and stamped ready to be posted. Jack noted that the envelope on top of the pile was addressed to Elliot Wetlock. Hannah was sitting in her highchair crumbling a buttered scone into tiny pieces and then licking them off the table.

Through the kitchen window, he saw Penny in the back garden pegging out multiple wash-loads. Maggie was tidying the kitchen worktops.

'Well . . .' by Jack's tone, Maggie knew something sarcastic was coming. 'If we're inviting everyone we've ever crossed paths with to our wedding, there's a cleaner on our floor at the station I'd like to invite. He talks a lot about Plymouth Argyle and he's programmed to wash dirty mugs on sight so, you know, he'd be interesting and useful. Unlike Wetlock.'

'Some of these invites are just for the evening do.' When Maggie turned to face Jack, she had a few stray scone crumbs on her cheek held in place by a tiny bit of jam. 'And Elliot Wetlock will more than likely say no. He's still got his hands full with Tania, but currently he's my boss, so I'm inviting him.'

Jack moved to Maggie's side, brushing his hand across Hannah's hair as he passed. He stood close to Maggie, leant in, making her pucker in expectation – then licked the jammy crumbs from her face. He followed this up with a kiss, so she knew that he still loved her, regardless of how much money she was spending on their wedding.

After dinner, Jack and Maggie retreated to the lounge with a plate full of cakes to sample and a bottle of red wine, whilst Penny headed upstairs to bath Hannah and put her to bed. 'There's a guy at work – Josh – he's from Alabama. I've invited him for dinner one night.' Maggie said this was fine by her and asked if Jack wanted everyone to be in or out when he came. 'In. He's on his own. He's missing some home comforts.'

'Saturday would be good, then. And Sunday's my hen night, don't forget.' Jack stared at her with a blank expression. 'I did tell you, Jack. Penny is with me, Hannah's with you. And next weekend is your stag night.'

'What stag night?'

'Well, I don't know. That's Simon's job. But the date for it is next weekend.'

'Oh my, God Maggie, why didn't you remind me that the best man does the stag night *before* I asked Ridley!' Jack threw his head back onto the sofa in total dismay. 'We'll end up at a museum!'

* * *

By 7 a.m. Jack was on the road to Hove. Ridley had given him the clear instruction to find Adam Border and so Jack was heading back to Hester Mancroft as she was the only point of contact they had for him.

As he drove, Jack tried to contact Ridley, but he wasn't answering – yet another thing that Ridley never did before his decision to retire – so Jack called Laura instead and asked her to tell Ridley that he'd be back for the afternoon briefing, hopefully with a solid lead on Adam Border. She was pissed off that he was heading to interview someone she'd already spoken to: if he'd found additional information or evidence that warranted a second interview, she would have accepted that, but he hadn't. 'Repeating my work makes me look stupid if you have no good reason to do it, other than you think you can do a better job.'

'Nah, I just want a day at the beach.' Jack tried to be flippant but Laura's silence told him that he had genuinely offended her. He was about to try and placate her when a call from Josh appeared on his mobile screen waiting to be either accepted or rejected. Jack spoke fast. 'I have a hunch, Laura, and I need to follow it up face to face. What I'm doing says nothing about the quality of your initial interview. But, if you're pissed off, take it up with Ridley. He's the one who told me to find Adam Border.' Then he hung up and pressed accepton Josh's call. Too late.

A text from Josh quickly followed:

Hurry up and invite me already! I'm starving!

Within a couple of text exchanges, it was settled that Josh would come to dinner on Saturday night.

* * *

Jack could see Hester Mancroft approaching the front door through the pane of frosted glass. She took forever but, with the sound of the sea behind him, he really didn't mind waiting.

Hester pressed her face to the glass and asked who it was. Jack shouted his name and said that he was a police officer, but she couldn't hear him, so he had to shout again. In the end, she opened the door anyway, on the assumption that a doorstep conman would not draw attention to himself by shouting his name numerous times in the street.

Hester took Jack directly into the kitchen and set about making a cup of tea. It was a lengthy operation and Jack doubted that it would be ready by the time he had to leave. She put a rusty old stove-top kettle on the gas, washed two of her best china mugs, then spent the first five minutes of their conversation trying to find a clean tea towel. She was a good-looking woman who, in her day, must have been very attractive. She was dressed smartly and had done her hair and make-up regardless of the fact that, until Jack turned up, no one would have witnessed the effort she'd made.

'Have you been to Hove before, Mr Warr?' Her voice was low and aristocratic, matching her smart appearance, but Jack wasn't at all sure she had the upbringing to back it up. 'The name is rarely heard without the words "Brighton and" before it, but I think we have the better esplanade. That lovely expanse of greenery in front of the beach is the perfect place to sit and watch the world go by as you eat fish and chips. It takes away all your worries and sorrows. Do you work with that lady who came to see me last week?'

'Yes, I do. I wanted to ask you a couple more questions about Adam Border if you don't mind. To see if we can figure out what happened to him.'

'I'll try to help if I can, yes. He rented a room from me when I ran a little B&B in Chelsea. I eventually sold it for far less than it was worth and moved here. My ex-husband was furious that I was offered three quarters of the asking price, which I found delightful, so I accepted. And it was enough to buy this place outright, which is all I really wanted to do. It was my mid-life crisis, I think. But you'll know this already from your lady friend, won't you?'

'Yes, I do.' Jack smiled to indicate that Hester's waffling wasn't a problem, then he guided her back to the subject he needed her to talk about. 'Adam was a friend of your son's, who's now deceased? I was sorry to hear that, Mrs Mancroft.'

'Thank you.' An old yet still poignant sadness spread across Hester's face. It seemed to Jack that the passing decades had not helped her to get over the death of her son. 'Adam and Julian were quite similar, so they got on. Adam only lived with us for a few months. He was charming, handsome, helpful around the house. He was a decent young man, I'd say. I took several students in over the years – on one occasion, don't ask me the date because I won't know – Julian had gone into one of the girl's bedrooms. She kicked up a stink as you might expect, and Adam calmed things down for me. Julian was a little worse for wear at the time. Her parents arrived the following morning to take her home and Adam helped me to dissuade them from calling the police.'

The screech from the kettle's whistle brought a pause to the conversation and Hester hit the side of a bag of sugar on the kitchen worktop to break up the solidified grains inside. Jack said he didn't take sugar, and when she sniffed the milk from the fridge, he quickly said he didn't take that either. Hester made a pot of tea, placed a hand-knitted cosy on top and joined Jack at the table.

'Julian's drug-taking was awful,' she continued. 'I felt so helpless. And stupid for not seeing it happening until it was far too late. At first, he just smoked weed . . . well, they all did at the time. I think Adam was a sensible boy, but when he moved to Amsterdam, that worried me. It's all legal over there, isn't it?'

'What can you tell me about Avril Jenkins?' Jack asked.

'Oh, Avril and I go way back. To a housing estate in Leeds. We were always in trouble. Well, she was, and I followed.' Jack hadn't known the connection between these two older ladies, but somehow wasn't surprised that, once again, Adam linked two disparate parts of this investigation. 'Avril was a real daredevil, although most of the adults would have just called her a devil. We'd spend hours trying to copy the hair and make-up in magazines.' Sadness descended once again. 'When she was 16, she ran off with a much older man. I think he was a carpet salesman. Those years without Avril felt . . . hopeless. But then she came back, without her carpet salesman. And she whisked me off to London! Oh, they were my best days, Mr Warr. I lived! She was doing photographic work and I got a job as a receptionist. Now, I never saw any of her photographs, but I expect you know what they were. She had lots of male friends swooning over her – she was exciting, you see. She felt dangerous.'

Hester got to her feet and got out a biscuit tin so old that the scenic picture on the lid had worn away around the edges where greasy fingers had opened and closed it a thousand times. She checked the dryness of the mugs by swiping her finger around the inside of hers and decided that it was time to pour the tea. It was as thick and dark as coffee, but Jack thanked her and politely declined a biscuit.

'Avril disappeared for a few years then,' Hester continued. 'I heard she'd gone back to Leeds. By then, some of her chutzpah had rubbed off on me and, one night in a bar, when a man asked me to dance, I said yes. That was my future husband. He owned a couple of second-hand car showrooms, which I thought was amusing and very "London". Turned out there was a lot of money in old cars.'

'Hester, do you know why Avril went back to Leeds?' Hester said no but Jack caught her hesitation. She wasn't skilled at lying. Jack gently pushed. 'I think she went back north because she had to. I think she was pregnant.'

Once Hester knew that Jack had figured things out for himself, she quickly spilled the beans. 'Avril had gone back home to give birth to a son. Then she'd stayed there and got a job at an estate agent's. Apparently, it hadn't taken long for the novelty of being a single working mum to wear off, and for the draw of the nightlife to call her back – the boy was often left with her parents whilst she partied. Not a good situation because Avril's mother was very unpleasant sober but drunk she was horrible, and her father had no time for the child. Ávril quickly lost her job and made the decision to relinquish custody to the boy's dad.' Hester recalled that over the years Avril's son did come back to live with her every now and then but generally she seemed to palm him off to various men who came and went in her life.

Jack asked if Avril's son was Adam Border and she confirmed that he was.

'His dad was in advertising, I think. Worked in London sometimes but lived in Amsterdam. Can't recall his name. He'd been a fling – well, they normally were with Avril. Until Frederick. I met up with her years later, just before my divorce. There was a big antiques emporium opening at the end of the street where I eventually moved to, and she was looking at a lovely velvet-covered armchair. I remember because it was very expensive, and she invited me to her flat to catch up on old times. She was living in a stunning little studio-type flat, all paid for by her boyfriend. Boyfriend! Sugar Daddy more like. She said she'd landed on her feet, apart from being petrified of him finding out that she had a son. Anyway, I had problems of my own with my divorce and so didn't see her again for years but I'm guessing he never did find out, because the next thing I knew they're married and she's living in a mansion.'

Jack took a sip of his tea, forgetting how long it had been sitting beneath the tea cosy. It was like tar. He raised the mug to his lips again and surreptitiously spat the first sip back into the mug. He then asked when Hester had last seen Avril.

'More than six months ago. We used to see each other quite often, but recently I've not heard a peep.' Hester became sad and reflective, as she had when talking about her dead son. 'Last time I saw her, she looked . . . I don't know . . . like a different person. She wore ripped jeans, a faux fur coat and she'd let her hair go grey and wild. She looked . . . well, she looked like the Avril I knew back in Leeds. Like she was trying to be 16 again. It made me think she might have a young man in the wings, but she said she didn't.'

'And she didn't mention that she had her son living with her?'

'Oh goodness, she never said a word. Maybe that was sparing my feelings because she knew I'd lost my own son. In fact, that was how we met up again because she wrote a very sweet letter. I know Avril can be difficult, but I do miss her when she goes into hiding on a whim.' Hester smiled and shrugged. 'She's my oldest and closet friend.'

These were unwelcome words to Jack's ears, because he knew that he now had the unenviable task of telling Hester Mancroft that her dearest friend had been murdered.

'Hester . . .' Jack made sure he looked into her eyes as he spoke. 'Hester, I'm sorry to have to tell you that Avril has died.'

Hester froze as Jack's words took their time to register. She swayed slightly in her seat, prompting him to place his hand on her shoulder and gently push her upright again. Hester quickly breathed out and then gulped in a fresh lungful of air, which she held on to. She brought her hand to her chest and her eyes filled with tears.

'Breathe normally,' Jack whispered. Jack stood, making sure she was steady in her seat, then went to get her a glass of water. He wanted to make her a sugary cup of tea, but that might be more stressful for him than telling her her best friend was dead.

Hester sat with her back to Jack, trying to remember how to breathe, as he ran the cold tap until the opaque water ran clear. In his search for a glass, Jack opened the cupboard above the kettle – inside was more medication than he'd ever seen outside of the pharmacy at Maggie's hospital. In amongst the prescribed tablets and medicines was a small brown bottle with a tiny cork stopper in the top. It was exactly the same as the one found in Jessica

Chi's make-up bag, except this one had a label: HEMP EXTRACT FULL-SPECTRUM CBD. And the handwriting was the same as in Avril's little red notebook.

Jack sat back down and was pleased to see that Hester was now breathing normally. He placed the glass of water in her shaking hands and hovered close by as she manoeuvred it to her lips. 'Hester, I need to ask you something and I want you to know that you won't be in any trouble. I need to ask you about the CBD oil in your cupboard. Did Avril give it to you?'

Hester finally let the tears overwhelm her. 'I've got such bad arthritis, Mr Warr. She gave me one bottle each month. It helps me no end. Medicinal is allowed, isn't it?'

Jack assured Hester that he wasn't interested in the oil itself, he'd just needed to know if she got it from Avril. 'She had a little greenhouse with a couple of plants, she said. It was only ever for friends, she said.' Jack showed Hester the photo of Adam Border that he'd been given by Jessica Chi. 'He was a teenage hippy when he stayed with me, but that's Adam, yes.'

Hester asked Jack to open the drawer beneath the kitchen table and pass her the photo album inside. It was a large, dark blue album in a dirty plastic cover and it was overflowing with a mess of memories. Every page was brimming with photos held in place by tiny white sticky corners, and then dozens of loose photos laid randomly on top, protected by thin sheets of tracing paper. This was the kind of album Penny used to carry around before Jack made all of her photos digital.

Hester thumbed through the pages, getting distracted at every turn by images of her and Avril as teenage girls, and by memories of Julian. About halfway through the album, she found what she was looking for: two photos of Adam and Julian, standing with their arms round each other's shoulders. They wore flared jeans and tight T-shirts, and both had shoulder-length hair. Then she picked out a third photo of Adam with a pretty, leggy blonde girl who stood a couple of inches taller than him. 'I can't remember her name. Something Dutch.' Jack took out his mobile phone and took pictures of the three photographs Hester had showed him. 'I need to go shortly, Hester. Is there someone who can come and sit with you?'

Hester leant heavily on the kitchen table and got to her feet. 'I don't have anyone. So I'd be very grateful, Mr Warr, if you'd walk me to the greenery by the esplanade. I'd like to sit there for a while.'

Jack offered his arm, which she gladly took, and he placed his free hand on top of hers. 'Actually, I fancy an early lunch, Hester. Would you join me for fish and chips? My treat.'

CHAPTER 16

When Jack finally entered the squad room, ready with his rehearsed excuse about traffic jams, only Laura was at her desk. She knew he was there, but she refused to look up. 'The DCI had to go. He said write up your interview with Hester and put it on his desk. He'll read it when he gets back.' Jack asked when that would be. 'Well, I don't know, Jack. I'm not his secretary.'

Jack hated the impersonal nature of handing over vital information via a written report. He was adamant that you couldn't properly convey priority and importance in words on a piece of paper. Jack was far better at verbal handovers, which is why he decided straightaway that he would stick around until Ridley got back. After a good twenty minutes, Jack could still feel Laura's eyes burning into the back of his neck.

'Go on then,' she snapped. 'I mean, you're writing one hell of a report over there, Jack, so, go on, tell me what she said to you that she didn't say to me.'

'Avril Jenkins was making and selling hemp oil.'

Laura leapt from her desk and rushed to Jack's side, hands on hips. 'What the hell! Avril Jenkins is our drug dealer?!'

'No . . . well, the cannabis might be hers, but the other stuff's in a different league.' Laura asked how Hester knew about Avril's drugs empire and why she didn't mention it during her first interview. 'Because you weren't there asking about Avril, you were asking about Adam. And I expect she didn't want to get her friend into trouble.'

'Oh, but she mentioned it to you!' Laura huffed.

Jack's growing impatience with Laura's petulance finally flared up. 'Laura, Avril wasn't dead when you spoke to Hester.' He took a couple of seconds to regain his composure. 'Nothing about my interview will reflect badly on you . . . so chill out and make us both a coffee.'

Laura spun on her heels and headed for the coffee machine. She wouldn't have taken such a sexist comment from anyone but Jack: the impromptu demand for hot drinks was normal. It was what partners did. In fact, he made coffee for her far more frequently than she made it for him.

At 7.20 p.m., Ridley walked into the squad room and it was plain to Jack that he'd forgotten all about their planned catch-up. Jack figured that whatever Ridley had been doing must have been important, so he ignored his frustration and started their handover with the big bombshell that Adam Border was indeed the son of Avril Jenkins.

'Yes, well, we knew that really, didn't we?' Ridley said dismissively. 'Hester was just confirming it.' Ridley walked straight past Jack and into his office. Jack couldn't believe the blatant lack of interest. Nonetheless, he again gave Ridley the benefit of the doubt and followed him.

'There's a further connection to Amsterdam, sir. It's where Adam's dad lived, and he was perhaps dating a girl from there. And of course, Jessica Chi had an address in the Netherlands.' Ridley listened in silence, without his usual questions and challenges. 'Hester confirmed our theory about Avril producing hemp oil for sale. The bottle found in Jessica's bag is with toxicology to determine its strength and if it could actually be made from the plants in Avril's greenhouse. But there's no reason to doubt Hester's statement. And the hundreds of small bottles that SOCO found in the outbuildings make sense now.'

Ridley rubbed his brow as though he was fending off a headache. 'I'll hand all of this over to Steve in the morning. Can I have your report, so I don't forget anything? How do we think the cannabis connects to the class A stuff we found?'

'I was thinking this through on the drive back,' Jack said, pulling up a chair. 'This cannabis factory could have been a mother-and-son endeavour, with Avril and Adam making CBD oil for medicinal purposes to sell to a small group of people. They'd make a decent profit, but nothing life changing – not after the debts Avril was left with and with that huge house to run. Adam could have been selling it in Amsterdam, maybe with Jessica Chi, maybe with the as-yet-unidentified Dutch girl. It would have been far less risky to do it there than here. At some point, I think Adam must have attracted the attention of dealers who offered him the opportunity to think bigger. I mean, he had access to a mansion and extensive grounds, he already grew cannabis without detection, and his eccentric mother kept visitors at bay better than a Rottweiler. Then maybe Avril started to get scared. I've seen the guys who attacked her and – although there's no footage of her murder – it has to have been them who did it. She had gang members taking over her home. Her life. Adam either left or was removed from the picture, so she was on her own. I think this is when she started calling us. She wanted our help but couldn't tell us the whole truth for fear of arrest.'

'Write it down. Add it to your report.'

Jack was stunned by Ridley's lukewarm response. 'None of it's fact, sir. It's just speculation. We need the evidence to back it up. We should bounce the theory round, 'cos it might have holes in it.'

Jack was getting worried about the integrity of the case. They were working closely with an exceptional team at the Drug Squad and if they presented ill-considered, half-arsed theories with nothing to support them, they'd be a laughing stock in no time.

'Sir, are you OK?'

Ridley repeated his request for Jack to write up his report, including his theory about the movement and distribution of the cannabis oil. 'We'll use the experience of the Drug Squad and trust them to check out the suggestions we're putting forward. That's what *they* do. They won't provide us with murder theories in their entirety – they'll pose questions and expect us to find the solutions. That's what *we* do.' Ridley pressed his fingertips down on the desk, leant forwards and pushed himself to his feet. He was trying to look calm but Jack's desire to work on when it was already so late was starting to piss him off. 'I know working with outsiders isn't your forte, Jack, but they are on the same team as you.' Ridley pulled his raincoat off the coat rack in the corner of his office, bringing the conversation to an end.

Jack answered back before he'd given himself time to think.

'It's not the outsiders who are the problem, sir.'

Ridley froze with his back to Jack and waited for whatever was coming next. Jack replayed the words that had just emerged, unedited, out of his mouth. There was no taking them back, so he ploughed on. 'Working with you on this case is like working with any other DCI in the nick – and that's not good enough. You're supposed to play devil's advocate at every turn and make me work hard for every step forward in the case. You're supposed to question me and doubt me, so that I double-check every detail and make certain that I never let you down. Since when do you just go through the motions? It's like you've already retired.'

Ridley spun to face Jack. 'Who do you think you're talking to? You think we're friends in here? I'm your boss! And if naming ceremonies and wedding invitations are confusing the issue, then it all stops. *Right now!*' Ridley slid his hand into the inside pocket of his raincoat and spun his wedding invitation through the air towards Jack. 'I'm not your partner, DS Warr, Laura is. You need a pat on the head, get it from her. Stop being so fucking needy.'

Ridley left his office without another word.

Jack was in shock. At first, he tried to make sense of what had just happened, then he realised that the far greater issue was how the hell they'd find their way back from the insults they'd just thrown. Jack stood in the middle of Ridley's office for what seemed like an age and finally decided that there would be no way back for them.

He looked up to see Ridley standing in the doorway. His eyes were lowered, and they flicked around the worn grey carpet, searching for the words he needed.

'I'm not retiring. I've got cancer.'

CHAPTER 17

Jack stood with his arms round Maggie's waist and his head on her shoulder as she soaked the oven dishes and explained the three-course menu Penny had planned for Josh's visit. Throughout her chatter, Jack stared out of the window in silence. 'Chicken and beef, Yorkshire puds. A load of veg, six or seven, one must be creamed mash according to your mum. Stuffing. She'll make two gravies from the meat juices and, what else, oh yes, bread sauce. She was thinking of doing apple pie and pecan pie, you know, the sort of puddings your new friend might like from home, but then she decided on our old-school favourites. So she's doing jam roly-poly and treacle sponge.' Maggie looked up from the sink and saw Jack's reflection in the blackness of the kitchen window. 'Are you going to tell me what's wrong?'

Jack and Ridley stood in silence for what could only have been five seconds but during that time Jack relived the last days of his dad's life before his cancer finally took him, quietly and unannounced in the middle of the night. Ridley finally spoke. 'I was going to tell you, but when I didn't suffer that many side effects from the treatment, I thought . . . no one needed to know. Superintendent Raeburn knows. And I'm doing OK.' Ridley paused and Jack made no attempt to fill the silence, letting Ridley find the words. 'My emotions are so close to the surface at the moment, Jack, that sometimes . . . sometimes I just need to be on my own in case . . . in case the anger and frustration – and the fear, if I'm honest – in case it all boils over and I say or do something I can't take back.' Ridley took a step forward and picked his wedding invitation up off the floor where he'd thrown it. When he stood upright again his eyes were red and glistened with the threat of tears. His voice had reduced to a whisper. 'Can I take this back?'

Of course, Jack had said yes, and Ridley had gone home. And that was it. Jack hadn't asked any questions and Ridley had done all the talking he was prepared to do for one day.

Now Jack kissed Maggie on the neck. 'Bad day. The menu sounds great.' Jack kissed Maggie again, told her that he loved her and went upstairs for a shower. Maggie knew something more was wrong. But she also knew that whatever it was, he wasn't ready to talk about it.

* * *

Ridley led the morning briefing with his old methodical, laborious attention to detail. He was back. He was strong, encouraging, purposeful and leading from the front. He relayed the highlights of his interview with Terence Jenkins, then he handed the room to Jack so that he could relay his conversation with Hester Mancroft – finishing with the revelation that Adam Border was Avril Jenkins' son.

'So,' Ridley summed up, 'the Amsterdam connection needs following up. Who's the blonde girl pictured with Adam? Where did his dad live? Is it anywhere near the address we have out there for Jessica Chi? Laura, ask Anik to find out what Josh knows about Amsterdam. Then, if you're not treading on Drug Squad toes, talk to the Amsterdam police and find out if the name of Adam Border is known to them. Jack, my office, please.'

The conversation in Ridley's office was . . . normal. Ridley's moment of sharing had seemingly been enough for him, and Jack was thankful to be talking about a double murder, rather than Ridley's health. Ridley made two coffees as he spoke. 'Anik's daily reports are, well . . . I thought I was thorough. He's found his mojo, that's for sure. I know it was tough for us to hand the lead to Steve, but Anik's doing a good job at reporting back, so we're getting what we need.'

'You know, guv, I sometimes think that Steve and his mob are holding stuff back. I mean, when I was over there looking at the footage – which they admitted was not in chronological order – they mentioned that the same men had at some point arrived in a Range Rover. They didn't show me that clip, just said they had traced it and it was a stolen vehicle. We should have been privy to that – just makes me wonder what else they are withholding.'

Ridley handed Jack his coffee and they both sat. Ridley made no secret of getting two bottles of pills from his jacket pocket and taking one tablet from each. 'I will look into that. In the meantime, it'd be useful to find a list of customers for her hemp oil.' Jack thought about the secret contents of his own jacket pocket, namely Avril's little red notebook. 'Painkillers and an anti-emetic. In case you were wondering. They don't impede my ability to work.'

'I know you wouldn't be here if they did, sir.' Jack took the opportunity to say the only thing he felt needed saying. 'I'm not going to pry. But if you need anything, from me or from Maggie, you must ask. The answer will always be yes.'

Jack came out of Ridley's office, coffee in hand, and stopped by the whiteboards. He was looking specifically at the photos they'd collated so far because, frustratingly, most of them showed people they couldn't yet identify. Pinned up were two photographs that had recently been added. Avril Jenkins' Range Rover and the Porsche. Beside the photographs was the updated information from the team allocated to check for fingerprints.

'When did these come in?' Jack asked Laura.

'Early this morning. The Range Rover had numerous prints, mostly Avril Jenkins', and others checked out. The vehicle had some kind of fault and had been taken in a few months back to the Range Rover dealership in Thames Ditton. The two mechanics that had worked on it were tested and matched. Avril was told that she would need to have the diesel pump changed as it was clogged, but apparently, she only drove it on short journeys and it would be quite costly to replace, so she told them to return it as she was not going to pay for the repair. They left it in her garage parked behind the Porsche.'

Jack was becoming impatient. 'What about the silver Porsche that we know was driven by Adam Border? Any prints would be vital for us.'

'I know that, and the forensic team were very thorough but it had been cleaned inside and out. Not one print was found. They even tested the tarpaulin on both vehicles but neither had prints.'

Jack gritted his teeth.

'That kid . . .' Laura waited for Jack to acknowledge that she was still talking to him. 'It's her brother. The principal from her school got back to me. David Summers. He's twelve years younger than Avril. We're putting a trace out. I'm making progress on Jessica Chi's background, just a couple more ducks to line up there. But I haven't found out who that bloke in military uniform is yet.' Jack suggested that she run the photo by Terence Jenkins to see if he could provide them with an identification. Laura joined Jack at the whiteboards. She seemed fed up. 'Apart from Hester's anecdotes and dateless memories, I've still got nothing of substance on Adam Border. And I mean nothing, until he rocked up at Chelsea Art College. Which means . . .' Laura gave Jack the honour of saying the words out loud.

'Adam Border didn't exist before that? We've been chasing a false identity.' Jack took a snap of the unknown man in military uniform on his mobile. 'Let's pick up the pace. First one to identify this guy gets a three-course canteen lunch bought for them by the loser. Go!'

* * *

Hester Mancroft's phone rang for so long that it cut out and went to voicemail. Twice. When she did finally answer, Jack explained that he'd texted an image to her mobile and he needed her to try and identify the man in military dress. Getting her to open the image, however, was like trying to get a cat to play the piano.

Meanwhile, Laura had FaceTimed Terence, having isolated the one relevant photograph so that Terence couldn't see all of the case evidence. Laura could hardly keep a straight face as she listened to Jack in the background trying to explain to Hester how to view an image at the same time as speak – she accidently hung up on him once and he had to call her back.

Terence was certain that he didn't recognise the man. 'You know the uniform's not British, don't you?'

Jack looked up from his pointless conversation with Hester, who was currently running through Avril's long list of old boyfriends to try and recall an army officer amongst them. 'I collected militaria in my time,' Terence continued. 'It's the only thing I did inherit from Father! This reminds me of the old Dutch get-up.'

Laura retained her composure, seeing as she was on FaceTime but, behind her back, she gave Jack the finger. She was about to win a free three-course lunch! She asked Terence if he was certain of the uniform's origin.

'Back in 2018, or 2017 maybe, the Dutch government encouraged people to join the armed forces by doing a campaign where they asked their serving military to wear their uniforms in the streets. Anyway, their current uniform is a modernised version of the one they wore in the seventies. That's what's in your photo.'

Laura thanked Terence for his help, wished him a good afternoon, then hung up. She spun round to Jack, wearing a huge grin. She sauntered towards him, ordering soup, followed by whatever the fish dish of the day was, ending with a double helping of

Bakewell tart and custard, then perched on his desk swinging her feet. Jack held his mobile away from his ear to muffle the noise of Hester talking at him.

'I didn't hear Terence identify the man in the photo,' Jack said.

'Oh, come on. He's Dutch. That's more information than you're getting. Could be Adam's dad?'

'Adam's dad was a carpet salesman from London.'

'Says who?' Laura nodded towards Jack's mobile. '*Her?*'

Hester suddenly became loud enough for Laura to hear despite not being on speaker.

'Oh, I've opened the photo, DS Warr!' There was a pause while she looked at it. 'No, I've no idea who that is.'

Laura giggled her way back to her own desk, as Jack thanked Hester for helping. 'I'm enlarging the insignia on this guy's uniform to send to the Dutch military,' she said. 'I'll let you know his name by lunchtime, Jack. Reserve me a table by the window.'

* * *

In his office, Ridley was himself now on speakerphone to Terence Jenkins, clarifying that Avril Jenkins' body was ready to be released. Terence asked if Ridley would be attending the funeral. 'Yes please, Mr Jenkins. Myself, DS Jack Warr and DCI Steve Lewis will be there, if you don't mind.'

Steve paced the area in front of Ridley's desk, hands behind his back, listening. Terence explained that it would only be a small gathering. He had two old friends he wanted to be there as support for him, and he thought it right to invite Avril's immediate neighbours and a couple of her friends he knew of. He estimated that there would be no more than ten or twelve people. Terence went on to say that although probate was still pending, he was allowed to be in the property and, amongst other things, could finally create a definitive inventory. With this in mind, Terence then asked if he could host the wake at the house. Steve didn't pause his prowling as he nodded to Ridley. 'Yes, Mr Jenkins. You can have Avril's wake in her home. Your home.'

As soon as Terence had hung up, Steve told Ridley what he was going to do. 'We'll run the cameras in the downstairs rooms during the wake and record every move of every person there. We might even change the outgoing loop to live action, so the drug dealers can watch too. Briefing in Staines? Zero eight hundred?' Steve left with no further niceties, leaving Ridley's door wide open.

Jack walked across and asked if he wanted it closing, as was his preference in recent months. 'Leave it open. Thanks, Jack.' Ridley screwed up his nose as though a terrible smell had just wafted his way. 'He used the 24-hour clock. What a prick.'

Jack and Ridley shared their first smile in weeks.

* * *

Before he could turn and leave, Laura appeared behind Jack with a notepad in her hand and a smile on her face. She'd found another piece of their complex puzzle. 'Jessica Chi. Daughter of Henrick and Matilda Chi, née Dovrick. Both alive and well and living in an artists' commune in Amsterdam. They're currently unaware of their daughter's death. This, together with the Dutch military uniform on that bloke standing next to Avril in the photo might just be adding up to a trip to Amsterdam, sir.'

Ridley quickly agreed. The notification of death definitely had to be done face to face and in conjunction with the Dutch police.

As Laura was quietly running through her wardrobe in her head to see if she needed to shop before flying out, Ridley announced that, first thing tomorrow, he'd get Anik back from Staines and send him to Amsterdam. Laura's chin almost hit the floor.

'I need you running the show here, Laura, whilst Jack and I are at Avril's funeral. The press release announced her death was the result of a robbery gone wrong. There's an undercover presence at her home, but no uniforms. To the outside world, everything's back to normal at that house. It's the exact time for someone to get complacent . . . and it's not going to be us.'

CHAPTER 18

The chef's curly brown hair was scraped back off her face and hidden beneath a hair net. She was unpacking and arranging four different types of shop-bought canapés onto large silver platters ready to be taken out into the small gathering of mourners. Two waitresses, dressed immaculately in black and white, waited for their instructions. They all looked the part, down to the last detail – if it hadn't been for the earpiece, barely visible beneath the chef's hairnet, no one would have suspected that they were all Drug Squad . . . as was the gardener raking leaves from the front lawn and the woman waiting at the bus stop on the main road at the end of the private lane entrance. She could clearly see any passenger getting off buses in both directions and would radio in to the duty officer outside Avril's house.

In the driveway, a white catering van was tucked against the bushes out of the way. This also belonged to the Drug Squad. Inside the van, Moley and Sergeant Mike Tulley monitored the system of hidden cameras inside the property. As planned, the external feed from the cameras was now live rather than looped footage, just in case any of the drug dealers were watching.

Ridley stood near the open fireplace in the drawing room, holding a champagne flute filled with fresh orange juice. From there, he could see the front door where Terence diligently met every guest and directed them to the circling waitresses, one carrying canapés and the other carrying a tray of champagne flutes. Ridley could also see the bottom of the staircase, which had been blocked by a red barrier rope, making the upstairs look mysterious, like the private area in a nightclub or exclusive bar, rather than the scene of a horrific murder.

Jack had positioned himself at the opposite end of the room, so he could watch all of the cars arriving. He could see Hester Mancroft sitting alone in a far corner of the drawing room, looking at the photograph of Avril chosen to adorn the front of the order of service. She cried quietly behind a freshly ironed hanky. Her seat was surrounded by a few of bouquets of flowers, all of which were destined for the old people's home on Kingston Hill. Jack wanted to go and ask if she was OK, but he couldn't risk getting stuck talking to her. If the day passed uneventfully, he'd spend a little time with Hester before she journeyed back to Hove.

* * *

As Jack looked out of the front window, a Jaguar with tinted windows pulled into the grounds and parked behind the catering van. Jack perked up and actually stood taller, like a meerkat having spotted something potentially dangerous. The smart-casually dressed driver got out of the Jag and headed for the house – and immediately behind him, Mike Tulley, dressed in a smart black suit, stepped from the catering van and followed him in. The driver had been clocked and was now under discreet surveillance. He was a tall slender man, not dissimilar in appearance to the man who'd arrived at the house on the night Avril was murdered, but without facial recognition there was no way of knowing. Whilst Jack did a quick trace on the Jag's number plate, he casually moved closer to the doorway of the drawing room so he could hear Terence greet the driver.

'I'm sorry for your loss, Mr Jenkins. I'm Jason Marks. I met Avril through her husband's business dealings. Your brother and I shared an affinity for beautiful art.'

'Are you a collector, Mr Marks? I don't mean to sound crass but, if it interests you, I'll be selling much of the house's contents, once I'm allowed. I can't take most of it back to the States with me, so . . . I would like it to go to a good home. An art appreciator, like yourself.'

Jason Marks kindly offered to speak with Terence at a time more convenient to him and mentioned that he'd happily value and catalogue the contents of the house and help him to avoid being ripped off during any house clearance sales. He then headed into the drawing room, collecting a flute of champagne on the way.

Jason walked straight past Jack and settled into a wingback chair positioned next to the fireplace where Ridley was still standing. He was already eyeing the antiques: his gaze caressed the Moorcroft Flambe Eventide vase that sat inside the fire grate, the wall-mounted brass fire poker, and the handwoven Persian rug beneath his feet. You could almost see him totting up his percentage . . .

Ridley, currently less than ten feet from Jason, had just been collared by Arnold Hutchinson, who was talking about Avril's will, Terence's inheritance and the associated timeframes relating to probate and the ongoing police investigation. The information that Avril had been found dead in her own home was in the public domain, so it didn't matter if that was overheard by Jason, but Ridley was fearful of Arnold unwittingly referring to him as 'DCI Ridley', so he put a gentle hand on Arnold's elbow and steered him away whilst saying something about trying the canapés.

Meanwhile, Jason continued to not-so-subtly peruse the room from behind his champagne flute – clearly window shopping. His eyes paused again on a pair of antique Sevres Bisque figurines depicting grape gatherers, one male and one female. He couldn't help but get up and take a closer look. Under the guise of heading for the waitress with canapés, Jack moved casually towards him. Pointing to the large sun-bleached outline on the wallpaper above the Sevres figurines, where a painting had once hung, he said, simply, 'Criminal.'

'Art theft?' Jason looked quizzically at Jack. 'Yes, it certainly is.'

'Jack Warr,' Jack introduced himself. 'I was part of the investigation into Mrs Jenkins' missing property. Art's not just a financial investment to most people, is it? It's an emotional one. You have to love something to spend . . . what would this set you back?' Jack picked up the female figurine.

'They're about a thousand a piece. Nothing compared to some of the items in this room. I'm a bit of a collector.' Jason Marks offered his hand. 'Jason Marks. I recently worked alongside Mrs Jenkins' insurance company. Freddie had a great eye for quality.'

'Not Avril?'

Jason smiled. 'I think buying with your heart is admirable. Although perhaps not profitable. I was closer to her husband, as we both had the misfortune to be involved in the Icelandic crash.' Jason Marks adjusted his perfect tie, allowing Jack to notice that he was wearing a heavy gold-and-cornelian ring on his pinkie finger.

As Jack made polite conversation about various antiques around the room, Mike made his way to Ridley's side and questioned Jack's decision to actually introduce himself to the man who may have been lounging in this very drawing room, whilst Avril was murdered and dismembered upstairs. Ridley didn't even crack a smile. 'It's almost as though it might be the last thing he'd expect a policeman to do, don't you think?' Mike scowled, reminding Ridley that this case was being led by DCI Lewis and the Drug Squad, so their preferred tactics should be respected. 'As far as I'm aware, DS Tulley,' Ridley said, emphasising Mike's rank as a way of putting him in his place, 'DCI Lewis isn't here.' He walked away without another word.

Jack didn't stay with Jason Marks for longer than a couple of minutes before he excused himself and headed for Hester. Jack crouched in front of her, so she could see his face. It took a few seconds for her to remember how she knew him but, when she did, she immediately started to cry. 'I never thought she'd go before me.' Hester smiled through her tears. 'She was always the last to leave a party.' Jack gently placed his hand on top of Hester's. Before leaving her, he made sure she had a full glass of champagne, and that she had the means to get to her hotel after the wake drew to a close, but she was actually was very well organised. She'd even decided to order a pizza and a bottle of stout for her dinner at the hotel, in memory of Avril's favourite meal from their youth.

Over the next hour, the drawing room continued to hum with conversation. When Terence had finished greeting people as they arrived and started to mingle, Ridley and Jack slipped out, one at a time and ten minutes apart.

Ridley's car was tucked down the side of the house, away from the main area designated for parking. Ridley was reading about Jason Marks on his mobile phone. 'No record. He's worked in the banking world all of his adult life. Climbed quickly. Some investments, like Frederick Jenkins, so that stacks up.' At that moment, a phone call came through from Steve Lewis, which Ridley put on speaker.

'Simon, look, I'm out for lunch, so I'll keep this brief. Your man, Jack Warr, I need you to keep him on a tighter leash. Jason Marks, if he's involved, is a small part of a much bigger picture. We can't have him being tipped off and blabbing to the higher-ups.' Steve snorted. 'There's nothing "undercover" about walking up to a suspect and introducing yourself, Simon. I know Warr's probably not well versed in this sort of work, so best leave it to us, eh?'

Ridley agreed wholeheartedly with every word Steve said, wished him a pleasant afternoon and hung up. He then turned the sound off on his mobile and put it into the central compartment between the front seats. 'Don't give that little hissy fit a second thought,' he said.

Jack's mobile pinged as a result on the Jag's number plate came through. 'It's a rental.' Jack let out a long whistle as he scrolled through the hire prices. 'From a very high-end Knightsbridge company. They've also got an underground car park at Number One Hyde Park. Bentleys, Rolls-Royces, Range Rovers, Maseratis, Ferraris, Jags . . .'

At this point, people began filtering out of Avril's house. Terence retook his place in the doorway and, just as he had done when people entered, he now thanked them again as they left. Jason Marks shook Terence's hand, left him with a business card and headed for his Jag. Close behind Jason was Mike Tulley, who clocked Ridley and Jack tucked down the side of the house. He briefly stared daggers at Jack as he walked to his unmarked BMW 5 Series and followed Jason out of the gate.

'They've all got really big bollocks over in Staines,' Jack joked.

Ridley started the engine. 'Yeah. I don't know how they sit down.'

CHAPTER 19

In the squad room, Laura was working at her computer with her earphones in. Tinny instrumental music could just about be heard as Ridley and Jack walked past. She removed the headphone cable from her phone and allowed the synthesised Baroque muzak to escape. 'I've been on hold with this particular department for twenty minutes. The music's driving me insane. I'm still trying to track down the military insignia the guy in the old photo with Avril is wearing.' Laura plugged the headphone cable back into her mobile and took out one of her earphones, so she could multitask. 'I've given Anik a copy of the photo in case he can find something out whilst he's in Amsterdam.'

Ridley asked if Anik had checked in since getting on the Eurostar. Laura's voice went up an octave and stayed there. 'Oh my God, sir, if he checks in one more time, I'll delete his number! He's been upgraded, so will not *stop* checking in. He's had a croissant for breakfast, and for lunch he had a jambon and Gruyère baguette with a Mediterranean pasta pesto salad. I mean, that's just a ham and cheese sarnie with a side salad, right?' Ridley waited for her to answer his question properly. 'He arrived at a quarter past one, sir. He's to meet with Lieutenant Garritt Visser who'll act as translator if he needs one. Jessica Chi's parents were away last night at a family birthday, and don't get back till 5 p.m.'

'Good, thank you, anything else?'

'Yes, we are still trying to trace David Summers, that's Avril's young brother. I'm waiting for call backs.'

* * *

Visser was a striking young man with vivid blond hair and high cheekbones. His English was perfect. 'Welcome to Amsterdam, Lieutenant Joshi.' Anik didn't correct Visser on his rank. 'I'm Lieutenant Garritt Visser. I spoke to Mr Chi on the telephone and they're on track to arrive at Il Kantine cafeteria at 5 p.m. Do they know why you're here?'

Anik confirmed that the Chis knew it was about their daughter, but that they were not yet aware of her death. It had been kept out of the newspapers due to the wider drug operation.

Visser nodded. 'Mr Chi's English seems very good, so I won't step in unless you ask me to, or unless I sense that either of them needs clarity. Does that sound OK to you?'

'That's perfect. Thank you, Lieutenant Visser.'

'Call me Garritt. Please. The NDSM ferry takes us directly to the cafeteria, so we'll be about an hour early. Would you like to look around?' Anik declined, saying that he'd rather spend the time getting himself prepared for the conversation with the Chis. But he added that afterwards, he'd appreciate being escorted to Zee-heldenbuurt as that's where his B&B was located. 'The rest of my day is for you. We can do whatever you need to.'

Il Kantine was a large converted warehouse, now a three-storey venue with meeting rooms, bar, restaurant and extensive terrace overlooking the docks. It retained much of its industrial look, with the high ceilings and huge windows adding to the character. It was 4 p.m. when they got off the ferry and walked the two minutes along the waterside footpath. Garritt suggested that Anik sit at the corner window table, as it would be the most private area. Then he got menus and two glasses of iced water until they were ready to order. Most of the other customers were young and looked like art students; probably connected to the many art colleges and galleries they'd passed on the train and the ferry. It was one of the very few occasions in his life that Anik had felt old. Garritt returned with a jug of iced water, two glasses and two menus. He asked if Anik would like to eat before meeting with the Chis.

'I don't think I could. Just a cappuccino, maybe.' He neglected to mention the two meals he'd already had on the train. 'It'd be nice to find somewhere to eat afterwards, though.'

For the next hour, Anik and Garritt spoke about anything other than the death of Jessica Chi. They got on well, being of a similar age, and with similar interests: namely Wimbledon, cars, women and being a police officer. Garritt was from a police family going back four generations. He'd never considered any other path in life. He was saddened by Anik's route into the police force: 'My family thought it was suicidal for me to join the police – they're not popular where I'm from. My dad's not spoken to me in nearly three years, 'cos when I joined up, his mates said he had to choose . . . me or them. He's ashamed. Skin colour's still a big issue in some parts of London; add a uniform and you get racism on a professional level. And not just from the public.'

Garritt shook his head, as if in shame at belonging to the white demographic. 'So, I left the uniform behind as soon as I could and the squad I work with now is brilliant. I love it.' Anik knew that he sounded doubtful. 'I gave up so much to pursue this job. I expect too much back, too quickly. I know I do. But this job owes me.' Anik laughed at how weighty the conversation had suddenly got. 'I appreciate days like this. I don't get them as often as I'd like.'

Garritt got the coffees, then occupied himself by catching up on emails before stepping outside to make some calls, leaving Anik to prep for the meeting.

* * *

At a quarter to five, Anik looked up from his notebook to see Garritt speaking with a couple in their late fifties. The man looked very trendy in light blue jeans, biker T-shirt and trainers, with his grey hair pulled back into a ponytail. The woman wore a long skirt and high-collared blouse with a large brooch at the neck, a fringed shawl draped around her shoulders, and wooden clogs that looked as though she'd hand-painted them herself. Her long black hair was twisted into a low knot down her back. Garritt shook hands with them both, then led them indoors.

By the time they reached the table, Anik's heart was beating out of his chest. He surreptitiously wiped his right palm on his trouser leg as he stood to greet them. The man introduced himself as Henrick and his wife as Matilda. Anik offered to get them a drink, but Henrick said that the iced water would be fine. They settled into their seats as Garritt went to the serving counter to get two clean glasses.

Matilda placed her hands together on the table and nervously picked at her nails. Henrick put his hand gently on top of both of hers, to stop her from fidgeting. 'We know why we're here.' Henrick's words stopped Anik in his tracks: how could they possibly know that their daughter was dead? 'We warned Jessica because we knew what the value was. She said she was told it was a copy, but I knew it wasn't.' Matilda gripped Henrick's hand and squeezed. Henrick continued, oblivious to the fact that Anik had no idea what he was talking about. 'I know that one of his last watercolours to come up for sale went for £2 million at Sotheby's. That's double the estimate, and that was back in 2014. It was bought by a private investor.'

Garritt returned to the table with a fresh jug of iced water and two clean glasses. As he poured drinks for the Chis, Henrick went on.

'Of course, anything from the Pre-Raphaelite period is worth a considerable amount, even more so as it was known that an oil version exists and is, I believe, in the Russell-Cotes Art Gallery in Bournemouth.' Garritt looked at Anik quizzically, confused by the conversation he'd walked in on. Anik gave a little shrug. 'So, you see, I knew it was authentic. Rossetti's nude *Venus Verticordia*. And I easily recognised his model as Alexa Wilding. I made Jessica tell me how she'd come by it. I knew it couldn't be legal.' Matilda brought her free hand quickly to her mouth and closed her eyes, fighting back the tears. Henrick looked at Anik in desperation. 'Jessica gave me her word that she'd return it. Did she? She swore to us. Please tell me she did.'

Anik had no option but to come clean. 'Mr Chi, I'm sorry, but I'm not here about a painting.' Matilda caught her breath and Henrick, clearly realising he'd just exposed a crime he needn't have mentioned, was wishing he could turn back time. 'I'm afraid I have bad news,' Anik continued. 'Five days ago, a body was found. I'm sorry to say that it was your daughter, Jessica.' Matilda continued staring, seemingly frozen in time. Henrick just shook his head. 'I'm afraid there's been no mistake. It was Jessica.'

Anik opened a small A5 file and slid Jessica's student travel card across the table towards her parents. The two sides of laminated plastic had come apart due to being submerged in the pond, and the colours of Jessica's passport photo had blurred slightly. 'It's wet.' Henrick's voice was panicked. 'Why is it wet? Did she drown?' As soon as he said this, Matilda's emotions finally burst free, and she began to cry loudly. As she fumbled in her shoulder bag for a handkerchief, Garritt tried to calm them in the language they knew best.

'We will require a formal identification if you could possibly come to London,' Anik continued after a short pause. He had done several death notifications in his years on Ridley's team, but this was the first time he'd had to use an interpreter to help him. He felt awful that these parents were basically hearing about their dead daughter twice, getting the facts from Anik, and then clarification from Garritt. 'Your daughter didn't drown, sir. There was a fire. We don't believe that Jessica suffered at all.' Anik knew this was a lie, as the post-mortem had clearly identified smoke in Jessica's lungs, meaning that she was alive as the fire raged around her. But Anik thought Mr and Mrs Chi were distressed enough without imagining that their daughter might have been burnt alive. 'Mr Chi, when did you last see Jessica?'

Henrick couldn't look Anik in the eyes. 'Two months ago. In London. I, er . . . I'm no good with addresses. I could drive there from the ferry, completely from memory but, I can't tell you . . .' Anik assured Henrick that they had Jessica's London address, but they didn't know whether she had a second home in Amsterdam. 'Jessica has a room in our apartment. Had.' Anik glanced at Garritt, who asked the Chis, in Dutch, if they'd like to take a short break. Henrick shook his head and took a deep breath before continuing. 'She had an on-off boyfriend. Adam, I think. He had a property here which she sometimes stayed at, but I don't think he has it anymore. He was pleasant. Polite. I never saw his place, but the part of town it was in is good. So, we knew he had a good job and could look after Jessica. I've not seen him for almost a year.' Henrick then asked Matilda to look through her address book and find the address for Adam. She snapped into action and obediently did as she was asked, seemingly relieved to have a task so she didn't have to listen to the conversation.

'Mr Chi . . . you thought I was here about a stolen painting. Rossetti's *Venus Verticordia*.' Henrick's eyes quickly filled with tears once again, as the thought occurred to him that his silence over his daughter's illegal art dealings might have contributed to her death. 'I need you to help me now, please. By telling me everything you know.'

Henrick showed Anik several pictures of the painting in question on his mobile phone and repeated that he was certain Jessica had returned it after he warned her that it was genuine. He also insisted that, if the painting was stolen, Jessica had not been the one to steal it: she'd insisted that she'd been given it and he believed her. As the interview came to an end, Anik asked if he could see the bedroom in their apartment reserved for Jessica.

* * *

The scenic walk to the Chis' apartment was marred by the awful conversation they'd just had. Anik had come to Amsterdam and shattered their lives into a thousand pieces ... and he wasn't done yet.

Jessica's bedroom was an attic space with a balcony that provided a view of the docks. There were a few clothes and one pair of shoes in the single wardrobe, but nothing else. Jessica hadn't stored anything personal there: no documents or personal effects, and the only two photos Anik found were both from childhood.

Back in the main area of the apartment, which looked and felt like an art studio, Anik had one more line of questioning to pursue before he could leave the Chis to their grief. 'I'm sorry to ask you this, but do you know if Jessica was ever involved in drugs?'

Henrick seemed so emotionally drained that he couldn't muster any feelings of offence. 'She dabbled in cannabis, as is the way for many people in Amsterdam, young and old. She never took anything stronger, if that's what you're asking.' Henrick handed Anik a piece of paper, with a handwritten address. 'My wife has written down the address for Adam, but I'm sure he no longer owns it. I think now we'd like you to go, please.'

Anik was more than ready to leave. He told them that once they were ready to come to London to do the formal identification of Jessica's body, they should contact Lieutenant Garritt and he'd help them. Garritt gave them a sincere smile that said 'I'm here for you' and they both left.

Garritt walked Anik towards his B&B in Zeeheldenbuurt, whilst reading the address written in shaky, grief-stricken handwriting by Matilda. 'This apartment is on the way. From memory, I think the whole building is now being rented to the business sector.'

Garritt was right: the address was for a tall, narrow building with four floors and a roof terrace. The top apartment that had been occupied by Adam was now the temporary home of a German businessman in Amsterdam on a three-month training contract. He had no knowledge of any tenant who had been there before him. He was able to direct Anik and Garritt to the owner of the building, but all he could remember about Adam Border was that he was polite, quiet and lived in London for most of the year. Although he did assume that Adam was Dutch, because he spoke it fluently.

Once the short interview with the owner of Adam Border's old place of residence was over, Garritt uttered one, incredibly welcome word: 'Beer?'

*　*　*

Anik and Garritt sat at a small waterfront bistro table sipping cold beer and eating a giant pizza between them. Apart from compiling his notes, Anik had nothing to do and the rest of his evening was free, while Garritt's only instruction from his boss had been to look after the English policeman. Then Anik made the mistake of turning his mobile back on. Dozens of messages and images pinged through from Laura, asking him to try and identify the uniform being worn by the unknown soldier. She'd provided names and addresses of training academies, army barracks and army hostels. And she'd been sure to mention that, although she was the one texting, the request had come from Ridley.

CHAPTER 20

Penny had been cooking since 2 p.m. The ingredients for the avocado and pear starter sat in a shady corner of the kitchen top, as they would be the last thing she prepared.

The meats were in the oven. Penny had added a lamb shoulder to the menu, as well as the chicken and beef, because she had a sachet of Moroccan lamb mix and some peppers that she wanted to use up with the leftovers. Penny did this all the time: she planned a week's worth of meals, rather than cooking from day to day. This meant that she didn't waste a single item of food and, each month, she saved Jack and Maggie a fortune on their shopping bill. She'd also swapped the planned treacle sponge for bread-and-butter pudding because the loaf in the fridge would shortly be 'on the turn'.

She sent Jack to the shops with Hannah, to buy two specific bottles of red wine, a decent brandy and some cheeses – whilst Maggie was given the task of setting the table. She was under strict instructions to use their best glasses, one for wine and one for iced water, and their white cotton napkins normally reserved for Christmas. Penny was firmly in control, with Maggie and Jack acting like the hired help.

Maggie slinked from the kitchen and raced out of the front door, desperate to catch Jack before he vanished down the street towards the shopping precinct. 'You know what day it is, don't you?' They both knew that her question was pointless: Jack had no clue what she was talking about. 'We said we'd do something really special this year because she helps us beyond words. And now look! We've both forgotten.'

'Oh, shit!' Jack had stopped in his tracks. 'Mum's birthday.' His attitude changed in a flash as he became Mr Fixit. 'Don't worry. I'm on the way to the shops. I'll sort it. You get back before she notices you've gone.' As Jack hurried off down the street, Maggie was under no illusions that he would come back with something that screamed 'last-minute gift'. But they'd both forgotten Penny's birthday, so she'd have to bear her fair share of the weight of the embarrassment that would accompany whatever Jack chose.

By the time Jack got home, the kitchen looked and smelled magnificent. Maggie took Hannah up for a bath, then bed, whilst Penny unpacked the shopping. Jack kept one bag back without her noticing . . . then he slipped away whilst Penny chose which bottle of red wine she wanted to serve first and removed the cap to let it breathe.

By 7 p.m. Hannah was asleep and Maggie was in the lounge trying to find out what Jack had bought for his mum so she'd know how apologetic she'd need to sound. But he was giving nothing away. Their mini-argument was brought to an abrupt end by a firm knock on the front door that echoed down the hallway. Penny spun and looked at the kitchen clock – Josh was bang on time. She whipped the pinny from her waist and threw it into the washing machine.

As Penny stepped into the lounge, straightening her skirt, her enthusiasm for hosting a home-cooked meal made Jack smile with pride: all he'd told her was that a friend from work, who was originally from Alabama, missed his mamma's cooking, and this was the result. Penny had taken on the role of surrogate 'mamma' and decided to cook up a feast. All to make him feel at home in a foreign country. *And* on her birthday which, right now, she must be presuming would pass by without a mention.

Josh had brought a bottle of the exact same red wine that was currently breathing in the centre of the table – and a treacle sponge!

Penny took this as a sure sign that he was a lovely, well brought-up young man. And she *loved* his accent. 'Thank you, ma'am, for cooking for me tonight. It smells amazing.'

Penny thanked Josh for coming, poured four glasses of wine, then instructed everyone to go into the lounge whilst she prepared the starter. Once in the lounge, Jack said they had around fifteen minutes to talk about the case.

'Well,' Josh began, 'no one's tried to get their drugs out of the cellar yet, which means they're either happy to lose that amount of product or they know we're watching. My gut tells me they don't know we have surveillance on the property. There's no sign that anybody's getting twitchy; the private plane hasn't moved in weeks.'

Jack was still finding it hard to gauge the size of this particular operation. But Josh, from past experience, had a better sense of scale.

'They're small. At the top, I mean. There are a lot of tentacles spreading across UK cities, which makes it feel like a huge gang, but only a handful of real decision makers. That keeps them safe, but it can also make them slow on the ground. The fire, for example: they should have swooped in and cleaned that place out before the ashes were cold. The fact they didn't suggests they might not have the resources. They're smart though: all we're seeing are the low-lifes, sneaking around in balaclavas, mixing, cutting and bagging the drugs.' Josh chose his next words carefully. 'They're hired drug workers, doubling as muscle who'll get rid of witnesses thinking they're . . . oh, what's that thing you guys say? Oh yeah, thinking they're the dog's bollocks.' Josh, fleetingly embarrassed by his own language, flicked his eyes to Maggie. 'Pardon me, ma'am. They're not the dog's you-know-whats. They're the expendable dumb asses . . . pardon me again.'

Maggie assured Josh that she wasn't offended by bad language; although Penny would object if he did it at the dinner table. 'Oh Maggie! The dinner table is for polite conversation; no drugs talk, no murder, no swearing.'

Josh went on to explain that, in the US, the drug gangs have an army of lookouts employed to do nothing but sit outside houses like Avril Jenkins' and report on who comes and who goes. And if the lookout failed to spot a drug factory being infiltrated by the cops, he'd be shot. No questions asked. 'This gang, apparently, doesn't even know that we put their own security system on a loop, so they can't see us moving around inside.' Josh took a mouthful of wine, clearing half a glass in one gulp. 'There are inconsistencies. Contradictions. Sometimes I think they really got their shit together, sometimes I can't believe we haven't caught them yet!'

Jack picked up the conversation as Maggie refilled everyone's glasses, emptying the first bottle of wine. 'I get that this might be small-fry to you, Josh. But getting this volume of lethal drugs off the streets is a big win for us.'

'It's all relative, Jack. I'm not playing this down. What I think you have here is a dealer who's been around a long time. He knows how to play the game and, crucially, he knows when to fold. My guess is that he started as a runner and worked his way up, thinking he could do things better . . . and he is. He'll have hundreds of properties like Avril's place. From the outside, there's nothing to see. But inside . . .' Josh sucked in a long whistle, then smiled. 'But, like I said, it's all relative. I come from a country where neighbours get all "high noon" over a parking spot. If our gang had succeeded in getting rid of Avril Jenkins, and shipped their haul off her property, we'd be none the wiser. Some big-time shit hit some big-time fans for them that night because a fire started. The top man must be pissed off and those small-fry further down the chain will be shitting bricks round about now. We want to get those small-fry while they're scared and offer them a way out.'

Penny's voice sang out from the kitchen: 'Rea-dy!'

*　*　*

In Amsterdam, Garritt had spent Saturday morning investigating the leads that Laura had texted across, and had narrowed Anik's search down from the seven locations she had sent him to one: the cadets' training college. 'I did two years as an Army Cadet and the man who taught me . . .' Garritt shook his head as though there were no words to describe his old mentor. 'Sergeant Bosch . . . there's nothing he doesn't know.'

Twenty minutes later, Garritt was driving to the college. He asked Anik what the uniformed Dutch man had to do with a murdered Chinese girl and a stolen painting. Anik had to admit that he didn't know. 'This case has taken several twists and turns which we hope will all eventually lead to the same place. And the same person. The woman in the picture, next to the Dutch military officer, was murdered in the same place as Jessica Chi. And each time we ask a question, we get an answer we didn't expect – like the fact that Jessica had a stolen Rossetti. I dread to think what your old mentor is going to tell me.'

The cadet training college was closed, and the only sign of life was the elderly man in an ill-fitting security uniform sitting in a security booth drinking coffee from a flask. Garritt parked just short of the booth and got out. As soon as the men saw each other, they beamed the biggest of smiles and exchanged a tight embrace.

'Anik, this is Sergeant Bosch. He should have retired many years ago, but he refuses to leave.' As Anik stepped closer, he could see that Bosch's uniform was in fact, not security, but military, and he displayed a line of medals across his chest. 'Sergeant Bosch, Anik is a policeman from England. I'm helping him to find murderers and drug dealers and a missing painting worth millions.'

'You always did exaggerate, Garritt.' Bosch shook hands with Anik and asked how he could help. Anik got out his mobile phone, showed Bosch the photograph of Avril Jenkins standing next to the young Dutch military man and asked if he could help to identify the uniform. Bosch patted all of his pockets, and even felt on top of his head. Garritt, knowing his old mentor inside out, popped his head inside the security booth. Sure enough, there was the daily paper with a half-done crossword, along with a pencil and a pair of glasses. Garritt handed the glasses to Bosch, who was then ready to take a look at Anik's photograph.

'Andre Boogaard.'

Bosch removed his glasses and sipped his coffee. Anik couldn't believe it.

'Told you he knew everything.' Garritt smirked.

Anik snapped into action, opening 'notes' on his mobile. 'Bogart? Like Humphrey Bogart?'

'B-o-o-g-a-a-r-d. Andre Boogaard. I kicked him out on his ass. He was no good. I only have time for people who want to learn, want to grow, want to achieve. I'm fussy about who I teach.' Bosch leant towards Anik and whispered loudly enough for Garritt to hear. 'Don't tell him. It will go to his head.'

* * *

Josh laid his knife and fork down on his plate. 'Oh, my goodness me! I don't know what to say. You almost got me in tears, Penny. I've not tasted food like that in months.' Penny was actually blushing – which Jack and Maggie found hilarious. Jack emptied the third bottle of wine into everyone's glasses, whilst Maggie cleared the dinner plates and put dessert bowls in the oven to warm. Penny asked Josh about the work he did. 'Ah, well now, I'm not sure that's table talk.'

'Josh, my son is a policeman, and my soon-to-be-daughter-in-law is a doctor. There's nothing you can say that will shock me.'

'Well, OK, ma'am. But you stop me if that proves to be wrong. I'm a consultant with the police in the US and, in recent months, in the UK. My specialty is drugs. I move around making sure we got joined-up thinking, 'cos that's the only way we're gonna shut 'em down. I'm the one that gets down and dirty with the bad guys. I learn the tricks of their trade, so I can show people like Jack how to use those tricks against them. Then we can predict what they're gonna do next and get there first.' The wine was now getting the better of Penny because, quite unexpectedly, she asked if Josh carried a gun. 'Not at the dinner table, ma'am,' Josh joked. 'Back home I carry a Glock at my hip and a little Ruger on my ankle. I do have my weapons over here with me, but I save them for special occasions.'

Jack jumped in as the moment presented itself. 'Talking of special occasions.'

Maggie gulped her wine as Jack pulled a gift bag out of the pasta cupboard where he'd hidden it earlier that evening. God, she hoped this last-minute gift wasn't too shit. Josh saw the 'Happy Birthday' tag and Penny's delighted face.

'Nooo!' Josh looked genuinely horrified. 'Jack, why didn't you tell me!'

Penny reached across the table and tapped the back of Josh's hand. 'You're here. That's enough.' Jack kissed Penny's cheek and handed her the bag. Then he refilled everyone's glasses whilst she gently pulled the red ribbon that held the handles together. Inside the bag were a series of images, downloaded and printed from the internet, then wrapped in tissue paper and tied together with another ribbon. Out of context, the first few images of landscapes and rolling fields were confusing, but then came an image of the city farm situated ten or so miles outside of London ... then an image of sheep with their newborn lambs. The next page was laid out like an adoption certificate:

Charlie – due to be born in spring, 2023. Adopted by Penny Warr.

Penny's voice quivered, 'You bought me a lamb?'

'You can be there when it's born,' Jack said. 'And you can visit anytime. I thought you and Hannah might like to watch Charlie grow over the years.'

Penny leapt from her chair and into Jack's arms. Her breathing faltered and her shoulders shook, and Jack hugged her close as they took a moment to remember the lamb's namesake: Charlie Warr, her late husband and Jack's adopted father. As Jack held Penny, Maggie gave him a silent round of applause. She had no idea how he'd done it, but he'd superbly grasped victory from the jaws of defeat.

Jack had also bought a chocolate birthday cake, which Penny decided to keep until the next day when Hannah could join her in blowing out the candles.

Whilst they tucked into mammoth helpings of bread-and-butter pudding with homemade custard, Penny suddenly picked up the earlier conversation from where it had left off. 'Do you think guns give people a false sense of power, Josh? Making it more likely that they'll get into trouble, rather than less?'

Josh grinned at the astuteness of Penny's wine-fuelled question. 'If I had my way, I'd educate gun owners in the same way a karate sensei educates his pupils. Having the power to defend yourself, should be treated with respect. It's for defence, not attack. Unfortunately, yes, you're right, some people can't handle that power.'

'Can I ask, Josh . . .' Maggie was as hypnotised as Penny by Josh's smooth Alabama accent. 'How are the drugs moving around so easily from China, New York and now Europe?'

Jack rolled his eyes and got up to open the brandy that Penny had sent him to buy earlier.

'Well, you see, in Brazil there are these places called favelas – they're shantytowns mixed in with open markets where anything can be sold. Anything. Dealers sell drugs and guns, and they're protected by armed gang members 'cos it's big business. These places are no-go areas for law enforcement. They're huge mazes, anyways – even if the police could find their way in, they'd never find their way out. Not alive, anyhow.'

Penny gave an audible gasp. Josh gave Jack a quick sideways grin: he was playing to his audience and loving it!

'It'd be a massacre if the cops went into the shantytowns of Mexico and Brazil. They have hundreds of shootouts every month, and that's just between rival gangs. Some parts of the drugs world are lowbrow mayhem, and some parts are quiet, smart, confident men and women willing to risk everything for the money that's on offer. Whilst the dumbasses, pardon me, are making a whole lotta noise over there . . .' Josh made a spiderlike shape with his left hand, followed by another with his right hand, 'the smart guys are quietly moving around over here. The cops go where the noise is. One way this gang gets drugs across borders is decoys. They hire someone with a drug habit to move through customs with ten pellets of cocaine up his . . . whilst the real payload crosses elsewhere. The guy goes to prison and gets put on a free detox programme, his family gets a large payout, the gang moves their drugs. Everybody wins.'

'Do you know what I think, Josh?' Penny sounded like she was about to solve one of the biggest international law-enforcement problems this century had ever seen. Josh gave her his full attention. 'I think that if drugs were made legal, it would take away all of the mystery and excitement and people would get bored of it very quickly. When Jack was twelve, I caught him at the bottom of the garden drinking from a bottle of cider. I took him indoors and we all shared it over dinner. It wasn't mysterious or exciting anymore, so Jack wasn't interested. And, to this day, he doesn't drink to excess, do you, darling?'

Jack popped the cork from the brandy and poured four glasses.

Jack placed a large brandy in front of Penny and handed a second to Josh. 'People don't take drugs because they're mysterious and exciting. They're addicts who can't stop by themselves and who need help. They're the ones we do this for.'

Penny swirled her brandy around the bowl of the glass. She knew she'd said something naive and didn't know how to backtrack. So she did the only thing she could: 'This is Remy Martin, Josh. A favourite of my late husband's. Do you like it?'

Josh smiled and raised his glass. 'I think your husband was a connoisseur, Penny.'

CHAPTER 21

Jack woke to a silent house. Josh had made his way home around midnight, after making a friend for life in Penny. She adored his polite American way of calling her 'ma'am', and how he said words like 'gosh' and 'heck' instead of, as she put it, 'the base words my son feels the need to use'. Josh had wholeheartedly agreed with her that cussing was a sign of weakness in a man, confident that Jack and Maggie wouldn't snitch on him for effing and blinding in the lounge earlier that evening whilst they'd all been out of Penny's earshot.

Maggie and Penny had taken Hannah to church. It wasn't a weekly ritual for any of them but every now and then Penny felt the need to reaffirm her faith. With all of the recent wedding plans and with the big day getting closer, she was becoming acutely aware of the fact that she would not have her husband by her side. Maggie's parents were lovely people, but there were two of them, while the wedding photos would show that Penny was a widow, which simply wasn't fair. Not for her, but for Charlie. He should be by her side, crying with pride as their boy married the woman he loved.

Jack made a large mug of tea and checked his messages and emails. Andre Boogaard was now a name being traced by Laura in the UK and Anik in Amsterdam. Between them, they were checking births, deaths and marriages to track his family and personal history, and they were checking for any international movements over the past thirty or forty years. There was a possibility that Boogaard could be Adam Border's father; this, in turn, could explain why Adam had been so hard to track down. Maybe he had been born and lived mainly abroad, regardless of what Hester thought? Maybe

Boogaard was his birth name, explaining why they could find so little information for Adam Border prior to him attending Chelsea Art College. And why they couldn't find him now. Jack called Anik.

'Lieutenant Visser, Garritt, saved my arse yesterday 'cos he knew this guy, Sergeant Bosch, and he knew Andre Boogaard. Once we had the military link, it took ten seconds. But if I'd not had Garritt with me, I'd still be trawling through all the crap Laura sent my way.' Anik was on a roll, so Jack didn't interrupt. He just put his mobile on speaker and made himself some toast. 'I'm still tracing his timeline from the photo, to now. The Chis – God, I hate telling people that someone's dead – Garritt's keeping in touch with them over the next day or two and he'll help them sort travel to London. They definitely need interviewing again.' Jack opened his mouth to ask if that was because they had information on Adam Border, but Anik spoke first. 'Not because of Adam Border – they didn't know much about him – but because of some stolen Rossetti painting they caught Jessica with.' The toaster popped in Jack's kitchen. 'You only just having breakfast?' Anik mocked. 'I've been up and working for an hour.'

As Jack raced upstairs, he pointed out that Amsterdam was one hour ahead, so that made them quits. Anik mentioning a Rossetti painting had instantly jogged a memory in the back of Jack's mind. Whilst Anik continued talking, Jack rushed into his office, grabbed Avril Jenkins' red notebook from his jacket and headed back down into the kitchen.

'The Chis are both artists,' Anik continued, 'so they knew this painting wasn't a copy, as Jessica claimed, but the real deal. They told her to return it to the original owner. That's why they thought I was in Amsterdam. They thought I was gonna tell them that I'd nicked their daughter.' Anik's mobile peeped in his ear. 'Listen, Jack, my battery's going. I'm about to send a full report of everything I just told you. I need to know how long Ridley might want to me to stay out here. Only my petty cash float has gone, so now I'm spending my own money and I can't . . .' Anik's mobile died.

*   *   *

Before Jack settled down to work, and before he forgot, he sent Laura a quick text message:

Thx for printing that stuff last night. Saved my skin. Went down a storm!

Jack flicked through the red notebook until he found the list of items Avril had reported as stolen. Top of the list, which was ordered by value, was a Rossetti painting. Then a connected thought occurred to him. As he flicked through the notebook he was mentally kicking himself for not looking sooner . . . and there it was. On a torn page, close to the back of the notebook, was an art gallery address and a scribbled-out phone number for Jason Marks.

Currently, no one knew that Jack had Avril's red notebook, and nor did he want them to. It was the one piece of evidence found at the house that seemed more relevant to the murder than the drugs, so Jack was eager to keep it away from Steve Lewis until he'd got everything he needed from it. And Ridley didn't need to be bothered by unsubstantiated hunches. Jack would fill him in, in good time.

Jack wrote the name 'Andre Boogaard' on a piece of paper and slipped that inside the notebook. Then he went upstairs for a shower before his girls came home.

Jack cooked Sunday brunch for everyone, which consisted of sliced sausages, bacon and mushrooms being fried together. At the last minute, Jack broke eight eggs into the same pan so that the fried egg whites held the entire breakfast together as one, and he then slid the whole thing out onto a chopping board for people to slice up like a pizza. He made sure that each 'slice' contained one fried egg plus a good selection of everything else. Charlie had taught him to make breakfast this way and claimed that it made your basic fry-up look like a piece of artwork on the plate. In truth, it was so he only ever had to wash one pan. Hannah's slice of breakfast pizza was laid face down in the still-hot frying pan for another thirty seconds, to make sure that the yolk was cooked through.

Today was Maggie's hen night. She'd insisted on it starting in the early afternoon, because some of her friends were on night shift and she would be up with Hannah at 5 a.m. There was no way she was still going to be awake past 10.30 so, to get in the required number of drinking hours, Penny and Maggie were starting with a film and a bottle of pink champagne at 2 p.m.

By 6 p.m, Maggie and Penny were ready to head out. Maggie wore a black T-shirt with sparkly pink lettering on the front boasting BRIDE, and Penny wore one announcing her as MOTHER OF THE GROOM. Jack and Hannah kissed them both goodbye, then they headed upstairs for Hannah's bath, bedtime feed and story.

As she fought sleep, Hannah's eyelids would close, and then her eyebrows would lift, dragging her eyes open again. Her stubborn refusal to sleep, even though she was exhausted, made him giggle. Eventually, Hannah's body relaxed and felt heavy in his arms, and he knew she was asleep.

Jack slouched on the sofa with the red notebook, half a bottle of red wine left over from the previous evening, and half a bottle of Remy Martin brandy. He committed the rest of his evening to going through the notebook from cover to cover. Towards the back of the book, in tiny writing was a list: *alcohol, steel stock pots, stainless steel rice cooker, electric cooling pan, plastic funnels, coffee filters, large syringe* ... then the list stopped abruptly where two pages had been torn out at the spine.

* * *

Maggie was cringing in the corner of a little pub in Richmond as her friends tunelessly shouted the words to 'Another One Bites the Dust'. The other customers had quickly moved on from smiling and congratulating Maggie, to now wishing the hens would leave. Penny was mildly embarrassed, but that was waning with each glass of prosecco. As the song hit the second chorus, two men carrying car keys and wearing Hackney Cab ID lanyards entered the pub and, in unison, their eyes settled on the raucous hen party and their hearts visibly sank. One young hen, spotting their drivers, leapt to her feet and screamed, '*Party!*' then downed her drink and led the way out of the pub. Penny was last out and, as she passed their taxi drivers, she apologised in advance for how loud the journey to the Blue Bird Café in Chelsea was about to be.

* * *

Jack sat reading the red notebook, with his brandy glass propped on a cushion.

Hannah was sound asleep next to him, hanging on to the teat of her bottle with her teeth for comfort. Over the previous couple of hours, Jack had received several texts from Maggie:

The monkfish is to die for. Me and you will have to come here x . . . Ha Ha. Your mum's in the kitchen demanding a recipe off the chef . . . They're playing our song. I miss you.

I'm moshing like we did at Bohemia in Torquay! x . . . I love you. Wait up for me x . . .
Back in 200 x

. . . which Jack presumed was meant to be twenty.

At half past ten, there was a knock on the door. As he made his way across the lounge, Jack presumed that Penny had left her door key in her bedroom, as she often did, and that Maggie couldn't find hers amongst all of the unnecessary items in her handbag.

Jack opened the door . . . to Tania Wetlock. Her dress was as skimpy as the last time she'd dropped by uninvited, and she seemed to be equally pissed, stoned, or both. 'Don't worry, Jack,' she slurred, 'I'm not here for you. I want to speak to Maggie.'

Tania tried to push past him, but he stood firmly in her way and told her to go home because Maggie was out.

Tania pushed his chest, but he didn't move. There was no way Jack was going to let a drugged-up unpredictable teenager into his home when Hannah was asleep on the sofa.

'I know she's here. Maggie! Maggie!' Hannah began to stir and grizzle. Jack gripped Tania firmly by the shoulders and pushed her back out onto the doorstep, then shut the door in her face. Hannah was now lying face down with her knees tucked up to her chest and her bottom in the air. Jack rubbed her back and made 'Shhh' noises in an endeavour to stop her waking up.

When Tania kicked the front door, Hannah and Jack both jumped. Hannah began to cry. Jack gently picked her up and, as she naturally put her head against his chest for comfort, he put his hand over her exposed ear and headed upstairs, while Tania continued kicking the front door and shouting for Maggie. Jack put Hannah in her cot but, as predicted, she immediately stood up and screamed to be held again. She had no clue what was happening and needed to be in the arms of her dad. Jack kissed Hannah several times on her cheeks, promised to be back, and then closed the bedroom door. Hearing her scream as he rushed back downstairs was heartbreaking.

Jack flung open the front door and stepped out, forcing Tania backwards onto the pavement. 'If you don't shut up, right now, I'll have you arrested. Go home!'

Jack backed towards his front door, not wanting to take his eyes off her. He didn't care about leaving Tania out in the cold this time, he didn't care how vulnerable she might be, all he cared about was his daughter. And Tania could see that. She suddenly rushed him.

'I'll scream on your doorstep, Jack Warr. Me and your kid will have a screaming competition. And I'll win. I'll scream things you don't want the neighbours to hear. RAPE! RAPE!' Jack grabbed Tania by the wrist and dragged her indoors. The instant his front door was closed, she fell completely silent. She'd got what she wanted. Jack dragged her to the sofa, pushed her down, leant in and shoved his finger in her face.

'You move, touch anything, shout out, and I'll shut you up. You're trespassing now, and I have every right to defend myself and my property against intruders.' The smirk slowly dropped off Tania's face as she tried to decipher whether Jack was seriously threatening her. He held her stare. He needed her to be scared of him. Because he needed to go and comfort his crying daughter.

As soon as Hannah was in his arms, she stopped crying and settled. She was emotionally exhausted and within two minutes was back asleep. When Jack returned downstairs, Tania was also asleep, curled up on the sofa in the foetal position, with her knickers on display. As Jack looked down at the small, vulnerable teenage girl, he knew he should feel sorry for her; but he couldn't. She frustrated him beyond comprehension. She was a spoilt little bitch and she was disrupting his life. He had zero responsibility for her, yet here she was again, invading his home. Jack took himself into the kitchen to make a cup of strong coffee and calm down.

He leant the palms of his hands on the kitchen top, fingers splayed, knuckles white. He closed his eyes and listened to the comforting sound of the coffee machine dribbling out a double espresso.

'I've changed my mind.' Jack's eyes shot open. He spun round to see Tania leaning against the kitchen doorframe, finishing the remnants of his brandy. 'It is you I want after all.'

Jack hadn't counted to ten in his head since he was at school, but he was doing it now. He took the espresso from the machine, calmly walked up to Tania and swapped it for the now-empty brandy glass. She looked him straight in the eye and launched the small coffee cup across the kitchen, smashing it against the wall. Her throw was so cack-handed that she spilt most of the coffee all over herself and him.

That was the last straw. He grabbed her arm and dragged her through the lounge towards the front door. Rather than go with him, Tania dug her heels in and fought. She grabbed at the cushion on the sofa, and her handbag fell onto the floor where the contents spilt out across the carpet. Jack stopped in his tracks: amongst the expected items such as make-up, mobile, purse, and keys, there was also a bundle of cash held together with a small black clip. Tania wriggled free from Jack's grasp and dived onto her knees to collect her belongings. 'You're a bastard!' she screamed. 'Just like the rest of them. A fucking hateful bastard!'

From upstairs, Jack could hear the distinctive sound of Hannah crying and knew she would be standing up in her cot. He hauled Tania off the floor, opened the front door and threw her out – just as Maggie and Penny were stepping out of a taxi.

Tania stumbled down the driveway, toppling off her heels, already trying to call someone on her phone. But when she saw the cab, she dropped the call and thrust the top half of her body in through the taxi window. 'Take me home,' she whimpered. Then she climbed in the back seat and the taxi sped away.

*   *   *

Penny walked straight past Jack and upstairs. She didn't care what had happened, she just wanted to hug Hannah and stop her from crying.

Jack closed the front door and double-locked it. No one else was going to invade their home tonight. 'I told him about her, Jack . . . I . . . swear I did,' Maggie slurred. 'How bloody dare she come round . . .' Maggie suddenly became transfixed by a smudge of lipstick on Jack's shirt. She poked it hard with her finger. 'Bitch.' Then she effortlessly shifted from being furious to practical. 'Whip it off. I'll soak it.'

Jack took Maggie by the hand and walked her upstairs. Once in the bedroom, she became clumsily amorous, trying to remove his shirt, catching it on his nose as she yanked it off over his head. 'Now you undress me.' She dropped onto the bed and lay back. Jack knew she was trying to be sexy, but as he took her skirt and tights off her flailing, unruly legs, he couldn't help but think that this was akin to changing Hannah's nappy! By the time he'd thrown Maggie's clothes across the room towards the linen basket, she was asleep. He swung her legs onto the bed, her head onto the pillow and covered her with his half of the duvet. He then tipped the contents of the plastic wastepaper bin onto the carpet and put it next to the bed in case she woke in the middle of the night and reached for something to be sick into. He stood looking down at his lovely drunk wife-to-be – and realised how quiet it was.

Penny stood in the nursery, rocking from foot to foot with Hannah asleep on her shoulder. She was staring at the photo of Charlie on the wall: Jack had put it up before Hannah was born, so that his dad could watch over his daughter in the night. 'I should probably move out, darling.' Penny's words came as a total shock. 'You'll be a proper family soon. I can't live in your attic forever.'

'We're already a proper family,' Jack said. Penny lowered her eyes and Jack knew she was crying. He turned her to face him, shaking his head as if he had no clue why she didn't understand. 'This is your home, Mum.'

CHAPTER 22

Jack and Maggie only really kept coffee in the house for visitors because she disliked the taste of it, even on Jack's lips when he kissed her. This morning, however, the smell of strong coffee coming up the stairs was exactly what she needed. Maggie could also hear the welcome sound of paracetamol tablets bursting through foil and held out her hand as Jack dropped two into her palm. She crunched them up without lifting her head. 'Are you meant to chew them?' Jack asked. Maggie said that the only risk from chewing was that it released the drug more quickly into her system, which was exactly what she needed. Jack told Maggie that her coffee and toast was on the bedside cabinet, then he began getting ready for work.

After about ten minutes, Maggie's head started to feel a little better, so she sat up. She looked around the bedroom. Her clothes from last night were on the floor next to the washing basket. Why could Jack not walk across the room and open the lid? She saw the lipstick on his shirt and a memory came flooding back. 'Did I see Tania here last night?'

'She was demanding to talk to you.' Jack turned to Maggie, so she could see how serious he was feeling about this topic. But her eyes had closed again. 'This has to stop, Mags. If there's a next time, I'll have her arrested. Hannah was downstairs and could have been hurt.' Maggie's eyes jolted open and she squinted in pain at the sunlight coming in through a gap in the blinds. 'Tania threw coffee across the kitchen. She's volatile.'

Maggie reached for her now-tepid coffee and swigged it down. The deep furrows around her make-up-smeared eyes, showed she'd got the message loud and clear, and was now figuring out how to handle Dr Elliot Wetlock.

In the kitchen, everything from the worktop was on the table and Penny was wiping the last of the coffee off the wall tiles. She heard Jack walk into the room behind her. 'When you sweep up broken crockery, darling, always vacuum as well. The tiny bits could get into Hannah's little knees.' Jack apologised for not cleaning up properly. 'And I'll make sure Maggie's up and about by eight. Luckily she's got a ten o'clock start.'

Jack asked if they'd had a nice time. 'Oh, she had a wonderful time.' Penny threw the coffee-stained cloth into the kitchen bin and started to move everything back to where it belonged. 'Regina sang – what's the word, you know ... she sang on her own, no musicians – in front of the whole restaurant. She's just stunning. And so brave. And I got the chef's recipe for tarragon glazed carrots. So, I'll do those tonight.'

Jack was glad that his mum no longer sounded worried about her place in his home. As he headed for the front door, she shouted after him, 'A cappella!'

*　*　*

When Jack entered the squad room, Ridley was already in his office, door open, organising a file for the morning's briefing. The two men nodded to each other and Jack headed for his desk. 'Anik's staying in Amsterdam for another couple of days,' Ridley shouted. 'Trying to get more on Andre Boogaard. You're thinking he may be Adam Border's father?' Jack walked into the doorway of Ridley's office and leant against the frame. 'His old landlord told Anik that he thought Adam was Dutch, so you might be right, Jack. I've got Anik Zooming into the briefing this morning to hand over everything from his interview with Jessica's parents.'

As the team filed into the squad room behind Jack, Ridley gathered his file and stood. He had a look of frustrated discontent on his face, reminiscent of the man he was months ago, before his decline into apathy which Jack now knew was due to his ill-health. 'The elusive Adam Border seems to be the son of a drug-dealing mother, and the boyfriend of an art-thieving girlfriend. Both of whom are now dead. We must find him, Jack. We're starting to look incompetent.'

Ridley walked past Jack and started the briefing. Jack smiled. The old Ridley was back.

*   *   *

The first half of the briefing was led by an increasingly enthusiastic and annoyingly arrogant Anik on camera. He got the team up to speed regarding all of the new information he'd turned up in Amsterdam – namely the stolen Rossetti and Adam Border's possible birth name. He revelled in having all eyes on him. The team knew he'd be bloody unbearable when he got back but, conversely, they also felt an odd communal pride that their little boy was finally growing up.

The second half of the briefing centred around the team's shaky relationship with the Drug Squad. Ridley was doing his best to play second-fiddle to Steve Lewis, but it didn't come naturally. The truth was that as the best DCI in the Met, Ridley would never have rolled over so easily under normal circumstances, and now his decision was coming back to bite him.

'I'm going to see Steve Lewis this morning, as he's not volunteering much without being asked. We have now been sent the video footage showing the prelim to the murder of Avril Jenkins. Go through it with a fine-tooth comb. We need to identify those men. And the man who arrived in the Jag. A Jag driver cropped up at Avril's funeral, Jason Marks, but we don't know if they're one and the same. Mike Tulley from Steve's team followed Marks away from Avril's funeral, but we have no idea what came of that. I'll find out about that too. Anything else I need to get from Drug Squad?'

The question, which was directed at the room in general, was met with a sea of shaking heads. Ridley brought the briefing to an end and returned to his office. Jack followed him.

'Sir, on the list of items Avril Jenkins reported stolen to Kingston nick there was a Rossetti painting.'

'And you think it's the same Rossetti mentioned by Jessica Chi's parents?'

'I think it's at least worth a conversation with Arnold Hutchinson.' Ridley told Jack to hand that conversation to Laura, as he should stay with the task of tracking Adam Border. 'Sir, this *is* about tracking Adam Border. He's the one Avril accused of stealing it, and Jessica is the one seen in possession of it. If it proves to be the same painting, of course.'

Ridley rubbed his forehead. 'Jack, pace is important in this case. You're not the only one who can interview people, you know.' Ridley looked up and could see that Jack really didn't want to delegate this particular interview. 'Fine. You speak to Hutchinson.'

* * *

As Jack was leaving the station, he bumped into Laura coming out of the ladies'. 'I'm off to interview Arnold Hutchinson then heading straight back.'

'OK, and by the by, I have information about David Summers, Avril's brother. He's in Strangeways, been there for eighteen months, with two more years to go. He was arrested for stealing a van and selling stolen lead from a church – he's got a long sheet of petty crime.'

Jack shrugged, and suggested she run it past Ridley to check if they needed to interview him.

Jack didn't call Arnold Hutchinson's office to make an appointment because he didn't want to be told that he'd have to wait until tomorrow or next week. When he arrived, he was told by the rather frayed receptionist, May, that Hutchinson was with a client – their heated conversation could in fact be heard from the reception area. Jack threw her a reassuring smile, ignored the muffled verbal sparring coming from the next room and sat down to wait. May initially tried to small-talk over the growing argument but, when she finally gave up, Jack heard a familiar voice.

'I've done everything asked of me. And I needn't have, Arnold, I bloody needn't have. This is totally unacceptable. I will be taking legal advice. Mark my bloody words on that.'

Hutchinson's office door flew open and Terence Jenkins strode out with his head down, jabbing his mobile screen as he dialled a phone number. He marched out of the main door without noticing Jack. May had an awkward smile on her face as she stood up. 'Please give me five minutes, DS Warr. To make sure Mr Hutchinson is free to see you. Then I'll make us all a nice cup of tea.'

Arnold Hutchinson was sipping from a tumbler of water when Jack was finally shown through. The pot of tea and two cups were already on the desk, brewing. 'The will of a client has become . . . complicated,' he explained. 'My apologies if you overheard any unpleasantness.' Hutchinson poured the tea. 'So, how can I help you, DS Warr?'

'You could tell me about Avril Jenkins' will becoming complicated.' Hutchinson realised that Jack must have met Terence on a previous occasion and recognised him as he'd stormed out, but insisted the details of Avril's will were confidential. 'This is a murder investigation and so I need you to please tell me if anything has happened that could be significant in finding Avril's killer. I understand about client confidentiality, but as the client is deceased, you can use your discretion.' Jack could see that Hutchinson was wavering, so he gave one final push. 'Help me, to help her.'

After a few seconds' thought, Hutchinson nodded. 'A second will has surfaced. More recent than the one with Terence Jenkins as the main beneficiary.'

'So, Terence no longer gets what he was expecting to receive?'

'I'm still verifying its legality. And he's contesting.' Hutchinson paused to drop two sugar cubes into his tea. He then chopped at them with the tip of his teaspoon. 'If the new will is legitimate, everything goes to Adam Border.'

Jack let out a low whistle. The house, its contents and the grounds were a substantial inheritance – no wonder Terence was so angry. Jack asked if he could see the new will but Hutchinson shook his head. 'I do want to help you and to see justice done, Detective Warr, but my loyalty lies with Avril Jenkins, irrespective of her death. She and her final wishes are my priority. I won't speak out of turn, and so until I've verified the new will, I'll say no more on the subject. I hope you understand.'

Jack did understand. He also knew that he couldn't legally compel Hutchinson to share the will, so he had to persuade the details out of him. And now was not the time for that.

'The reason I'm here, Mr Hutchinson, is to ask about the Rossetti painting that Avril included in the list of property allegedly stolen from her home.'

'I remember it being valued some years ago for insurance purposes. I seem to remember that the authenticity of this one came into question. I can't recall the outcome, although the insurance company will be able to tell you. I can find their number. Freddie bought and sold artworks beyond retirement, you see – he said it kept him out of trouble.' Hutchinson snorted a gentle laugh down his nose as he fondly recalled Freddie. 'It didn't work. He lost on investments, as you know. Which is why Avril was forced to sell some pieces after he died. I lost track beyond Freddie's death, because Avril would privately sell items without informing me or the insurer. She got through some insurance companies, I can tell you! They simply refused to work for her.'

Hutchinson suddenly felt uncomfortable, as if he'd said too much. He stood and went to a tall, four-drawer cabinet from which he removed a file. He took out two pieces of paper that had been stapled together. As Hutchinson diligently picked out the staple without ripping either sheet, he spoke of his friend, Frederick Jenkins.

'Freddie and I go back decades. I'd never have put him with Avril but, well, she made him . . . bloom. Can men bloom? Or is it just women? Anyway, she made him happy.' He shrugged his shoulders. 'There's no accounting for taste. I'll get May to photocopy this insurance inventory for you. I also have a recent inventory from Terence Jenkins, so if you compare the two, I guess you'll come up with a third list of items that have gone walkabout. Sold, stolen, mislaid. Who knows?'

As May photocopied the relevant pages and placed them into a manila envelope, Jack asked his final question. 'Did Jason Marks value any of the artwork in Avril's home?'

Hutchinson said that the name sounded familiar, but he didn't know if Jason Marks had ever supervised any actual sales. He did, however, know that Frederick Jenkins only ever dealt with the likes of Sotheby's, so if 'this Marks person' moved in lesser circles, then it was unlikely he'd have been trusted to do the selling.

* * *

Jack sat in his car outside Hutchinson's office and digested the new information, trying to make it align with what they already knew. If Avril had redrafted her will, and if Adam Border knew about it, why did he disappear? Why not stick around to collect what was his? This begged the question of whether or not Adam Border even knew that Avril Jenkins was dead.

Or worse, it begged the question of whether or not Adam Border was still alive to collect his inheritance. He too could be dead. He could even have been the first to die. If this gang of drug dealers had managed to complete the dismemberment and disposal of Avril Jenkins, the police would never have learnt about the drugs den beneath her home. It was only the impromptu fire, set on the same night that Avril died, that had brought the emergency services in to expose a murder scene.

The more Jack thought about the viciousness of Avril's murder, the more he disagreed with Josh's assessment of this gang being amateurs. Jack thought that Josh's past experience in the US was not necessarily a useful benchmark. This was not America. Shootouts were not daily occurrences. And dismembering pensioners was not par for the course. Josh might be complacent about the level of criminal activity they were dealing with here, but Jack refused to be. Josh spoke of drug deaths as casually as Penny spoke of new carrot recipes. Jack never wanted to get to a stage in his career as a police officer where death was 'expected'. Avril's death was horrific. Jessica's death was horrific. And if Adam Border was also dead, that would no doubt have been horrific too. Irrespective of what side of the law these people had been on, Jack didn't believe that any of them had actually deserved to die. If Adam was out there somewhere, Jack wanted to find him alive.

CHAPTER 23

Before Jack returned to the station, he took a detour to Portobello Road and the art gallery listed in Avril Jenkins' red notebook next to the name of Jason Marks. There was a sign on the door saying VIEW BY APPOINTMENT ONLY but, after turning up at Hutchinson's office unannounced and learning something integral to the case, Jack was in the mood to try the same tactic again. In his experience, surprising people often proved more fruitful than giving them notice of your arrival.

The small shopfront was not particularly impressive, and Jack noticed a business card wedged into the wooden frame of the door. JASON MARKS – ART VALUATION EXPERT. There was also a phone number which differed from the one crossed out in the red notebook. Above the gallery was a row of three windows which – because of the flowers on each of the sills – looked as if they belonged to a flat. The shutters were closed and, when Jack knocked on the shop door, there was no answer. It looked as if a second impromptu visit was not going to be as productive as his first.

* * *

At the station, Laura and Anik were liaising via Zoom about the Boogaard name. Anik had found a birth certificate dated 1987. The father of this newborn baby boy was identified as Andre Erik Boogaard and the mother as Avril Summers. At the time the certificate was issued, the baby had not been given a Christian name and so that section was blank. Anik had also found a death certificate for Andre, dated 1998. As yet, they had not been able to trace a marriage certificate between Andre and Avril.

Currently, Laura and Anik were exchanging notes on passports issued under the name of Boogaard, in the hope of fully identifying the baby boy. So far, they'd worked their way back to the 1990s, but with little success. Whilst searching for a passport being used by any male named Boogaard since 1987, Laura and Anik had repeatedly come across the name of Ingrid Boogaard. They'd tracked her birth certificate and found the father to be Andre Erik Boogaard. So, there was a sister, or half-sister in the mix too. Laura called the Royal Netherland Registry Department to find out as much as she could about Ingrid Boogaard. Within seconds, she was placed on hold listening to muzak.

When Jack walked into the squad room, he was confused to hear Anik shouting his name from somewhere. Then he saw the laptop screen sitting at the end of Laura's desk.

'Hey, Jack! What's the deal with that painting? Do you know yet?' Jack relayed his conversation with Hutchinson from that morning and explained there was a doubt about its authenticity. Anik reiterated Henrick Chi's certainty that it was genuine. 'And . . .' Anik's tone was cocky, almost mocking, 'when it comes to authenticating paintings, I'll take the word of a professional artist over a solicitor any day.' Anik giggled at his own retort and glanced sideways at Laura in an invitation for her to join in. She didn't.

Jack leant towards the screen, placing his hands on Laura's desk, close to either side of the keyboard and spoke so that only Anik and Laura could hear him.

'You know what, Anik, you're right, I don't know what I was thinking listening to Hutchinson's opinion. You're right, of course you are. Well done. In recent months, you've proved yourself to be a real . . .' Jack tapped the touchpad and cut Anik off. As he headed back to his desk, he finished his sentence: '. . . tosser.'

The person on the other end of Laura's phone finally returned and her conversation began again. 'No, no, as I told the first two people I was put through to, I'm calling from the Metropolitan Police, London. I need to contact Miss Ingrid Boogaard.' Laura covered the mouthpiece, and in a heavy whisper, she let off a little steam in Jack's direction. 'They're annoying me now. And it sounds like the same woman just putting me on hold, then coming back again. She's taking the piss . . . ah hello, yes. Oh brilliant. Thank you.' Laura quickly snatched up a pen and paper. 'And this is Ingrid Boogaard's current address? Perfect. Yes, go ahead.' Laura wrote down the address, which was a lengthy process as she had to ask for most of it to be spelled out. 'And do you have a phone number for her as well?' As Laura listened to the reply, the enthusiasm vanished from her face, and she screwed up the piece of paper she'd just written on. Her nostrils flared and she kept her lips pursed shut to keep her frustration in. She tried to sound as calm as possible: 'Just a suggestion, but perhaps that should have been the first thing you told me?' She then slammed the phone down. 'She's dead. Cancer. Last year.' At that moment, Anik's name popped up on her screen as he attempted to FaceTime again. Laura clicked accept.

'We got cut off.' Anik always got flustered by temperamental technology. He was very tech-savvy until something went wrong, and then he was useless. 'Is Jack still there? I missed what he said.' Jack stood just out of view, shaking his head. 'He said I've proved myself to be a real . . . something. That's where we got cut off.'

'Asset.' Laura spoke with a completely straight face. 'He said you're a right asset.' Anik looked as if he didn't quite believe her. 'Listen, Anik, Ingrid Boogaard is a dead end. Literally. When are the Chis arriving with us?'

'They were on the 2 p.m. flight, so they should be with you soon. I don't need to stay out here any longer, do I?' Laura said that she'd confirm with Ridley whether or not Anik could head home. 'Cool. Thanks, Laura . . . oh, and tell Jack I think he's a right "asset" too!' Anik cut Laura off so that he had the joy of having the last word.

* * *

For the next hour, Jack and Laura discussed possible next courses of action. They now had the lists from Hutchinson, showing insurance companies involved with the Jenkinses through the years, an inventory of items insured, and the more recent inventory given to Hutchinson by Terence Jenkins. They also had the Leeds connection – although the boy in the school uniform from the photo had turned out to be Avril's brother David and not Adam Border as they had originally suspected. However, that didn't mean that Adam never went to school in Leeds. Laura said she'd approach the school again and ask if they had ever had any children called Boogaard.

As it got to lunchtime – Jack was more than ready to take a break from sitting at a desk staring at paperwork – a uniformed PC entered and announced that Mr and Mrs Chi had just walked into reception. Jack asked that they be taken into the soft interview room. 'They've not long landed from Amsterdam. Please make sure they're looked after – tea, sandwiches, whatever they want. On us, of course.' Jack then turned his attention to Laura. 'Foxy knows they're coming today, right? Anik did tell him?'

Laura grabbed her coffee and headed out with Jack. She said that she'd stretch her legs by running over to the mortuary to tell Foxy that he was about to have visitors, and Jack should keep the Chis occupied until she texted him to say that Jessica was ready to be viewed. She'd then meet them there in case Mrs Chi needed a shoulder to cry on.

* * *

In the soft interview room, Henrick and Matilda Chi sat huddled together on one sofa. Her arm was linked through his and she held a cup of black coffee tightly in both hands. Henrick's hands lay flat on his knees in an attempt to seem calm. He wasn't. Neither of them had really accepted that their daughter was dead. They'd heard the words from Anik, and again in more recent days from Garritt, but their brains were simply not ready to process the information and accept it as being true. For now, they were on auto-pilot. Neither of them moved or said a word when Jack entered and introduced himself. In the time it took Jack to walk across the room and sit down on the sofa opposite, he'd noticed that, between them, they'd brought one artist's folio case and one lady's handbag. They looked at Jack like lost children waiting to be told what they were meant to be doing next.

'I'm Detective Sergeant Jack Warr. I'm one of the officers tasked to your daughter's case. We have a short wait before we can go and see her, so . . .'

'No questions.' Henrick spoke quickly and then swallowed a short, sharp gulp of air. Jack thought he might be about to be sick. 'We're here to see our daughter. That's it.'

Jack had seen this so many times before with bereaved family members. He knew that, as soon as they did see their daughter, the realisation that they'd been keeping at arm's length for days would suddenly hit them and, from that moment on, they'd be gibbering wrecks and of little use to him at all. He had to question them before they saw their daughter.

'I'm afraid we have a short wait regardless, Mr Chi. I won't ask you anything if you don't want me to. You can ask me any questions you like. Or not. You're in charge of what we do today.' Jack smiled in heartfelt solidarity. He took his mobile from his pocket and placed it face up on the seat next to him. Then he sat back and laced his fingers. 'They'll text me when it's time.'

Jack knew that it would take Laura at least ten minutes to even get to Foxy. If he knew about the viewing, then Jack had about twenty minutes with the Chis; and if Foxy didn't know, then Jack had anything up to an hour. Either way, he was banking on the silence eventually becoming too awkward for the Chis to bear.

Matilda appeared very calm although it could have simply been the shock of thinking she was so close to her dead daughter. She clung to Henrick as though her life depended on it and never took her eyes off the coffee. Jack thought she was unlikely to be the one to break the silence. Henrick, on the other hand, looked angry. 'Are you treating her as a criminal?' he asked.

'Definitely not, sir.' Jack spoke simply, using as few words as possible. 'Your daughter is a victim. This case is about catching her killer. So that she has justice, and you have answers.' In a few short sentences, Jack had aligned himself with the Chis and set himself up as the person who was going to give them the answers they yearned for. Jack now felt he could ask his own question. 'Could you describe Adam Border to me please, Mr Chi?'

'Do you think Adam was involved?' Henrick said with a surprised expression.

'My job is to trace the movements of each and every person who came into contact with Jessica in the last few months. This is how I rule people out as well as in. For now, I'm asking about Adam purely because we haven't yet discovered his whereabouts.'

Henrick nodded. 'Six feet tall. Slender. Shoulder-length blond hair, usually swept back into a ponytail. Striking blue eyes; they almost look like they're painted. Adam's polite and charming. He wears fashionable clothing and he always carries a small briefcase, which would look odd on someone less . . . cool. He's a quiet man, at least he seemed quiet at the side of Jessica.' Henrick couldn't stop the small smile from creeping across his face. 'She's so vibrant. Enthusiastic.'

Jack ignored the fact that Henrick was talking about his dead daughter in the present tense. He knew that probably wouldn't change until they actually saw her body.

'I don't know how old Adam is. Thirties? He's comfortably off. I know this because of his old Amsterdam apartment and because of his choice of wine in restaurants. I like him.' Jack asked what Henrick knew of Adam's life before he and Jessica met. 'Nothing much. He had no parents. He speaks Dutch, German and English like a native. And he has a love for and great knowledge of art.' Henrick glanced up at Jack, instinctively knowing what the next question was going to be.

'The Rossetti was a shock to me. I knew it was authentic because of the frame.' As he continued, Henrick got out his mobile and began searching for something he wanted to share. 'It was very old and the canvas was tacked onto the back of the wood frame. On the back of the picture, there were two unique stamps. A little worn, but legible. One related to an art exhibition and the other to a gallery. They served to help age the piece, just as the wooden frame did. I couldn't price the Rossetti that Jessica showed me, but another – *Pandora* – went for over £10 million.' Henrick handed his mobile to Jack. 'Scroll left. They're all authentic Rossettis. The one called *Lady Lilith*. I've held that. I know what authentic feels like.'

Jack returned Henrick's mobile to him. He certainly sounded convincingly well informed about the art world. So much so, that Jack almost felt bad for hanging up on Anik earlier.

Mr Chi continued: 'Rossetti was an exceptional creative artist. His poetry was as beautiful as his painting. He even buried a book of poetry with his deceased wife.'

Henrick touched his wife's hand to let her know that he was still there and that everything was going to be OK. She remained motionless, apart from a small tremor in her hands. Jack asked Henrick if he believed his daughter thought the painting to be a copy, or did she know it was authentic.

'Jessica wouldn't have known. But Adam would. He and I spoke about art many times. Detective Warr, do you think Adam was not the man he purported to be?'

'When I find him, Mr Chi, I'll ask him.'

Henrick nodded. 'Please, call us by our first names. You must understand, Jessica is a good girl. I told her to take the painting back and she said she would. I wish . . . I wish I was a rich man so that I could have helped her. We live modestly, being dependent on income from exhibitions. Many artists are in the same precarious position, of course, now more than ever because of the global pandemic.' Henrick lowered his head and took a moment to control the tears that Jack could see building inside him. 'Jessica even helped us with the rent in recent months.' His voice faded to a whisper. 'I should have realised something was wrong.'

'Henrick, I need to ask, to your knowledge, did Jessica ever use drugs?'

Henrick was open about the fact that Jessica used to smoke cannabis and also that, many years ago, she had a heroin habit. But he knew that she had gone through rehab four years ago and had been clean since.

The screen on Jack's mobile phone lit up and stopped the conversation dead in its tracks.

* * *

Jack led the way down into the car park at the back of the station, where a patrol car was waiting to take them to the chapel. It was perfectly walkable, being only two minutes along the same road, but bereaved families were always taken by car. Matilda hung onto Henrick's arm and walked with tiny, careful steps – as though she was on a tightrope and might fall if she lost focus for a split second. Henrick kept pace with her, giving her all the time in the world. Jack thought they looked like a strong, loving couple who were about to be shattered into a thousand unmendable pieces. He wasn't relishing getting to their destination.

The chapel was a white room with no windows, clinical in appearance, with one bed right in the centre. On the bed, Jessica lay beneath a crisp white sheet. Laura held the door open and waited for Matilda and Henrick to enter and take up position at their daughter's side. She then left Jack to do the identification.

Jack asked if they were ready, and they nodded. All three of them took a deep breath – Jack had not seen Jessica since the greenhouse, so the image in his mind was of a badly charred corpse. He slowly pulled the sheet down from Jessica's face and rested it on her shoulders. Foxy had perfectly wrapped her scalp in a manner reminiscent of a nun's wimple, so that only her pretty young face was on show, concealing her burnt hair and skull. Jessica's face was also expertly made up. Foxy's team had worked a miracle, Jack thought gratefully. Jessica even looked warm, as though blood still flowed beneath her skin adding a glow to her cheeks and a depth to her features. Jack knew it was all an illusion, but as far as the Chis were concerned, their daughter looked like a sleeping angel.

Matilda gasped and the tears came quickly. Henrick remained steadfast whilst he fulfilled his duty to Jack. 'Yes, Detective Warr, this is our daughter Jessica.' And then he too crumpled. Matilda sobbed as she took Jessica's face in her hands and kissed every visible inch of cold skin, repeating certain words over and over, sometimes in English, sometimes in Dutch: 'I'm sorry. 'I love you. Goodbye my darling.' In contrast, Henrick looked at the ground, statue-like, and allowed the tears to effortlessly fall from him. He couldn't look at Jessica and he certainly couldn't touch her. After a few minutes, the pain got too much for Matilda. She walked out of the chapel and collapsed into a chair in the corridor, sobbing into a hanky and numbly accepting Laura's comforting arm around her shoulder.

Henrick finally looked at this daughter.

'I'd like to sketch her,' he whispered. 'To paint later. To . . . to bring her back to life. Paintings are about immortalising those you love. May I? Please.'

Jack completely understood Henrick's need to turn this horrific moment into something else. Something beautiful that would be easier to revisit. He suggested that Henrick sit with Matilda, whilst he collected Henrick's art folio for him.

'Two days ago, I was a father. Now, I'm not.' Henrick looked Jack dead in the eyes. 'Are you a father?' Jack nodded his reply. 'I need to feel sad and mourn . . . and instead I feel anger and hatred. But the truth is, if the man who took my daughter was standing in front of me now, I'm not sure what I could do. I'd like to think I would tear out his heart with my bare hands . . . but I'm not a bold man, Detective Warr. Not like you. This . . .' Henrick laid his hand on Jessica's arm, gently at first, before instinct took over and told him to grip tightly onto her and never let go. He closed his fingers around her wrist and sobbed. 'This is wrong. Please make it right. Not as a policeman. But as a father.'

Henrick then walked into the corridor, where Matilda stood to meet him. He cradled her head against his chest and rocked her in his arms.

Jack stared at Jessica's wrist – Henrick's finger marks were still visible as indented white lines where her lifeless skin had not bounced back into shape when he'd finally dared to let go. How he'd let go at all was beyond Jack.

Jack covered Jessica's hand with the sheet to stop thoughts of vengeance-by-proxy filling his mind. He could not think like a father, as Henrick had asked. He had to think like a policeman. Although he didn't know if he'd still be so logical when he finally faced the person behind the brutal murders of Avril Jenkins and Jessica Chi.

CHAPTER 24

Jack and Laura huddled together at the far end of the chapel corridor, whilst Matilda stood at the window watching her husband sketch their dead daughter. 'You've got to get back to the squad room, Jack. Ridley texted when you were in there with Mr Chi. He's not happy about something. Again! He's so volatile recently. Anik thinks he's been dumped, but my guess is the male menopause.' Jack frowned as though to say she was talking rubbish. 'It's a thing!'

Ridley had been Laura's guilty crush for more than six months. At first, she was frightened of him not feeling the same, then she was frightened of him feeling the same, then she decided that the reality would not match the fantasy and that she loved the thought of him more than anything else. Now she had Josh.

Laura told Jack that he'd better head back, before Ridley came down to the chapel and caused a scene. She'd look after the Chis until they went back to their hotel, then she'd pick up with Interpol. 'The likes of Hester Mancroft thought Avril could have been married before she met Frederick Jenkins, but even their solicitor doesn't know for sure. We don't know if she was married to Andre Boogaard, they could just have had a kid together.'

Jack was about to suggest that Laura make a second visit to Hester, but then decided against it. So far, he'd kept her cannabis oil use out of the investigation and, for now, wanted it to stay that way. Using home-grown cannabis oil was illegal and he might need Hester again, so he wanted her to know that he was someone she could rely on to keep her secret. Instead, Jack suggested that Laura and Anik extend their international enquiries to Germany, as that was a key European country in Josh's bigger-picture investigation. Laura whispered her ranted reply, so as not to disturb the mourning that was occurring just ten feet away.

'You've got to be shitting me, Jack. How the hell is Adam Border-slash-Boogaard-slash-whatever staying under so many radars? He's done a uni course, for fuck's sake. He's been seen by dozens of neighbours at the Jenkins house, digging and pruning, and driving round in a bloody Porsche. He's been investigated for B&E, theft and stalking. And we have nothing. No employment or unemployment records, no benefits, medical records, car insurances or parking fines. Adam Border-slash-Boogaard-slash-whatever doesn't exist. Not here. Not in Amsterdam. And you now want me to look into tracing him in *Germany*?' Laura let out a heavy sigh and turned her back. 'Oh, just piss off back to the squad room.'

Jack smiled and said thank you.

* * *

Ridley sat at his desk washing down two tablets with a bottle of water. He waved Jack into his office and told him to close the door. 'I just received a call from DCI Steve Lewis. He was surprised to see you appear on undercover surveillance footage from the workplace of Jason Marks.'

Jack pursed his lips and the tiny muscles under his eyes twitched. Of course he knew Jason Marks had been followed from Avril Jenkins' wake, but he didn't know that he was under constant surveillance. Jack said nothing as Ridley laid into him.

'He's a suspect in a dual investigation. We don't know anything about him yet, he could be vital, and you're strolling up to his front door and knocking on it. Embarrassing me is one thing, Jack, but embarrassing a DCI from another division can get you removed from this case.'

'Sir . . .'

'Don't speak!' Ridley's shouted instruction cut Jack dead. 'Lewis is leading an investigation which requires an ongoing agreement to share information. What you did is an infringement of that agreement and jeopardises our position in the case. He can have me removed, Jack. And if I go, you go.' Ridley sat back in his chair and laced his fingers on his lap. It was now Jack's turn to speak.

'Sir, I would never intentionally embarrass you or threaten your position. And if the Drug Squad *was* sharing information, then we'd have known that Jason Marks was under surveillance. I'm investigating the murders of Avril Jenkins and Jessica Chi. Avril listed a Rossetti painting as being stolen from her home, she accused Jessica of stealing from her and Jessica was seen in possession of a stolen Rossetti. Seeing as Avril and Jessica are both dead, of course I was going to question the only art dealer connected to the case.' Ridley sat in stony silence as Jack explained in more detail. 'It could have passed through his hands. He could have it. Or it could have gone up in flames alongside Jessica. I don't know. But approaching him was a perfectly legitimate step in my investigation.'

Ridley gave a long sigh, turning away from Jack, shaking his head.

* * *

Laura stood next to Matilda at the chapel window and they both watched Henrick seated next to Jessica, sketching her face. He looked happily lost in the moment. The image of Jessica that was slowly appearing on Henrick's sketch pad was astonishingly beautiful and serene. Not dead – just waiting to wake. Like Sleeping Beauty. She possessed a long-gone life, that was clearly coming from Henrick's memory.

'He can capture the essence of a person.' This was the first thing Matilda had said since arriving at the station. 'It's more accurate than a photograph. He only has to see a person once and he can see their truth.'

An idea came to Laura. Now all she had to do was find the right moment to ask . . .

* * *

There had been such a long pause that Jack was unsure whether to say something. He was about to when Ridley turned to face him. 'You have a go at Steve Lewis for not sharing information with us, Jack . . .' Ridley stood, throwing his chair back against the wall. 'Yet why is none of what you just told me about Jason Marks, on that incident board?' He headed for the corner of his office and started to make himself a cup of ginger tea in an endeavour to calm down. 'You're a law unto yourself. Once again! Well, now I've got a DCI from Drugs thinking that I'm either in on your insubordination, or not even aware of it. Which makes me look at the very least incompetent.' Ridley then returned to his desk and stared at the light brown liquid in his cup. 'This shit tastes like peppered water.'

For a moment, Jack watched Ridley as he blinked rapidly and took in short, sharp breaths.

'How are things? With you.' Jack's question sounded weak in light of what Ridley was going through. Not that Jack actually knew what Ridley was going through, because he was such a private man. Jack didn't even know what kind of cancer Ridley had been diagnosed with. And he would never ask. Ridley had spoken as much as he was prepared to, and Jack respected that. 'I'll get my reports up to date now. I didn't want to bother you with it because Jason Marks wasn't there anyway.'

'You had a go at me for not being there for you, Jack, so don't have a go at me now for being all over you like a rash. You can't have it both ways.'

A small smile crept over Jack's face. 'I'll take being dragged over the coals by you above being ignored any day of the week. Sir.'

Ridley pushed the cup of ginger tea away from him across his desk. 'Make me a coffee. Decaf.' As Jack flicked the kettle on again, Ridley asked if he'd seen Foxy at the chapel. 'I'd like to be able to give Mr and Mrs Chi some news on their daughter's death before they go back to Amsterdam. The fire brigade are now saying that it could have been a leak from one of the gas tanks used to power the infrared heaters. I need to know if it was an accident or murder.'

Jack's mobile pinged with an image from Laura. He was shocked to see a photo of a sketch of a young man with three words beneath: *Meet our ghost*. The sketch was frightening. Not only was it instantly recognisable as Adam Border – based on younger photos they already had and on verbal descriptions they'd received from people who'd met him – it also felt like an insight into the man himself, and that's what made Jack wince. The version of Adam Border on Jack's mobile screen looked powerful, strong and enigmatic. He also looked hollow – like there was nothing behind his eyes.

The A4 sketch of Adam Border was even more disturbing than the photo Laura had sent through. She had her head cocked to one side as they both looked at the sketch pinned to the evidence board. 'He's magnetic. He's the boy your mum warned you against. If he was in a crowded room, you'd see him first.'

'Then how is he invisible?' Jack moved the two photos they already had of Adam Border closer to the sketch: one of him as a teen, from Hester Mancroft; and one of him as an adult, from Jessica Chi. 'In both photographs he looks like a boy. Henrick's drawn the man.'

'Matilda said that Henrick captures a person's essence. Their truth.'

'That's what this is, Laura. The camera does lie: it tells us that Adam is a handsome, wholesome man who parents see as son-in-law material. But this grown man with those unfathomable eyes . . .'

Jack tapped the sketch with the tip of his finger. 'This is who we're looking for.'

* * *

Laura had been working on the insurance lists and inventory from Arnold Hutchinson for much of the afternoon. One insurance company had said that they were involved with Frederick Jenkins in the early days, but he was a difficult client to manage because he always thought he knew best. He could buy, insure and sell an item within the space of a month if the market was ripe. He was an avid collector of an eclectic range of works – silver, porcelain, furniture – and his exceptional, ever-expanding knowledge meant that his judgement usually turned out to be right. He was just very tricky to keep up with because he could be so spontaneous. He used to say that the art world moved quickly, so you always had to be ready to move with it, or it would leave you behind. Conversely, when circumstances dictated patience, he had it in spades: many a time he bought up the work of an up-and-coming artist and held on to it until they'd made their name. Due to his constant buying, selling, and disagreeing with advice given, he eventually changed brokers.

The second insurance company also found Frederick Jenkins to be a difficult client as, by then, he knew his trade as well as, or better than, some of the experts. If he felt that a valuation was inaccurate, he'd demand a second or even a third opinion. But he was also a man that insurers wanted to work with because his private collection was so high-end: at his peak he owned a Modigliani, a Rossetti and a Van Gogh.

But the insurance company unlucky enough to be in the Jenkinses' employ when Frederick died described Avril as being ten times worse to deal with. For months they could not gain access to the private collection and so had no clue what items were still in her possession, and yet she constantly questioned the level of monthly cover she was being quoted. In the end, the insurance company wrote her a letter stating that they could not work with her unless she allowed them access to her home in order to assess whether the current security levels were adequate. Three letters were sent in total, warning Avril that although many of her smaller valuables fell under her contents insurance, her incredibly valuable paintings would not be covered unless she cooperated.

This was why the insured property inventory from Arnold Hutchinson did not match the inventory held by the last company to insure Avril, and that, in turn, did not match the inventory of stolen items she wrote for the Kingston police, making it impossible to discern what Avril had sold, what had been stolen, and what should, in theory, still be in the house.

Jack looked at the mess of insurance and valuation information sitting on Laura's desk. Laura shrugged. 'Terence Jenkins has got one hell of a mess to unravel.'

Jack suddenly remembered that he hadn't written up his notes from his visit to Arnold Hutchinson, so currently he was the only person in the squad room who knew there was a second will. Laura recognised the look on his face and asked what it was that he'd just remembered he'd forgotten. Jack turned, so his back was to Ridley's office door, then lowered his voice.

'Before the Chis arrived, I was with Arnold Hutchinson. He mentioned a second will written by Avril Jenkins. If it's legitimate, it'll override the first, meaning Terence Jenkins isn't the beneficiary of her estate.'

Laura's mouth dropped open. 'Don't tell me. Adam Border? Oh, my actual God, Jack. Terence is gonna be so pissed off when he finds out!'

'He was. He was in with Hutchinson when I arrived. Avril did it online apparently.'

Laura gave a sly look towards Ridley's office and sniggered at the thought of Jack having to relay news that was now more than five hours old.

'I've not had time, Laura. The Chis arrived, then he distracted me with a bollocking about going to see Jason Marks, who just happens to be a suspect under constant surveillance by Drugs.'

Laura hid her face behind her hand in case he saw her laughing. She suggested that Jack give Hutchinson a quick call to see if he'd found anything out for sure yet about the new Will. Ridley would go a lot easier on him if he went armed with all the answers.

*　　*　　*

Hutchinson was out of his office, and his secretary refused to divulge where he was due to client confidentiality. Jack had no time to play legal games with her. 'May, if he's with Terence Jenkins, say nothing. If he's verified the authenticity of Avril Jenkins' new will, say nothing. You see, May,' Jack was using his best smoky tone, reserved for his more susceptible interviewees, 'Arnold has already told me everything he knew as of earlier today. What I don't yet know are the names of the witnesses. Now, he will tell me when I ask, but it'd make my life a lot easier if I didn't have to wait for him to return. Asking his permission would be nothing more than a formality, as I'm sure you already know. He's been sharing information at every stage to avoid the need for issuing warrants to obtain it. He'd hate for that to happen simply because he's out of the office.'

May hesitated and then said quietly, 'I only know one of the names. Mrs Hester Mancroft.'

*　　*　　*

Jack left the office and walked to the train station to catch the 3.15 p.m. from London Victoria to Hove. He knew he would get the most from Hester Mancroft by talking to her face to face, and for the sake of a one-hour train ride, Jack was more than happy to travel down to the coast to see her in person.

Hester took an age to walk the length of the hallway. In fact, Jack was sure that she was being slower than the last time he visited. Eventually, he heard bolts slide back. Hester's face seemed anguished, and her tired, reddened eyes took a moment to focus. The sight of Jack brought a smile, but her brow remained creased from the pain she was clearly in. Jack held up a bottle of gin . . . and her brow relaxed, ever so slightly.

In the kitchen, Hester sat herself at the table whilst Jack found two glasses, which he rinsed and dried before joining her. Hester watched him pour one large gin, with an equal measure of tonic, and one glass of just tonic. As she sipped on her generous G&T, Jack got straight to the point.

'I need to ask you, Hester, about the will you witnessed for Avril Jenkins.' Initially Hester looked blank, but then she recalled that Avril had handed her the back sheet of something and asked her to sign it, which she'd done without asking what it was. Hester said that was about six months ago when she'd gone to London to collect . . . Her sentence trailed off and she gulped a large mouthful of gin and tonic, which was now nicely numbing the pain from her arthritis. Jack topped up her glass, adding ice and a slice for her this time. She smiled coyly, claiming it was a tad early for her to drink, but that it would be rude not to be sociable after he'd come all this way and brought her such a lovely gift.

'Hester, the last time I was here, we spoke about the possibility that Avril was already married before meeting Frederick Jenkins.'

'Oh, yes, well, she could have been. I think if the right man asked her, she'd have just up and done it. Then regretted it, or not, later. *Oh!* Do you think she was married before Frederick and never divorced? Nothing would surprise me, DS Warr. She rarely did things in the right order. But, as I think I said last time, from what I know of Freddie, he was more concerned with whether or not Avril had a child. Because he was protective about his money, you see. He didn't want an heir popping up uninvited.'

Hester had not mentioned this the last time at all, but Jack wasn't going to pick her up on it. She was doing her best to recall events, some of which were long ago. Hester lifted her gin glass halfway to her lips and then laughed, slamming it down onto the table again.

'She called him a tight-fisted old bastard! Which I thought was deeply unfair considering how quickly she could go through his money. She only had to ask. Range Rovers, jewellery, furs.' Hester shook her head. 'Avril never appreciated what she had. Things came too easily, you see. Spoilt. Which is not something often said about a person from the arse end of Leeds.'

Hester dragged the lemon wedge up the inside of her empty glass with her finger and pushed the glass towards Jack. He refilled it for her and topped up his own tonic at the same time. Then he returned to his seat and set Hester off on a new topic. 'She had a younger brother, David – did you ever get to meet him?'

'Well, I knew him when we were in Leeds. He was a bit – to use Avril's words – *mentally challenged*. He was never at school, was a lot of trouble, I think, and Avril once told me he had been in prison, and was an embarrassment, so she never mentioned him to me again. She could be quite cruel, you know, and I think after she married and had money, she was very protective of her new image so would probably not even acknowledge her brother if she passed him in the street.'

Jack nodded, knowing Avril had never acknowledged Adam as her son. 'Tell me about the first time Adam Border came to your B&B in Chelsea.'

*　*　*

As Ridley headed upstairs to Raeburn's office, he expected he'd been summoned to give her an update on his health. It was about that time. Every week, she had to make certain that he was fit enough to be on active duty. Raeburn was the only person who knew the details of Ridley's illness – that he'd been diagnosed with early-stage prostate cancer and was receiving radiotherapy as an outpatient. She also knew that his prognosis was good, although the ever-present fear during the early stages was that they'd discover it had spread, most likely to his lymphatic system or bones. Neither had happened yet and, as the weeks passed, metastasis became less and less likely.

When Ridley opened Raeburn's office door, he was surprised to see Steve Lewis standing in the corner casually stirring sugar into his freshly brewed cup of tea.

*　*　*

'Describing it as a B&B is underselling the establishment,' Hester snapped. 'I had to call it that because there are boxes to be ticked to qualify as a hotel and, well, I can't recall what they were now but . . . what did you ask me?' Jack patiently repeated his question, this time without saying 'B&B'.

'I expect Adam read my advertisement in the *Evening Standard*. He was very impressed with what I'd done to the place. He said I had a stylish eye for detail, which I thought was lovely coming from an art student.' Hester became tearful as she reminisced. 'I'd used my entire divorce settlement to purchase and convert that house. And Adam was right, it *was* beautiful. I chose every single piece of furniture, every picture frame, every rug. And I must have single-handedly kept that emporium at the end of the road going for a good few years. I spent so much of my money there. Oh, I loved my time in that house, DS Warr. I imagine it would be triple the value now if I'd been able to maintain it.' Mentioning the emporium suddenly brought back a memory. 'That's where I bumped into Avril again. We had a little catch-up over shopping. My news was that I'd just taken my shit of a husband for everything I could in a divorce, and her news was that she'd just escaped a drunken Irishman. They lived in Dublin together for a while, as I recall. It wasn't long after that Adam came to stay with me.'

That was the last useful thing she said. Jack's decision to ply Hester with gin to get her to talk more freely about Avril was now backfiring. All she wanted to do was chat about décor and how she could have studied art if she hadn't been tied to her bastard husband through her most adventurous years. She became morose and tearful as she recalled having to sell up all her treasures as she got herself into debt, and was forced to lose her lovely house.

Jack made his excuses, thanked her for talking to him, and left her to finish off the bottle of gin by herself.

* * *

When Jack got back to the squad room, Laura was putting on her coat. Jack launched into his handover. 'There's a connection to Ireland. I need you to trace the movements of Avril Jenkins between—'

'Whoa! It's six thirty. I'm going home.' Jack looked at Laura as though he thought she was slacking 'I'm happy to help you tomorrow,' Laura said, picking up her handbag. 'But just as a reminder,

Jack, I'm a DS too. So, try asking me, not telling me.' She headed for the door. 'I'm glad Hove was productive. See you bright and early, when I'll be raring to go ... Night, sir.' Jack spun to see Ridley standing right behind him.

Ridley started the conversation by pointing out that Jack had already got the team running around making enquiries in Amsterdam and Germany ... and now Ireland? 'We're thin enough on the ground as it is, so you'll need to convince me it's a good use of resources.' Ridley slid his hands into his pockets and perched on the edge of the nearest desk. 'You're off for the rest of the week now, right? Step away, Jack. Take the time to enjoy your stag night and your wedding.'

'Actually, sir, Ireland is this new lead which I—'

'No,' Ridley said firmly. 'Hand it over to Laura tomorrow, as she suggested. You think every new lead will end with Adam Border. Maybe this time it will. Maybe it won't. But you're getting married, Jack. The job isn't that important in the big scheme of things, believe me. Take some leave. A week. Take Maggie on honeymoon.'

Jack didn't understand where all of this was coming from, but suspected Steve-sodding-Lewis was throwing his weight around again. Something was happening higher up than Ridley and now Jack was being kept out of the loop.

CHAPTER 25

By the time Jack reached his car in the police station car park, he was no longer so pissed off by the conversation he'd just had.

Perhaps Laura and Ridley had the right idea – she'd decided to actually have a life outside of the job and Ridley wasn't sacrificing his current health for it. Jack was days away from getting married, for God's sake, yet he was more excited by the prospect of heading to Ireland and tracking down the elusive Adam Border than spending time with his wife-to-be.

Jack called Maggie on FaceTime. When she appeared on his screen, she was in scrubs with her face mask pulled down and tucked beneath her chin. 'You OK? I got one minute for you. Or can it wait till I come out of surgery?'

'One minute is all I need.' Jack couldn't wait to see how surprised and happy Maggie would be when he told her his news. 'I've got a week's leave. So, we can get married, spend the day being sociable then, as soon as everyone's gone home, we can disappear off on honeymoon for a few days. I'll sort it with Mum. Where would you like to go?'

The smile that appeared on Maggie's face wasn't the sort he was hoping for. He'd amused her rather than delighted her. She said that, firstly, they had a suite booked for the wedding night, so they couldn't take off straightaway. And secondly, why did he take a week off without first making sure that she could do the same? She ended by saying, 'I love you,' and then hung up.

Fuck, Jack thought to himself. He could cope with a week off work if it meant spending time with Maggie, but if it meant spending time alone, stewing in his own juices . . . that would be carnage.

* * *

As Jack pulled up outside the house, Penny was on the pavement trying to lift an Amazon parcel over the doorstep, whilst shouting into the house telling Hannah not to crawl out of sight. 'Come back, darling. Hannah! Grandma can't see you.' Her voice was light and sing-song, so as not to make Hannah think she was being told off, but Jack could hear the stress in it. Jack swept up behind Penny and took the weight of the parcel from her, leaving her free to run inside and catch up with Hannah.

As Jack put the parcel onto the kitchen table, Penny felt the need to launch into an explanation. 'I wanted to get it indoors because it was in full view of the street, and you never know who's walking past. Some people just take parcels off the doorstep. And Hannah's so fast now! And strong-willed. Maybe we should get one of those doorbell cameras.'

Jack glanced into the dining room, where Hannah had pulled herself to her feet using a pile of unopened packages. She was slapping her hand down on a small piece of face up sellotape and scream-laughing at the feel of it. Jack asked what on earth Penny had been buying.

'They're wedding presents, darling. You and Maggie need to open them one evening soon, when you're together. I've bought you some thank-you cards. And I've bought wrapping paper for the gifts you need to buy.'

'Who am I buying gifts for?'

'The bridesmaids and the best man.' The way Penny looked at Jack reminded him of when he was a boy and he'd asked a stupid question like why he had to wear shoes to school. 'It's traditional to thank them with a gift. An item of jewellery for the bridesmaids and perhaps a good bottle of single malt for Simon. I can buy them for you if you don't have time.'

'No, no. I've got plenty of time on my hands.' Jack ventured into the dining room and picked up Hannah. As soon as she was in his arms, she strained to be down again, so he stood her on the tallest box, held her by the hands and let her bounce up and down on it.

Penny shook her head. 'Let's hope that's not a crystal decanter!' Her sarcasm went unheard. 'Hannah and I were about to go to the park,' she went on. 'Would you like to come? Some fresh air?' As soon as Hannah heard the word 'park', she reached for Penny. Jack winced: Hannah was now the third person in a row to blatantly reject him. Jack knew that he wasn't good company right now, so said that he needed to shower. Penny squeezed his arm and gave him one of those pitying smiles that only a mother could get away with. Then she gave him the space he wanted.

Jack stood in the shower, allowing the water to pound his scalp and reinvigorate his mood. By the time Penny got home, he was feeling far more sociable. Hannah had fallen asleep in her push-chair, so she was parked in the dining room amongst the parcels whilst Penny put the kettle on. Jack sat at the kitchen table.

'So, what still needs doing?' Penny looked at him as if she didn't understand the question. 'For the wedding. What still needs doing? I've got a week off, so I can ...' Before Jack could finish, Penny started to giggle. She pressed her fingers against her lips and apolo-gised, then quickly tried to think of jobs she could give Jack, to make him feel useful but also to keep him out of her way. Jack picked up on what she was doing. 'Great!' Jack said. 'Is there anyone who *does* need me around?'

'Oh, stop that,' Penny said. 'You caught me unawares, that's all. There's still plenty to do, and I'd be very grateful of your help, dar-ling. Oh Jack, you should see everything Maggie's managed to pull together. She's worked so hard. I'll make a list of what's left and give you some jobs. There might be a lot of fetching and carrying, if you don't mind. Things I can't do.' Penny chattered on as she started preparing the organic vegetables for dinner. 'The menus are all done. Maggie's been extremely clever with them because two of her nurse friends are vegetarians, two are vegan and one is on the paleo diet, whatever that is when it's at home! Something to do with cavemen. But she didn't want them to feel singled out by having something on their plate that looked different. So, she's been very careful to choose a menu that means everyone's dinner looks the same. The flowers are arriving first thing on Saturday morning, and the car taking us all to the registry office is booked for an hour beforehand. It's a Mercedes S-Class.' Penny paused meaningfully, and Jack pretended to be suitably agog at how well she and Maggie had done to choose such a beautiful vehicle. 'Everyone else is getting there under their own steam. Maggie did toy with the idea of a double-decker bus to take everyone, including us.'

'A bus?'

'Open top. They're all the rage.'

'For winning football teams, maybe. I prefer the Merc.'

'I think she wanted a solution to people getting from A to B, being able to drink and not having to worry about driving. When's your stag do, darling?' Jack hadn't given it a second thought – and he was fairly sure Ridley hadn't either. Penny smiled. 'I bet Simon's got it all planned. He's the organised sort. Now, Jack . . .' Penny pointed the vegetable knife in his direction. 'I want to give you some money for behind the bar. I know you said you'd do it but, well, you know what policemen and nurses are like with a free bar. I insist.' Penny then turned back to her chopping board and fell silent. He could tell by the way her shoulders had tightened that she was crying.

'I remember when you and Dad knew that Maggie and I were for keeps,' Jack said gently. 'Dad said that when the time came, a free bar would be his gift to us.' Jack put on his dad's deep, West Country accent: *A free bar is a powerful thing, son. People won't remember the wedding, but they'll remember you forever.* You don't have to take on Dad's promise, Mum. You've done so much . . .' Jack corrected himself. 'You *do* so much.'

'I miss him at times like this,' Penny said, sniffing. 'I don't want to sit at the front on my own. I want to be on your dad's arm. I want to hold his hand and watch our son get married to the best girl in the world.'

Jack got up and stood just behind her.

'Be on my arm.' Penny turned to face him. Her glasses were steamed up and tears rolled down her cheeks. 'There's nothing to say that I have to start off at the front. Walk me down the aisle, Mum. Give me to Maggie.' Penny rested her head on Jack's chest and put her arms round his waist. He rested his chin on the top of her head and hugged her. 'I miss him too.'

*   *   *

When Maggie arrived home, Penny was upstairs watching *Midsomer Murders* in her bedroom, Hannah was asleep, and Jack was pretending to keep an eye on the cottage pie that Penny had made. He was flicking through the list of things already organised for his wedding, and the list of things that still needed tackling – clearly a mammoth amount of work had happened without him even noticing. It made him feel bad for not pulling his weight, but as he looked at the work still to be done, he just couldn't muster any enthusiasm. He wanted to marry Maggie and he wanted a wedding day to celebrate his love for her in front of all of their friends . . . he just couldn't be arsed with the rigmarole of it all.

Jack had moved all of the unopened wedding gifts into the living room and opened a bottle of red wine. He'd handed Maggie a full glass and sent her upstairs to soak in the bath that he'd already run for her. Some things Jack *was* good at. Pampering Maggie was one of them.

Jack sprinkled cheese on top of the cottage pie then put it back into the oven. Then he moved to the fridge where a magnetic white scribble pad had pride of place. In the centre of the pad, was a handwritten list.

6 p.m.: turn the dish as the back of the oven is hotter than the front. 6.30 p.m.: add cheese & turn down to 140. 7 p.m: ready.

Jack plucked the magnetic board rubber from the fridge door and wiped everything off the scribble pad. He then turned the oven down to 140 and returned to the lounge.

Maggie was now sitting in his large towelling robe, feet tucked underneath her, wine in hand. He loved how she looked, fresh from a bath. She had glowing, rosy cheeks and soft wrinkled fingertips. And she smelt of mandarins. Jack proudly announced that tomorrow he was going into town to shop for bridesmaids' gifts, and something for Ridley.

Maggie gave him a gentle smile. 'It's done. I went out on my lunchbreak and bought a silver bracelet each for Regina and my sister. I was going to get a gold tie pin for Simon but, seeing as he's retiring, I got him a subscription to a Scottish distillery instead. He'll get their Whisky of the Month for a whole year.'

Jack thought about the timeframe: a whole year. For all he knew, it could turn out to be a gift that didn't get used. Jack realised he was desperate to share Ridley's cancer news with Maggie, but instead, he handed her the first wedding gift to open.

As she picked at the packing tape, she brought up the subject of Jack's week off work. 'I can't get a week off with you, Jack. I did ask but it's just too short notice. I can get three days, so we could have a long weekend somewhere. On the wedding night, we booked a suite at Soho House, remember?' Jack admitted that he hadn't remembered. 'If you wanted to go out of town for three days, I can cancel it? What do you want to do?'

'It doesn't matter, Mags. I just got this week off and thought . . . well, I didn't think. It was stupid. Sorry. Let's just stick to the two-week honeymoon later in the year.'

Maggie leant across the gift on her knee and took hold of Jack's hand. She spoke gently. 'You know, Jack, it *was* stupid. Because we both work shifts, so why on earth wouldn't you have asked me before taking a week off? Answer: you didn't take a week off. You've been told to. You've pissed Ridley off again, haven't you?' Maggie smiled, then rocked forwards on her knees and placed a long kiss on Jack's lips. 'I love you, Jack Warr. For a whole week, I get my man waiting at home for me, running my baths, pouring my wine.' She punctuated her fantasy list with another kiss. 'And Ridley will forgive whatever you've done.' Maggie rocked back onto her bottom and, as she took the final piece of tape off the first present, she instructed Jack to write down what she said. 'Aunt Jane. Book-ends.' She then put on her best pretend-excited voice. 'Oh, Jack. One's got your name engraved on it and the other's got mine!'

'Well, shit, that makes them impossible to sell on eBay!' Jack typed the notes into his mobile. 'Now I'm going to have to buy a fucking bookshelf.'

Maggie picked up the next gift. 'You want to talk about what happened with Simon? You've not been suspended, have you?' Jack explained that Ridley had pushed him off the case, using the wedding as an excuse. He'd not been suspended, but only because he hadn't dug his heels in. 'Well, he couldn't suspend you for no reason. Is Simon wrong to keep you away from the case? If he is, you *should* dig your heels in. What's stopping you?'

Jack couldn't tell Maggie about Ridley's illness and so made out that taking a week away from the case was more of a mutual decision.

'It's hard for Ridley because we're working under another team. He's not the one ultimately in charge, so lines have to be toed.' Maggie sucked her teeth. She knew that toeing lines wasn't something Jack was very good at. He continued, 'The investigation is being headed up by Drugs and, sometimes, as they pick up the pace, we have to slow down so that our investigation doesn't get in the way of theirs. Only I'm so close to finding this one particular guy, Mags, and he's crucial to our murder investigation, I just know he is. So, sitting on my hands for a week could be a disaster.' A darkness came into Jack's eyes as his true feelings about the case surfaced.

'I know that I get blinkered. But I get obsessed with one train of enquiry because I know – I *know* – it's leading me in the right direction. There's this guy, Adam Border. His name keeps coming up, but no one can find him. He might be connected to the drugs, but he's definitely connected to a second line of enquiry around the art world. 'Course, Drug Squad aren't interested in that, because Josh is filling their heads with how *big-time* this sort of gang crime is in the US. They're saving the world and all I'm doing is getting justice for two women who are already dead and gone. But they matter, Mags. And I seem to be the only one focussed on that. Everyone else is double checking every move they make with Steve-bloody-Lewis.'

'Why is Simon rolling over?' Maggie asked. 'He should be fighting for his case, shouldn't he?'

'Drug Squad's chasing their very own Pablo Escobar, and they're ignoring Adam Border. Because he doesn't fit their profile. But criminals come in all forms. I've met jockeys scarier than Jack the Ripper, and old women who'd give Ronnie Biggs a run for his money. Rule number one: follow the evidence. If I can find Adam Border, I know things will fall into place. He could be a killer, or a drug dealer bringing lethal concoctions to the streets and filling up your ED with young kids who don't know what they're taking. Right now, he's a ghost. But I can feel him just out of reach. If I stop now, I could lose him for good.'

Maggie sighed. 'I can see why Simon wanted to give you some headspace. Please, please, let's take the three days that I've been able to get off work and let's just go somewhere. Me, you and Hannah . . . or just me and you if you like. You scare me when you get this fixated. I can see it in your eyes, Jack. The anger.' Maggie stroked Jack's cheek with her warm fingertips. 'I love your beautiful soft brown eyes. Not these dark pools that I'm looking into now.'

Jack kissed the palm of Maggie's hand and whispered, 'I'm sorry.'

'Never be sorry for who you are.'

When Jack looked up again, his brows were raised and his eyes looked kinder and infinitely more alluring. 'Do I really scare you?'

'Oh, Jack, no, not in that way. I feel safe with you. Protected.' Maggie rested her hand on Jack's chest and smiled into his now gentle, loving eyes. 'My Jack.'

Jack threw the gift box onto the floor and crawled along the sofa towards her. She scooted down underneath him so that he could lay down between her legs. As he kissed her, his hand moved from her ankle and slid effortlessly up her freshly shaved shin, over her knee, up her thigh and beneath her robe. Maggie gasped as he touched her . . .

The doorbell made them both jump, and then freeze in the hope that whoever it was would go away. Jack's mobile buzzed. 'Fucking hell!' he whispered. 'It's Ridley.'

Maggie kissed Jack's cheek. 'Oh, Jack . . .' she whispered.

'I can't leave him out there, Mags.' Jack looked down at his beautiful wife-to-be and strained to control his body. 'God. I wish I could.'

'That's not what I was going to say. I was going to say . . . I can smell something burning.'

CHAPTER 26

Maggie peeled the burnt cheese from the top of the cottage pie in one big strip, then sprinkled more grated cheese on top of the potato and started the process again. She set an alarm on Jack's mobile for fifteen minutes and headed upstairs, leaving Jack and Ridley to talk in private.

Ridley stood in the middle of the lounge holding a large gift-wrapped box with a white envelope sellotaped to the side. He placed it amongst the other gifts as Jack brought two glasses and a bottle of whisky through from the kitchen.

'Sorry to disturb your evening. I need to explain a few things. Such as why I pulled the rug out from under you earlier.' Jack indicated that Ridley should sit down. Ridley sipped his whisky. It was so smooth and warming, that he couldn't help but take two more sips before continuing.

'The Drug Squad has been joined by the National Crime Agency. They have covert ops tracking a haulage firm from the Netherlands to Ireland via the UK. With the help of informants along the entire route, the NCA, slowly but surely, is tracking drug labs on an industrial scale. Their biggest single haul being twenty-seven arrests in Northumberland, confiscating twenty blocks of cocaine and 380 blocks of cannabis travelling from Holland to Ireland. SOCA's involved, too, mainly monitoring the M6. They're working towards a massive swoop but so far the only arrests they've made are some lower-strata dealers and distributors. That's the way it always goes. They believe the kingpin is a man originally from Leeds. He's been seen at a large property in Spain, but that gave them nothing they could use. He's smart. Uses a different burner phone each day. And none of the low-level gang members will give him up: they either don't know who he is or are too scared to say. The NCA even has one of his accountants, and they normally turn pretty quickly, but this one's practically mute. Two days ago, they got a tip-off from a woman that he might be hiding in Lithuania. She's now in a safe house somewhere on the south coast.'

Jack whistled. 'Wow. And this smuggling operation – worthy of the National Crime Agency and the Serious Organised Crime Agency – is using Avril's home as one of their bases?'

'Just as Josh said they would be.' Ridley emptied his glass. 'They utilise small-scale bolt-holes across the UK and Europe. Usually homes, and often occupied. It's a sort of cuckooing approach. They're basically hideouts from where they can still do business.' Ridley sat forwards in his seat and let his empty glass dangle from his fingertips. 'Some of the gang already caught are hired muscle – even hired guns. Steve Lewis thinks our killers are amongst them.'

'Then we should be the ones to interview them, sir.'

Ridley shook his head. 'They're connected to his drugs case. He'll only pass them across to us when he's finished with them.'

Jack gave a long, heavy sigh. 'Sir . . . do they think Adam Border is their kingpin?'

Ridley shrugged. 'That conversation is above my pay grade.' He swung his empty glass, unsubtly drawing Jack's eye. Jack emptied his own glass, then refilled both. 'I did remind them that we have an established connection between Avril, Adam and Leeds, but . . . the thing Steve keeps coming back to about Adam Border is that he's an art student turned gardener. Can he really be the brains behind an international drug cartel?' Jack smiled his answer: anyone can be anything. 'Steve Lewis told me all of this in a FYEO meeting yesterday. He told me to tell my team nothing, except to ask before they do anything in case they inadvertently tip off the wrong people. But you? You, he told me to send home for a week. Because you never ask before you do anything. If we tread on their toes or tip anyone off or do anything to compromise their investigation, we're both gone.' Jack put the fresh glass of whisky into Ridley's waiting hand. 'One place I'm asking you not to tread, is Ireland. Not now it's been identified as the destination of a multi-million-Euro drugs haul. That is an order, Jack.'

Ridley sipped his drink and sat back.

'So . . . what do I say in this best man's speech?'

CHAPTER 27

Jack's Friday began with a phone call from the jeweller who was resizing Maggie's wedding ring. She'd seen a stunning platinum band with a line of delicate, 2.4 mm diamonds that spiralled round like a DNA helix. Maggie had spotted the ring from across the other side of the shop and had joked that it 'spoke' to her. DNA was the make-up of each human being and Maggie always said that loving Jack was in her DNA, just like the colour of her eyes and the kink in her hair. The ring had been far too expensive, but Jack had encouraged her to try it on anyway – just to imagine what the perfect wedding ring might feel like. Then they'd chosen and ordered a very pleasant, but not heart-poundingly beautiful ring, together with a matching man's version. Both had required resizing, so were left at the shop. Later that day, Jack had called the jeweller's and ordered the DNA ring for Maggie, and the 'very pleasant' ring for himself. Jack was thrilled to start the day with news that Maggie's dream wedding ring was going to be ready in time.

After collecting the rings, he went to the venue in Fulham where the reception was being held. He was under orders from Maggie to tell them to expect the table flowers to be delivered around eight on Saturday morning and also to have one bottle of champagne, one bottle of red and one bottle of white on every table for when the guests arrived. All drinks had to be vegan friendly. Mrs Kasabian was as patronising as the first time she'd met Jack: 'You can tick me off your little to-do list, Mr Warr. Tell your wife that everything will be perfect.' Jack was annoyed with her – not for presuming him to be an unreliable, untrustworthy man who needed his wife to give him a list because hadn't the first clue about planning a wedding . . . he was annoyed with her for being right.

From Fulham, Jack went to Soho House to extend their stay in the bridal suite to include the Sunday night. He also arranged for champagne and flowers to be in the room when they arrived on the Saturday night.

Then Jack headed to Hazlitt's, a truly stunning little hotel booked by Maggie's parents. Maggie had sent them a list of mid-priced B&Bs and guesthouses in the immediate area, but they'd opted for the £250-a-night Hazlitt's as a wedding gift to themselves. Jack welcomed them to London and asked if they needed anything from him prior to the big day. They were a pleasant enough couple, but talking to her dad, George, was like pulling teeth. As he relayed the details of their train journey, Jack couldn't help but worry about the length of the 'Father of the Bride' speech.

*   *   *

Back home, Penny was moving all of the unopened gifts back into the dining room. Maggie came downstairs with Hannah in her arms and quickly apologised to Penny for making even more work for her. The gifts were meant to be open by now, and a thank-you list should have been made. 'Simon turned up. I left them to talk on the proviso that today and the whole of the weekend is a work-free zone.' Penny raised her eyebrows and blew a raspberry. This made Hannah laugh, so she did it again. 'Daddy can't forget about work for a whole weekend, can he?' she said in a baby voice. 'No, he can't. Silly Mummy.' Hannah reached for Penny and Maggie willingly handed her over. 'Jack and I will open the gifts tonight and make a thank you list. I promise.'

'OK, darling.' Penny didn't sound convinced. She had gone from being uptight and ultra-efficient to being relaxed and fatalistic. All of the big things were now organised – if some of the finer details fell by the wayside, so be it.

* * *

By 3 p.m., Jack was sitting on the bed staring at the zipped wedding gown bag hanging on the back of his bedroom door. Beneath it, almost hidden, was his black suit. Jack held the open jeweller's box containing Maggie's DNA ring. His 'very pleasant' ring was on his finger. He turned it with his thumb, feeling the cold metal glide over his skin. It felt like it was going to fall off. It felt like he wouldn't be able to keep it safe once he was back in the real world. It felt like he'd never get used to the feel of it and always be distracted from what he was supposed to be doing. He didn't like it. Jack put his ring back into the box alongside Maggie's, just as she entered the bedroom.

'Oh, the rings! Has he done a good job of resizing them?' As Maggie reached for the jewellery box, Jack dropped it onto the bed directly behind him, gently grabbed Maggie's wrists and stood up. He swept her arms behind her back, forcing her body tight against his. He leant down and kissed her neck, turning her on the spot until she stood with her back to the bed. Jack continued kissing Maggie's neck as he unbuttoned her blouse.

Maggie sighed. 'We're supposed to be opening presents, Jack.'

'I am.' They fell back onto the bed, laughing. His amorous mood then subsided and he became almost subdued in her arms. 'Thank you for sticking with me,' he whispered. 'Thank you for not giving up.'

'I would never give up on you. That would be like giving up on life.' Maggie ran her fingers through Jack's thick black hair and gazed deep into his eyes.

Jack breathed the words, 'Do you have any idea how much I love you?'

'I do.'

*   *   *

Jack took his time getting ready for his stag night because he didn't want to go. Maggie reassured him that whatever Ridley had organised, it would be fun – and if it wasn't, then at least Jack knew it'd all be over by ten as Ridley was an early-to-bed-early-to-rise kind of man. A message pinged through on Jack's mobile. 'Ridley's texting me the venue.' Jack read his message. His head dropped. 'It's at the bloody pub up the road from the station!' Maggie wrapped her arms round him, and he let his head fall onto her shoulder. 'Don't make me go, Mags. I want to stay here with you.'

*   *   *

Jack entered the main bar of The Red Dragon. The only person in the entire place was Morgan. He beamed and waved his half-empty pint glass in the air. 'Gerrus another, eh, groomy.' Jack strode to the bar with a face like thunder. Dave had owned The Red Dragon for around eight years. He was five feet tall, with the physique of a jockey. Not that you'd guess his height from the customer side because he stood on the specially made raised platform that ran all around the inside of the bar. Behind Dave, above the optics, a cheap banner reading STAG PARTY was Blu Tacked to the mirrors along with inflatable antlers at either end.

Jack was stunned into silence. He ordered two pints of lager and a double whisky which he downed whilst the pints were being pulled. 'There's nibbles in the back.' Dave rarely spoke and, when he did, he used very few words. 'In the pool room. A few sarnies and crisps.' Dave nodded his head towards Morgan, who was now texting on his mobile. 'I didn't let him in, 'cos he'd eat it all before you arrived. But you can go through now. I'll send others through as they arrive.'

Morgan drank his pint on the move, as he led the way through to the pool room. Drinking and walking at the same time was slow going, but Jack couldn't overtake him as he filled the narrow corridor that led to the back of the pub. As they got to the door, Morgan turned and waggled his eyebrows. 'I hope no one else comes. I'm starving.' He then walked backwards into the room, grinning and drinking as he nudged the door open . . .

Dozens of hands holding drinks rose into the air and a raucous cheer echoed through the room. Ridley stood square in the middle of the crowd, holding two glasses of whisky and looking very smug. The pool room was unrecognisable. It was now a casino. Gaming tables had been brought in, male and female croupiers wearing red waistcoats and red bowties were at their posts ready to deal, and a small bar had been set up in the corner of the room. The smile on Jack's face had appeared from nowhere, but now it wouldn't go. As he made his way across the room towards Ridley, dozens of his fellow officers from every division in the station gave him their best wishes – or their condolences, depending on whether they felt like being sincere or sarcastic.

Ridley handed Jack a double whisky, keeping one for himself. 'People wanted to pop in as they came off shift. This seemed like the most sensible venue.' The two men clinked glasses and sipped the well-chosen single malt.

For the next two hours, people drank far too much, ate from the constant supply of pizzas that kept coming out of the kitchen, sang along to a steady stream of nineties music and lost money at the tables.

Foxy spent much of the evening with Anik, trying to ascertain why Laura was the only woman in London who was immune to his charms. Anik draped his arm round Foxy's shoulders and talked beer fumes into his face. 'Foxy, Foxy, Foxy. She's high maintenance mate. Men like me and you need someone for a good time, not a long time.' Anik then set his sights on the blackjack croupier.

At eleven, Dave gave a 30-minute warning and, over the following half hour, the croupiers gradually brought each game to a close, then hid each table beneath a closely fitting branded pastic sheet. It took another thirty minutes and numerous tannoy announcements from Dave for everyone to clear the pool room and filter through to the main bar.

During the evening, Jack had been pleasantly surprised by the fact that scores of people had come and gone. In truth, they only amounted to a small percentage of the station's workforce, but they were the important percentage – the people who Jack liked and respected. Even Angel popped her head round the door at just gone ten. She put a tequila slammer with salt and a slice of lemon on the rim into Jack's hand, then clinked his shot glass with hers, necked her tequila, kissed him smack on the lips and said she couldn't stay as she was on her way to a domestic triple murder-suicide.

Jack put his hand on her arm. 'One second, Angel, just a query: do you know if anything of interest was found in the bins from the Jenkins house?'

'Nope, just rotting food, old newspapers and old cardboard boxes from Amazon. But we took DNA from the cigarette butts, though it might be no good due to them being sodden. I have to go.'

* * *

Jack had parked his car round the back of the police station, so the first thing he and Ridley did on leaving The Red Dragon was head across to collect Jack's overnight bag and wedding suit from the boot. Both men then embarked on the short walk to Ridley's flat, where the groom would hole up overnight, so as not to risk seeing the bride on the wedding day until the moment she arrived at the registry office.

On their way back to his flat, Ridley insisted on 'treating' Jack to sausage and chips from Carlo's Takeaway, which looked like someone's front room with the wall knocked out. But Ridley insisted that Carlo sold the very best chips in London, so Jack went along with it. Jack paced the wide kerb edge whilst waiting for Ridley to buy their impromptu supper, which neither of them really needed as they'd been eating pizza since nine.

'What's in the weird bag?'

Jack turned to see a group of five young lads, all wearing black hoodies beneath various styles of denim jacket. Instinct kicked in and in the time it took for Jack to reply that it was a suit bag containing his wedding outfit, he'd moved around so that his back was to the window of Carlo's Takeaway. He placed both bags on the ground behind his legs and he put his hand into his jacket pocket and closed his fingers around his house keys, manoeuvring his Yale key in between his fingers. Jack was now certain that if this gang were looking for trouble, he could keep them at bay until Ridley twigged what was happening and joined him.

'Show us it.'

The leader of the group stood with both hands in his pockets, and spoke with a frightening degree of confidence. The remaining four lads hung back, waiting for their instructions. Even though none of them were much older than seventeen, they were all fit young men who, Jack presumed, would be in far better shape than himself or Ridley.

Jack was the epitome of calm. 'My mate in there says these are the best chips in London. Fancy some?' The leader shuffled his feet slightly, showing how Jack's question had thrown him off guard. 'You see, I'm not going to open the bag. So, I'm hoping I can just buy you some chips and we can all head home.' Ridley stepped out of Carlo's holding a paper carrier bag containing two portions of sausage and chips. The instant his feet were on the pavement, he knew what was happening. Jack nodded to him. 'I was just saying to these lads that the best way for tonight to end is with us buying them some chips.' Jack stared the leader dead in the eyes. 'Anything else would be stupid.'

The lad smirked, and removing his hand from his pocket he pressed the button on the handle of his flick knife.

In the next split-second, Jack took his hand from his pocket and punched the lad on the top of his right arm. The Yale key penetrated his skin by an inch and, before he pulled it out, Jack twisted it, tearing the puncture wound into a jagged hole. The lad screamed in agony and his damaged bicep immediately became too painful to wield the knife.

Jack quickly and fiercely pointed his bloodied finger at the other four lads. 'Go home! Before you really start to piss me off!'

All five lads looked at each other and, with one united nod, they made the wrong decision. In the time it took for Ridley to put the bag of food on the floor, more flick knives were out and pointing in their direction. Ridley deftly slipped his open jacket off his shoulders and wrapped it round his left forearm just as the blade of a knife sliced through the material. With one lad now within arm's reach, Ridley landed a single powerful punch to his chin, cracking his jaw. The three remaining lads now froze to the spot. They pointed their knives, but none had the courage to use them. The lad with the broken jaw knelt on the pavement, cradling his face and crying in agony. Ridley took out his mobile and called for an ambulance as Jack stepped towards the remaining three lads.

'I'll say it again – go home.' They didn't need telling a third time.

As the leader watched most of his gang running away, he glared up at Ridley 'I'm gonna kill you,' he spat. He was on his knees, bleeding and abandoned, but he couldn't bring himself to surrender. 'You hear me?' the boy grinned through dirty, stained teeth. 'Enjoy his wedding . . . 'cos next thing will be your funeral.'

A darkness descended behind Ridley's eyes and his fingers closed tightly around his mobile phone until his knuckles turned white. Ridley stepped towards the leader of the gang and lashed out with the hard edge of his mobile, striking the open wound to his bicep. The boy screamed in pain and crumpled onto his back. Ridley raised his fist again, but Jack caught his wrist in mid-flight. In the blink of an eye, sanity returned, and Ridley seemed to deflate. The fight had drained him and now he could hardly breathe. He was in shock. He stared at Jack's fingers wrapped around his wrist. There was blood on his shirt cuff and on the edge of his mobile. Ridley looked at the blood as though he had no idea how it had got there. Jack let go of Ridley's arm. He then picked up his bag of food and they headed for home.

For a good fifty yards, Jack walked behind Ridley. Then Ridley stopped. 'I get these rushes of anger. I'm so fucking angry, Jack. And I'm scared. I'm fighting, and winning, I think. But what if it's spread? What if it comes back?' Jack and Ridley stood in the middle of the pavement, forcing the drunken stragglers from pubs and clubs to walk around them. 'Who would care? For long, I mean. People would be sad for a bit, but nothing more than that. My only relative is a mother who doesn't know who I am. Two months ago, I wrote my will. I have a flat with a mortgage and a few savings. I got an estate agent to value it, and it's worth about fifty grand, but then it dawned, I've no one to leave anything to. Do you want it?'

Jack shrugged. 'Sure.' It took a second, but then both men were quietly laughing as they resumed walking towards Ridley's flat.

By 3 a.m., Jack was still lying awake in the spare room. The little white box gave nothing away: no pictures, no colour, no personality. There was nothing except for a white single bed and a white set of flatpack bedroom furniture. It was like a hospital room.

Jack had been awake for so long now that he was beginning to get a headache. He got up and crept into the bathroom to try and find some paracetamol.

The contents of Ridley's medicine cabinet were not encouraging: temazepam, dolasetron, protein powders, oramorph and at least ten bottles of various vitamin supplements. Jack felt useless, seeing the stark reality of his friend's illness.

* * *

The next morning, Maggie opened her eyes and spent the first five minutes of her wedding day staring at the empty pillow next to her. Then Penny entered carrying a cup of tea, some buttered toast with poached eggs and two glasses of bucks fizz on a tray. Maggie sat up and Penny perched on the edge of the bed. They clinked glasses and sipped the fresh, tangy champagne.

Penny's eyes filled with unexpected tears. 'Since the first day I saw you and my son together, I knew you'd become a Warr one day. It just took a bit longer than I expected,' Penny joked. 'And I know that taking a man's name doesn't mean what it used to, and that's no doubt a good thing, but ... Oh, Maggie, I've waited so long to call you my daughter-in-law. You fill me with such pride.'

Maggie precariously hugged Penny over her breakfast tray, then they gulped down their first drink of the day.

* * *

Ridley stood at the front of the modestly sized room, tightly clutching the ring box. Although the bride's family were seated on the opposite side of the room to the groom's, many of the guests knew each other because Maggie and Jack had grown up in the same corner of Totnes, so their parents had mutual neighbours and friends. The rest of the guests were from various parts of the emergency services, so again paths had crossed many times before. Wetlock was seated towards the rear of the room on his own, next to the door in the 'quick escape' row of seats. He had his head down, checking his mobile, avoiding conversation with his neighbours.

There was a ripple of unrest running around the forty-three guests, due to the fact that Jack wasn't standing next to his best man – but this was quickly replaced with joy as the doors at the back of the room opened . . .

Princess and Hannah both wore layered pink dresses with lace trim and matching pink hair bands. Princess sat in a Little Tikes Cozy Coupe, which Hannah was pushing whilst also dropping petals onto the floor, and Mario steered.

By the time they reached the front of the room, most people had tears in their eyes. Regina swept Hannah up into her arms and Mario steered Princess to the side of the room, before lifting her out and joining Regina and Hannah in the front row. All eyes returned to the now-open doors at the back of the room, where Jack stood, on the arm of his mum.

Penny beamed with pride and made a point of meeting every single tearful eye as she walked her only son down the short,

makeshift aisle. By the time she was at the front, all of her neighbours from back home had their handkerchiefs out. Ridley took
Penny by the hand and led her to her seat in the front row, near
Regina. As soon as Penny was seated, Hannah scrambled into her
arms. And once Jack was in position at the front of the room, the
music began, and Maggie entered on her dad's arm.

She looked stunning in her long-sleeved white satin dress. It
hugged every curve of her athletic body. The neckline was ele-
gantly revealing, plunged just far enough to meet her cleavage.
Jack was speechless, in awe of the fact that Maggie had somehow
managed to make herself even more breathtaking than usual.
As she continued towards him, they never took their eyes off
each other.

The ceremony was blissfully short and sweet, with all of the
superfluous, old-style wording removed. Before Jack knew it, Ridley was being asked if he had the rings, and the second he opened
the box and Maggie saw the DNA ring, she burst into tears, throwing her arms round Jack's neck. The guests, although confused,
knew that something special had just happened so responded with
laughter and a round of applause.

*   *   *

Mrs Kasabian turned out to be true to her word. The venue was
perfect down to the very last detail. Champagne was opened on
cue, and no one had an empty glass for longer than two seconds
before a teenager in immaculate black-and-whites swooped in and
filled it up.

Ridley led Penny in on his arm, and asked what she would like
to drink. Penny smiled at the fact that he was prepared to keep her
company. 'Don't you worry about me. I'm going to pop over to my

old Totnes friends and reminisce about what tearaways the bride and groom were as children.' She reached onto her tip toes and kissed Ridley on the cheek. 'Thank you, Simon. You are kind.'

Ridley watched Penny walk across the room, into the open arms of a big group of loving, attentive, lifelong friends. Ridley thrust his hands into his pockets and, no longer needed, headed to the bar on his own.

The early part of the evening was filled with old friends reconnecting, joyous dancing, hundreds of photos being taken, and dozens of bottles of wine being polished off. The teenage waiters seemed to be under strict instructions never to allow a glass to fully empty, so people quickly lost track of how much they'd actually drunk. At 5 p.m., Mrs Kasabian turned the music down and asked everyone to make their way to the tables. Wine glasses were filled, and the father of the bride stood to make his speech. He announced himself as being a man of few words, which thankfully turned out to be true, as he was also incredibly dull. He received a polite round of applause and Jack got to his feet.

'Thank you all for coming. It's great to see so many friends here, old and new. Thank you to George and Hazel for allowing me to marry your daughter. Thank you, Mum, for . . . God, where do I start? You saved my life, Penny Warr. I love you. I love Dad. I wish he was here with us.'

Penny mouthed the words, *He is.* She'd been in tears from the moment Jack stood up, but now she was in full flow. Her hanky was out and she was soaking up the tears before they fell, so as to minimise the damage to her make-up.

Jack took a deep breath. 'Everyone, I'd like to introduce you to my wife, Maggie Warr. I've wanted to say that since I was nineteen. To me, the name means love, safety and belonging. I hope it means the same to you, Mags.' Jack said very little more. He didn't need to.

He handed the thank you gifts out to the bridesmaids and to Ridley, then the guests raised their glasses to the bride and groom.

Ridley could stand in front of every officer in the Met and deliver a faultless briefing. He could stand in front of the national press and give a word-perfect speech. But this . . . this was so much harder because it was personal. Ridley was the most mysterious man in the station, with a private life that no one knew anything about, and now he had to say how he felt. Beneath his immaculate black suit jacket, his armpits were wet, and he could feel sweat running down his spine. Ridley had tried and failed to prepare, so now he was winging it, which was something he'd never done before in his life.

'I don't know why Jack chose me to be his best man. Some of you would be able to tell hilarious stories from years ago – I can't do that. Some of you will have spent holidays and leisure time with Jack – whereas I only work with him. In fact, I'm his boss.' The excited anticipation of a hilarious stream of embarrassing anecdotes instantly vanished and an awkward silence settled on the room. 'If best man means "oldest friend", that's not me. But I think that every now and then, someone comes into your life who has an impact that you didn't see coming. They fill a gap you didn't know was there. And they provide support you didn't know you needed. That's how Jack and I rub along together. As unexpected friends. So . . .' Ridley raised his glass and the now captivated, obedient room did the same. Ridley's simple honesty now had everyone in the palm of his rather sweaty hand. 'Maggie . . . thank you for allowing me to step into your life. Jack . . . thank you for stepping into mine. I have never known such a perfect couple. To the bride and groom.'

As the room stood and repeated those words for the third and final time, every nurse who had swooned over Ridley at Hannah's christening was right back in that moment. He hadn't said much, and he hadn't been remotely funny, but he'd made the biggest impact.

Ridley sat at a table with Laura and Anik, and six guests from Totnes. It wasn't the table he was meant to be sitting at, but an old friend of Penny's had arrived by herself and announced the recent death of her husband. Ridley had willingly given his seat to her so she could be with Penny, meaning that places got shuffled round and, somehow, he'd ended up at the back of the room.

It was an eight-seater table catering for nine, so was all far too intimate for Ridley's liking. He also wasn't feeling his best and had only eaten half of each plate put in front of him. As the occupations around the table ranged from hairdresser to accountant to estate agent, the three 'coppers' were clearly the most interesting people to talk about and everyone felt the need to confess their crimes: shoplifting, speeding, protesting. A large tattooed man boasted about attacking multiple policemen at a Wake. 'Coppers was called to a bunfight once and I ended up lamping all six of 'em. Got a right slap on the wrist for that.'

Ridley figured that his evening wasn't going to get much better than that, so he made his way outside to get a taxi home.

For the next three hours, the guests slowly thinned out as people got too tired or too drunk to stand up. At nine, Penny headed home with Hannah. And at ten, Jack and Maggie snuck out and headed off to the Soho Hotel.

* * *

The bridal suite was perfectly adorned with flowers in the same colour scheme as the wedding bouquets, with a rainbow of petals on the bed and a bottle of champagne chilling in an ice bucket. As soon as they entered the room, Jack and Maggie leapt onto the bed, settled into the extraordinary number of feather pillows and FaceTimed Penny and Hannah. They were both in their pyjamas and Penny was nursing a mug of cocoa whilst Hannah played peek-a-boo behind the arm of the sofa. It was their special bedtime game because Penny didn't have to move, and it wore Hannah out very nicely.

After a chaotic conversation with everyone talking over everyone else, but all saying the same thing – what an amazing wedding it was – Hannah brought the FaceTime to an end by gripping the arm of the sofa like a vice and straining so hard that her face went purple. 'Oh, she's making room for her bedtime milk,' Penny joked as she gulped down the last of her cocoa. 'That's my cue to go. I love you both, have a wonderful couple of days away from real life, and I'll see you on Monday.'

Once they'd hung up the phone, the large bridal suite fell silent. Jack and Maggie looked around at the immaculate room, where every detail had been considered and everything was geared towards man and wife not having to leave the room at all if they didn't want to: room service dinner for two was included, and the contents of the mini-bar were free. They looked at each other and the weight of expectation made them giggle. Jack and Maggie, in unison, slid down in the bed so that, by the time they were comfortable, Maggie was lying on Jack's chest, and he had his arm around her shoulder.

'Do you know,' Maggie said, 'fifty-two per cent of newly married couples don't have sex on their wedding night.'

Jack exhaled a silent laugh, making Maggie's head bob on his chest. 'Thank God for that.' He kissed his new wife on the top of her head. 'I love that that door over there isn't our front door, so no one's going to knock on it. I love that my mum and my daughter aren't in the next room. I love that neither of us has got work tomorrow.'

Maggie turned on her side, so she could see Jack. 'You know what I'd love to do?' Jack grinned, knowing full well that she was about to suggest the most perfect way for them to spend their wedding night. 'I'd love me and you to drink that bottle of champagne in a hot bubble bath. Then I'd love to order room service. You have surf and turf, I'll have the beef lasagne, and we'll go halves. For pudding, I'll get pavlova, you get cheesecake. Then, I'd love to curl up in bed with you and watch a film that hasn't been made by Disney. It's got to have loads of swearing, violence and sex. And if we're still awake, we can have a quickie before sleeping through the whole night undisturbed.'

Jack pulled Maggie closer. 'God, I love you, Mrs Warr.'

*　*　*

Sunday was spent walking round London and taking the time to actually visit places that they'd walked past a thousand times. They made a pact before they left their hotel that they'd see one park, one museum, one total tourist trap, and then treat themselves to a very expensive lunch cooked by a Michelin star chef. Hyde Park became their first port of call, followed by the London Eye, followed by Tate Modern, and finally they spent a fortune on a snack at Skylon on the South Bank.

When they got back to their hotel, they were so exhausted that they set their alarm for 5 p.m. and settled down for an afternoon nap. Dinner on the second night wasn't included in the wedding package, so they were slightly more reserved with the budget. After spending two hours eating and drinking, Jack led Maggie into the lift and pressed the button for the penthouse suite. As the lift politely announced each floor, Jack backed Maggie into the corner and kissed her. This was to be their last night together in a hotel before heading home. Everything suddenly felt illicit and exciting. The lift opened directly opposite their suite and, within seconds of entering, they were desperately undressing each other. Maggie fell back onto the plush mattress, Jack stood between her legs and, still half-dressed, they made frantic and noisy love, relishing the freedom to pant and moan as loudly as they wanted. It was over quickly, but that night, they woke and made love again.

* * *

Jack and Maggie returned home around ten, to the noise of Penny rifling through the pots and pans cupboard to find the one she needed. This racket was occasionally drowned out by the equally horrendous noise of a high-pitched American voice singing 'Baby Shark', and Hannah screaming along. Jack kissed Maggie. 'Welcome home.' Then he took their suitcase upstairs whilst she braved the kitchen chaos.

The day was spent with all four of them opening the rest of the gifts that had been piled up in the house for weeks, and any new ones which had been brought to the venue on the day of the wedding. Ridley and the team had bought an expensive set of six knives in a block. Penny particularly liked the fact that the back of the block doubled as a stand for a recipe book or for her iPhone.

In the early evening, their wedding photographer posted a USB stick through their letterbox with a handwritten note explaining that none of the images had yet been 'touched up', none of them were downloadable and all of them currently had his watermark plastered all over them. Basically, this was his polite way of saying that the images were impossible to steal. Maggie set up her laptop so the images from the USB displayed on their TV screen. Each image had a number in the bottom, right hand corner, so Penny designated herself as note-taker and, as they scrolled through, she jotted down the numbers of the photos they wanted printing. Maggie suggested they try to choose the best hundred.

An hour later, Penny was in the kitchen making a cup of tea, and Maggie and Hannah were both snoozing next to Jack on the sofa. He was now the one in charge of jotting down the numbers of the images he considered worthy of printing. He was scrolling back through some of the group photos taken at the party, trying to find a nice one of all the hospital staff, because Maggie wanted to give Regina a print of her old work friends. The problem he was having was that these photos had been taken late in the day, so most included drunk police officers, or people purposefully disrupting the shot by doing rabbit-ears behind someone's head or, worse, by flashing their arses.

Jack scrolled back to earlier in the day when people had still been sober. Outside the registry office, there were some lovely, posed shots where the photographer had put people together in groups around the bride and groom. Jack smiled at the fact that the hospital staff made for a far prettier bunch of human beings than the coppers!

As Jack scrolled through several similar images to try and find the best one, he noticed the same woman standing at the edge of each of the hospital group photos, half hidden behind the wall of the registry office . . . just watching. Jack would have put her down as a nosey passer-by if she hadn't seemed so familiar to him.

He kept looking at her, allowing his mind to slowly find the memory he needed. Associated words popped into his mind, and he desperately tried to make sense of them: tall . . . long black hair . . . horses . . . children – no, not just children: orphans.

Julia Lawson!

The name hit him like a ton of bricks. Julia Lawson was one of the women who committed the biggest train robbery the UK had ever seen and, decades later, she'd finally got away with millions in cash. Because of him. He let her go. He let them all go. Not only that, but he also accepted some of the stolen cash and used it to buy the house they were now sitting in. Jack could hardly breathe, his rapid heart palpitations making him physically shake. He jumped up without waking anyone and grabbed himself a brandy which he drank far too quickly, the alcohol burning all the way down to his stomach. Julia Lawson. Julia Lawson . . .

Julia Lawson was one of the few people alive who could bring Jack's world crashing down and put him behind bars. He had to find out why she was back. And why she was watching him.

CHAPTER 28

On Tuesday, life returned to normal. Jack kissed Maggie goodbye and she ran to work with a change of clothes in her backpack. Maggie had a locker at work where she left her uniform and work shoes, which gave her the freedom to run in whenever she felt the need – and after looking through all of the wedding photos and seeing herself next to some much younger, much more svelte nurses, she was feeling her age.

'I'm not going to let myself go just because I've bagged my man,' Maggie said, gently patting Jack's stomach. Then she dashed off before he could spout some excuse about working long hours and eating on the run.

Once he was alone, Jack flicked the TV on. The last photo that he'd looked at the previous evening was still on the screen. Ridley being forced to give Jack some time off was now acting in his favour, but he had to find Julia Lawson fast, before Ridley expected him back on the Jenkins case.

For the life of him, Jack couldn't figure why any of the women would risk coming back to the UK. But the more he thought about it, the more he realised that the only one who'd left something valuable behind was Julia. She'd left her children. The care home Julia had run looked after some of the most vulnerable kids in the north-west of England. She hid them from abusive parents and from violent lives. She gave them the respect they needed to understand that their lives actually meant something. She taught them that they were worthy of saving, worthy of a future and worthy of love. If she was back, it would be for one of them.

The problem Jack had was that many of the children from back then were under strict protection orders, so as soon as he started digging, his actions would show up. He wanted to remain below the radar so as not to have to explain why he was searching for a woman who, as far as the police were concerned, had gone to ground somewhere in Europe. Although he wanted to find Julia Lawson, it was certainly not his intention to start a trail that others could follow. Jack recalled three names of children who Julia had been particularly attached to: Sam, Suzie and Darren. He'd met each of them when he'd gone to her care home in Chester to interview her about the train robbery, but he never learnt any of their surnames.

Jack started his search with Julia; and with any child called Sam, Suzie or Darren, who was either sent to her from the Juvenile system, or who went into the Juvenile system after she disappeared aboard – it was a negative assumption to make, but an accurate one as many of the kids were indeed known to the police at some point. The dubious upbringings of these youngsters normalised things which should never be normal to a child – violence, abuse, crime. Jack found two boys from the Chester area named Samuel, and three named Darren . . . one of which immediately stood out. In November 2019, Darren Winstall, aged just 17, was found hanged in his room at the Juvenile Detention Centre. If this was the same 'Darren', then perhaps Julia came back for his funeral and stayed? There was a lengthy report detailing how Darren slowly retreated into his shell until he was nothing more than a mute, violent, pitbull of a boy who never let anyone get close to him. During his short stay in juvenile detention, Darren was visited numerous times by Daniel Karina, who Jack remembered being a carer at the home Julia ran. Daniel had seemingly tried to get Darren out of juvie and back into his care, but he'd failed. Darren had burnt too many bridges, meaning he had then been stuck in a system that saw him as a criminal rather than a damaged child.

Daniel Karina was still working in social care, and, from his annual DBS reports Jack was able to find his home address and contact phone number, but he couldn't just call and ask if Daniel knew Julia was back in the UK. Nor could he ask for the surnames of Sam and Suzie. Daniel wouldn't willingly give him any of that information. Whilst Jack pondered the best course of action, he absentmindedly searched the internet for Julia Lawson, Daniel Karina and Darren Winstall in the vain hope that something would pop up and trigger a lightbulb moment.

Sure enough, Daniel's Facebook page was a mine of information. He was an avid photographer, posting snaps of his food, clothes, bike and, most importantly, his holidays. Daniel had posted discreet images of himself and Julia at Formby beach and nature reserve, which Jack immediately recalled was where they used to take the kids on holiday. These dated back as far as 2017, so weren't useful, but Daniel's more recent holiday snaps were.

In July 2020, as the country came out of lockdown, Daniel posted photos from Wales. He talked about an 'old friend', although he never gave them a name. A couple of the images were taken outside a rural property with horses roaming a field in the background. It was called Winstall Farm. Jack googled it and found the postal address. It was just outside Aberdovey in a small village called Cwmystwythe.

It was a five-hour drive, but he knew he had no choice. Once he was on the A40, he called Maggie, assuming she'd be furious that they hadn't even been married a week and he was heading off to Wales. Instead, she launched into a moan about how she was now covering Wetlock's surgery list because he had gone AWOL – something to do with his daughter. Maggie expected Tania had been off causing havoc somewhere again.

'So long as she doesn't come back to my house, offering my husband sex on a plate. Keep in touch, Jack. I'll meet you on the sofa at nine for takeaway and wine.'

The bulk of the drive to Wales was motorway, giving Jack plenty of time to play out various scenarios surrounding Julia's surprise return. Darren's funeral did seem to be the most likely reason for her being back in a country where she was still in danger of being arrested and sent to prison for the rest of her life – she'd certainly risk her own freedom for one of her children and the fact that Jack was now heading to a farm possibly named after Darren supported his theory. But why had she been in London, at his wedding, watching him? That was deeply concerning to him.

*   *   *

Once Jack had crossed into Wales and begun hitting smaller country lanes, he began to rely on his sat nav to get him to Cwmystwythe. This was a stunning part of the world. Narrow, winding roads cut through rich green farmland, edged by drystone walls. The clouds created shadows that moved down the hillsides and through the valleys, changing the landscape from light green to dark green and back again. Occasionally, Jack would spot the ruins of a small stone building, which he presumed had belonged to long-ago farmers. Like much of rural Wales, there was an almost prehistoric feel to the place.

Eventually, Jack stopped at a small grocery shop in Llanidloes to grab a sandwich and make certain that he was on the right road for Winstall Farm. The elderly lady behind the counter knew exactly where he was heading.

'It's not a farm anymore. But you're on the right road, yes. Past Devil's Bridge. Past Pont-Rhyd-Groes. The next place you see on the right, will be Winstall. I tell you what . . .' She dipped beneath the counter and reappeared with a white plastic carrier bag. 'You can take this with you, if you don't mind. Save either of them coming to get it.' Jack took the bag of shopping and paid for his sandwich. 'Lovely couple, she continued, counting out Jack's change. 'Both ladies, but that doesn't matter these days, does it? Winstall is on a blink-and-you'll-miss-it sort of road, so keep your eyes open for a gatepost with no gate, followed by a cattle grid.'

Within twenty minutes of driving, Jack passed over the cattle grid and saw a hand-painted sign saying WINSTALL FARM. A single-track road led to a decent-sized stone farmhouse with two corrugated metal outbuildings and a wooden stable block. The fields on either side of the track were home to several horses and Jack recognised this part of the property from the images Daniel had posted on Facebook, so he was now certain that he was in the right place.

Outside the main house was an old Jeep and a small tractor. There were children's swings, bicycles and two scooters, as well as a large greenhouse beside a burgeoning vegetable patch. Looking at this place made Jack smile. It reminded him of the pictures he'd seen of the would-be children's home owned by Dolly Rawlins back in the eighties. Julia had always said she wanted to fulfil Dolly's dream and now, seemingly, she had. Jack parked next to the Jeep.

*　*　*

Through the net curtain of the kitchen window, Julia watched the unknown vehicle drive towards her. They rarely got visitors and strangers were a rarity. She began to feel frightened. But it wasn't until Jack got out of the car that her legs gave way, and she had to grab onto the white Belfast sink to stay upright.

Jack Warr . . .

Instinctively her fingers closed around the handle of a small carving knife on the draining board.

Julia stepped out of the open front door. She looked stern, very wary and uncertain. Jack held out the white plastic bag. 'I've brought your shopping.'

She wore a pair of scuffed boots and jodhpurs, with a heavy knit sweater. Her long, thick hair was now grey and she wore it tied back in a loose braid. To Jack, she seemed to have aged a lot in the three or four years that had passed.

Julia stared at Jack for a moment longer, trying to decide why the hell he'd come all the way out here. It certainly wasn't to deliver a bag of groceries. 'What are you doing here?'

'I've come to ask you the same thing.'

Julia moved swiftly to Jack's side, looking around as she moved. Regardless of the fact that she and Jack had bonded over weak parents and shitty starts in life, she remained highly suspicious of him. He seemed to be alone, but she'd learnt not to trust policemen. She took the shopping and told him to get inside. 'The kids will be out trekking until three. You can't be here when they get back.'

Julia's kitchen was huge, spanning the depth of the property, and seemed to be split into zones. Kids' toys were strewn all over the floor, but only in one corner. Baking was in mid-flow, but only on one bench. Herbs were being re-potted, but only by the back door. It was impressively organised chaos. And at the heart of the chaos was a long wooden table. Jack and Julia stood at either end. Both cautious, both needing answers.

'Did you come back for Darren's funeral?' Jack asked. Julia lowered her head as the pain of losing him rose to the surface. 'I'm sorry, Julia.'

'I'm not Julia anymore.' This short statement told Jack that their past was not up for discussion. This was as comforting to him as it was to her. 'His death is my fault. I showed him what it was to be loved . . . and then I abandoned him. I knew I shouldn't have named the farm after him, but I couldn't help myself. I assume that's how you found me? Is anyone else coming?'

'No. And if they ever do come, it won't be through me.' Julia nodded. She flicked the kettle on, then pulled a tray of cookies out of the oven. Jack knew exactly how vulnerable Julia felt right now. His fellow officers were as dangerous to her as her fellow criminals were to him. Any one of them could ruin his life. 'Have any of the others come back?'

'I very much doubt it. We swore never to contact each other again, then went our separate ways. I hope they're living the lives they deserve.' Julia looked Jack square in the eye. 'I know I am.'

Jack was genuinely pleased for her. As he held her stare, she sensed that she was still safe. He then brought the conversation swiftly around to the reason he'd travelled the width of two counties. 'Why were you in London, watching me get married?'

'I wasn't.' Julia put the hot cookies onto a plate. 'I was buying horse blankets from the stables in Hyde Park that are closing down. I had an hour to kill, so I walked for a while. Weddings always draw your attention – congratulations, by the way. A group of guests were being ushered into position by your photographer and I saw someone I recognised. A bad memory from more than thirty years ago. Then I saw you and . . . well, needless to say, I ran for my life.'

Jack asked who it was that she saw, and she almost spat out the name of Elliot Wetlock. 'We were medical students together. He was two years ahead of me, but he got invited to all the parties because . . . he could get forged prescriptions.'

Jack didn't try and hide his surprise. 'He was a drug dealer?'

'Nembutal, barbiturates, steroids. Even chloral hydrate. He was into everything. And had no qualms about getting others into everything too. Once he qualified and started climbing the ladder towards surgery, he stopped all of that. Well, most of it. He was still addicted to demerol and heroin when I knew him. He's not the reason I ended up in prison, that was all me, but he's the reason I became addicted. Last I heard, he'd gone straight because he bagged himself a beautiful young girlfriend – titled, I think. Then I read that she'd OD'd on sodium pentothal.' Julia shook her head in disgust. 'Wonder where she got that from.'

'How did he get away with it for so long?'

'Do you know how many medical students drop out because of stress, tiredness, ill health, mental breakdowns? One of Wetlock's specialities, when you were run ragged and dead on your feet, was to give enemas. It's the fastest high and carries you through your shift. You'd see a junior doctor speed-walking up the corridor and you'd think, *There goes another one of Wetlock's clients.* And if anyone opened their mouth against him, DC Warr, their career would be gone. Self-preservation kept everyone quiet.'

'I'm a DS now,' Jack smiled. 'Just so you know.' Julia glanced at the clock. Ten to three. She said that she'd give him another ten minutes, as long as they continued their conversation outside.

Jack opened his car door and leant in to retrieve something from the glove box. As he did, Julia noticed the clips for a baby seat in the back. 'A promotion, a wife and a child. You're going up in the world.'

'Do you know anything about growing cannabis?' he asked.

'No comment.'

Jack opened Avril's little red notebook at the page which seemed to show a detailed recipe for cannabis oil, and he asked Julia for her opinion. She took her time to decode all of the scribbles and crossings-out.

'This person sounds pretty knowledgeable. And from the amount of alcohol in the recipe, they were making a serious amount. Back in the day, I tried this, but failed miserably. You can use a rice maker now – that keeps the heat nice and low as you cook the grass.' Julia paused. 'I assume this is connected to a case. Are you going to tell me more about it, or do you just want me to keep talking?'

'Just keep talking please, Julia.'

'Well, this would have to have been cooked somewhere with good ventilation. The resin glands contain CBD trichomes and they get you high. The buckets in this list must be for washing and rinsing as it thickens . . . and see, they've even listed coffee filters because you pour and strain through them so none of the seeds seep through. It looks to me like they were making decarboxylate cannabis oil. That's why the rice maker's temp control is great, 'cos the mixture must never boil. It's got to stay between 210 and 230 degrees Fahrenheit.'

Julia slapped the book shut and handed it back to Jack, then gave a throaty laugh.

'Take a photocopy. When you retire, get yourself a greenhouse and a rice maker, and you'll have yourself a nice little cottage industry.'

She perched herself on the footplate of the tractor while Jack sat in his car with his feet outside. 'From what I remember, you're like a dog with a bone.' She spoke in a low, calm voice, as though she was soothing one of her children. 'Whoever you're after, you'll find them. You were the only one who found us.'

As they sat in the brilliant sunshine, being cooled by the breeze coming down from the surrounding hills, Jack felt a million miles away from the stresses of the case. He felt safe talking to Julia because they were mutually bound by silence. But they were also bound by an understanding that they both came from bad places and had beaten the odds by not succumbing to the dark side of life. They both knowingly and willingly existed in the vast grey wilderness of good people who had done bad things.

'I'm obsessed with tracking this one guy who I think is the key to everything,' Jack said. 'He was a nomadic kid because of his mum's lifestyle. He got dragged from country to country, person to person. His mum got into the habit of denying he was even hers. When she was younger, that was because the men she was with didn't want someone else's baggage. But when she was older, I think she denied him almost out of habit. She told the neighbours he was her odd-job man – even encouraged the gossip that he was her toy boy.'

'Sounds like half the kids I've looked after over the years.'

Jack smiled. 'Sounds like me if I'd not been adopted.' Jack had told Julia about being a foster child when they'd met previously. But that's all she knew. She didn't know that Jack's birth dad had turned out to be Harry Rawlins. Or that he had been shot to death by his wife, Dolly Rawlins, the very woman who happened to be Julia's mentor and role model. Jack was the product of an affair with a woman by the name of Trudie Nunn, a weak and highly unstable woman who hung around in all the seedy clubs waiting to be rescued by someone half decent. She struck lucky with Harry, but it was short-lived. Trudie died of a brain tumour when Jack was too young to remember her, though her death was the ultimate blessing in disguise.

'Being saved, as you were, is why you're so good at your job,' Julia observed. 'You know the look. You saw it in each one of us. I see it in the ten kids I've got here right now. That pain of knowing that this life isn't as good as it should be. We got out, Jack; me and you. But it leaves scars. My scars draw me to kids like these, your scars draw you to people like your missing man. We know them because we're always seconds away from being them.'

The wind from the hillside carried the distant sound of children shouting and laughing down into the farm. Jack took it as his cue to leave. 'It was strangely nice to see you again, Julia.'

'You too, DS Warr.' Over the crest of the hill at the back of the farm, a woman appeared followed by several children of varying ages. The youngest two rode ponies and were being led by the older children. 'Jack? Please don't come back.'

Jack smiled. 'Take very good care of yourself.' Then he got into his car and turned it round. As he drove away, he could see Julia in his rear-view mirror. The woman greeted her with a kiss and the children swarmed round her legs all talking at once as they relayed their adventures. Julia was a good soul. For her, freedom did not come from fleeing abroad with tens of millions of pounds – freedom came from coming home. Jack was sure that he would think of Julia often, but he'd never see her again. And he'd never tell a soul that she was home.

CHAPTER 29

As Jack hit the M40 back to London, his radio display changed from RADIO 4 to MAGGIE. He thought that he should alter it to say WIFE and that made him grin. Jack was in a good mood. His visit to Julia had been unexpectedly positive and productive: he'd learnt that she was not back in the UK to ruin his life, and that the enigmatic Elliot Wetlock used to be a drug dealer and was still possibly a drug user. It made Jack happy to know that the doctor whose eyes and voice could make Maggie swoon was not perfect after all. But Jack would not tell Maggie any of this for now.

'Hi, Mags. ETA 7 p.m. I'll sort the takeaway as soon as I'm home. You want your usual? . . . Listen, Mags, what does canteen gossip tell you about Wetlock's private life? From way back. Possibly from before he came to work.'

'Are you driving?'

Maggie sounded sad and Jack's mind immediately leapt to his mum. 'What's happened? Everyone OK?'

'Everyone's OK. We found out why Elliot Wetlock has gone AWOL. He found Tania's body late last night. She'd been dead for days.'

'Jesus, I'm sorry. I know she was a pain in the arse, but . . . sorry, Mags. He must be devastated.'

Maggie said that she'd still be home at the expected time and that she'd be needing a hug that might have to go on all night, depending on how depressing the rest of her shift turned out to be. Jack asked if Maggie wanted to be picked up from work, but she was actually looking forward to the run home as a way of clearing her head. Maggie didn't volunteer any of the details surrounding

Tania's death, so Jack assumed that she either didn't know or didn't want to go into the gruesome details over the phone. So, Jack didn't ask any questions. He simply kept saying 'I love you' until Maggie felt strong enough to hang up.

Jack assumed that Tania had OD'd, as he'd only met the girl twice and she was high both times. His drive home flew by as his mind raced to make sense of everything he now knew. Jack wondered whether Wetlock was her supplier. But, if he was, would he really bring the police into their lives? No, Jack thought Tania had been more than capable of ruining her own life. She was clearly a deeply unhappy girl, who dreamed of being rescued from a life she couldn't escape on her own. That's why she lived in a fantasy world – because it was better than reality.

Before Jack had spoken to Maggie, he'd been under no pressure to share what he'd learnt about Wetlock's lifelong connection to drugs, but now, with the death of his drug-abusing daughter, it would all have to come out. Jack knew that he'd have to think of a way to explain how he'd come by the information.

As Jack's family car sluggishly made its way back along the motorway, his thoughts shifted to a second car. Something nippier, more sexy and less homely. Seeing Julia again had reminded him that on a couple of occasions he'd stumbled across money during a case which didn't belong to him but which he'd gratefully taken, on the basis that it didn't belong to anyone else either. He'd been drip-feeding this money into his daily life ever since, his wedding's free bar being the latest example. A new car would certainly be an asset now that Hannah was getting bigger and would soon be taking part in more and more social events such as Caterpillar Club and Buzzy Bees Gymnastics, both of which Penny had found being advertised in the library. Jack spent the rest of the journey home figuring out how to raise the subject of a new car with Maggie, who he knew had her heart set on a luxurious honeymoon. He wasn't convinced they could do both – not in style.

When Maggie walked through the front door, flushed from her run, she saw Jack standing in the kitchen doorway and her eyes instantly glistened with tears. Jack held open his arms and she walked into them. He squeezed her tightly. 'Takeaway will be here at nine. Go grab a shower. I'll open the wine.'

Maggie had taken to wearing Jack's dressing gown because hers had permanent crusty patches on both shoulders where, over the months, Hannah had dribbled or puked into the fleece. Jack thought there was something very sexy about seeing the woman he loved wrapped in his oversized clothes.

Maggie, wine in hand, sat cross-legged on the sofa, facing him.

'He was coming down from the third floor where he'd been getting the Management up to speed, and I got in the lift with him on my way back from x-ray . . . God, he looked awful. She'd stopped answering his calls or responding to his text messages about three days ago. And because it wasn't unusual for her to go off the radar, he never thought anything of it. Then yesterday . . . oh God, Jack. Imagine finding your own daughter dead.'

* * *

Elliot Wetlock threw his house keys into the wooden bowl on the hallway table. As he took off his coat, he looked at the space in the row of shoes beneath the table. Tania's shoes had not been there for three days. Nor had her coat. He went into the lounge and poured himself a glass of brandy, which he took into the kitchen and sipped whilst he made himself a chicken and avocado sandwich. He flicked on the TV and watched the ten o'clock news. Wetlock tidied as he moved, so by the time he'd settled to the breakfast bar to eat his sup-

per, the kitchen looked like it hadn't been used. It looked like part of a show home. Soulless and unloved.

As the news ended, Wetlock put his plate in the dishwasher, popped into the lounge to refill his brandy glass, then headed upstairs. This was his routine. He used the hallway, lounge, kitchen, his bedroom and his en suite which, together, constituted a quarter of the property. The remaining three quarters were unused, except when Tania deigned to come home. Father and daughter lived separate lives under the same roof, and he hated it. But he had to endure it because otherwise, she'd never come home at all.

When Tania was not squatting back with Daddy due to lack of funds, she was in her own flat across town. Tonight, for some reason, his usually well-hidden fatherly conscience made him put his coat and shoes back on and actually head over there to see if his daughter was OK.

Wetlock had always had a spare key to Tania's flat but rarely used it. He allowed her to live her own life, but in recent months she'd been behaving in a way that made him worry. At the top of the stairs on the third floor, he turned right towards Tania's flat which was the last on the left and occupied the highly sought-after corner suite. As soon as he opened the front door, his nostrils flared in response to the heady smell of drains. He opened the bathroom door first, because it smelt like he might be faced with a backed-up and overflowing toilet. Everything was normal. Except for the now heightened smell of faeces coming from the next room.

He ventured towards Tania's bedroom and – never imagining that she'd actually be on the other side amid such a terrible stench – opened the door. The smell instantly intensified. Wetlock brought his hand to his mouth and nose, and his gaze locked on Tania. She lay in the centre of the bed, curled up in the foetal position, shoes and coat on. The white floral duvet cover beneath her body was stained with urine and excrement. Wetlock stared at his daughter in abject horror – not because her bladder and bowels had emptied, but because her skin was white apart from the cheek that lay against the pillow. He couldn't see it fully, just enough to notice it was purple with lividity, telling him that she'd been dead for more than eight hours.

Despite this certain knowledge, Wetlock raced to his daughter's side and pointlessly felt for a pulse. Then he shook her by the shoulders and screamed her name. Her ice-cold body moved freely beneath his hand. His doctor's brain now also knew that she'd been dead long enough to go into and come out of rigor – that meant three days – but his father's brain was telling him to never stop shaking and never stop screaming.

* * *

Maggie pushed her noodles round her bowl, while Jack couldn't help but tuck into his because he was starving after his expedition to Wales. But he ate quietly, taking small mouthfuls, in case he needed to say comforting words.

'She'd been there three days and he had no idea. She'd OD'd. The paramedics had to leave her there, in her own excrement, because the police want a post-mortem.' Maggie found a small piece of chicken which she decided to nibble at as she continued. 'Apparently, there was one locked cupboard in her bedroom which Elliot gave the police permission to force open. They found a couple of half-empty champagne bottles, some prescription pills, some illegal drugs and a diary. I don't even know why he told me all of this, Jack. I didn't know what to say. Maybe he wanted me to relay it all to you.'

'Did he tell the police about the talent scout?'

'Oh, he's probably *still* telling them about him . . . Poor man. Poor, poor man.' Jack now knew that Wetlock might not be a 'poor, poor man' at all. But Maggie didn't need to learn the truth about her mentor tonight. She looked up at Jack for the first time since she'd started relaying Wetlock's terrible ordeal. 'He told them about you.' Jack froze mid-chew. 'They know Tania came round here a couple of times. That she threw herself at you and—'

'Wetlock told them that his daughter threw herself at me? And how exactly did he know that?' Jack knew that the information could only have come from Maggie. Instead of defending herself, she began to look tearful, so Jack stopped himself before he lost his temper. He couldn't believe it: with one misplaced conversation, he was suddenly a person of interest in the suspicious death of a teenage girl who had been to his house twice and offered to have sex with him both times.

He recalled her first visit – and the taxi driver who'd seen her crying and dishevelled as she left his home. And her second visit had been even more damning because she'd stood on his doorstep and screamed, 'RAPE!' And the only way he could shut her up was to drag her inside his house. It would only take one of his neighbours to have witnessed that and he'd be up shit creek. The job he loved would be gone in the blink of an eye.

CHAPTER 30

Maggie went to bed before Jack, whilst he stayed up seething and drinking. Today had certainly been one for the books: he was bound to be questioned in connection to Tania's unnatural death, and he was harbouring one of Britain's most wanted in rural Wales. *And* he had to work out how to share the damning information he now knew about Wetlock's connection to drugs without divulging where that information had come from. The only thing he was certain about was that he'd never reveal Julia's whereabouts. Self-preservation dictated that, but she was also a guiding light in the otherwise dark lives of the children in her care. And Jack knew first-hand how much that mattered.

Maggie had been a little sheepish when she'd kissed him good-bye and driven to work. She'd offered to leave him the car – regardless of the fact that it was her day to have it – so he knew she felt guilty for blabbing to Wetlock.

Jack sat at the breakfast table, head down, going through notes he'd made on his iPhone in the early hours of that morning. He'd made a big mistake not reporting Tania's visits to his home. He'd have to explain that decision, without it looking like he had something to hide. And he'd have to explain why he asked Laura to go and speak to Tania without making it official first.

'Watch her, Jack. She's showing you what she can do.' Jack looked up to see Penny staring at him. She nodded towards Hannah, who was sliding an upside-down spoon along her cheek towards her gaping mouth. The thick porridge was currently defying gravity . . . Penny and Jack willed the spoon towards her mouth before it was too late! Success was greeted with a cheer and a round of applause. Hannah beamed with pride as she lifted her arms into the air, just like Daddy was doing, and cheered her own cleverness. Then, focussed and determined, she went in for another spoonful of porridge.

Penny asked if everything was OK between Jack and Maggie.

''Course. Yeah. It's work.' Jack toyed with the idea of not telling Penny about Tania's death. But the truth was that he'd be better positioned if someone other than him could give a statement about how volatile she was, and how he did nothing inappropriate. 'You remember the girl who was here when you and Maggie came back from the hen night?'

'Do I?' Penny scoffed. 'Maggie told me all about her the next day.' Penny made a disapproving tutting sound as she recalled just how out of control Tania had been. 'She was hysterical! Stumbling out of the front door looking like she'd been dragged through a hedge backwards. Effing and jeffing, calling you the B word. The sofa cushions were all over the floor and Hannah was scream-ing her poor little head off. It took me an hour to scrub the coffee off the kitchen walls. And I had to soak your T-shirt where she'd smeared her lipstick across the shoulder.'

Jack immediately regretted mentioning it. If his mum told the police any of that, she'd end up being a witness for the bloody prosecution.

'She died, Mum.'

Penny's attitude immediately changed. She put her hand on her chest. 'Oh, the poor girl.'

'I'll be giving a statement today about the two occasions she came here,' Jack continued. 'If I don't have to mention you as a witness, I won't, but if I do . . . you can see how everything you've just said could make me look at fault. Yes, she was hysterical, but if you say that, they might think I did something to make her hysterical.'

Penny laughed and said that obviously Jack would never do anything to hurt anyone, not grasping the seriousness of the situation.

'The officer who interviews me, won't know me. Tania's dead and it'll be his job to find out if it was foul play. That's all he'll be interested in. Did she have a run-in with anyone? Did anyone not like her? I'm a detective, Mum. This could lose me my job if it goes the wrong way.'

Penny said that she understood and promised not to do or say anything that would make him look bad. Jack had visions of her telling the interviewing officer that he'd always been a good boy, expecting that to be enough. He decided there and then that he'd do everything in his power to keep Penny's name out of it.

*　*　*

Jack didn't know how to start his day in earnest. Maggie, Penny and Hannah were all out of the house and he had various options in front of him. He never had options! He normally just got showered, dressed and headed to work. Today, if he felt like it, he could go and buy a paper, or go for a run, or sit in the garden. The problem with all of those choices, however, was that Jack didn't want to do any of them. He wanted to be at work.

When his mobile rang and he saw Laura's name appear on the screen, he answered before it had rung twice. 'What the hell, Jack,' Laura mocked, 'bloody Tania's dead and you're in the mix – again!'

Jack hated the fucking police grapevine. He should have known the news of Tania Wetlock's death would get back to the station before he did. He asked if Laura had called purely to take the piss.

'I wish I could say yes. Drug Squad has made an arrest. They clocked some guy in the vicinity of the Jenkins' property every day for the past week. Sometimes more than once a day. He sits at the bus stop on Kingston Hill, walks a dog, or jogs through the main private road, the security bloke at the barrier there smiles and waves, and he then runs towards the open grounds just north of the woodland behind the Jenkins' back garden. They took a few days to ascertain that it's always the same guy. He's low-hanging fruit, that's their description, in other words a junkie. Anyway, Josh thinks he can turn him.' Jack heard Laura let out a girlish little titter. 'Josh could turn anyone.'

'All I can say, Laura . . .' She let out a sigh and waited for Jack to rib her about falling for the wrong man again. '. . . is that you've chosen another man who you can't possibly end up with because he doesn't even live in this country, so you might as well enjoy it whilst it lasts. Have fun. He's a good guy, I think.'

After the call, Jack sat at the kitchen table, cradling a cup of tea and watching the drizzle run down the windowpane. The lines of water annoyed him as they took the path of least resistance down to the sill below. As he sat there contemplating how predictable certain courses of action were, his mind drifted back to Julia and the thought of her made him smile. He would never have expected her to come back to the UK. Yet there she was, living the life she'd always dreamed of, completely invisible to the police. *Being predictable gets you caught*, Jack thought to himself, *like the man who went back to Avril's house again and again.*

Jack now started thinking about the second witness signature on Avril Jenkins' will. Who was she in frequent enough contact with to ask? Not Adam, because, as beneficiary, he'd be prohibited from also acting as witness. Not Hutchinson, as that would be a conflict of interest. As Jack watched the rain slowly stop, the sun took over and created miniature rainbows in the water trails on the glass. It was beautiful. *Like a work of art . . .* Jason Marks? That would make sense as an option.

Jack dialled Arnold Hutchinson's office number and received a cheerful greeting from May. 'Good morning, May. DS Jack Warr. I wanted to talk to you about Avril Jenkins' new will, as witnessed by Hester Mancroft and Jason Marks?' Jack put a slight inflection on the end of his sentence to make it sound like a question, in the hope that the first thing May would do was confirm that he'd got the details correct.

'That's right, yes. How can I help you?'

'Has the new will been verified yet, please, May?'

She was proving to be very trusting so far and therefore quite easy to manipulate. Jack continued to use her first name in order to make the conversation sound like a casual chat. She confirmed that as she understood it the Will was now certified as being genuine. Jack laughed out the next few words: 'Oh, I bet Terence had something to say about that!' May joined in the laughter, saying that Terence certainly could swear for such a respectable-looking man. Jack made another casual comment about will-contesting taking such a long time, and May replied that Terence was prepared to do anything to get back the personal property that had once belonged to his brother. He cared less about the house, not to mention the tat Avril had purchased in more recent years.

Jack and May finally exchanged brief opinions on the weather, and she assured him that the sun was now due to stay out, so their afternoon would be delightful. Jack thanked her for her time and said goodbye. He'd got everything he needed from the lovely May, and she'd only learn that she'd broken confidentiality when she informed Arnold Hutchinson of their conversation.

As soon as Jack ended the call with May, a text message from Ridley appeared on the screen:

DC Daniel Lyle. Hammersmith police station. 11 a.m. Interview re: Tania Wetlock.

Jack swore – just the fact that Ridley was privy to the situation was enough to make him more than pissed off. The next call he made was to Foxy.

'How's married life, Jack? You know you only get sex once a week from here on in, don't you, mate? Friday. Tea, *Inspector Morse*, sex, then you can stay up and watch *Match of the Day* whilst she's upstairs reading *Fifty Shades*.'

'*Match of the Day* is on Saturday, and Maggie read that novel when it first came out!' Jack responded, making Foxy laugh out loud.

'Are you doing the post-mortem on Tania Wetlock today?'

'I don't recall seeing your name on the paperwork, DS Warr, so I can't tell you anything in relation to the post-mortem of Tania Wetlock. Let's catch up properly over a pint after work . . . that's if the old ball and chain will let you out unescorted. Four o'clock. Prior to that, I'll be in the lab with my newest patient.' Foxy hung up before Jack could thank him. His day was suddenly filling up.

Jack now knew that whilst he was being interviewed by DC Lyle about Tania Wetlock, Foxy would be examining her corpse. By four o'clock, Jack and Foxy would be comparing notes, and hopefully he'd find out whether or not Elliot Wetlock had anything to do with his daughter's death.

CHAPTER 31

Jack wore a smart suit and tie and sat in the soft interview room at Hammersmith nick. It was bigger than theirs, but not as nicely decorated, and the camera which would be used to record the interview was on a tripod at the end of the sofa rather than being hidden behind a two-way mirror.

DC Lyle wore thin wire-rimmed glasses that made the lenses seem as though they were floating on his face. He looked smart, fresh-faced and trustworthy – but the tiny beads of sweat on his baby-smooth upper lip gave away that he was nervous. Lyle brought no complimentary hot drinks into the soft interview room, nor did he offer to get any sent in. In front of him was a thin file, a notebook and a pen. He poured two glasses of water from the jug on the table between them, and then jumped straight into the interview by asking Jack to describe his relationship with Tania Wetlock.

'Relationship isn't the correct word,' Jack replied evenly. 'Tania Wetlock was the daughter of Elliot Wetlock, who works at the same hospital as my wife, Maggie.' Jack's own words made him pause. This was the first time he'd described Maggie as his wife. And the moment was horribly tainted by the fact that he was being interviewed in connection to the suspicious death of a teenager. 'Elliot Wetlock claimed to be worried about her. He thought she was being led astray by a talent scout, whose identity I never discovered. He'd tried to send her to therapists, but she wouldn't comply. He wanted a female police officer to speak with Tania in the hope of . . . I don't know . . . there's no mother on the scene and Wetlock seemed out of his depth.'

'So, you asked DS Laura Wade to speak with her . . .' Lyle opened the file he'd brought in with him and pulled out a single-sided A4 piece of paper, indicating that he had already spoken to Laura. 'Off the books?'

'I didn't know if there was anything to investigate. In hindsight, I should have told Wetlock to go through the proper channels.' Jack didn't apologise for his decision. It was the least of his worries. 'Tania came to my home twice. Both times uninvited and unwelcome.'

'But you let her in on each occasion?'

'She was intoxicated, and in my opinion she was also high. My decision to let her in was more about not wanting to leave her wandering the streets alone. She was vulnerable.'

'Let's talk about the first time she visited you, Jack. Tell me everything you can recall.' Jack could see that the file in front of Lyle's contained at least seven or eight sheets of paper which, he assumed, were all statements. So, he chose to be open about everything.

Jack explained how on her first visit Tania had wanted help to get her dad off her back, so that she could follow her dream of becoming a Hollywood star. He told Lyle how one minute she was offering him sex, and the next she was crying like a baby; and how she shifted between 'Marilyn' and Tania in the blink of an eye. He explained how she seemed to be a confused mess of a girl, who'd lost track of who she was.

'She was more challenging the second time. Perhaps because I was, too. I flatly refused to let her in, regardless of her again seeming to be drunk and high, because my daughter was asleep on the sofa.' Jack took a deep breath as he got to the more potentially damaging moments of her visit. 'I closed the door on her. She kicked it numerous times, forcing me to go back and open it.'

Lyle took a second sheet of A4 paper from his file and placed it on top of Laura's statement. 'Your neighbour looked out of his window at this point.'

'Then my neighbour would have heard Tania shouting, "Rape!" and seen me dragging her inside.' Lyle smiled his appreciation at Jack's honesty. Jack continued to relay the facts with absolute confidence that he had nothing to hide. 'I've never seen Tania straight. I don't know what she was actually like. But the volatile, frightened child I met was disturbing to be around. Because regardless of the fact that I wanted to help her, I was a man alone with a sexually aware young girl. I was more vulnerable than her on both of the occasions she came into my home.' Jack glanced at the file. 'I expect you have a statement from the taxi driver in there.' On cue, Lyle pulled a third sheet of paper from the file and laid it face up on top of the neighbour's statement. He then took a fourth sheet of paper and handed it to Jack. Much of it was blacked out, but some of it was readable.

'Elliot Wetlock managed to get Tania to a couple of therapy sessions over the years.' The information Lyle chose to volunteer came as no surprise to Jack. 'It was suspected she may have been experiencing the onset of schizophrenia, possibly triggered by excessive drug use. They didn't see her again, so she was never properly assessed and diagnosed. Mr Wetlock never returned to them, nor did he approach his community mental health team.'

'She tried to call someone for a lift both times she left my house. Can you get her call history?' Jack asked, trying to keep the impatience from his voice.

'That's in hand.' Lyle slid all of the paperwork back into the file, suggesting that the interview was almost over. But instead, he kicked things up a gear. 'Did you ever see Tania anywhere other than at your home?' Lyle's casual tone had been a clumsy ruse to lull Jack into a false sense of security.

'No, I did not.'

Lyle then asked if Jack had had a sexual relationship with Tania Wetlock.

'No, I did not.'

Jack knew that Lyle was clutching at straws, but this sort of empty tactic really pissed him off. It was amateurish at the best of times, but to use it on an experienced DS was insulting.

'I only ask,' Lyle continued, 'because we found two bottles of champagne in Tania's bedroom. One had your fingerprints on it.'

Jack sprang to his feet.

'You ran my prints! Does DCI Ridley know?'

'This isn't his investigation. Sit down please, DS Warr.'

'She brought the champagne bottle with her and she was swinging it around. I understand that my interactions with her need to be looked into, but that's the last ridiculous accusation I'm responding to, DC Lyle. If you want to question me as a suspect in the death of Tania Wetlock, then you read me my rights and we'll do this properly.'

From where Jack stood, he could see more sweat glistening on Lyle's forehead as he swallowed nervously. He knew he'd got carried away and overstepped the mark.

Jack tried to control his rising temper. 'I didn't like Tania, but she was a kid. She could have changed. If it was foul play, I want to help you.'

'My apologies, DS Warr.' The play acting was over. Lyle had snapped out of the role of the interviewer trying to outwit the suspect and now started to sound like an actual policeman. 'The volume and variety of drugs found in the deceased's bedroom suggests . . .' Lyle raised his brows and shook his head. 'I don't know what it suggests. Medical. As well as street. Nembutal, chloral hydrate, demerol, various barbiturates such as amytal. Cannabis and cocaine. Some of the bottles had her name on them, some had no labels. We don't know if this was a suicide, accidental or otherwise, but we suspect that a third party was at least aiding her addiction. With your fingerprints in her bedroom, we had to consider . . . I mean . . . you could quite easily have access to prescribed medication.'

'Maggie? You think I could have got the unlabelled prescription drugs from Maggie? Have you met my wife? She would never jeopardise her job, even for me. Surely your first port of call with that train of thought would be Tania's father.'

DC Lyle shook his head. 'He's not being as cooperative as you. For now, we're treating him as the grieving parent, while also seeking court orders to access his office, his home, and even his hospital locker.' He then held out his hand for Jack to shake. 'I may need to see you again, DS Warr. Please don't . . . my apologies, but I have to say these words out loud to you . . . please don't attempt to leave the country.'

Lyle made his parting line sound like it had not come from him, which of course it hadn't. It had come from much higher up. Meaning that Jack was still very much on their radar.

*　*　*

By 3 p.m., Jack was sitting in The Red Dragon eating a family-sized slice of microwaved frozen lasagne accompanied by some chunks of lettuce, tomato, cucumber and onion. Dave was no chef, but the portions of food served here catered for a healthy appetite. It was a coppers' pub, with fast food and cheap beer. As Jack drained his pint glass, his mobile phone lay on the table in front of him, chattering away on speaker as Laura told him all about her evening with Josh. She was clearly in lust, but Josh was a great guy as far as Jack could make out. Dave leant on the bar in an otherwise empty pub with a deeply confused frown on his face. It was only when Laura started talking about the case, that Jack took her off speaker.

'Josh was telling me that the low-hanging-fruit guy they arrested at the Jenkins' property is starting to open up. He's a long-time drug user, which is exactly the sort of person this gang uses. He admitted driving the Range Rover they had nicked; he was given cocaine as payment, and told they might need him again. Anyway, Josh has offered him rehab followed by relocation. His alternative is to be let back on the street, which he knows would be a death sentence. He's scared rigid they might find out he's been arrested and will rat on them.'

Jack smiled at Laura's use of the word 'rat', instead of 'grass' or 'inform'. She really had been spending too much time with Josh.

Laura continued: 'Josh is now liaising with the Dutch police about . . . oh God, bloody Anik! if he tells me one more time that *his* Dutch policeman is now helping the Drug Squad, I'll bloody kill him. Lieutenant Garritt Visser, he's called. Josh says he's good. Between them, they've isolated both ends of a small but well-established supply route. They're currently identifying weak links and picking them off one by one. Nobody that low down the pecking order has any idea who Mr Big is but – and this is interesting, Jack – a couple of the weak links arrested at the Dutch end were recruited in Leeds.'

'Listen, I've got to go, Laura, thanks for keeping me up to speed, I'll be in touch.'

* * *

Foxy was waiting for Jack in the reception area of the mortuary. He was impeccably dressed for a man who'd just spent his day opening up Tania Wetlock. As soon as he saw Jack enter, he joined him and they took a taxi to have a late lunch and a good bottle of red at La Famiglia. The idea of eating again made Jack feel sick, but he needed to know what the post-mortem had revealed.

Jack picked at a steamed sea bass, whilst Foxy tucked into a huge plate of spaghetti bolognese and joked that Maggie had clearly got Jack on a diet already, before switching to discussing the post-mortem.

'She'd ingested enough drugs to kill an elephant. Some of the capsules were still whole, so I can tell you that she took or was given barbiturates amongst other things. Toxicology has got the contents of her bedside cabinet to confirm that the drug on the label of each bottle conforms to what's inside.'

A beautiful teenage waiter, wearing immaculate make-up, and with his shoulder-length blond hair scraped back by an Alice band, appeared behind Foxy to fill the empty glass in front of him. But Foxy didn't pause the conversation.

'And I've given them urine, blood and stomach contents. Plus slices of kidney and liver to take a look at. When I cut through the stomach wall, I could smell booze.'

The young waiter hurried back to the kitchen, with his hand over his mouth.

'There was a considerable amount of congestion and haemorrhaging to the stomach lining,' Foxy continued, 'again suggesting an overdose of barbiturates. Such a shame. She'd done a bloody good job of hiding the damage she'd done to herself – cheek and breast implants, lip and eye fillers, teeth all capped. She didn't even have needle marks.' Foxy dabbed his mouth and chin with a napkin, then sighed. 'But you can't hide the damage on the inside. She'd been abusing drugs and alcohol for a good seven or eight years and – considering that she was only 17 – my guess is that she had help. Kids don't know how to get their hands on the stuff she had in her possession.'

'You said she had no needle marks,' Jack said. 'So, here's a question for the lunch table, Foxy: did you examine her colon?' Foxy gave Jack a puzzled look. 'Drug enemas might be the preferred method of someone she knows,' Jack explained.

Foxy nodded. 'It's certainly a highly effective way of getting drugs, usually benzodiazepines, into the bloodstream quickly.' Foxy drained his wine glass and moved onto his third, as Jack still nursed his first. 'Not that Tania needed to do that, because she seemed not to have sporadic fixes like a junky, more like one long, continuous maintenance dose. But I'll certainly check for you.' He stood and thanked Jack for lunch. 'Right, got to dash. Toxicology reports on our first two ladies are with Laura.'

Jack sat back in his chair and sipped at the remains of his wine. After eating a gigantic lasagne followed by steamed sea bass, and drinking a pint followed by a glass of red wine, he felt uncomfortably full. He asked the waiter to bring the bill while he dialled a number.

'Laura, Foxy says you've got the tox report on AJ and JC.' Because Jack was seated in a public place, he didn't use the full names of their two victims. Laura didn't have long as she was heading into a briefing. She confirmed that Jessica Chi had heroin in her system and Avril Jenkins had cannabis, demerol and MDMA in hers.

Jack immediately recalled the video Mal had shown him, and the replica rubber MDMA tablet. When the masked men carried Avril upstairs, had they drugged her? Demerol and cannabis were no doubt part of her normal routine, but MDMA?

'Thanks, Laura. I think TW could possibly be murder. Foxy's checking for the presence of . . .' Jack was about to say the words 'drug enemas' when he looked up to see the waiter hovering with a card machine in one hand and a small silver plate in the other, with the bill and a couple of mints. Jack chose not to traumatise the poor lad any further.

* * *

As Jack walked through his front door, he was greeted by the normally beautiful aroma of fish pie. But tonight, the thought of any more food made him feel sick. He'd have to come up with an excuse for not eating.

In the kitchen, Hannah was banging a wheel-less toy car down onto her plate, while Penny drew patterns in the potato topping on the fish pie with the back of a fork. 'Your favourite!' she beamed with motherly pride.

Jack smiled and nodded, doing his best to pretend that he was hungry.

'Look at this, darling.' Penny moved towards Hannah, who instinctively raised her arms to be picked up. Penny took Hannah's socks off, stood her on the floor and told Jack to kneel down a short distance in front of her. He knew what was coming. He knelt down, held out his hands to his daughter and encouraged her to come to him. Hannah gripped one of Penny's fingers and wobbled back and forth at the hips. Her perfect little toes curled downwards in an endeavour to grip the lino. Her mouth gaped open under the effort of concentration. When she was ready, she let go of Penny's finger. Hannah stood like a starfish, legs wide and arms out to the side. Her hips wobbled every time she shifted her weight slightly in an attempt to lift one foot and take that first step. She'd achieved this wobbly stage about one week ago but until now she'd always just dropped to her knees and crawled because it was quicker. Today was different. Today, she wanted to walk. After a few seconds of working herself up to the big event, Hannah took her first step. She screamed, reached for Jack's outstretched hands and made a stuttering run for it. Four steps later, Jack threw her into the air and loudly announced that she was a genius.

Ten minutes later, Maggie came home from work. Ten minutes after that, she and Jack were kneeling on the kitchen floor encouraging their daughter to walk between them. By the time she was ready for bed, Hannah could walk twelve whole steps.

* * *

After dinner, which Jack had not had the heart to refuse, he and Maggie tidied the kitchen whilst Penny had an early night. 'A DC Lyle called the hospital today and asked if he could speak with me. I couldn't. Not today, because of the workload Mr Wetlock's absence has left us with. But he's asked me to go to the station tomorrow afternoon.' Maggie fell silent for a second before continuing. 'Penny says you asked her not to mention how bad Tania was when she came here.'

Jack was firm about the fact that he'd not asked Penny to lie. 'I asked her to stick to the facts and not be over-dramatic. They found a champagne bottle with my prints on in her bedroom. And they asked me not to leave the country. They know my wife is a doctor so assume I have access to prescription drugs. Police work, Mags, is a process of elimination, but until I'm eliminated from their enquiries, Mum telling them that Tania ran out of this house looking like she'd been attacked, crying and calling me a bastard, isn't going to help my case!'

'Well . . .' Maggie whipped the tea towel onto her shoulder and began putting the clean plates away. 'Fortunately for you, I was too drunk to be able give your DC Lyle a coherent statement.'

CHAPTER 32

Jack lay on his back with one arm tucked beneath his head and the other wrapped around Maggie. They often fell asleep cuddling, then he naturally rolled away at some point during the night. But, tonight, Jack had not yet been to sleep, so their position had not changed.

There was so much his team didn't know because they weren't leading. There was so much deemed irrelevant to the murder investigations, yet relevant to the drugs investigation. But Jack didn't trust anyone except his own team to make such important calls. Jack hated being so far away from the front line. He had to focus! Which was hard because his mind didn't move in a linear fashion. Jack was happy to be distracted by details when they leapt out of a pile of evidence like luminous signals screaming, 'Follow me!' When the evidence spoke, you listened. Always. But some officers didn't know how to. Steve Lewis certainly didn't.

A thought from days ago suddenly resurfaced in Jack's tired mind. *'Last I heard, he'd gone straight because he bagged himself a beautiful young girlfriend – titled, I think. Then she OD'd on sodium pentothal.' Julia shook her head in disgust. 'Wonder where she got that from.'*

Jack was suddenly wide awake and thinking hard. It was 3.42 a.m. when he looked at the clock for the last time before finally falling asleep.

* * *

As soon as the clock on Jack's mobile screen ticked to 7.30 a.m., he deemed it a sociable enough time to phone Laura. He needed her to send him copies of all documents given to them by Arnold

Hutchinson pertaining to the inventory of 'stolen' items from Avril Jenkins' home, and all insurance companies involved with the Jenkins property across the years.

'Why are you working, Jack?' Laura asked. 'Why aren't you . . . gardening? I'm not saying this for your benefit, you understand, I'm saying it, so you'll stop distracting me from the work I'm meant to be doing.' Jack thanked her for making time to indulge his hunches.

Jack sat at the rear of the library in front of a microfiche machine. He was now working on two trains of thought at the same time: firstly, he wanted to try and find the beautiful girlfriend who had tempted a younger Elliot Wetlock back onto the straight and narrow, before herself OD'ing on sodium pentothal. Julia had implied that she would have needed a trusted and constant supplier, which described Wetlock perfectly. Jack suspected that it was also the role he played in his daughter's life – the similarities between the deaths were too striking to ignore.

Jack did not have any dates to help him in relation to the girlfriend's death, although he did know from Maggie that there was nothing in the hospital's gossip mill about dead girlfriends. So, it must have been long ago. Jack searched back thirty years with no luck, so he took a break, opened his mobile phone and downloaded the insurance attachments sent from Laura in relation to the Jenkins case.

The various lists of precious items were so contradictory that Jack went right back to the original inventory from Frederick Jenkins. This had to be the list that all others should be measured against. Jack spent a couple of hours scrolling through paintings, antiques and other collectable items including valuable books to get an accurate steer on the overall value of the Jenkinses' collection. At which point, he was starting to get hungry. He joined the library and took all of the relevant art books home with him.

It took him forty minutes to walk home, and all the while he was desperately trying to figure out how high-value items could vanish from one list to the next, whilst seemingly not being recorded as sold or reported as stolen. He decided the truth must be that many items had never been listed and never insured: that's how they vanished without raising any kind of alarm. As Jack rounded the corner into his own street, he looked forward to being able to think things through properly.

Jack's office at home was his sanctuary. His pure, serious thinking space into which normal life was not allowed to intrude. Or at least, that's what it was supposed to be.

As he sat at his desk beneath the window, his blinds angled so that he could see the world, but the world could not see him, his eyes were drawn to the pile of boxes and bin bags in the corner of the room. Bloody Maggie! Within weeks of Jack getting his office up and running, she'd started using it as a storage space for all the clothes and toys that Hannah had already grown out of. 'They'll go on eBay when I get the time,' Maggie had said. 'Just ignore them.'

* * *

Jack glanced at his small radiator bedecked with *Paw Patrol* babygrows. As he tried to get down to work in his office-cum-laundry-cum-store cupboard, Maggie FaceTimed. He opened the call on his laptop to see Maggie standing outside Hammersmith police station.

'Lyle's an intense young man, isn't he!' Maggie had decided to open with a joke in case Jack was worried about her being interviewed. In truth, he'd forgotten she was due at Hammersmith today. 'I told him that it was me who let Tania into our personal lives by trying to do her dad a favour. I never expected her to show up at our home, pissed and stoned, and you had every right to be angry with her. And with me.'

Maggie's words were occasionally drowned out by the noise of the wind blowing across the microphone on her mobile, but he got the gist of what she was saying. She hadn't bothered to deny Jack's anger at Tania – the neighbours and the taxi driver had all given statements saying as much – but she'd vehemently supported his right to be angry.

'He told me that Tania had finger bruises on her wrists and upper arms. I don't know what he thought I might say to that – maybe he imagined I'd break down and tell him you're an abusive husband. I said that you would only have responded physically in defence of yourself and our daughter, and that you would have used the minimum force needed to keep Tania from hurting anyone, including herself.' Maggie smiled. 'I told him that Tania was lucky that you were the one who opened the door to her, because I would not have been so understanding about having our home invaded by a volatile, drunk teenager. I'm so sorry for all of this, Jack. I know Mr Wetlock was an unobservant, absent father, but he'll blame himself for that for the rest of his life.'

Maggie seemed particularly saddened by the situation after reliving it with DC Lyle so Jack, once again, refrained from telling her the truth about her esteemed mentor. 'God, I hope this isn't what he's remembered for, Jack.' Maggie ended the call, saying that she had to get back to work as she was picking up another one of Wetlock's shifts whilst he was on compassionate leave.

Jack's mind was now distracted by the two vastly different versions of Wetlock he'd been given, one by Maggie and one by Julia. One Google search later, and Jack was reading about the great man for himself.

Wetlock was 62 years of age and had started his medical career as a GP in Hammersmith before returning to medical school to study his specialism. He divorced from a woman called Katherine Mercer fifteen years ago, and Tania Katherine Wetlock was born two years before that. Jack could find nothing more about Wetlock's private life. Everything else was in reference to his meteoric rise through the ranks. When Jack searched for the name of Katherine Mercer, he found nothing to tell him whether she was even dead or alive.

Jack looked at an image on his screen of the young Dr Elliot Wetlock graduating from medical school. He looked like a man who knew exactly where he wanted to be in life and knew how to get there.

A text message then appeared in the top right-hand corner of Jack's screen. It was from Ridley.

Meet me at Staines station. Drug Squad found the kingpin.

CHAPTER 33

Jack and Ridley stood together in the darkened room. To their left, Anik stood with Josh, Mal, Moley, Mike Tulley, Edgar Matthews and Steve – his new team.

The blackout blinds were drawn and the seven screens showed the view from seven body-cameras. Seven officers, all dressed in black, carrying what looked like AR15 semi-automatic rifles crouched in a circle, each filming the others. There was no sound as six of the officers intently listened to the one in charge. On a specific instruction, each officer placed one hand on the back of the person to their left and ripped away a black velcro flap of material to reveal the word POLICIJA.

The seven officers moved quickly along the bare brick exterior wall of a block of flats. A gloved hand input a numbered sequence onto the main door's keypad, and they crept inside. They immediately ran to the concrete spiral staircase and, without pausing, they slammed their backs against the wall, pointing their guns at the higher floors as they crept upwards. Once they'd passed the door marked 1 AUKŠTE, the officer at the rear turned for a moment to make certain that no one came through the first-floor door and ambushed them from behind.

He did the same again as they moved passed the second floor. At the third floor door, the team kept low as they snuck through and into the corridor. They crouched for a second, quickly scanning left and right before setting off again. Outside flat number 23, they split and crouched in two groups of three on either side of the door. The seventh officer took up his position directly opposite their target flat. Guns were raised to the shoulder and the door was silently opened with a copied key card.

A slender young woman with a small protruding baby-belly, sat on the sofa watching TV with her feet up on a footstool. Although no sound came from the screens, the speed with which she jumped up showed that she was being shouted at to comply. Two officers aimed their guns at her and she dropped to her knees and placed her trembling hands on her head. She laced her fingers, bowed her head, and sobbed.

Seconds later, a door from within the flat opened and a shirtless man stepped out. He was a handsome man in his sixties, with black stubble and thick, iron-grey hair. He seemed calm but was tight-lipped with anger. He shouted through the line of guns at the officers beyond as he inched forwards, pointing at the terrified woman on the ground. It was only when one of the officers lifted her to her feet and sat her back on the sofa, that their target appeared to relax. He then turned his back to the guns, knelt down and allowed his hands to be cuffed behind his back.

Steve Lewis high-fived his 'A-Team' before moving to Ridley and Jack. 'That's Michael Mahoney. Not sure who she is, 'cos his mistress is in protective custody after we found her in his three-acre Spanish hideaway last week. She's pregnant, too, and wouldn't give this scumbag up because he promised to leave his wife and marry her.' Steve smirked. 'I bet she talks when she sees his pregnant Lithuanian mistress.'

The lights flicked on, and Jack could feel the sting around his retinas as his pupils shrunk away from the sudden, fluorescent brightness.

'Come into my office, guys, and I'll get you bang up to speed,' he said cockily.

Jack noted not only Steve's disrespect for Ridley but also the fact that he was supposed to have been keeping them up to speed on a daily basis.

* * *

Steve's office was as neat as a new pin and his shiny new coffee machine made every type of caffeinated beverage you could wish for. It was style over substance, Jack thought: *Just like Steve.*

'When we brought in . . .' Steve tutted at his own memory lapse. 'I'll get the name for you . . . his three-acre-Spanish-hideaway mistress, she gave us the Lithuanian steer. Their police force was already watching flights between Vilnius Airport and London, not knowing they could be observing anything as big as what we've got going on. We quickly identified flight patterns – Vilnius to London, sure, but also Vilnius to Leeds Bradford. Mahoney took a flight from Leeds to Vilnius the day after Avril Jenkins was murdered. He's being extradited tomorrow. Then he's ours. We'll break him.' Steve set his extravagant coffee machine going. 'We may have just brought in the head honcho of an international drugs ring, and the man who ordered your double murder.'

The small hairs on the back of Jack's neck bristled. *If Ridley were his normal self, right now,* Jack thought, *he'd put you back in your sanctimonious cage.*

'One of the low-hanging fruit,' Steve continued, 'one we've been softening up for a couple of weeks, has a passport that goes nowhere other than Belgium. We combined forces, using Visser as our liaison and, two days ago, we seized a huge shipment destined for the UK: 34 kg of cocaine, 470 kg of cannabis and 15 kg of cutting agent, hidden inside metal rollers used to make industrial conveyor belts. Once we knew what we were looking for, we found evidence of eighteen similarly sized shipments, moving in exactly the same way over the past two years. That's an estimated 68 million pounds' worth on the streets. Once the shipments hit the UK, they got split and distributed across the country and on to Ireland.' Jack made a mental note of yet another mention of Ireland. 'As well as numerous small-fry, we arrested fourteen gang members from higher up the ladder. Some of them are already talking, pass-ing the buck and doing deals for easier rides. It seems . . .' Steve left a dramatic pause in order to build the tension, 'amongst the arrests, we have one of your trio of killers.'

* * *

Jack and Ridley drove back to their own squad room, both silently churning over the idea of interviewing Avril Jenkins' potential killer. They were both pissed off not to have been in on the arrest . . . or more to the point, not to have even *known* about the arrest. But none of that was worth agonising over now. Now they had to get justice for Avril.

Ridley broke the silence. 'What the hell is the link between all of that and Avril Jenkins? Why did they choose her and why did they kill her? And Adam Border . . . how does he fit in?' Ridley's questions were the exact same ones that were swimming around in Jack's head.

'Sir, from what I understand, DCI Lewis has got Mahoney down as kingpin because someone told him that's who he was. We should reserve judgement. Lewis moves far too quickly. He's arrested dozens of people and has no actual clue who he's got.'

Ridley nodded, and then took a deep breath. 'Unless the top guy is our missing Adam Border – which I doubt, because I think he's long dead. That's the reason we've been unable to trace him.'

* * *

The whole of Ridley's team – including key uniformed officers from early on in the investigation – were gathered in the squad room ready for the big update. Ridley didn't say too much about the drugs angle, but instead focussed on one of the men suspected of Avril Jenkins' murder who was being escorted across to their station in the next two hours.

'Jack and I will interview. Anik, stay on top of whichever member of the Drug Squad you think will be the most forthcoming.'

'That'll be Moley, sir.'

'Fine. Keep on him. Hour by hour if you have to. And if DCI Lewis feels the need to get involved, you let me know. Regardless of the lack of communication, we are where we need to be. Our job now is to find every existing connection between the new names – such as Mahoney – and the Jenkins house, including confirmation whether Adam Border is deceased. These are threads that the Drug Squad will have no interest in tying up. Anik, feed everything back to Laura and we'll figure out the relevance from here. Thank you, everyone, for your patience and hard work. It's been disjointed, but you've all stuck with it, aiming for the bigger picture. We're nearly there.'

Ridley's mobile pinged, telling him that their suspected killer had just arrived in the custody area.

'Ready, Jack? I don't know about you, but one out of three isn't good enough for me.'

CHAPTER 34

Ridley sat in the observation room looking through a two-way mirror into the interview room where Jack sat opposite Avril Jenkins' alleged killer. Two uniformed officers stood just inside the door, sentry-like, in case Jack needed assistance.

On their way to the custody area, Ridley had made the decision that the interview would initially be done by Jack alone. This gave them the flexibility to introduce a second officer halfway through proceedings, to make the prisoner feel either more or less relaxed, as needed.

The man sitting in the interview room across from Jack was white, in his mid-40s, with shaved greying hair and three-day stubble. His close-set eyes were brown and, due to being slightly overweight, he seemed to have no wrinkles at all. He wore a gold stud in his right ear and a badly made friendship bracelet on his wrist suggesting that somewhere there might be a child who loved him.

'Your passport says your name is John, so that's what I'll call you.' Jack planned to start gently, regardless of the acid revulsion he could feel building in the pit of his stomach. If this guy did turn out to be one of the men who so brutally murdered Avril, Jack wasn't sure he'd be able to hold his temper. But for now his tone remained light. 'Unless you want to choose something else. I'm sure John's not your real name and four days of being called something you don't like could get tedious.'

The man didn't flinch at the thought of being kept in police custody for four days. He'd clearly done it before.

'How's about Dave?' He grinned, showing a small gold implant in his right lateral incisor. Jack grinned back. Not because he'd taken a step towards bonding with the low-life in front of him, but because he'd got him to speak, and now he knew 'Dave' was a Leeds man.

'You're facing possible charges that – when proved – will see you sent down for life,' Jack began. Dave folded his arms, sat back and said nothing. 'Did you know there were cameras in the house?' The tiny muscles beneath Dave's eyes twitched. 'Now you're trying to work out if I'm telling the truth. But do you know what you should have said? "What house?"' Dave remained impassive. 'What part of Leeds are you from?' Dave's lips curled into a half-smile. He thought Jack was funny, and he was definitely not afraid.

Jack pushed onwards, asking Dave about his upbringing, if he had a drug habit, if he ever met the person who gave the order to kill. He even offered Dave a deal and protection if he gave them the top names. 'Who made the friendship bracelet for you? A daughter? Niece? You must have people you care about. I know how this works. You think you have to keep quiet to keep them safe. That's not how you protect your family – you do it by helping us.'

Dave was 'no comment' from the very start. The only words he had spoken in forty minutes were, 'How's about Dave?'

Jack instructed the two officers to take him back to his cell.

* * *

In the observation room, Ridley was on his mobile.

'Thank you, Steve, I appreciate that. Yeah, I'll send them both back to you once we've got what we need.' Ridley slid his mobile back into his pocket. He stared into the empty interview room. 'The second individual called Soren Bech has just been given up for Avril's murder. So, we could have two of them now. Anik's escorting him across.'

'They're scapegoats, sir,' Jack said. 'Dave wasn't even listening to me. He glazed over right after my comment about him being from Leeds. From that moment . . . nothing. No twitches, no micro-gestures. Nothing. He's going to go into custody for a few months, whilst we look for hard evidence and then he'll be released. And he knows it. He's been told to go "no comment" and hold his nerve. And meanwhile, this Michael Mahoney – we believe him to be the sharp dresser in the Jag and the Drug Squad are certain he's the main man, but I reckon he will vanish into thin air. Dave and Soren may well be two of our killers, but they're not scared of being arrested.' Jack paced the tiny box-like room. 'And I don't blame them! We've got nothing.'

Ridley released a long sigh. He knew that everything Jack said was true. 'Let's interview Soren Bech. Then we'll see.'

Jack and Ridley watched the police van park up in the rear yard. It rocked slightly as the people inside stood up and moved towards the doors.

The back doors of the police van opened and Anik walked down the steps. He then turned and reached up into the van as a scrawny man with greasy hair and sunken eyes stumbled forwards. He reached out his cuffed hands and leant heavily on Anik whilst he navigated the two small steps to solid ground. He looked weak and terrified. Anik led him slowly inside.

Jack and Ridley stood by the custody desk, watching Soren's relentless shaking; his muscle control was weak and he was soaked in sweat, every inch of him pining for his next fix. Ridley rolled his head on his neck as though fending off a headache. He then addressed the custody sergeant: 'Get duty doc to see him. If he needs to go to hospital, source two uniformed officers. No less than two, please. Keep him safe.'

Soren tried to move towards Ridley, who he now perceived to be the man in charge, but Anik held him at a distance. '*De ramte min lille pige.* They hit my little girl. With a truck. Now she can't walk. I have two more children back in Amsterdam. Please. They kill my baby. I'm sorry. I didn't want to do it. I'm sorry.' Soren stumbled heavily into Anik's arms. A PC stepped in, took some of Soren's negligible weight, and helped Anik take him towards the cells.

Ridley was seething at the fact that Steve hadn't sent Soren Bech straight to hospital. 'He doesn't want to waste any of his officers on the escort, that's why! Look at him, Jack. We won't be able to interview him for hours and, when we do, he'll be "no comment" as well. All of this . . . this garbled half-confession is inadmissible.'

Ridley wasn't telling Jack anything he didn't already know, he just needed to vent. Jack led the way back towards Ridley's office with a suggestion of tea and brainstorming. Then they'd figure how to get their case back on track.

* * *

When Ridley and Jack arrived back in the squad room, Steve Lewis was perched on the edge of Jack's desk, his arms folded tightly across his chest. Behind him were two crates of beer. And Foxy, choosing to stand alone, had adopted much the same position on the edge of Laura's desk.

'Simon . . .' Foxy held a file in the air and got to his feet. 'I have more information for you on Jessica Chi.'

'Thank you.' Ridley checked his watch – half past six – then invited Steve, Foxy and Jack into his office whilst the team had some well-deserved downtime.

Steve took the main seat opposite Ridley's, leaving Foxy with the smaller, harder chair and Jack standing up. Jack opted to make himself useful by putting the kettle on as Foxy indicated that Steve should speak first.

'Here's what we've got from our interviews so far. Mahoney's northern empire has migrated south over the past three years. As we have discovered, he and his gang were notorious for using large, out-of-the-way homes as bolt-holes. Only instead of targeting vulnerable users who could already be on our radar, they targeted respectable members of the public who are on their way out, physically or mentally.'

Jack wanted to defend Avril's character, but he didn't bother. He figured that Steve Lewis would probably just say 'Avril who?' Jack put a strong coffee in front of Steve and a weaker, decaf coffee in front of Ridley. Then he made Foxy and himself a cup of tea whilst Steve continued.

'The reason I've come in person is to share some video footage. I hope it's a kind of full stop for you on the death of Jessica Chi. We were only recently able to uncover the links due to the delay clearing all the debris from the fire, and subsequently put together further surveillance footage. There's a file in your inbox, Simon.'

Ridley downloaded the file and pressed play.

Jessica Chi walked down the street that ran adjacent to the east wall of the woodland area beyond Avril Jenkins' property. She wore the clothes that her charred corpse was found in, and she carried a duffel bag on her shoulder. Once she headed down the footpath by the side of the golf course, she was no longer trackable . . .

The video changed to footage from the hidden camera inside Avril's conservatory. The view through the conservatory window was of the extensive garden, and the expanse of high trees that stood in front of Avril's greenhouse. Nothing happened for at least thirty seconds. But Jack could tell by the smug grin on Steve's face that something was about to. After eighty-seven seconds of watching nothing more than trees blowing in the wind, a brilliant red flame burst skyward, like a single rocket and then a huge plume of smoke rose into the air from the rear of the garden, beyond the thick foliage of the treeline.

'That's the greenhouse going up in flames.' Steve's enthusiasm was hugely inappropriate seeing as this was also the moment that Jessica went up in flames, but Foxy jumped in before anyone could take issue with it.

'When I examined the lining of Jessica Chi's lungs, I found a substance I couldn't immediately identify, so I sent samples away to be analysed.' Foxy opened the file he'd brought with him. 'Cyanobacteria, commonly known as blue-green algae, is a micro-organism that lives on the surface of unhealthy water with low-quality ecosystems. The untended pond in the woodland behind Avril's home was like this near to the banks, where the water was shallow and could become stagnant. Cyanobacteria can make the surface of the water visually merge with the surrounding greenery of the woodland floor.' The immediate change of expression on the faces of Jack and Ridley, told Foxy that they'd caught up with his train of thought. 'Jessica Chi inhaled water from that pond. My guess is that she wasn't watching her footing and in she went.'

Steve jumped in, so he could join the final dots. 'The greenhouse would already have been warm. So, she paused there to dry off. But it looks like she then flicked on the one remaining heater which was found next to her body. That heater had been left off for a reason: we had it tested and, even with the fire damage, it proved to be faulty. It took one and a half minutes for the gas levels to become combustible and . . .' Steve inflated his cheeks and then let the air escape. 'She'd probably not have smelt it over the skunk.' Steve sat back and waited for the plaudits to come his way.

Jack deliberately ignored him. 'Do you take sugar, Foxy? I can't remember.'

'No thanks, Jack.' Foxy moved to Jack's side under the guise of collecting his drink, but he also took the opportunity to speak privately whilst Steve stewed in his own juices. 'You were right about the enema, benzo and diazepam probably. Indicating, as you say, the potential for a second person to have been present. But be careful, Jack, because the current evidence floating about suggests that the other person could have been you.'

Steve slapped his hands down firmly on the arms of his chair and got to his feet before exiting Ridley's office without another word.

* * *

As the evening drew on, Ridley ordered several large pizzas and let his team chill out with the supply of beer provided by Steve Lewis. He and Jack sat in his office nursing a small whisky each. Ridley asked Jack how things were going with the investigation into the death of Tania Wetlock. Jack knew there was nothing concrete to incriminate him but that certain aspects of the case didn't make him look good – the champagne bottle in her bedroom being one of those things. And the bruising to Tania's wrists and upper arms being another.

'Tell Lyle everything, Jack. There's nothing worse in cases like this than for details to come out later on. The tiniest thing can make a man look guilty. You taking some leave, regardless of it not being your decision, will help here.'

Jack shook his head. 'I don't fucking believe it.'

'You have to, Jack. If you were at work, Lyle could be forced to suspend you, and I need you back with me as soon as possible once this is all cleared up. Keep your head down. Bide your time.' Then Ridley smiled, adding, 'Do you actually know how to do both of those things?'

CHAPTER 35

In the squad room everyone had gone home with the exception of Laura and Ridley. She was absentmindedly dismantling the incident boards, and he was watching her from his office as he pulled on his coat. He knew what she was thinking. 'It's not over, Laura.'

'It feels over, sir. DCI Lewis has his kingpin due to arrive and we have two of the killers who seem to be victims themselves. And I don't like the fact that we weren't involved in all of that. Today feels like someone else's victory.'

Whilst Laura voiced her feelings, Ridley moved to her side.

'We won't stop until we know for certain if this man Steve claims is the kingpin, is the same man who stepped from the Jag on the night Avril was murdered. And we won't stop until we have Adam Border. Nothing's over.'

'Do you think he is alive, sir?'

Ridley frowned. 'It's possible, Laura, but if he is dead, we need to find his body. He's been a long time missing. No one can just vanish.'

*   *   *

Jack sat on the Underground, heading for home. As he listened to a lady shout into her mobile about the cost of play therapy being akin to daylight robbery, and watched a young girl snog her boyfriend with such desperation that anyone would think he was off to war, Jack finally made up his mind that he and Maggie definitely needed to be a two-car family.

As with Laura and Ridley, Jack also felt that this case was not ready to be closed. There were far too many loose ends which were currently being ignored in favour of celebrating the arrest of a kingpin who might or might not have been the top man, seeing as many drug gangs used decoy leaders who were paid handsomely to take the fall if ever the police got close. In Jack's far more analytical mind, there were still too many unanswered questions such as how Jason Marks fitted into the picture, and what part was played by Adam Border – two people who came and went freely from the Jenkins household, without anyone batting an eyelid. And who was the man seen driving the Jaguar, passing over items that could have been paper forensic suits, so no one was covered in Avril's blood when she was dismembered? From the footage of Michael Mahoney's arrest, Jack could not be certain that he was that man because they had no facial recognition. Steve Lewis was congratulating himself and his team, but they still had to prove Mahoney was their big-time drug dealer, and Ridley and his team still had to prove Mahoney was complicit in Avril Jenkins' murder.

Jack was also concerned about the death of Tania Wetlock, even more so now that Foxy had told him about the remnants of a rectal enema present in her body. When administering a rectal enema, a syringe would normally be used, and yet nothing was found at Tania's flat. But the biggest piece of evidence for Jack was the knowledge that Wetlock was not the sainted surgeon everyone thought he was. No one else was currently privy to the fact that Tania seemingly died from an overdose administered in the 'Wetlock way', or how he used to sell drugs to medical students when he was a much younger man – but Jack would need these accusations to be more than just hearsay before he could use them against Wetlock.

The Underground stopped at Holborn and there, on the wall of the tunnel, squarely framed by the window, was an advert for a Jeep Renegade. Now that was exactly the sort of thing Jack thought his family needed as their second car!

* * *

Maggie was lying face down on the floor of Hannah's playroom making growling noises and pretending to swim across the carpet, whilst Hannah strode around, arms in the air for balance, screaming at the top of her lungs. Watching from the doorway, Jack was very unsure of the rules of this particular game.

'She thinks I'm a shark or something,' Maggie explained. 'Doesn't matter. Really, we're just practising her walking whilst she's on the carpet where she's safe. Did your mum tell you about the day nursery on the way to the hospital?' Jack's blank expression told Maggie that this was the first he'd heard of it. Maggie started talking again before he could ask the one question she knew he would. 'It's not expensive compared to most round here and, yes, she does need to start going. She's mobile now and needs to be socialising with other babies. Your mum is amazing, Jack, but we've got into the habit of just assuming that she'll say yes when we need to pick up extra shifts or work late. Apart from her night classes, your mum's got no time to herself. She's like a live-in nanny. And she's still young.' Jack frowned, uncertain if Maggie was insinuating that his mum should get back out there and find herself a new man. Again, she could read him like a book. 'All I'm saying, is that she needs friends her own age. Just like Hannah.'

All the while Jack and Maggie had been talking, Hannah had been running in circles and screaming with her hands high in the air to counterbalance her still-wobbly legs. Now exhausted, she wrapped her arms round the outside of Jack's knees and wedged her head between his thighs. She then panted and giggled whilst she got her breath back. When Jack gently tried to move away towards his office, she stepped on top of his feet, so he had to take her with him. As father and daughter waddled along the landing, Jack told Maggie that his leave would more than likely be extended if the Tania Wetlock investigation was ongoing.

'I can't believe they're treating you like a suspect!' Maggie said.

He tried to explain that the champagne bottle found in Tania's bedroom was potentially damaging as it had his prints. 'But Ridley knows I'm not guilty of anything: he's given me leave to protect me from suspension.' Jack then prised Hannah off his legs, kissed her several times all over her face and handed her to Maggie. 'If I need to stay out of sight, I will.'

As Jack disappeared into his office and closed the door behind him, Maggie suspected that his relaxed reaction to being kept away from the squad room meant that he was up to something on his own which Ridley probably knew nothing about.

*　*　*

As the days passed, Jack's office got messier by the hour and none of it was his doing. While he sat at his desk, researching artists such as Modigliani, Degas and Picasso, his peripheral vision was assaulted by items which had no business being here. Half-used pots of paint, pinboards waiting to be wall-mounted, and dozens of old toys waiting to be advertised on eBay – together with the recycled boxes, envelopes and padding that would be used to send them to their new homes –made concentration on the task at hand difficult. But eventually he managed to tune them out.

Amedeo Modigliani was a fascinating artist who seemed capable of painting a captivating portrait including none of the sitter's personality at all. He was, in Jack's eyes, the exact opposite kind of artist to Henrick Chi, who managed to capture the very soul of a person. Although Jack had never heard of Modigliani, he knew who Degas and Picasso were, and both were listed as being in Frederick Jenkins' original collection, authenticated by none other than Jason Marks. Jack immediately decided that now Marks was no longer a person of interest to the Drug Squad, there would be no conflict of interest if Jack asked for his input.

* * *

On Wednesday, Jack arrived at the Casa Manolo on the King's Road in Chelsea, about twenty minutes before Jason Marks, instantly noting that the Spanish food and wine selection looked fabulous.

Jason walked in wearing tan chinos and a pristine white T-shirt. Over one shoulder he wore a man-bag and, over the other his jacket hung from a finger. Before sitting sat down at the table, he ordered at the bar a selection of dishes from the tapas menu and a bottle of Beronia Gran Reserva Rioja, all of which he'd clearly ordered numerous times before.

'I hope you don't mind. You'll thank me when it all arrives,' he said. Jack's quick smile hid the fact that he had been hoping for a beer and a meal that came on a plate which would only be touched by him.

Jason sat a little way back from the table with his legs crossed, and looked at Jack with a defensive gaze. 'This is completely informal, Mr Marks,' Jack assured him. 'You don't have to answer any of my questions, but I'd appreciate it if you did.' Jason straightened his knife a quarter inch, so it was in line with his fork. Then he seemed to relax. Jack got straight to the point. 'Did you witness a will for Avril Jenkins?'

'Several months ago, I do believe I did,' Jason replied. 'That is to say, she put a piece of paper in front of me and thrust a pen into my hand. There was a name in the header, which told me it was something from a solicitor. I can't recall the name.'

Jack asked if Jason knew the name Adam Border. He nodded vaguely. 'Arnie Hutchinson let it slip that he's the new beneficiary of Avril's will. And that he's gone AWOL. Or he's dead. Either way,

Terence is preparing to fight for what he firmly believes is his. Terence claims that a son can't exist because Frederick would have known about him. He's also banking on the fact that Avril was a bigamist.'

Jack asked what evidence Jason had of that. 'Chinese whispers. Someone said to someone. All I can say is that nothing would surprise me about Avril Jenkins. If she was already married when Frederick proposed, I have no doubt whatsoever that she'd lie about it. She had a childlike view of life. She'd have spoken without thinking and worried about it later.'

'Did you ever meet Adam Border?'

'I met the man who tended her garden. I never asked, or was told, his name. But if that was him, she didn't treat him like he was her son. She treated him more like he was her toy boy. An unseemly ruse if he was her offspring.'

The wine and food arrived, and all conversation paused whilst Jason tasted and approved the bottle chosen, then visually checked the tapas dishes he'd selected, shifting the tiny bowls until they formed an aesthetically pleasing pattern on the table.

'In truth, I was Freddie's friend and only really dealt with Avril after his death,' he said. 'Freddie could be a tricky customer at times. Moody. Probably bipolar, in hindsight. He could be paranoid, too, which is why he rarely relinquished control of the reins with investments. He questioned my valuations and expertise, but he also paid me well so I could live with it. Freddie did have a stunning ability to spot an up-and-comer. He'd follow the careers of students, attend their little local art exhibitions, then pounce on collections he guessed would one day be worth money. And he was right most of the time.'

Jason fell silent again while he selected a spoonful of food from each of the tapas bowls, arranging them in neat piles on his plate, like paint on a palette. It was only now Jack realised that Jason had ordered food by colour and not by content.

'What was I saying? Oh yes, Freddie. He learnt from his dad, who really *was* an art collector. The old boy spotted Andy Warhol early, but his real passion was the Dutch masters. Mr Jenkins was the real talent, and an obsessive collector. After he died and Freddie inherited the lot, he learnt fast – but then, dear God, Avril was a nightmare. She was one of those people who bought and sold based on whether she liked the look of something. Preposterous! She stopped insurance payments and sold on a whim. She decimated poor Freddie's vault.'

Until this moment, Jason had been providing information that Jack already had, which was exactly what Jack wanted him to do, so he could be certain that he'd not overlooked anything. But a vault? What vault?

Jason explained that during a bout of paranoia, Frederick Jenkins had had a secret vault built beneath the cellar in order to safely store his art collection. 'Avril moved Rossetti's *Venus Verticordia* from the vault to above the fireplace. I told her not to. The heat, I said. The heat will destroy it. She couldn't care less. She liked it, so that's where it was to live.' Jason became almost mournful. 'Her worst crime was selling a Degas pencil drawing without seeking my advice first. And a rather unusual Van Gogh which, thank the Lord, turned out to be a fake. I would have given my eyeteeth to have been allowed just one peek inside that vault. What a vision it must have been to see it filled with masterpieces! I only knew of its existence because once when I was in the hallway, just about to leave, he came out of the kitchen carrying a canvas that needed to be authenticated, and he said he had been down in the vault. He said no one, not even Avril, was allowed down there.'

Jack sipped from his glass of wine to give himself a moment to think. So the vault beyond the cellar – which they'd all assumed was built to be used as a secret drug factory – was in fact a private art gallery which had been in existence decades before the drug dealers showed up. Once again, Jack was privy to information that no one else had, simply because his gut had told him to keep probing with someone who'd been dismissed from the inquiry days ago.

But did it mean the art angle was now more pivotal than the drugs?

CHAPTER 36

Jack was still hungry when he got home. On the kitchen top was a large pork casserole with one scoop missing, so Penny had clearly eaten earlier. Seeing as it was Wednesday, that meant that she was now at the college learning how to . . . Jack couldn't recall. It was something to do with the garden, that's all he knew.

As Maggie put two plates in the oven to warm, Jack was eager for the upcoming feast. This was the kind of food that suited him best: home-cooked, on its own plate and shared with the women he loved. The £6.99 bottle of Merlot was also far more to Jack's liking than the £50 bottle Jason had so pretentiously chosen.

Jack's mind was now firmly on Elliot Wetlock because he knew he wouldn't be able to focus on all of the loose ends belonging to the Avril Jenkins case until the weight of accusation surrounding Tania's death had been lifted from his shoulders. And the only way that was going to happen was if her killer was identified. Maggie didn't understand why Jack was the only person who was referring to Tania's death as a murder and not a suicide. But Jack wasn't going to share his suspicions about Wetlock until it was far more than just a hunch based on the revelations of a fugitive. So far, all he had was Foxy's evidence that Tania had taken drugs anally. Jack's current theory was that she had taken a cocktail of drugs orally, but not enough to kill herself, then a second person had administered the lethal additional dose anally which brought on the OD.

'How would you get a rat out of a hole?' he asked suddenly.

'Cheese!' Maggie beamed. But the grin on his face suggested that she was way off the mark. 'Oh, you mean a person rat. Not a rat rat,' she said. 'Well, swap cheese for whatever it is that your rat likes best. Then,' Maggie continued, pouring two glasses of wine, 'close off all escape routes barring the one you're waiting at. Then scare the shit out of them and wait till they come to you.' Maggie grinned, impressed with her own ingenuity. 'I know, I should have been a copper. Also, for your information, Penny and I were discussing getting one of those doorbell camera things, and I am going to order one online, for the front and back door.'

'Let me sort that out,' Jack suggested. 'But you're right: lesson learnt from the bloody Tania Wetlock situation.'

'OK. But don't say you're going to do it and then forget.'

'I won't, promise. Now let's eat – I'm starving'.

Maggie went to bed around ten, as was her routine when she needed to be up at five in order to run in to start her shift at seven. At eleven, Jack was still lying on the sofa wide awake: all he could think of was Dr Elliot Wetlock. He was a rat who had been hiding for far too long.

* * *

Jack went into the kitchen, where Maggie's rucksack was by the back door next to her running shoes ready for the morning. Inside the rucksack was her handbag. And inside her handbag was her mobile phone. Jack had never in his life looked in Maggie's handbag, and he'd certainly never looked at her mobile. Yet he felt no guilt as he flicked through her contacts looking for Wetlock's details. He could have asked Laura, of course, as she'd been to Wetlock's house, but that would have made her an accomplice to what he was about to do.

CHAPTER 37

The following morning Maggie was in the kitchen stretching for her run, and Jack was sitting at the table with his coffee and toast, watching her every move. On normal workdays, Jack would be running round the house looking for his car keys or shoes or both. This morning, however, he was loving just watching his amazingly beautiful wife bend and flex her body, readying it for the three-mile run to the hospital. Jack wasn't even aware that he was smiling.

'I'll be home by two,' Maggie whispered seductively. 'If you're here, you can watch me warm down.' As Maggie bent forwards, keeping her legs dead straight, and pushed the palms of her hands flat onto the lino floor, Jack stepped up behind her and placed his hands gently on her hips. She held her position for a second or two before standing up into his arms. He kissed her neck and she headed out.

Jack went upstairs and grabbed a quick shower before dressing in a tight black polo-neck jumper, dark jeans and black trainers. He pulled on a lightweight black running jacket and stuffed a ski hood into the pocket. In the top drawer of his desk was a burner phone he'd purchased many months ago to infiltrate the violent world of a London jeweller, who had a sideline in masterminding high-end burglaries in the Cotswolds. He had never imagined he'd need it again but had kept it regardless. Jack was ready. Although he had been left the car, he'd not be using it this morning in case it was picked up on CCTV.

Wetlock lived in a substantial three-storey house on Cheyne Walk in Chelsea. Jack stood on the opposite side of the road with his mobile to his ear as though he was talking to someone. He started walking, giving himself time to check out the immediate area for CCTV cameras, both private and public. They were everywhere in this particular neighbourhood, and they were definitely on the front of Wetlock's home, positioned just beneath the upstairs windows. Without moving his mobile from his ear, Jack took several photos. He was desperate to get inside Wetlock's home and find something incriminating, but there was no way to avoid being captured on security camera. He was about to leave when he saw Wetlock draw up in his BMW and park in one of two residents' bays right outside his front door. As Wetlock went inside, Jack moved round the property and down a small alley framed by two silver birch trees. He covered the lower half of his mobile in his ski hood to muffle his voice, then called Wetlock's land line.

'Hey, Elliot.' Jack kept his voice low and spoke slowly so that Wetlock would not miss a single word.

'Who is this!' Wetlock immediately sensed that the person calling was not someone he knew or wanted to know.

'I wondered if you still had your business on the side?' Jack said. 'I could do with a little help to get through my med finals.'

It was a while before Wetlock responded, but when he did, Jack was impressed by how cool he sounded. 'You have the wrong number.'

Jack jumped in before he could hang up. 'Listen! If you don't, the police will.' Wetlock didn't utter another word, but the heaviness of his breathing told Jack that he was listening.

'I get why you did it. She was embarrassing and you've got a hard-earned reputation to protect. But you made a mistake, Elliot. And I found it.' Again, Jack left a pause, which Wetlock didn't fill. There were no questions, no indignation, no threats to call the police – all things that an innocent person would do. Wetlock was silent. He *knew* what Jack was talking about. For now, that's all Jack wanted to know.

Walking home, Jack passed a Mercedes showroom and there, in the centre window, was a Mercedes Benz G Class. It was a ridiculously large car for London but – with the adrenaline still surging through his veins after threatening Wetlock, and still being dressed from head to toe in black – Jack was feeling bold. His eyes refocussed from the classiest-looking Jeep he'd ever seen, to the pristine salesman beaming out at him. The salesman was waiting, respectful and attentive, to make Jack an espresso and try to sell him a £50k vehicle.

As Jack struggled to hold the tiny handle of the espresso cup, he listened to the man list what was included and what were added extras. The salesman's attentive smile waned slightly when Jack asked if he had a second-hand version of the same model – then he reconsidered and decided that a £30k Merc was still an excellent commission. The last second-hand model in the showroom was black, had an excellent low milage and one very careful retired gentleman owner. Jack asked if there was a further reduction if he paid cash, at which point the salesman stepped up a gear. He looked furtively around the showroom, openly making sure his boss wasn't in earshot, then reduced the price by £5k 'just for Jack'.

As Jack pondered whether they had £25k to divert from daily living to the purchase of a second car, Maggie called. She asked where he was and when he lied, the salesman deflated on the spot. Jack had clearly not asked his wife about getting a new car, so there would be no sale today.

'I'm going to be late again, Jack. Something else has just happened with Wetlock, God knows what this time. Anyway, he's called in. I'm staying on till they can find cover.'

After the call was done, Jack could see that the salesman had lost faith in him as a potential sale and now just wanted him to leave.

* * *

Hammersmith police station had recently had an impressive overhaul. Jack was led through freshly painted corridors towards a spacious second-floor room where CID were housed. It was bright, fresh and open plan, creating an invigorating atmosphere in which to work. It made Ridley's squad room look very neglected. It was too neat and tidy for Jack's liking, however: it looked as though no work was being done.

Lyle was sitting behind a large modern desk which had been split into zones for his computer, his reading and his phone calls. Again, this was far too tidy for Jack – to his mind, a police officer's desk should be a busy, active place where they endeavour to spend as little time as possible, in favour of being 'out there', actually doing the legwork. But it was still one hell of a desk for such a young officer. Jack asked for an update on the investigation.

'You know I can't discuss that with you, sir.' Lyle wiped his sweaty brow with a handkerchief. 'The aircon in here doesn't work. The window behind me is south facing and the blind's knackered, so it's like an oven some days. Sorry, I haven't offered you a drink. Would you like some water?' Jack declined and asked Lyle if he had received the latest pathology from Foxy, pointing out that he wasn't asking Lyle to share the contents of the report; he was just after a yes or no. 'I have had a recent update from pathology, yes.'

'Then you'll know about the rectal diazepam.' Lyle's initial shock at Jack being privy to the contents of the path report was soon replaced by indignation. 'I was the one who told Foxy to look for it, DC Lyle. Which is something you could have done if you'd been more vigilant.' Jack softened his tone. 'We both know that I'm no longer your prime suspect. I'm trying to help you.'

'Well . . .' Although Lyle knew that he shouldn't divulge any more information, he also wanted to know what Jack knew about Elliot Wetlock, so he hedged his bets. 'It looks like accidental suicide. She had several prescriptions written by various doctors, medical and psychiatric. She had a diagnosis of anxiety, and she was known for storing her drugs in order to take them all at once for one big hit. It's looking like this one went wrong. And regarding the enema, you can administer those yourself.'

'Not if you're unconscious,' Jack said. 'And the level of drugs in her system strongly suggest that she would have been.'

Lyle didn't even know enough to be embarrassed by Jack's insinuation that he'd got a key part of the investigation wrong, so carried on. 'The talent scout seems to have been a figment of her imagination. Supporting the probability of schizophrenia, perhaps. It seems that her only actual brush with fame was being on the books at a local lookalike agency, and they stopped using her when she turned up at a job as high as a kite. The rest was fantasy. We're about to release her body, DS Warr, so if you have hard evidence against Elliot Wetlock, you need to share that with me now.'

'I've already told you, DC Lyle, you can't self-administer an enema if you have the amount of drugs in your system that Tania did. Someone else delivered the fatal dose, so you've got a murder on your hands. You catch yourself a killer and your DCI will never forget your name again.' Jack took a gamble that Lyle had, at least once in his short career, had to reintroduce himself to his own DCI. Lyle, now looking like a wounded puppy, confirmed that Jack was right. He again asked Lyle to accept his help.

Lyle stood up from his desk, leaving a sweat line on the leather seat. 'Are you sure?' he asked quietly. Jack nodded, prompting Lyle to make a quick confession in the hope that Jack could help him rectify his mistake. 'I've given them the nod to clear the crime scene.'

* * *

Considering they were now against the clock, Lyle was driving like a middle-aged aunt. Jack couldn't comprehend his need to obey the speed limit when he had a siren and lights at his disposal. Lyle had called the officer in charge of clearing the scene and halted the operation, but that order would take time to filter down to the officers on the ground and, until they arrived, Lyle had no idea if his crime scene was still secure.

They eventually arrived at a small block of newly built flats facing the riverside just along from Hammersmith Bridge. Lyle pulled into a resident's bay, put his Met police card on the dashboard and led the way to the glass entry. Lyle quickly got the attention of the uniformed lady standing behind the small desk. He slapped his badge against the glass and she rushed to let them in.

Jack and Lyle rushed up the stairs two at a time, closely followed by the receptionist carrying her master key. When they got to the top floor, Flat 9 had no crime tape across the door because it had never been considered a murder scene. But the lady from the desk could guarantee that the cleaner had not been in since her shift started four hours ago, though she had no idea what had happened before that. Fortunately, as soon as Jack entered, it was more than obvious no cleaner had been near the place for weeks. Their crime scene was secure.

Lyle sounded like an estate agent as Jack made his way around the small, two-bedroomed flat. 'This is one of the most sought-after blocks of flats in London. There's a large gym and lap pool on the lower ground floor, but no car park. Each flat has a post box in reception. We checked Tania's, of course: nothing of interest. And that . . .' Lyle pointed towards a small, locked cupboard built into the wall just inside the front door. 'You put small kitchen waste bags in there and they get collected from the outside. We looked through the contents.'

Jack had to admit the flat was stunning. The large living room had a balcony overlooking the river. The beige carpet matched the oat-and-cream-coloured armchairs and sofa and large ornate mirrors were positioned to make the room feel even bigger. There was a flatscreen TV and a stereo system stored in a cupboard with the doors open. Lyle took two pairs of nitrile gloves from his jacket pocket and handed one to Jack.

The kitchen was small and compact with a skylight view. Lyle pointed to a tiny fridge freezer, saying that there had been nothing at all inside the fridge, not even a pint of milk.

A glass-fronted cabinet was filled with white china on one shelf and wine glasses on another. Everything was laid out like a show home. The cooker top looked unused and the oven smelt as clean as the day it was bought.

The spare bedroom was very small and was being used for storage, but the master bedroom with en suite was fabulous. The entire space was an *homage* to Marilyn Monroe, complete with framed photographs and posters covering almost every inch of light-silver wallpaper. The wall-to-wall, mirror-fronted wardrobe doors were slightly open, and clothes spilt out all over the carpet. Designer shoes and handbags were thrown in piles in every corner. Underwear and negligees were draped over every surface and poured out of the open top drawer. Discarded takeaway cartons, pizza boxes, paper coffee cups and Coke cans completed the picture. The stench of old food hung heavily in the air, making it hard to breathe freely.

The king-size bed had been stripped of sheets and pillowcases, and the silk bedcovers lay in a heap beside it. The bedside tables had various ring marks from glasses and mugs, and there was a selection of face creams and lotions. Jack moved carefully around the room as Lyle read off the list of items that had been removed by the police, including bed linen, certain items of underwear, champagne and wine bottles, as well as her diary, laptop and all of the medication and drugs. Lyle explained that the mattress and bedsheets were spattered with numerous old stains such as menstrual blood, semen, faeces, urine and make-up. There were also patches of bleach all across the carpet.

'Prints belonged to her, her father, a lad who we've eliminated due to the fact that he's been dead five months – from drugs. And . . .'

'And me.' Jack completed his sentence for him. 'On the champagne bottle, I know. She had it with her when she came to my house. But you won't find my prints on anything that belongs inside this flat.'

Underneath the bed and littered across the room were hundreds of photographs of Marilyn Monroe, as well as stacks of books about her life and career, most of which had Post-it notes attached marking pages of interest.

'He said she was lying on her side, curled up like a baby,' Lyle said. 'Mr Wetlock could see she'd been dead for days but apparently tried to revive her anyway. He called an ambulance and then us.' Lyle watched Jack as he stood still and silently took in the scene as if he was replaying events in his mind to see if they added up. 'I know you think it was her father, Jack, but I can't see it. I took his statement. He was distraught. You can't fake that.'

'I'm sure he was distraught.' Jack leant down and cautiously felt along the underside of the mattress. 'I'm sure he loved her. I'm also sure he killed her. Did you find a syringe?'

'She didn't inject. The PM report indicates no track marks, recent or historic.' Lyle began to sound pissed-off at Jack's constant contradicting of his investigative findings. He might be young, but he wasn't stupid. 'We looked for needles. There were none.'

'Not a needle. I'm looking for a syringe. The type used for anal insertion.' Lyle clearly didn't know if they had specifically looked for that type of syringe or not, but he insisted that no medical-looking equipment of any kind had been found. 'Hospitals use them all the time,' Jack said. 'Wetlock would have been able to pick one up anytime.' Jack left Lyle with that thought as he continued searching around and underneath the mattress. 'How long was it before the emergency services arrived?'

'We're local, so maybe ten minutes before we got here. And the ambulance was a couple of minutes ahead of us. Her father was in shock. He just kept repeating that there was nothing he could do. We moved her pretty quick because she was lying in her own . . .' Lyle leant on the doorframe and watched Jack continue his search. 'He'd tried calling her a couple of times earlier that day and when she didn't answer, he came round. He was in two minds because although he was concerned about her fragile mental state, he was also used to her ignoring him. He thought she'd been doing OK.'

'What did the person on the front desk say about visitors?'

'She never had any. Apart from her dad and he'd not been for four days.'

Jack stood bolt upright and stared at Lyle in disbelief. 'He was here four days before he found her body? Around the time she actually died? *Think*, Lyle. No father walks into this flat and thinks their kid is "doing OK". Does this look like the place of someone who's doing OK? She was at my house twice in the space of a week, pissed, high as a kite and offering herself on a plate.'

'As far as I understand it, he didn't know that.'

'Four weeks ago, he asked my wife to ask me to help him protect his daughter from being groomed by an unidentified talent scout—'

'Who doesn't exist.'

'DC Lyle!' Jack finally snapped. 'I respect any officer who sticks to their guns in a case, but if you're just going to spout bullshit irrelevancies, then I'll find the evidence against Wetlock myself and take it directly to your DCI. Elliot Wetlock, a loving father and medical professional for more than thirty years, sees his mentally ill daughter living like this, surrounded by more prescription and street drugs than any one person should take in a lifetime, and he walks away? 'Course he fucking doesn't. And he *did* know that she'd been to my house causing trouble because he was the one she called to come and collect her. I know she ended up in an Uber, but he'd have had a missed call and a voicemail from her.'

Now that Lyle was on the back foot and feeling like a fool, Jack softened his tone. He continued searching on and around the bed as he spoke. 'Tania Wetlock was a liability to his career. This isn't me guessing, DC Lyle: I know because my wife told me. This flat – it's not about giving his daughter independence and responsibility, it's about keeping her out of sight. You know he pays for it all, right?'

Lyle nodded. Everything was in Wetlock's name, and he paid all of the bills.

Jack continued. 'I know he looks like a doting dad on the surface. So you have to dig. Find his ex-wife. Find his old mentees from years ago.' Jack got out his mobile phone and disappeared beneath the bed. Lyle moved round to keep him in sight.

Jack was sprawled on his belly on the filthy floor, half underneath the bed. 'Get down here.' Lyle reluctantly joined Jack, sensing that he'd found something that he and his team had missed. Jack held his mobile on its side, so that the torch shone into a gap between the ill-fitting skirting and the floorboard beneath it. Inside the gap, was a plastic wrapping. Jack took two photos of it in situ, before Lyle took a pencil from his pocket and hooked it out.

The wrapping read: *Diazepam Rectal Gel 20mg.*

Lyle and Jack lay side by side beneath the bed with the springs above them on the mattress pressing on their hair while Jack air-dropped the two photographs he'd just taken to Lyle's mobile, and

Lyle snapped several more whilst Jack shone his torch on the single piece of evidence that they both knew could put Wetlock away for the murder of his daughter. Lyle secured the wrapper into an evidence bag, then both men got to their feet, brushing the dust and cobwebs from their clothes.

'Dig into Wetlock's career history,' said Jack. 'Look for him being unexpectedly promoted out of one hospital and sent to another. Look for recurring names on recommendations and for him being protected by the same people again and again. Anything that doesn't feel right. I'm guessing it won't take you long. Then get that rushed through for prints before going to your DCI with any new evidence. Say that in the process of eliminating Elliot Wetlock from your enquiries you made one final sweep of Tania's flat. Don't mention me.'

Lyle silently absorbed every word of Jack's instructions. Jack then reiterated what his policeman's instinct was telling him. 'Maybe Wetlock had reached the end of his tether. Maybe he finally wanted peace – for Tania as well as for himself. Wetlock was seen here four days before she died, which is roughly the timeframe for her OD. Everything he did from that moment on was calculated playacting. When he came back days later and "found" her, the scene was set for him to play the grieving father. If you go after him in the way I've suggested, you're raising the bar. Your guv will expect you to leave no stone unturned from this second on. If you're not good enough, now's the time to admit it.'

Lyle raised his chin and pushed his shoulders back, then nodded.

'Good.' Jack smiled. 'Your career just got a lot more interesting.'

CHAPTER 38

When Jack got back home he printed out the two photographs he'd taken of the rectal diazepam wrapper and slid them into an envelope. He then returned to Wetlock's property, where he could clearly see his BMW parked in his designated resident's bay. Jack wore his ski hood rolled up like a beanie hat, pulled up the collar on his jacket and posted the envelope through Wetlock's letterbox.

Jack knew that although Lyle was now firmly on Wetlock's case, it could be days before he gathered enough evidence for an arrest, and Jack wanted this sorted now, so he could clear his head and go after Adam Border.

Jack texted Wetlock from his burner phone:

Check your post. Your mistake is with the cops. Go to them before they come to you.

* * *

Jack walked home with the intention of meeting Maggie off her run and seeing if she was still in the same flirtatious mood as she'd been that morning. He then had the idea of taking her to shop for a new car – ideally the black G Class Merc he'd fallen in love with and knew he could get for £25k. Then he'd round off his hugely productive day by preparing to use the last few days of his leave to go to Ireland and track down Adam Border.

Jack was still on a high when his mobile rang.

Unfortunately for Jack, Maggie had other plans for the rest of his day.

* * *

Maggie had forgotten all about her early morning flirting and instead had arranged for Jack to meet her outside the small local nursery. It was located in the back garden of a large property just around the corner from their home and catered for no more than fifteen children. If Hannah did end up attending, Maggie and Jack would be given the password to the nursery's security cameras and so would be able to log in and watch Hannah playing with her new friends. Maggie was excited about the prospect of their daughter starting to explore the world without them. The thought gave Jack palpitations.

Maggie and Jack were greeted at the locked gate by a pleasant middle-aged lady called Margo Berry. She invited them into the playground and walked them around the outside of the building. Most of the windows were partially obscured by paintings Blu Tacked to the inside of the glass.

'On the south-facing windows, the children's artwork acts as shade without completely blocking the view of the outside world. And the secondary purpose is to hinder people from looking into the classrooms. We're not that close to passing foot traffic and people aren't likely to pause and look in but, well, "there's always one" as my mother used to say.'

Jack wasn't remotely comforted by the strategy of using children's paintings to stop local sex offenders ogling his daughter. And he knew for a fact that there was definitely more than just one. Maggie tightened her grip on Jack's hand as she felt him tensing.

The play areas, however, indoors and out, were fabulous. The neat little kitchen was immaculate. The dining area, filled with low tables and tiny chairs was bright and cheerful. And each classroom was complete with a matted sleeping area in a windowless corner. It was a very impressive nursery with bubbly, polite staff and all mod cons.

Even so, Jack couldn't help himself. 'Do you do enhanced DBS checks on all of your staff, or the regular ones?'

Margo didn't flinch. 'Enhanced. We have coded locks positioned high on all exterior gates and doors, and the code is changed weekly or whenever a staff member leaves. All windows only open four inches unless a special catch is released which can only be reached from high up on the inside. We have twelve security cameras and in my office is a panic button linking us directly to the local police station. Two community support officers loop this area twice daily, coinciding with the beginning and the end of each day so they can learn the parents' faces. You'll meet them if you choose us for your daughter. We also play our own little version of hide and seek, with prizes given to the children for keeping very still and very quiet: the children love it and aren't aware that they're practising for the highly unlikely event of a targeted terrorist incursion. I'm happy to answer all of your questions, DS Warr, and you're welcome to inspect our security for yourself.'

Jack flicked his eyes to Maggie who was purposefully not look-ing in his direction. She'd obviously warned Margo Berry that Jack was a police officer. Margo continued in her best teacher's voice.

'The moment you hand your daughter to a stranger and walk away, even if it is only for two hours, it can be very difficult. I advise you treat it like ripping off a plaster. Bring Hannah one morning next week at 9 a.m., go to the café at the end of the road, and come back here at 11 a.m. I promise that she'll have had a far less stressful couple of hours than you.'

As Jack and Maggie walked away from the nursery, he glanced back to check what he could see from outside the tall fence. Margo was right about the paintings in the windows: Jack couldn't see any of the children in their classrooms, so he had to admit that the whole set-up felt very safe. Maggie linked her arm through Jack's and brought their walk to a halt.

'I've been thinking, Jack . . . we might need a second car.'

Jack's face became animated. It was as though Maggie had read his mind! 'I was thinking the same! I've found a . . .' Maggie glanced towards the road, not listening. Behind Jack, parked in the street adjacent to the nursery, was a pea-green Nissan Micra.

'One of the junior doctors has taken a placement in South Africa and so needs to sell it quickly. He said we could keep it overnight, to see how we feel about it.' Maggie pressed the key fob in her pocket and the Nissan's lights flashed into life. 'It's four-door. Really economical. The boot's not huge, but we only need it for shopping. And Hannah would love the colour! It's a bargain, Jack.' Maggie slid her arms round Jack's waist. 'You don't have to drive it. And it'll be easy for your mum to find in the supermarket car park.'

As Maggie drove the bright-green monstrosity back home, she casually explained that, according to the rumour mill, Wetlock was meant to attend an HR meeting today but had rung in sick at the last minute. This had prompted an emergency managers' meeting to discuss the option of ultimately replacing him. He was still on compassionate leave at the moment, of course, but there had been growing doubts about his ability and commitment since his daughter had started going off the rails. Jack didn't tell her that Wetlock would have cancelled the HR meeting at the last minute due to an anonymous threat of exposure if he didn't confess to his daughter's murder. Instead, he asked how the 'rumour mill' knew such confidential information about a senior consultant.

'Sofia. She cleans the managerial floor. They think she can't understand English, but she relays the hospital's secrets to whoever sits next to her in the canteen at lunch . . . I heard that Tania's body will be released soon. Does that mean it's all over?'

Jack said that the police station grapevine was nowhere near as efficient as the hospital one, so maybe she could ask Sofia and then let him know!

*　　*　　*

Lyle stood in front of his DCI with his hands in his pockets, trying his very best not to look uneasy. His DCI was a middle-aged go-getter who was all about the clear-up rate of his team. He sat slouched in his chair, tapping at his keyboard and with an irritated frown as Lyle explained himself.

'In the process of crossing the ts and dotting the is, I came across something in the father's background. In the mid-nineties, he was investigated in-house and cleared of supplying drugs to medical students. His senior consultant at the time was a man by the name of Jasper Filpin. He moved Wetlock sideways to another hospital and buried the internal investigation records. Filpin's name came up twice more in the following four years in glowing references, which allowed Wetlock to be promoted on from one hospital to another. Filpin's long retired and won't lie for Wetlock now, sir. Then there's the rectal diazepam. Tania couldn't have self-administered.' Lyle then paused, waiting for the information to sink in. 'Someone else was with Tania Wetlock within minutes of her dying.'

The DCI didn't congratulate Lyle for going the extra mile. Instead, he began barking orders about making the victim's flat a crime scene and getting round there before the cleaners destroyed any missed evidence.

'I did that as soon as I knew something was amiss, sir. I found the wrapping from the rectal diazepam. That's with forensics. I'm confident they'll find the fingerprints of Dr Elliot Wetlock.'

Lyle's DCI was at a loss. He couldn't snaffle victory or kudos at the last moment, as both clearly belonged to Lyle. All he could do was congratulate his young detective on a job well done.

*   *   *

Jack gazed out of his small office window, down at the pea-green Nissan parked on the driveway. Hannah was sitting on Maggie's knee, yanking the steering wheel left and right, and screaming – he could hear her through the triple glazing. And Penny was walking around the outside of the car, kicking the tyres like she knew what she was doing. Jack let out a sigh so deep and long that he steamed up the window. It was possibly the most horrible car he'd ever seen.

On the desk behind Jack was a laptop, open on a page for Ryanair. Later that night, Jack planned to first of all agree to buying the Nissan, and then he'd ask Maggie if she wanted to go to Ireland for a couple of days before he returned to work. Jack knew that she wouldn't be able to, due to covering for the absent Wetlock, and he also knew that she'd give her blessing for him to go alone. He would reluctantly agree, and the trip would sound like her idea in the first place.

Jack didn't know for sure whether Adam Border was in Ireland, but he was going to find out.

CHAPTER 39

Jack and Maggie had promised each other that their first venture back out into the wider world beyond the pandemic would be their honeymoon. Yet here he was, flying to Dublin to get closure on a murder case, whilst she was working overtime to cover for her absent surgeon boss.

Once Jack had landed, he went straight to collect his hire car. He'd asked for a Mercedes Jeep which they didn't have, so he settled for a BMW M3. He knew that by the time he got home, Maggie would have purchased the horrendous pea-green Nissan, so he'd decided that he owed it to himself to at least spend his short time in Ireland driving something nice.

Jack headed straight for the red-brick council building, where he used his police ID to get some help searching local births, deaths and marriage records to find out if Avril Summers had married anyone else before Frederick Jenkins.

He knew that Adam Border was around 35 now and he also knew that Adam was around five or six when Avril was in Dublin. So, if she had quietly married here, it would have been between 1992 and 1994. Jack was left alone at an archive computer, with instructions on how the system worked. Two and a half hours later, he found what he was looking for. In the spring of 1994, Avril Summers married Shaun Joseph Donal Border.

Jack was then sent from one department to another in order to find an address to go with the name. Shaun Border, it eventually turned out, was the part-owner of a building company in Sandymount, two and a half miles south of Dublin. He suffered a back injury at work when he was in his thirties and was forced to sell his business and start claiming benefits. He was also paid compensation for his injuries. He'd been registered with various benefit offices from Cork to Killarney, which is where his death was registered in 2002. There was no record of Shaun and Avril getting divorced, which meant that Terence might well be back at the top of the list to inherit all of Avril's estate. Jack searched for a short while longer and found a nephew for Shaun Border. Seamus was still in Ireland, running a dairy farm in Cork.

Jack drove for just under three hours along the M7, then the M8 towards the Border Dairy Farm. It was a small, family-run business working out of a large house with several attached barns and sur-rounding fields, accessed via a long, well-maintained gravel path just wide enough for two cars to pass.

Jack parked in front of the impressive four-storey house, next to a quad bike. There were large, cracked plant pots boasting fabu-lous looking grasses on either side of the wide front door which was opened by a woman wearing dark green wellington boots over blue jeans, and a cotton floral shirt stretched tight over her heavily pregnant stomach. One hand leant on the thick wooden door frame and the other pushed into the small of her back, trying for a more comfortable position.

Jack asked if it was possible for him to speak with Seamus and she gave him the option of walking around the outside of the house via an uneven footpath full of potholes containing muddy rainwater, or driving back down to the road, taking the first left and heading around the outside of the house that way. Jack chose to drive.

Within minutes, Jack was regretting his decision because of the mud that was being thrown up onto the back window of his hire car from the rear tyres. The noise of stones hitting the underside was also concerning, as he envisaged not getting his deposit back.

In the distance, Seamus was waiting outside an enormous milking shed, hands on hips, watching Jack's BMW bounce over the uneven ground. He was a large man with broad shoulders beneath his old rollneck sweater.

Jack parked short of the milkshed, for fear of totally ruining the BMW's suspension by driving any further. As he stepped down into the mud, Seamus spoke first. 'Kathleen said you wanted to speak to me.' He had a broad Cork accent.

'My name's Jack Warr, Mr Border. I'm a DS from the Met in London.' Jack walked towards Seamus with his hand extended and his eyes on the ground, carefully avoiding mud puddles and cow pats. Seamus, who was less concerned with where he stood, strode forwards, his broad hand swamping Jack's as he shook it hard and corrected Jack's assumption that his name was Border. He was a Benton; his mother's maiden name was Border. Seamus then led the way into a lean-to office which contained nothing more than a desk and a chair. Seamus perched on the desk and gestured for Jack to sit. Jack chose to remain standing. 'I'm trying to locate Adam Border. I have some good news for him.'

'I don't know what I can tell you. I've not seen Adam in years. And not properly since school. Last time was, more than twelve years ago? Something like that. What's the good news?'

Jack said that he'd need to speak to Adam before anyone else, then casually asked Seamus to elaborate on family history, in the hope of stumbling across a clue as to where he might be now.

'His mother married my uncle Shaun. Patience of a saint, that man . . . which was lucky because Adam's mammy was a bloody battle-axe of a woman; I mean, she was good-looking, but a right handful. My uncle Shaun was very kind to Adam, giving him his name and all, so he'd not feel unwanted. I know Adam had spent the first five years of his life in Amsterdam with his da, so he was wiser than me, you know. I've been nowhere. As we grew up, he'd come and go with his real da, and sometimes she'd bring another man and take him away, and once he was left in some airport on his own, and Shaun had to collect him. He also spent time in Germany with I-don't-know-who, but he said it was his favourite place. Anyways the bitch Avril was long gone by the time he was a teen. He didn't seem to care, but never getting so much as a birthday card from your mammy has to sting.'

Jack nodded his agreement and Seamus continued. 'Adam was lucky to have Shaun, and, after the work accident, Uncle Shaun was lucky to have Adam. He did the heavy lifting and they both lived off the compensation, but there was friction between Shaun and my family, and you know he had to sell up at a loss. Shaun was forever getting cheques she was cashing, draining every cent he'd got left. My da said it was fraud and Uncle Shaun should get the cops onto her, but he wouldn't, and it was a big falling-out. I think Adam was with him until the end, then like his mammy he disappeared abroad. Anyways, we never seen or heard from him since.'

He sighed shaking his head. 'I can take a guess at what the good news might be . . . his mammy finally do the decent thing and die?'

* * *

As Jack was about to head back to his now-filthy hire car, disappointed that he'd had a wasted journey, Kathleen appeared around the side of the house. She was carrying a flask of tea and a Tupperware box filled with sandwiches for Seamus' lunch.

Jack shouted a thank you in her direction and she asked if he'd got what he came for. By Jack's polite but lacklustre reply, it was clear that he hadn't. Seamus joined Kathleen and apologised for not being very helpful.

'I told him we'd not seen Adam in such a long time, twelve or more years.'

'What about our Rachel's wedding? Remember?' Kathleen's words made Jack pause. 'My sister's eldest, Rachel, married an optician in Killarney back in April last year. I was driving out of the hotel car park when I saw a guy on a motorbike heading in the opposite direction. I swear on Seamus' mam's life that it was Adam.'

'Meaning she's not sure,' Seamus clarified.

Cork to Killarney was just over an hour's drive along the N22. As Jack drove, he called the Victoria House Hotel and booked himself in for the night. He'd selected a decent place to stay because – if it was as nice as it looked on the website – he'd suggest it to Maggie for their belated honeymoon. It was allegedly one mile from the town centre, overlooked a national park and had fabulous-looking suites. Tonight, Jack was staying in one of their 'Cosy Rooms', which he interpreted as 'small'. But that was fine for him on his own.

As he made his way through the luscious green farmland, he couldn't help but wonder if he was now on a fool's errand. He'd become obsessed with tracking this elusive man yet, if he was honest, it was based on nothing that would stand up in court.

Jack arrived at the Victoria House Hotel at 3 p.m., just in time to be allowed to check in. The concierge was shocked when she saw Jack enter carrying one small, tatty black rucksack and splattered in mud from his knees down – but the BMW M3 humming outside the main door waiting to be valet-parked allayed her fears. Once he'd signed in and left his card details, he was directed to his room. Jack looked through various leaflets for local attractions that had been left on the dresser, then FaceTimed Maggie. She was sitting in the staff room on DeBakey Ward, with her trainers off and her stockinged feet propped on top of the radiator. Jack held up a leaflet for Lough Leane in Killarney National Park so that Maggie could see the photographs.

She let out a long moan. 'That looks amazing. I'm desperate to get away, Jack.'

'It's a beautiful part of the country, Mags.' Jack held up more leaflets. 'Ross Castle. That's right on the edge of Lough Leane. A puffin colony? You fancy that?' Jack grinned, expecting Maggie to mock the idea of puffins being a tourist attraction at all. But she screeched, clapped her hands and said that she'd love to sit and watch puffins pottering about on the cliffside. 'Bloody hell, Mags. You really do need a break!'

Jack then held up a leaflet advertising the staggeringly beautiful Killarney beach and Maggie audibly gasped. Jack's trip to Ireland had suddenly been worth every second. His eyes then moved from Maggie's captivated gaze to the reverse side of the leaflet she was looking at: in the bottom left-hand corner was a hand-drawn picture of a hemp leaf, with a smiley face, doing a double thumbs-up.

'Promise we'll do it, Jack.' Maggie's words regained Jack's attention. He promised he'd definitely take her on honeymoon to Ireland if that's what she wanted. Then, with perfect timing, Maggie's tea break was over, leaving Jack free to find out where the hemp symbol might have come from.

From the hotel bar, Jack watched the staff come and go. He was trying to identify who might be most likely to be involved in the local drug scene. Halfway through his second cappuccino, Jack saw a young porter talking to a chambermaid. He strode over, flashed his Met ID badge and showed them the cartoon hemp leaf.

'There's a gang operating in this area, targeting hemp farms. Have you heard of anyone losing crops to thieves?'

The porter didn't seem to know or care too much, but the chambermaid was outraged by the audacity of it all. She 'fucking hated thieves' and was eager for Jack to make sure that her friend's farm, not five miles down the road, hadn't fallen victim. Jack got accurate directions and assured her that he'd make sure her friend was safe.

* * *

As Maggie tied the laces on her trainers and walked back out onto the main ward, she noticed four suited men standing in the reception area, one of whom she recognised as DC Lyle. He looked different to how she remembered him – authoritative and rather serious, which gave him a rather attractive air of mystery which she'd never imagined he could possess. He looked like a man not to be taken lightly. As they passed and nodded to each other, Maggie realised he reminded her of Jack two years ago.

CHAPTER 40

Ridley was wrapping up for the evening, after spending all afternoon preparing his team for tomorrow's onslaught when they were expecting thirteen prisoners to be transferred from the Drug Squad to be interviewed. Some of the prisoners had already been charged with drug offences, from importation to mixing, to distribution; and some were addicts who, after giving evidence against the drugs gang, had been charged with nothing.

However, some of them had admitted to being taken to Avril Jenkins' home at one time or another, and so needed to be interviewed by Ridley's team. And they still had a thick file of unidentified fingerprints. He wanted to make absolutely certain that they had all the evidence possible against the two men they had in custody for Avril's murder. He needed to work out if they were Alpha, Beta or Gamma; and he was, of course, still looking for the third member of the trio. It was going to be a long and exhausting couple of weeks.

Anik was coordinating the transfers and the logistics of detaining so many suspects. Those who'd been charged would wait in cells and those who hadn't would be held in the canteen under police supervision until it was their turn to be interviewed. Anik was liaising with Moley and – as far as Ridley could make out – neither of them was using the time strictly for talking about the job at hand. In fact, Ridley distinctly heard Anik use the words 'Rainbow Six Siege' which he knew was an online multiplayer game. Ridley called Anik into his office and asked to see the interview list.

'I've put me and you down to interview the higher-ups from 9 a.m. tomorrow, if that's OK, sir. Me, because I've been through all the hidden security footage we had from the house so I might be able to pick out any lies. And you, because Jack's in Ireland.'

Ridley remained motionless. His fingers tightened around Anik's newly printed interview schedule.

'Remind me why Jack's in Ireland tomorrow.'

By the forced calm in Ridley's voice, Anik instantly knew that Ridley hadn't known about the trip. He quickly stuttered an explanation about Jack still being on leave, so he'd taken the opportunity to go to Ireland and check out honeymoon venues. He also made certain that Ridley knew this was all second-hand information from Laura. Within thirty seconds, Anik had scurried out of Ridley's office and Laura was now the one in the firing line.

'I think he just needed some downtime, sir. Tania Wetlock when she was alive was enough of a threat to his career, but now she's dead he could end up being sacked or even arrested.'

'I know all that. I'm asking why he's in Ireland. And don't tell me he's checking out honeymoon venues. Ireland is one of many onward destinations for the drugs. Ireland is one of Michael Mahoney's hideouts. We also know Ireland forms a part – no matter how small – of Avril Jenkins' past. So, Laura, correct me if I'm wrong . . . but, after being told by Hammersmith CID not to leave the country, Jack is now over there attempting to track down Adam bloody Border.'

Ridley stormed back into his office as his desk phone rang. He snatched it up. It was Steve Lewis and before Ridley could speak, he launched into an angry tirade about bringing in Michael Mahoney. He had a team waiting at Heathrow but there had been flight cancellations and it was costing a fortune to retain the armed guards and transport to bring him directly to the Drug Squad. He also complained that before they had even seen him, let alone questioned him, there were calls from his legal team demanding immediate access.

'I know he must be aware of all the arrests we've made, so he must be shitting himself, but I won't allow any fucking bigwig lawyer to get their hands on him before I have him.'

Ridley let Steve continue his frustrated vent before he interrupted to say that with all the arrests the Drug Squad had passed on to his team, they were stretched to the limit. He also said that they had not yet uncovered which of the suspects in custody had murdered Avril Jenkins. 'Which, obviously, Steve is our priority, not the transporting of Michael Mahoney – but thank you for the update.'

Ridley slammed the phone down before Steve could reply and picked up his mobile.

*　*　*

Jack's mobile silently vibrated on the bar table next to him.

He could just make out Ridley's name on the screen, half obscured by the glare from the setting sun. He sipped on a sixteen-year-old Bushmills and watched the sky changing colour. If Jack answered his mobile, Ridley would probably order him to come home, which Jack would refuse to do. So, he opted to ignore Ridley's call. Less than thirty seconds later, his mobile let out a single buzz indicating that Ridley had left a voicemail:

'*I presume the Garda don't know you're there? Be smart, be subtle and be careful. If you get caught on the wrong side of the line, either by the police over there, or by Hammersmith over here, I can't help you. If you succeed in finding Adam Border and you need backup, you call me, understand – no one else. Anytime. I'll send the cavalry. Again.*'

Jack smiled as he listened to Ridley's message for a second and third time. Not because it was surprisingly supportive, but because he sounded exactly like his old self.

The mattress in Jack's Cosy Bedroom was so soft that it was impossible to roll over. He'd slept like a starfish all night and woke more refreshed than he ever did at home. But the price of sleeping alone was too high: he missed Maggie.

* * *

Over a full Irish breakfast, Jack googled what he could about hemp farms in Ireland. There were several articles in the regional and national press about the Garda raiding small holdings and farm buildings. And there was a recent interview with a local MP who promised a crackdown on the sale of CBD products manufactured in Ireland. This interview was printed in one small column, on page three of the local newspaper; whereas the opposing view-point supporting making the production of CBD oil legal to be used medically to counteract pain, anxiety, inflammation and sei-zures, was front-page news for two days running, with numerous hemp farmers insisting that the plant thrives in Irish soil, aids the economy and helps reduce climate change. Oppositional quotes from the Department of Health reiterated that CBD products con-taining THC were illegal. The current legislation was strict and anyone growing hemp without the correct licencing could face prosecution.

Jack was fed, showered, dressed and back in his hired BMW before half past eight. The rain started after ten minutes of driving, so torrential it made visibility poor, and the noise of rain on the sun-roof was alarming. After another ten minutes, the rain stopped, and the sun came out. And the rainbow that followed was truly magical.

As Jack drove through a small village, he saw a dark blue mini-bus, showing no vehicle livery, stranded in a ditch at the side of the road. A burly man, wearing a tweed coat and cap, had his face out of the driver's window and was smoking a rollup. Jack pulled up alongside to check if he'd broken down and needed help.

'You offerin' to tow me out in your hired BMW, are ya?' Jack immediately saw the futility of his offer. 'I know I look stuck. But that's on account of the Garda. If they come along saying I'm not allowed to stop here for a smoke, I'll tell 'em the rain drove me off the road. How come you're out this way? You lost?'

'I'm here on business,' Jack lied. He couldn't introduce himself as a policeman from England because he was fairly certain from the faint aroma that the rollup was actually a spliff. Jack nodded knowingly to the dog-end between the man's lips. 'My mate buys his baccy from somewhere round here. Adam Border. You know him?'

For a second, the driver said nothing whilst he sized Jack up. Then he started his engine. 'Oh, I definitely think you're lost, my friend. I'd go back the way you came if I were you.' He drove off, coughing a plume of black smoke from his exhaust as the bus heaved itself out of the ditch. After a moment, Jack followed.

The roads were narrow and winding, so Jack frequently lost sight of the tweeded bus driver. As the rain came down again, he slowed to give way on a single-track humped-back bridge and, when he emerged on the other side, the blue bus was gone. He put his foot down but after a couple of minutes he still couldn't see it. Jack pursed his lips, furious with himself for mentioning Adam's name and spooking the bus driver.

Jack decided to head back to the village and start again trying to locate the hemp farms. He checked his rear-view mirror before pulling into a layby – and suddenly there was the dark blue bus, closing in fast. Not wanting to be challenged in a layby in the middle of nowhere, Jack quickly pulled back out onto the road and sped off.

Soon he came to a crossroads with a sign pointing back to Killarney. Perfect. He'd get back to civilisation, where he'd be more than happy to challenge the driver of the bus that was currently still hot on his tail. But Jack's move towards the Killarney turn-off was pre-empted and the bus cut him off, forcing him onto a single-track road. If anything came in the other direction now, it would be a head-on disaster. The bus sped up, forcing Jack to do the same.

Jack was now doing 40 mph around hairpin bends without a clue what might be coming the other way. He had to find a turn-off. Up ahead, beyond the roadside hedges to the left, Jack could see a farm building and realised there must also be a track leading to it. Jack sped up, skidding into the dirt track at 60 mph, sending a spray of loose pebbles into the path of the following bus. Jack spun the beautifully responsive BMW into a tight handbrake turn and ended up facing the road he'd just turned off. The blue bus slowly came into view. It was now stationary and, by the time Jack realised that the driver was no longer inside, it was too late.

The crowbar shattered the BMW's passenger window, forcing Jack to escape via the driver's door. A voice shouted, 'Why's an English businessman following me down country lanes? Which side of the law are you on, asking about Adam Border?'

Now that the tweed-clad bus driver was out of his cab, Jack could see that he was built like a hard-working farmer should be. Add the crowbar into the mix and Jack was most certainly on the back foot. Jack could now read the name badge sewn into the man's jacket. 'I'm nothing to do with the police, Greg,' Jack shouted back. 'I'm looking for Adam because I have some news for him. That's all.'

'Well, you can tell me, and I'll pass it on. How's that?'

'No. I need to see him for myself. I have news for Adam, good news. Connected to his family. You can check with a guy called Jason Marks if you like. He knows about it.' Jack threw the name of Jason Marks into the mix hoping it would establish a connection in Greg's mind between Jack and Adam. And, if the name meant nothing, then no harm done.

Greg got an old flip phone from his pocket. He stepped away from Jack and placed a call.

The rain came down again and Jack started shivering in the icy deluge. Greg, who was more hardened to the weather, didn't flinch. Finally, Greg closed his mobile and put it back into his pocket. 'Follow me.'

Greg's bus snaked effortlessly along back roads and narrow lanes while Jack, following closely behind, constantly dodged potholes and dried-out tractor ridges to avoid ruining his suspension or ending up in a ditch. A chill wind filled the car through the broken window, making Jack's wet clothes stick to his body.

They drove deeper into the countryside, passing dairy farms and smallholdings. Eventually, Greg pulled up outside a five-barred gate with thick hedgerows on either side.

Jack had no clue where he was. He pulled up a short way back from Greg's bus, leaving enough room between them to pull out and drive away if he began to feel any more unsafe than he already did.

Greg got out of the bus, opened the gate, walked to Jack's car and spoke through the broken passenger window. 'Follow the track till it splits. Then go left. Close this gate behind you.' He then got back into the bus and used the gap Jack had left between them to reverse and drive away.

Jack sat in his hired BMW with the broken side window, looking along the dirt track ahead of him. He knew once the gate closed behind him, he was on his own. Jack checked his mobile – no signal. Every ounce of common sense was telling him to drive away.

* * *

The dirt track was a network of deep tyre tracks that were impossible to avoid, so Jack drove, slowly. In his rear-view mirror, the closed gate got smaller until it finally disappeared out of sight.

The road forked and Jack turned left, as he'd been instructed. A few seconds later he saw a hand-painted wooden sign which read STUDIO. Then the track disappeared completely and was replaced by a steep but walkable path. Jack got out and started to follow it.

He trudged on, past thick hedges separating him from the lush fields beyond. After fifteen minutes of arduous walking, a slate-roofed bungalow gradually appeared.

Jack saw a quad bike and a motor bike were parked next to each other down the side of the building beneath a lean-to shelter, while an old army Jeep was parked around the rear wall.

Jack walked to the front door, again checking his mobile for a signal. Nothing. But he'd come too far to turn back now. His heart pounded in his chest. He'd made the assumption that Greg had led him to the home of the elusive Adam Border, but he'd only know for sure when he got inside.

There was no answer after the first knock, nor after the second. So Jack tried the black iron latch. It lifted with ease and the heavy wooden door pushed open. Immediately beyond the door was a polished pine wood floor.

Jack wiped his shoes on the grass, removing as much mud as he could, then ventured inside.

There were several doors leading off the hallway, but one in particular caught his eye. It was a double sliding door, slightly open, with a light shining from inside. He slid the door wide to reveal a vast room with dozens of paintings stacked along the walls. In the centre of the room was a large easel on a square of paint-splattered rubber, holding a big canvas draped in muslin. A small wooden table held a wooden tray of oil paints, brushes, glues, turps and a water jar. There was a worn, plum-velvet sofa, and two leather chairs placed within the bounds of a large Mexican-style rug. The rain rolled down the tall windows and – even as the dark clouds were forming outside – this room still looked magically bright and airy.

Jack heard footsteps behind him. He spun quickly to see a man standing between the open double doors, and instantly Jack knew he was finally face to face with Adam Border.

CHAPTER 41

Adam Border was a tall, slender man with long reddish-blond hair tied in a ponytail with a leather cord. He was dressed in jeans and a black sweater, and had fine gold bracelets on both wrists. He didn't look particularly like any of the photographs Jack had seen of him, but he did look like the sketch provided by Henrick Chi.

The men stared at each other, each waiting for the other to speak first.

Eventually Jack broke the silence. 'I've been looking for you for quite some time. It is Adam Border, isn't it?'

Adam gestured to the two leather chairs sitting about a foot apart on the Mexican rug, then sat down himself in one of them.

Jack had so much to say and so much to ask. But he had to be careful and steady, because there was still the possibility that this enigmatic man sitting opposite him could be an integral cog in a huge drug-trafficking machine and, possibly even a murderer. Jack chose to start by asking about Jessica Chi.

Adam spoke very quietly. The tone of his voice was soft and Irish, with a slight European lilt. He took his time, as though choosing his words very carefully. 'I read about her death in the papers. An accident, wasn't it? I assume you're a policeman.'

Jack saw no reason to hide the fact and nodded.

'I cared for Jessica very much. She was damaged . . . I seem to attract damaged people. Or maybe they attract me. She was clean when we met but relapsed over time. When that happened, I'm afraid to say that I walked away. I've learnt over the years that if I don't protect myself, then I'm of no use to anyone. Truthfully, I was very sad to read about Jessica . . . and my mother.' Jack could tell that Adam's sadness for Jessica was genuine, whereas his mention of Avril sounded very much like an empty afterthought. 'I don't know your name.'

'DS Jack Warr. I knew your mother briefly, when . . .' Jack realised that he didn't know how to end his sentence, other than by saying, *When I was investigating your thefts, psychological torment and death threat*, but that might have put an end to their so-far amicable chat, so he left the sentence unfinished. 'There's been a lot of speculation around your relationship with your mother. Lots of gaps. Would you mind helping me to fill them in?'

Adam laced his fingers on his lap, 'I bet you've heard that she was an eccentric, yet somehow loveable type. A free spirit who comes and goes on the wind, bringing fun and mayhem before drifting off into the sunset again. Until next time. That's all lovely, unless you're a five-year-old boy.' Adam gave a hefty sigh before he continued. 'I was left with various men who she'd married, lived with or just screwed. That, in her mind, meant they were obliged to show some sort of parental responsibility towards me which, to be fair, most reluctantly did. Others didn't. Mainly I lived in Amsterdam with my actual father, in Leeds with my grandparents, or in various places with her and her lovers. Until she came here and met Shaun.' Adam smiled. 'It seems you're familiar with all of the names I've said so far. You really have been looking for me for a long time.'

'Your name seemed to change quite a few times. That made it hard to track you,' Jack said with a smile of his own.

'Well, bloody well done for finding your way here. Do you want me to carry on with the family history?'

Jack said that he did.

'OK, my mother stole everything from Shaun that wasn't screwed down and vanished back to the UK, leaving me behind.

It was the only good thing she ever did for me. Shaun was the best father I've known, and he eventually gave me his name, so I'd feel like I belonged. And I did. For a time. I was fifteen when he died. I could have stayed here but by then I was ready to start life on my own. I went to London with the aim of going to art college. I needed a parent or guardian to sign some papers for that, so I had to detour through Leeds to track down my mother. My grandparents had died, but my uncle – her brother – well, he was no help on account of his psychological problems. She was horrified to see me. She launched into an explanation about her current man not wanting someone else's kid in tow. She was relieved to hear that I only wanted her signature. I think she must have felt guilty for being quite so harsh, because she gave me some money and the name of a friend who was renting out rooms. That's when I knew that her new man was rich. The next chapter of my life started when I began lodging with Hester Mancroft and Julian in Chelsea. You know about this?'

'From Hester, yes. But it'd be good to hear your version.'

'She's almost as idiotic as Avril, don't you think? I expect you can't answer that, being a policeman. Anyway . . .'

Adam turned away frowning, then he sighed, as if he felt some kind of pain in his soul. After a moment he continued. 'Her son Julian was another damaged person. Self-inflicted. Julian and I were inseparable for a time. As well as college, living and studying together. But when I quit, he sort of followed me, and we travelled through Amsterdam and lived in Germany. I can't remember the year, but he had to come home when Hester ran out of money and needed his help to sell the place in Chelsea. He OD'd – I presume you know that.'

Jack nodded without elaborating, as he didn't want to break the flow of Adam's recollections. As Adam filled in all of the gaps in the story so far, Jack was enthralled by his quietly engaging manner. With every moment that passed, Jack hoped more and more that Adam had done nothing at all illegal.

'After two or three years in Germany, I moved back to Amsterdam. By this time, I'd met Jessica. Her parents – well, her father anyway – was on the art scene. And while I was getting my life in order in Europe, my mother was doing the same in the UK by marrying the poor, oblivious millionaire, Frederick Jenkins.' Adam uncrossed his legs and sat forwards with his elbows on his knees. 'Here's something I bet you don't know, Jack. My father, Andre Erik Boogaard, was still married to my mother because she couldn't find him to divorce him.' Adam sat back, laughing. He rested his elbows on the arms of the leather chair and pressed the tips of his long artist's fingers together. 'Has he passed, do you know?'

Jack confirmed that, during their investigations, they had found a death certificate for Adam's biological father.

Adam's mobile rang and without a word he got up and left the room. Jack checked his own mobile again: now he was indoors he had a three-bar signal which was a huge relief. Jack reminded himself that this eloquent, charming man could be a heartless psychopath. Jack was alone with him, far from civilisation, with no backup. And at that moment he had no idea what Adam was doing.

Jack got up and wandered the room browsing the stacks of paintings, ornate empty frames, and the huge range of art materials. Then he spotted something that caught his eye: a silver picture frame containing a wedding photograph of Avril and Frederick.

'Why should she have fond memories when I have none?'

Adam was holding two ice cold beers. He handed one to Jack and retook his seat. Jack was desperate to know who Adam had just been talking to. Had Greg called to check that he was all right and was he now on his way, crowbar in hand? As Adam drank his beer, Jack asked about the artwork that surrounded them.

'A hobby. Buying and selling. Freddy could be a vicious, belligerent old bastard, but he was an exceptional collector. He'd not share his treasures, though; instead, he hid them away in his secret chamber so that he – and only he – could sit there, with his dick in his hand, enjoying them. My mother had no notion of their value or of the importance of their carefully documented provenance. She had money, jewellery and a fine house, but no brains to speak of. I felt sorry for her in a way: her dream of being cared for by a rich, respectable man and therefore being accepted into polite society, never happened. Jenkins mocked her ignorance, showed her little love and made her deeply unhappy. She gave up all of her friends for him, and yet was never lonelier than when she was living in that huge house behind iron gates.'

Adam laughed as he took a swig of beer before continuing.

'My mother suddenly needed me. After years of keeping me a dirty secret, she finally needed me. Well, that's not exactly true. What she needed was a gardener. Freddie after a few years began suffering with arthritis in his knees and the house had become a burden. God, how I wanted to reject her like she'd rejected me. But the truth was, she paid me to stay. She gave me money and a car, and all I had to do was not reveal that I was her son.' Adam looked away and emptied his bottle. 'Anyway, I expect that's about where you came in, isn't it?'

Jack decided there was no reason to delay the inevitable tricky conversation. 'Who grew the cannabis in the greenhouse?'

'Why are you here, DS Warr? Greg said you had good news for me, and I'm trying to figure out what that could be. Is it that you're looking to make an arrest for the cultivation of a class B drug?'

'If I was here to arrest you for growing cannabis, I'd have sent the local Garda,' Jack said.

'In that case, yes, I grew it. Her greenhouse was brimming with weeds and dead plants. I made better use of it. I can sell CBD oil in your country, but I can't grow the raw ingredients. I learnt how to grow the stuff out here, so I knew her greenhouse would be perfect. It was a modest enterprise.'

Adam stood sharply, as though he'd just remembered that he had to be somewhere. Jack's fingers tightened around his half-full beer bottle. 'Another?'

Jack declined, knowing full well that he shouldn't really have accepted the first. Adam popped out of the room to fetch himself a second beer. He shouted from elsewhere in the studio, 'Avril was grateful to have a little spending money of her own and Freddie, as time ticked by, was grateful to live and eventually die pain-free.'

Adam returned, beer in hand and returned to his seat. 'The cellar gallery became a neat space for bottling the CBD oil and, as money ebbed and flowed with crop cycles, whenever we were short of ready cash Avril started selling off the odd painting. She had no idea of the price of anything, of course.'

Adam went on to explain that after the first successful crop, he started shipping the CBD oil to Amsterdam and Germany – while, at around the same time, Avril had engaged the services of Jason Marks to value and sell some of the paintings. Between them, they were earning enough to pay off Freddie's eyewatering investment debts and maintain the house. Just.

'We started making enough money from the cannabis alone, so I wanted her to stop selling paintings. But Jason was taking advantage of her ignorance. That's when I started shipping them over here, out of harm's way.'

'You were stealing from her?'

'I was preserving history.' Jack's gaze swept around all of the artworks stacked against the walls. 'She didn't know what I'd taken or what she'd sold. She'd become more interested in the cannabis side of things. She went to California to stay with her brother-in-law, and I had the brief freedom to move more and more artworks, but then she came back with some grand ideas she'd learnt from some professional stoners out there. She wanted the enterprise to become, as she put it, "a fuckin' empire".' Adam stood, and as he walked across to the door he took a packet of cigarettes from his pocket. 'The smoke damages the canvas.' Then he disappeared outside, giving Jack no option but to join him.

The countryside surrounding the studio was truly stunning. Jack had never seen grass as green, or fields as rolling. Roads snaked through the landscape and over the horizon, urging you to follow.

Adam inhaled the smoke and let it drift from his nostrils. 'A year or so ago, I came back from Ireland and she'd been to a funeral in Solihull, where she'd met an old school friend.' Adam's speech was now slower and he seemed more tense. 'This friend said he could help her grow her business. Tenfold, was the word he used.' Adam shook his head and took a long drag on his cigarette. 'I warned her.'

Jack speculated on the identity of Avril's old schoolfriend. 'Mahoney?'

Adam claimed that to begin with he had not known how big a player Mahoney was, although he instinctively knew that he was too big for Avril. 'He was a smooth, two-faced bastard of a man, but like my mother he had gained some kind of veneer of sophistication. She was very enamoured, and he played her like a gigolo – he might have even fucked her to keep her sweet. I could see stuff going on, his so-called helpers coming and going in trucks. I tried to persuade her not to get involved, but she was too stupid to listen, so I eventually left her to it.'

'You kept going back for the paintings, though?'

Adam tipped his head skywards and laughed out a plume of smoke. 'I went back for the paintings, yes. And the frames. And the equipment. And the provenance.' He laughed again. 'And the odd curveball to keep her guessing. Like fairy duvet sets. I even put a couple of ornaments in her dishwasher once. She was a greedy bitch, greedy and stupid. But I knew she was growing scared of him, which made it even easier for me.'

The lifelong animosity Adam felt towards his own mother was deep-rooted and impossible to hide.

'Your turn, DS Warr. Why are you here?'

'She left everything to you,' Jack said. 'She made a second will. In the end, she did right by you. The house and contents are yours.'

Adam barked out another sudden laugh. 'Whatever will has been found is illegal. You need to be aware that only Freddie's is legitimate. She was a bigamist, and she had a pre-existing child – me. Being a criminal and being a whore were both clauses that would exclude her in his will. I know because he told me. Towards the end he hated her. She should have got nothing. So, it's not mine, it's Terence's. Give it to him.'

A momentary quietness descended. The men looked out across the landscape and seemed to share a serenity regarding Adam's decision as it brought a certain closure. During the silence, Jack replayed the last hour of conversation. At best, he'd expected to hear a confession about the cannabis, but the theft of the artworks ... that had come as a surprise. Jack watched Adam take the final couple of drags on his cigarette and stamp it out. Jack had to take control now. It was time to go.

'Let's go back inside, Adam.' Jack didn't want to appear challenging, not yet. He needed backup first. He needed to get indoors so that he had a phone signal. And then he needed to quickly work out how the hell he was going to bring Adam in.

* * *

In London, the convoy bringing Michael Mahoney to the Drug Squad's main holding cell was making its way from Heathrow Airport. Two motorcycle out-riders were in front of the white covered transport vehicle, while inside were Mahoney and two armed response officers. Tailing them was a patrol car, carrying an array of Gucci suitcases owned by their prisoner. There had been a barrage of reporters held back at the airport, as they tried to locate and track the convoy: news of a major international drug dealer being arrested had spread fast.

* * *

Jack was becoming incredibly wary. Adam exuded a disarming confidence, even when he was confessing to a variety of class B offences. He behaved as if he was untouchable. Maybe he was? Maybe Greg was just seconds away? Adam made no attempt to head back inside.

'Don't let's spoil things yet, Jack. I've got so much more to tell you.' Jack tried not to flinch for fear of Adam sensing his discomfort.

Adam perched on a drystone wall indicating that he was going nowhere. 'I had this old campervan. Jessica travelled back and forth with me to Amsterdam, to catch up with her parents, have a bit of a holiday. She knew the reason for the trips, but she was just a passenger, literally and metaphorically. I know you can't hurt her now, but I'm very fond of her parents so . . . they know she made mistakes. She took the Rossetti. Jessica never had money, which didn't bother me but did bother her. She wanted to pay her way and all she could think of was to steal from an exceptionally easy target.'

'Sounds familiar.' The words left Jack's mouth before he could edit them.

'No, no, no, Jack. I didn't steal from Avril because it was easy, I stole because she didn't deserve to have nice things. She had so much in her life that she should have cherished and looked after and kept safe, but no!' Adam clearly included himself in that. 'She had to treat it all like shit. I didn't steal, I . . . rescued.' Adam stared at Jack, challenging him to argue. He didn't. Instead, Jack asked a question that steered Adam away from his hated mother.

'What happened to the Rossetti?'

Adam took a second to regain his composure. 'It was stupid of Jessica to show it to her father, but I guess she wanted it authenticated. When she told me what she'd done, we argued. She wanted to use the painting to start a new life together, but I wasn't ready to leave. I took it from her. That was the last time we saw each other.'

Until this moment, Jack had not known the fate of the Rossetti. But now Adam was admitting that it had been in his possession, at least for a time. Jack would need to know its current whereabouts eventually, of course, but for now, there was a more pressing question that he wanted answered. 'What did you mean, *I wasn't ready to leave*?'

Adam lit another cigarette and paused for a considerable length of time as he allowed the nicotine to calm him down.

'Freddie Jenkins had an astonishing, lifelong love of art, acquired from his father when he was just a child. So, his passion was sixty years in the making. Pair that with a callous disregard for provenance and you have one of the UK's most prolific collectors – and forgers – of works of art.'

Jack couldn't believe what he was hearing. During the investigation, he'd been made aware that some works of art in Avril's possession were forgeries, but not once did he imagine that Frederick was the one who had painted them. Maybe that was because Frederick was already dead? Maybe Jack had elevated Adam into the position of mastermind because it suited him better. After all, he couldn't chase a dead man.

Adam continued.

'As Freddie became weaker, he asked me to act as a runner for him. Collecting and delivering, to and from dealers and other collectors.' Adam folded his arms and smiled, as he remembered. 'I'd buy boxes of oils, inks, parchments. And I'd buy up worthless paintings, beautiful centuries-old frames, complete with all the original canvases and nails. Then he'd copy an old master, including the provenance, and sell it on. He was a fucking genius.'

Jack found Adam's tale fanciful. 'I find that hard to believe. I mean, are you telling me that Frederick Jenkins fooled Jason Marks? Fooled the art world?'

'For decades. Let me tell you a story, Jack. In 2007, Prince Charles rescued an eighteenth-century mansion in Scotland with a £20 million loan. Dumfries House. Charlie was a hero, and, over the years, millions of people came from across the globe to view the ever-changing art collections that were loaned out to adorn the walls of the principal gallery. Collectors were desperate for their work to be seen there. In 2017, Dumfries acquired another collection. Seventeen paintings. Among them works by Monet, Dali, Picasso, Chagall. Again, millions of art fans, critics, collectors, amateur enthusiasts came to view them and bask in their stunning beauty.' Adam beamed a huge grin.

'Fakes. Painted by a guy called Tony Tetro, on his kitchen table. And, as I recall, valued collectively in excess of £100 million. Stick provenance on the back of a frame dating from the same time period as the original was painted, and bingo. Provenance comes from the French *provenir*, meaning *to come from*. Provenance is the dealers' gospel. The art world isn't stupid, but it's slow. It takes expertise and lots of man hours to spot a fake and sometimes months or years to prove a fake. But when no one's even looking . . .' Adam shrugged. 'Fakes can hang for decades on Prince Charles' wall, with no one batting an eye. Some of the collectors Freddie sold to might have known and not cared, I suppose. I think Jason knew. But he was on a nice cut, so . . .'

'So, what did Freddie do with the originals?'

'Locked them away in his dungeon, so that only he could enjoy them. Like he did with all beautiful, exciting things. The fakes would be delivered to their destination rolled up in my campervan and hidden, along with flasks of cannabis oil, amongst bedding, camping equipment and tins of baked beans. It was a tangled web, Jack. Because whilst Freddie was off his face on cannabis, Avril took the odd painting from rooms all over the house and – behind her husband's back – asked Jason to sell it for her. So, sometimes Jason was being asked to quickly and clumsily sell paintings which he knew to be fake. He couldn't refuse Avril, or he'd be kicked out of the house and lose his golden goose, and he couldn't tell Freddie for the same reason.'

Adam shook his head with laughter. 'He sold a Degas and I think a Picasso for her. She was involving galleries and dealers very close to home. Jason must have been shitting himself.' Adam finally noticed that Jack was not laughing along with him. 'You can go inside and make your call if you like. I won't run.'

Jack stood up. 'Come inside with me, please, Adam.'

'Who'd win, do you think, Jack? If I resisted arrest.'

'I'd win.'

Adam shrugged at Jack's self-belief as though it was a façade. He was revelling in a confidence that Jack needed to challenge. Jack casually put his hand on his hip, letting his fingers slide into his back pocket and fish out a black cable tie which he always carried with him. Jack was just about to grab Adam unawares, cuff him and drag him indoors to call for backup when Adam spoke again. Deadly serious this time.

'I've told you a lot of secrets today, Jack. But I've got one more. And after I've told you, you're going to let me walk away.'

'Really? That good, is it?'

'It's the only thing you really want.' Jack knew that there was only one more secret left to tell. 'I want my freedom, Jack and, in return, I'll give you my mother's murderers.'

Jack's mind raced as he tried to work out if Adam was telling the truth or if this was all just a ploy to distract him. How the hell could Adam know who had murdered Avril?

Adam got to his feet, slid his hands into his pockets and surveyed the landscape before them. 'I can't go to prison. I'd not survive without beauty. Nature, art . . . they keep me alive. I sold the Rossetti in the US, you know. It bought Seamus's farm for him, bought me a nice castle in western Europe, and bought this place together with land enough for the hemp farm – I'm joking about the castle.' Adam turned to face Jack. 'It took me a long time to find my place in the world, but I think this is it. It's important to belong somewhere, wouldn't you agree?'

'How do you know who killed Avril?'

'Are you still searching yourself, Jack, or have you found your place?'

Then it dawned on Jack that there was only one way Adam could know who the killers were. Jack had to take a deep breath before he could speak. 'You have the missing CCTV footage!'

Adam nodded, smiling. 'Jack, the cellar was Frederick's, not Mahoney's. The CCTV was Frederick's, not Mahoney's.'

Jack couldn't believe they'd missed something so obvious. Michael Mahoney and his gang took over Avril's home. They found the cellar, they stacked their boxes of guns and grenades in front of the rusty old filing cabinets and never gave them a second thought.

Jack continued to think out loud. 'If you knew the CCTV footage locations, that's how you got in and out of her property.'

'Most of the time, I was already inside when she locked up for the night. I told you, she was stupid. Freddie became obsessed with monitoring every room in the house. The camera in the bathroom he used to observe the steaming of parchment paper to age it.'

'Did she know about the monitors in the cellar?'

'Of course not. She only knew where the external CCTV cameras were, at the front and back of the property. I even showed her how to watch those on the laptop she had, and when Mahoney took over I guess she could have showed him. But neither of them ever knew about or had access to any of the cameras on the inside of the house.' Adam smirked. 'Mahoney must have been spitting feathers when he stared to see one patrol car after another turning up.'

'All the calls to the local police were down to Avril being scared.'

'She was in so deep and had no clue how to make it stop. She was jeopardising everything.' Adam cocked his head to one side. 'I asked you a question, Jack. Are you still searching, or have you found your place?'

'No more talking, Adam. Back inside.' Jack was reeling. He needed to get control of the immediate situation, but he was also desperate to learn the identity of the sharp-suited man who'd arrived in a Jag on the night Avril was so brutally murdered. And if he believed what he had just been told, Adam knew who it was.

'Are you still searching or—' Adam pressed.

'I found my place!' Jack said angrily.

With that reply, Adam was back in control. He could see the yearning for justice in Jack's eyes. He could see the guilt, and he knew he could now toy with Jack and he'd have to play along for fear of losing this golden opportunity to finally do right by Avril.

'Why were you lost? Was it an errant parent, like me? Or were you the errant one?'

Jack sighed and gave a small shrug of his shoulders. 'A little of both.'

'Parents!' Adam boomed. 'Fuck 'em!' He took a huge breath in, held it, then released. When he spoke again he was quiet. Quiet but full of venom. 'Boogaard was decent when sober but a nasty drunk. She did that. She did that to all of them. I'd like to have known him properly but, the truth is, I'm not even sure if he was my father. I took his name and I do seem to have his enviable hairline, so who knows?'

Adam put his hands on his hips and began digging the toe of his boot into the soft, wet earth. He started to sound petulant. Childlike. 'Perhaps it was Wolfgang Beltracchi, a man she once met in Germany and lived with for a long time or perhaps it was Chi in Amsterdam. The moment she landed in a country, she started shagging the locals, so anything is possible. Perhaps an Irish "uncle" is not an uncle after all. Perhaps Terence Jenkins is not so squeaky clean in the fidelity department. She lived in London for years – who knows, Jack? We could be brothers.'

This was the first time Jack had sensed any kind of vulnerability in Adam. 'Biological parents aren't all they're cracked up to be,' he said. When Adam looked up, he was fighting back tears. Jack kept the connection going – partly to keep Adam from doing anything rash, and partly because he felt compelled to. Jack felt as if his brain was turning cartwheels. Regardless of the fact that Adam was a criminal and was withholding the identity of a killer, they had an undeniable connection. It was an unsettling thought.

'I never met my biological father,' Jack volunteered. 'But the more I found out about him, the less I wanted to know. He was a criminal and was murdered because of it.'

Adam's pupils dilated, replacing violet with black. He tilted his head to one side, listening, so Jack continued.

'He had no love for my biological mum, even though she adored the ground he walked on. I have no first-hand knowledge of either of them and I'm no worse off for that. My foster parents are the people I called Mum and Dad. They're the people whose name I proudly use and that, Adam Border, is all you need to know.'

Adam looked directly at Jack. 'Darkens the soul, though, doesn't it?' He walked forwards and placed his hand flat on Jack's chest. 'I can feel the scars each time I take that first breath of a new day. Right here. It reminds me that I'm damaged. But also, that I'm so much stronger for it.' Adam lowered his hand and stepped back from Jack. 'I'm ready to go inside now.'

In the corner of the studio was a stack of laptops. He opened the one on top. Adam clicked to open a blank email account – one that had never sent or received anything – and he handed the laptop to Jack. Then he opened his mobile phone. A couple of seconds later, an email pinged into the inbox on the laptop. There was no subject heading and no content, but there was a video file attached. Jack opened it.

Avril sat in the middle of the sofa in her front room. Her knees were clamped together, her fingers were clenched in her lap. Her body was pure tension. She was sobbing and looked petrified.

Jack recognised the sharp-suited man from the Jag standing over her. His collar was now down, but he had his back to the camera. The two men named by the Drug Squad as Alpha and Beta entered the room; both men were wearing navy forensic paper suits, with the hoods down – and they looked as if they were enjoying the show.

The man from the Jag bent at the waist and pushed his face towards Avril's. She brought her hands up in a vain attempt to protect herself and begged him not to hurt her. Jag turned slightly, put his finger to his lips and with sinister calm shushed her.

This was the moment that Jack saw his face for the first time. Jack's mind leapt back to watching the grainy bodycam footage of Michael Mahoney's arrest in Lithuania. Was it him? Jack couldn't be certain, but facial ID would be.

Avril immediately did as she was told. As she sat there with no way out of the nightmare, Jag kicked her ankles apart and stepped in between her splayed legs. He then hauled her to her feet by her hair.

He gestured for Alpha and Beta to take her. They stepped forwards, grabbed an arm each and lifted her off her feet. Avril was hysterical as she hopelessly struggled against them. Jag took a small plastic bag containing MDMA tablets from his pocket, tipping one out, and as his men held Avril tight, he forced her mouth open and pushed a tablet into her mouth, holding her nose and choking her to make her swallow.

Jack looked across at Adam – he had one earphone in and was playing a game on his mobile. It was clear to Jack that he'd seen this footage and had no desire to see it again. Jack turned back to the screen.

Jag was now by the fireplace, leaning on the mantel as though this house was his domain . . .

During the following minutes of silent footage, Jack noticed the floor of Avril's lounge looked somehow different from when he'd been there. It looked out-of-focus somehow. When he finally worked out why, he felt the bile build in his stomach and his skin turn cold.

The lounge floor was covered in plastic.

When he was ready, Jag gave the nod to Alpha, who pulled Avril into the centre of the plastic sheet.

Jag took a pair of latex gloves from his pocket and pulled them on. He lifted an ornate poker from its mount on the wall and began doing practice swings, swiping it through the air again and again. Avril, now knowing without a shadow of a doubt that she was about to die, fought like hell.

Alpha and Beta held each of her arms high and wide by the wrists as Jag closed in. Then, with one fierce blow, he brought the fire poker down and split her skull. He then swung it wide one more time, this time virtually cracking her face open. Avril dropped like a stone. Alpha and Beta worked quickly, putting a plastic bag over Avril's head and securing it with a draw cord, tight around her neck. They wrapped her body in the plastic sheet and then carried her out of the lounge. Jag got a handkerchief from his pocket and wiped the poker clean of Avril's blood and his own fingerprints, then hung it back on its mount. He stepped back to check that it was straight, then removed the gloves, wrapping them in his bloodstained handkerchief and placed them into his pocket. He turned just as the poker slid to one side, so – with his index finger, he pushed the bottom of the poker a millimetre or two to the left. Perfect.

Jack was shaking as the screen turned to snow for a few seconds. Then it came back to life, showing Avril's en suite.

Avril lay on the floor. The bag on her head was filling with blood. Alpha and Beta were securing their hoods, to make certain that their black clothing was completely covered. Alpha then cut Avril's clothes from her body with a sharp, thin-bladed knife, tossing them to one side until she lay naked. He stuffed her clothes into a plastic bag, as

Beta removed the plastic bag from her head, blood quickly poured out, expanding across the white-tiled floor. Beta leant out of shot, then back in, now holding a small, single-handed electric chainsaw.

The video became snowy again for a moment before it jumped to a short insert of the exterior of the property. The night vision was poorer quality, but it clearly showed Jag hurrying from the house and then driving his car away down the drive.

After another moment of static, the video jumped back to the en suite camera. Now the horror was in full flow as the men hacked at Avril's lifeless torso.

Jack turned to Adam. 'Jesus Christ!'

Adam lifted his hand to indicate that Jack should continue watching. 'One minute more.'

Jack looked back at the screen and immediately realised why the men had left her part-dismembered body without completing the job. They were leaning over her head, saw in hand, when a flash of a red light suddenly illuminated the dark room. This was the moment the greenhouse had exploded. The video ended.

As Jack drew his hand back from the keyboard, it trembled beyond his control. The fury inside him manifested in a physical ball of intense pressure pushing against the inside of his sternum. He felt like he was about to explode. He leapt to his feet and moved quickly to the window, throwing it open and gasping the clean air while his mind replayed the very worst moment he'd just watched . . . not the moment that the poker split Avril's skull, but the moment she realised she was definitely going to die. She'd fought so hard. Jack was filled with such raw anger that, at that moment, he just wanted to kill. He wanted to stop those men from breathing with the same degree of callous disregard and torturous glee they'd shown Avril.

Adam put his mobile away and gave Jack his full attention. 'I think you must be an exceptional policeman, Jack, to muster so much anger on behalf of a woman you don't really know. God, it must be petrifying to be on the wrong side of you.'

Jack became distracted by a fizzing noise, combined with a single high-pitched tone. He glanced back at the video he'd just watched to see the image disintegrating. Jack raced to the laptop shouting, 'No!' as though that could stop his evidence from disappearing. Once the video was wiped from the laptop, Jack glared up at Adam.

'It must be obvious to you by now that I had access to – and am in complete control of – all the video footage from Avril's home,' Adam said. 'It's time now, Jack, I want a 24-hour head start. After which, I'll forward that video to your email account. And this time it won't corrupt and be wiped from existence after it's been watched.'

Jack couldn't contain himself. He charged towards Adam, fierce and uncontrolled. Adam responded by dropping to the floor, sitting on his heels, covering his head with his arms and freezing. 'Get it back!' Jack screamed. 'Get it back!' Jack stood over him, fist in the air, and slowly came back down to reality.

Jack walked backwards across the room until he was far enough away for Adam to dare look up. Adam smiled. 'I think you've got more of your father in you than you'd care to admit. Twenty-four hours, Jack. Once we make this deal, it's all down to trust. I trust you to give me a one-day head start, and you trust me to give you Avril's killers.'

Adam drove Jack on his quad bike, back to the single-track road where he'd been forced to abandon his hired BMW. He then opened the storage hatch at the back of the bike and handed Jack a cardboard tube. 'A gift,' Adam said. 'A thank you.' Adam held out his hand for Jack to shake. 'In the next life, Jack Warr, I have no doubt we'll be friends.'

CHAPTER 42

Adam had then sent a one-word text message from the quad bike as he hurtled back towards his studio:

Now.

This was an escape that had been planned from the moment he arrived, but he'd put it into action when he'd left his studio to take the phone call.

Adam moved quickly yet calmly, stacking all of the artwork into one single pile leaning against the wall nearest the back door. Ten minutes later, he was supervising the removal of his precious cargo. The painting on the easel was the last item to go – an almost finished Modigliani. Adam smirked at the thought of Jack being so close to it, without ever asking to see beneath the muslin. Frederick Jenkins had taught Adam well, and he'd been an exceptional and obsessive student.

From a wall safe Adam removed ten passports – more superb fakes. These were 'fog' passports, created during the genuine online renewal process, using the substitute photograph of a fraudulent applicant. He put all of this into a leather shoulder bag, together with around 300,000 in US dollars, Irish euros and English pounds. The castle that Adam had joked about wasn't a lie at all. It was a modest chateau in the south of France, complete with cannabis farm. And he also had a large apartment in Amsterdam; in fact, it was the penthouse apartment in the very building Anik had visited with Lieutenant Visser. Of course, neither property was in the name of Adam Border.

* * *

Jack got a direct flight back to London, using the one hour and twenty minutes to arrange his thoughts. He had originally assumed that his biggest problem when he returned would be justifying his Irish trip to Ridley. Now he'd have to explain why he let Adam go, for the sake of catching Avril's killer.

He hoped and prayed to any god who'd listen that Adam Border sent the video footage as he'd promised. Without it, everything rested on getting a clear print off the fire poker. It was now clear that the poker found in the en suite off Avril's master bedroom was not the murder weapon at all. Jack replayed in his mind the moment that Jag used one finger to straighten the poker on the wall, and the importance of it gave him palpitations.

Jack had packed very carefully, wrapping the cardboard tube in a plastic bag with the sole intention of preserving Adam Border's fingerprints. Jack would honour the 24-hour head start in order to get the video but, as soon as he had it, he'd make it his mission to find Adam and bring him in.

*　*　*

Jack strode from the airport, knowing that Ridley would be waiting for him. Jack had texted just before his flight took off:

Meet me at the airport. 3.15. I have our killers.

And sure enough there he was, parked in the pick-up area. Jack threw his bag and the cardboard tube into the boot then jumped in the front. 'We need to get to Avril's house, sir. I'll explain everything on the way.'

In the 30-minute drive to Kingston, Ridley didn't utter a single word. He just listened. Jack omitted the conversation he and Adam had had about parents, upbringing, absent fathers, but everything else was relayed in perfect detail.

Once at Avril's house, Ridley got a large evidence bag from the boot of his car and they headed towards the open front door. Arnold Hutchinson was sitting on the third stair up. 'Your call was most intriguing, DCI Ridley. Why are we here?' Whilst Ridley paused to thank Arnold for opening the house at such short notice, Jack continued into the lounge. The poker, like all of the houses' contents, was still in place, the entire property being in limbo during the wills dispute.

* * *

Jack pulled on a pair of nitrile gloves, lifted the poker carefully by the handle and lowered it into the evidence bag. Jack turned to Ridley.

This was currently their only chance of identifying Jag. The video footage would give them facial identification on all of the killers, and it would give them Jag's number plate when he drove away just before the greenhouse explosion – but right now, the poker was the only physical evidence they had. All they needed was a twelve-point match to Mahoney and they had him.

* * *

Jack headed out, followed by Ridley who thanked Hutchinson again for his cooperation.

Jack laid the poker carefully in the boot of Ridley's car. His cheeks were flushed. He was eager to get back to the station and hand the poker over to forensics. 'Go home, Jack.' Ridley was firm: this was an instruction. 'I'll rush the poker through with Angel. Tomorrow, get in early. By then we'll have a name on the print.

And, by midday if Adam's as good as his word, we'll have the video.' Ridley was desperate to clear the decks and take Jack to task over his unforgivable level of insubordination – from going to Ireland, to allowing an art thief to walk away – but, right now, he wanted Avril's killer just as much as Jack did.

* * *

When Jack got home, Maggie was on the sofa with her feet up, a white wine spritzer in her hand and a bowl of crisps balanced between her thighs. Hannah was curled up at the other end of the sofa watching *Peppa Pig* through very tired eyes. She was determined to stay awake, however, as Maggie had told her that Daddy was on his way home.

Jack bundled in through the front door, dropping his bag and the cardboard tube in the hallway. Hannah struggled to her feet, looked over the back of the sofa then bounced up and down on the cushions. 'Peppa! Peppa!' she squealed, which Jack, of course, heard as 'Papa! Papa!' He beamed, landing a huge kiss on her nose. Maggie crossed her legs, making room for Jack to sit in between the two of them. She was presented with a bottle of Tom Ford perfume and Hannah was given a teddy bear wearing a green hat. She wrapped it in her arms and settled back down to watch the television again.

Jack placed the silver Celtic brooch he'd bought for Penny onto the coffee table and leant over Maggie's crossed legs, spilling the precariously balanced bowl of crisps into her crotch. Neither of them cared as he gently kissed her. 'I missed you.'

'You hungry? I waited for you.'

Jack picked up a crisp from between Maggie's legs and ate it. 'So, I see.'

An hour later, Hannah was asleep, Maggie was scrolling through Netflix to find a horror film and Jack was ordering the Chinese takeaway. Penny had been and gone – her yoga started at seven, then she was heading to the pub for a drink with a group from her class. She'd tucked her brooch into the inside pocket of her handbag, so she could show it off later.

As was always the way when watching a film with Maggie, halfway through she worked out the ending, got bored and started talking, despite the fact that Jack was still engrossed.

'You'll never guess what's happened now.' Jack continued watching the film and eating, whilst he listened. He could guess what she was going to say. 'Elliot Wetlock's only gone and resigned. I mean, he's jumped before he could be pushed, I'm guessing, but you should have heard him. He was actually humble. He apologised to everyone for the inconvenience he'd caused by his constant absences and thanked us for our understanding and brilliant work during the pandemic. Then he did this.'

Maggie reached beneath the sofa cushion she was sitting on, and handed Jack the *Evening Standard*, already turned to page five. The headline read: SURGEON ADMITS TO HIS PART IN DAUGHTER'S SUICIDE. It was not what Jack had expected Maggie to tell him. Wetlock had presented himself at Hammersmith police station and asked to speak with the detective in charge of the case. He'd admitted supplying his daughter with barbiturates which, although illegal, he'd done on medical grounds to help her through some very tough times. He claimed to have had no clue that she had been storing them up with the intention of taking her own life.

'What a load of bullshit!' Jack shouted making Hannah stir in her sleep. 'He was keeping her addicted, the sick bastard and, in the end he . . .' Jack was just about to launch into a tirade of abuse about how criminal and perverted it was for a father to stick a diazepam suppository up his own daughter's arse with the intention of killing her, when he stopped himself. Maggie didn't need to know. Not tonight. And not from him.

She agreed that there was definitely something very wrong with Wetlock and his daughter's relationship, but she also clung onto the last remnants of loyalty she felt towards her old mentor. 'He was an exceptional surgeon whose training I'll value forever. Shame he also turned out to be a bloody weirdo. Based on his behaviour in recent months, the hospital breathed a communal sigh of relief that he's gone, if I'm honest.'

Maggie nibbled on the final piece of prawn toast as she got round to asking Jack about his trip to Ireland. What she specifically wanted to know about was the hotel he'd suggested might be nice for a mini honeymoon. Jack left her with the brochure whilst he went upstairs to unpack.

In his office, Jack laid the cardboard tube, still inside the plastic bag, down onto the desk. As he got a pair of nitrile gloves from his desk drawer, he was momentarily distracted by the contents of his rubbish bin. He rustled through screwed-up bits of paper and chocolate wrappers, uncovering a paper pharmacy bag inside which was a receipt for a plastic syringe. Jack found an old lighter and lit the edge of the receipt, then the bag. As each burnt down to his fingers, he placed them into half a cup of cold tea that had been on his desk since before he went to Ireland.

Jack stood in the shadows of the overhanging trees in the far corner of the doctors' car park. He was invisible from every angle so, when Wetlock drove into his parking space which was only yards from the trees, he had no clue that Jack was there. Wetlock got out of his car and, as usual, pushed his wing-mirror in so that it wouldn't get bumped by anyone using the footpath that ran past his driver's side. Angel had loaned her fingerprint kit to Jack on the proviso that he didn't end up asking her to run a set of prints 'off the books'. It was a time-consuming favour and she never got anything in return. Jack had promised. It took him thirty seconds to remove Wetlock's print from the back of the wing-mirror and ten seconds to clean away all of the powder residue.

Jack hadn't given his actions a second thought until he'd seen the headline in the *Evening Standard*. It pissed him off that Wetlock might get away with murder, and Jack decided that he would help Lyle to find enough ex-student doctors to come forwards and give evidence relating to Wetlock's historic drug crimes. Then the death of Tania could be reopened and Wetlock might get the sentence he actually deserved.

But right now Jack needed to refocus on Adam Border.

Jack kept the latex gloves on, and carefully cut the plastic bag from round the cardboard tube, so as not to smudge any fingerprints. Using the tips of his fingers, he pulled the white plastic cap out of the end of the tube and removed the rolled-up canvas scroll from inside.

The rolled canvas measured around fourteen inches by twenty and was frayed along each edge. It was slightly brown with age and small rust-stained holes showed where it had been attached to the original wooden frame. Once fully unrolled, Jack sat back and took in the image of a dark-faced young man with unruly hair. In the bottom right-hand corner was a faint signature in black paint: *A. Giacometti*. As he looked at the painting, Jack's heart pounded in his chest. What exactly had Adam given him? On the reverse of the canvas was a small gallery sticker with faded writing: *La Belle Epoque at Villa Massena, Art Museum Marseilles 1940.*

Jack rolled the canvas back up and searched through the stacks of papers he'd copied from the numerous inventory lists given to him by Arnold Hutchinson and additional information about various artists he'd found for himself on the internet and in the library. The original list of paintings acquired by Frederick Jenkins over his forty years as a collector was hugely impressive and complete with purchase dates, gallery names and provenance details. Of course, now Jack doubted everything he read. They could have been fakes for all he knew.

Van Gogh, Picasso, Warhol . . . then some more unusual names such as Zao Wou-Ki and William de Kooning. There were heavy black pencil rings around a Henri Matisse. Paintings listed often had a 'P' printed beside them and, under 'Pre-Raphaelite' was Rossetti, underlined. Towards the bottom of the list, Jack found what he was looking for. A reference to Giacometti. The painting Jack had just received was apparently part of a collection bought in a silent auction along with a Keith Haring and a Jean Michel Basquiat.

Jack glanced at the rolled canvas sitting on his desk and was certain it had to be a copy. Not that he could tell. But fake or real, what on earth was he supposed to do with it now? And why had Adam given it to him?

As Maggie's slow, cautious footsteps made their way upstairs, Jack knew that she must be carrying Hannah. He slid the canvas into a shallow drawer and decided that he'd research his newly acquired Giacometti properly tomorrow.

* * *

Maggie's 5 a.m. alarm woke them both with the gentle sound of harp music, which got less gentle the more they ignored it.

Jack took charge of the coffee, which was becoming more of a morning habit with each passing day, whilst Maggie got Hannah up and dressed. Maggie was running late – so when she came down with Hannah in her arms saying that she needed the old car as it had the car seat in it, Jack, without thinking, agreed. Maggie was out the door and away by the time he realised that if he intended to drive anywhere today, he'd be going in a pea-green Nissan Micra.

CHAPTER 43

The amount of time Angel spent at crime scenes was nothing compared to the amount of time she spent sat in front of a computer or hunched over a microscope. So, it wasn't unreasonable for Jack to assume that he'd catch her if he wandered into her office unannounced. Angel was in fact trying to unfold a wet piece of paper found in the suit pocket of a man pulled from the canal several hours earlier. Millimetre by millimetre, she was separating the layers and opening the whole thing out into what she hoped would turn out to be a receipt. Jack knew that she knew he was standing behind her, but he didn't disturb her until she finished what she was doing. The delicate job she was currently in the middle of could be make or break for the SIO. So, Jack waited.

Eventually, Angel looked up. 'Bloody bingo. At 1 a.m., he was buying chewy at a garage seven miles upriver from where he was found. And who lives seven miles upriver from where he was found?'

'Your prime suspect?'

'Got it in one.' Angel stood and stretched her spine. 'Simon's got your ID, you know.'

'Yeah, I'm heading there next.' Jack took the now-empty cardboard tube from its carrier bag. 'I need you to lift prints off this, please. One set will be mine, but I made a point of only touching the bottom. In the middle you'll find another set which might match the cigarette butts I gave you. That's it for now.'

Angel said she was glad to help and asked for the case number. Jack just gave her a sparkling smile. She took the cardboard tube and said that it would cost him a Thai takeaway as she was done with helping him for free. He didn't need her to clarify a potential timeframe: she was a fast worker – even with sneaky, off-the-clock favours.

* * *

Jack was the last to arrive in the squad room. He quickly entered Ridley's office and shut the door. Jack didn't need to ask the question.

'The print belongs to Michael Mahoney,' Ridley said. 'But it's only a partial, so it's weak on its own. Mahoney's been "no comment" all the way with the Drugs Squad and his brief is trying to get him bailed. So far not one of the men arrested has named Mahoney or implicated him in any way. This is his mug shot taken over twenty years ago when he was arrested in Leeds for possession – take a look at him, and tell me if he's the man you saw in the videos.'

Ridley pushed the mug shot towards Jack and waited. The young man in the photo had collar-length hair, blonder than Jag's, but he had similar features. Jack hesitated . . . then rushed out into the squad room.

Jack hurried to the whiteboard that still had numerous still-unidentified photographs pinned up. He turned to Laura and clicked his fingers.

'Don't you click your fingers at me, Jack Warr!'

'Sorry, sorry, this is important. The photographs we had pinned up on the board – ones of Avril's early years and the unidentified boy, not her brother or the Dutch guy, the blond kid.' Laura could feel Jack's impatience as she crossed to the banks of files already being logged and listed.

Jack hurried back into Ridley's office with two small black-and-white photographs. 'I might be wrong about this, but we never got to identify this kid.' Jack jabbed his finger down on the image of the small blond boy. 'Adam Border said that Avril had met someone in Leeds when she went back for a funeral, and he was the one she brought into the house . . .'

Ridley put his hand up to interrupt Jack, who hadn't noticed that he was on the phone. Jack placed the two small photographs down beside the mug shot and waited. Ridley thanked the caller and replaced the receiver. 'The Jaguar with the black-tinted windows was bought from their new dealership, posh showrooms by that big Costco store. The buyer had it customised and paid in cash nine months ago. We ran his name and address but it's a dead end. However, we have a pretty good description of him, and to me it could be that big bruiser we're holding – Dave with the tattoos. So, we'll get a warrant to search his house.'

'These bastards are too savvy,' Jack said, shaking his head. 'The Jag will be wiped clean.'

Ridley clenched his fist. 'I'm sick of hearing *no comment, no comment, no* bloody *comment!*'

Jack glanced down at the innocent face of the small blond boy. How does a child like that grow into Mahoney? 'After what Mahoney did, when he cracked open Avril's skull, they're scared, sir. They're all too scared.'

Ridley knew Jack was right. They needed to bring Mahoney down before the men under arrest would start talking. Ridley drew the photographs towards him. It was a real possibility that the boy from Avril's past was Mahoney. But time was ticking.

'Christ, I hope we get the footage from Adam Border, because I've already set the wheels in motion to transfer Mahoney across from Staines. In the meantime, figure out how on earth we can trap him without the videos.'

* * *

Within seconds of Jack settling to his desk, Laura had perched next to his keyboard. 'You look tense. Is that because Ireland wasn't as relaxing as you'd hoped, or because you just arrived in a car that looks like a peeled kiwi? The fruit, not the bird.'

'Both.'

'And, whilst you were over there, I don't suppose you stumbled across the elusive Adam Border, did you?'

Jack smiled and said that Adam Border's day would come, and much sooner than he imagined, but, for now, they'd just found evidence that Michael Mahoney was the man who struck the first blow in Avril Jenkins' murder.

'What evidence? Where from?'

Jack started accessing Mahoney's arrest record. 'He's being transferred for interview as we speak, Laura. Let me prep, OK. I'll explain everything when I've got more head space.'

Laura slinked away, whilst Jack tried to work out how he was going to break a fearless man with a mob of high-powered lawyers in his back pocket and a queue of people willing to lie for him, without the film footage from Adam.

Jack stared at his computer screen and the details from Mahoney's one and only arrest. From the date, he calculated that Mahoney would have been twenty-one years old, so younger than Avril by about ten years. He kept looking at the photographs he had taken from Ridley's office. Laura was leaning over his shoulder. When she saw the comparison Jack was making, she immediately saw the likeness too. 'Oh my God, the young blond kid is Mahoney!'

'He and Avril were kids together,' Jack said. Laura perched on his desk and asked how that information helped them. Jack sighed and shook his head. 'I don't know. Leverage? We're grasping at straws.' Jack glanced at the clock on the wall. The 24-hour head start was ticking down, and they'd soon know if Adam Border was an honourable thief.

* * *

The cavalcade bringing in Mahoney entered the building an hour before Jack and Ridley were allowed anywhere near him, because he was consulting with his banks of solicitors. Steve Lewis had insisted on being the one to escort him across and, whilst they waited, he insisted on giving Ridley a few tips.

'This is a man who preps his defence months in advance, Simon. He's got alibis coming out of his arse, for dates I've not even asked him about yet. He's fearless. If you want my advice . . .'

'Steve . . .' Ridley rubbed his brow, where he could feel the pressure building, 'just let me focus. In silence preferably.'

Steve quickly pointed out that he could insist on sitting in on the interview. Ridley had had enough.

'You won't, though, Steve, will you? Because you haven't got the intuition or the stamina to interview a murder suspect for several hours. Starting slow and gaining their trust. Giving them the time and space to back themselves into a corner before you pull the rug and hit them with the facts that contradict every word they just said on tape. You won't sit in on the interview because you have the patience of a small child. Would you like to report me and lose this murderer, or would you like to shut the fuck up?'

Ridley then dropped into a chair with his back to the room. If there were any consequences from his outburst, he'd tackle them *after* they'd secured their murder conviction.

* * *

Jack had a brief meeting with Ridley before Ridley went into the interview room, armed with the photographs and some notes made by Jack. Ridley had made the decision to lead. Jack was disappointed, but his priority had to be getting the video footage from Adam

As Ridley entered the interview room, Jack entered the observation room where he could watch live through the two-way mirror, as well as watch either of the two cameras currently filming Mahoney.

Mahoney looked confident. He'd been allowed to shave and put on a change of clothes, choosing a grey cashmere sweater and cord trousers.

Two male officers joined Jack in the observation room – they had been assigned to be in the interview room with Ridley, but he'd requested that they step out. Jack stared at Mahoney. It was definitely him! The man who had swung the poker with such enthusiasm down onto Avril Jenkins' skull. He was calm, expressionless and confident that they had nothing on him.

Jack watched Ridley as he laced his fingers on top of the file in front of him. 'Go on, sir,' Jack whispered. 'Get the bastard.'

After a lengthy pause, Ridley read Mahoney his rights and then got straight down to the questions, omitting any formalities of explaining that Mahoney could ask for a break or refreshments at regular intervals and could refrain from answering any questions if he so wished. Mahoney was an old hand at this, so didn't need telling. And besides, Ridley had already been given a statement from Mahoney's solicitor, Nathaniel Barker, that his response would be 'no comment' to all questions.

'When did you first meet Avril Jenkins?' Ridley asked, opening the file on the table in front of him. 'In your interviews over in Staines, your solicitor, Mr Barker, read out a statement claiming that you don't know Avril Jenkins, nor have you ever been to 27

Woodridge Place in Kingston.' Ridley paused. 'What about Avril Summers? When did you meet her?'

For a split second, Mahoney's intake of breath paused, before quickly resuming. It was a fleeting involuntary response in an otherwise perfect act.

In the observation room, Laura had joined Jack. Neither thought Mahoney was going to speak a single word today; the best they were hoping for was that his refusal to speak turned out to be equally as damning.

In the same relaxed, informal tone of voice, Ridley continued. 'It's been suggested that you have dozens of bolt-holes similar to Woodridge Place scattered across London. Possibly hundreds across the UK. And the same in Europe. I don't know: they're not connected to my case. I assume that part of your confidence in police interviews, Mr Mahoney, comes from the fact that you can't be forensically linked to any of those properties. I assume you've not even been to them. So, why did you go to Avril's house?'

Nothing from Mahoney.

'Had she changed much since the last time you saw her? In Leeds, I mean.'

Mahoney pushed himself back in his seat and crossed his legs. It was a small, natural movement, but now his relaxed disposition had gone, replaced with a more defensive stance. Mahoney was far from crumbling, but he was certainly getting uncomfortable.

Barker felt the need to justify his presence. 'My client has already stated that he does not know Avril Jenkins.'

'I know what your client has stated, but he's lying. Object to that if you like, but it's not speculation, it's a statement of fact.'

From the file, Ridley removed the old photographs that had been pinned to the whiteboard in the squad room. Images of Avril and a series of friends playing in back streets, playgrounds and fields, through summer and winter. He laid them on the table one by one, directly in Mahoney's eyeline so there was no way of him avoiding them. Ridley pointed to the teenage Avril, identifying her in each image. Then he pointed to the small blond boy. 'This is you. Facial recognition says it's you.'

Jack and Laura looked at each other. 'He's certainly a chancer!' Laura grinned.

'He's a bullshitter,' Jack corrected her. 'It's fascinating watching him working, though.'

Ridley had used the words 'facial recognition' carefully. They implied, but did not state, that he was referring to computer software, whereas in truth, he'd had no time to check the photographs properly. Like Jack, he was working on a hunch. But the likeness between the small blond boy and Mahoney was undeniable. Ridley placed the old mug shot of Mahoney onto the table, tapping it with his finger. Mahoney gritted his teeth but remained silent.

'When you bumped into her again, Michael, what did you think?'

Mahoney placed his hand flat on top of all the photographs. Barker was now faintly grimacing at the thought of the secrets Mahoney might be about to give away.

'It must have been very interesting when you met Avril more recently and discovered she was a wealthy widow.'

Mahoney's cheek muscles twitched almost imperceptibly.

In the observation room, Jack instructed the two uniformed officers to go and stand outside the interview room as Mahoney became visibly more tense. Ridley checked his watch. Eleven forty a.m. – the video footage that Adam had promised to send should be arriving shortly.

'Did she remember you, Michael? I mean, she wouldn't remember you in the same fond way that you remembered her, but did she remember you at all? Or did you have to introduce yourself? Did you finally make advances towards her?'

This made Mahoney look up and, for the first time, they locked eyes. Mahoney was clearly angry.

Ridley tapped the photograph of the young Mahoney looking at Avril with adoration. 'You look as if you were infatuated back then. So, tell me Michael, if you once loved Avril Summers, why did you kill her?'

Barker quickly stepped in, for fear of what Mahoney might say or do. 'Will you be presenting actual evidence at any stage, DCI Ridley?'

Ridley ignored the question and focussed completely on Mahoney. 'Mr Mahoney, do you still maintain that you never entered Avril Jenkins' home?' Mahoney's nostril's flared as he desperately tried to think what Ridley was working up to. 'Were you ever inside 27 Woodridge Place, Kingston?'

Again, Barker stepped in to protect his client. 'Mr Mahoney has already answered that question.'

'I'm asking him again because he's mistaken.' Ridley sat forwards, well within Mahoney's long reach. 'You know what I think, Michael? I think you knew she was going to die that night and you just couldn't stay away.'

Barker tried to butt in, complaining about fishing trips and unfounded speculation, but both Mahoney and Ridley ignored him. Mahoney now stared, dead-eyed, unblinking, allowing his anger to build. This is what Ridley was banking on. If he could tip Mahoney beyond the point of no return, they'd have him.

'I think you sent your men to kill her, then thought, *Fuck this, I'm gonna do it myself.* What did she do, Michael? Was she pissing you off by reporting thefts to the local police – patrol cars and uniforms coming and going, and you with a mega delivery ready for distribution? She was playing with fire. Playing with *you*! Didn't she know who you are now? Or did she still see that little blond boy? No respect. Is that why you picked up that poker and shattered her skull?'

Mahoney raised both his fists high above his head and slammed them down onto the desk, sending the photographs bouncing into the air. Barker jumped almost as high out of his chair.

Jack stood in the open doorway of the observation room, from where he could still watch Ridley. In the corridor, the two uniformed officers were like coiled springs, waiting for his signal to go in. He held a hand up – Ridley wasn't done yet.

'No fucking comment, you bastard, NO COMMENT!' Mahoney roared. His white-knuckled fists were pressed hard against the desk, as he tried to stop himself from lashing out.

Ridley gestured for Barker to sit down. Then he collected the photographs and replaced them in the folder.

'Mr Mahoney, you left one fingerprint in her home. The home you deny ever being inside of. We matched that one print to the prints in your file.'

Ridley watched Mahoney open his fists and spread his fingers and then clasp them together as he retained control of his temper.

'No comment.'

* * *

Jack perched on the windowsill watching Ridley make two decaf coffees. 'His outburst, plus the partial on the poker, plus the video should be enough. It means we've got him for another forty-eight hours, not that I think he'll say anything else.'

Jack sipped his coffee, grimaced and threw Ridley a filthy look. Ridley repeated the health benefits of decaf coffee and said it would do Jack the world of good to detox – then they both froze as Jack's mobile pinged and an email landed. They held their breath for the few seconds it took to open.

'Do you want two-for-one vitamin supplements from Holland & Barrett?' Jack asked.

Ridley headed for his desk and slumped into his chair. 'Fuck's sake.' The waiting was killing them both.

* * *

By 12.50, Jack's mobile had pinged another seven times. None of the emails were from Adam Border. He was now around an hour late in delivering on his promise but while Ridley was losing faith, Jack was still sure that Adam would be true to his word. He *had* to be. Three more insignificant emails landed. And by now the tension was mounting. Mahoney's brief had been demanding an explanation as to why their interview had been terminated without Ridley sharing any evidence regarding an incriminating fingerprint. He was told that they would be served refreshments and must remain in the interview room or Mr Mahoney could be taken to the cells to wait if he preferred.

Laura had remained in the observation room, watching their suspect become more and more angry, and demanding answers from his brief. Every time Mahoney moved from his seat, one or both officers told him to sit back down. He clearly hated being told what to do. He was almost ready to explode.

Ridley was beside himself, pacing the carpet. And Jack was sweating now.

Then, at 1.05, a video link arrived from an unknown email address. Jack clicked the link and a still image appeared.

Avril sat in the middle of the sofa in her front room. Her knees were clamped together, her fingers clenched on her lap . . .

Jack hurried to his desk to collect his iPad, then propped it on the desk in front of Ridley. 'I don't need to watch it again.' And with those words, Jack left Ridley to it, closing the door behind him.

Jack sat at his desk, sipping his vile coffee, watching Ridley's every move via the window in his office door. He could even see the reaction from Ridley when the video turned to snow and then he saw him concentrate as it jumped to the second video from inside Avril's en suite.

* * *

Inside his office, Ridley stared at the screen, motionless, for a good few minutes after the video ended. He then pushed his chair back, very slowly made himself another cup of coffee and retook his seat. He hovered his hand over the play button, took a deep breath and watched the whole thing again. Jack watched, his nerves on edge, but seeing Ridley replay the video told him for certain that Adam had also been true to his word about the video not corrupting after being watched once.

At that moment, Angel appeared in the squad-room doorway holding the cardboard tube in its carrier bag. Jack jumped up to meet her. 'There's one print on this – and it's yours.'

'That can't be right, I saw him touch it . . .' Jack's words faded to nothing. He knew Angel hadn't made a mistake – which meant that he had. Angel wished him luck with whatever he was up to, then left him to his thoughts.

Jack stepped into the corridor and hurried into the gents' toilet. He quickly called the local police station in Killarney and asked them to check the name Adam Border against the art studio's location. The last street name he'd noted was Runda Street, but the track that led to the studio itself had had no signage. He described the route taken from his hotel as best he could and said that it was also a cannabis farm. The officer he spoke to said he'd get back to Jack as soon as he had news.

Jack walked to the canteen hoping a change of scenery might help him think more clearly. And because he needed a coffee with caffeine in it.

He stared down into the car park at the awful pea-green Nissan, turning recent memories over and over in his mind. How could the cardboard tube have no prints on it when Adam had handed it to him?

He closed his eyes and tried to find the memory he needed.

When Adam left the studio to take a call, Jack had used the time to discreetly explore the studio. It was an intriguing space and – right in the centre – was the tantalising canvas hidden beneath a muslin cloth. Jack remembered how he had glanced at the door Adam had left through – nothing – he had then moved towards the easel, reached out his hand and caught the muslin between his fingertips. This was the moment he heard Adam's voice moving closer. Jack had dropped his hand and by the time Adam returned Jack was scanning the painting materials on the floor beneath the easel – brushes, paints, artists' glue, palette knives, pots . . .

'Glue.' Jack opened his eyes and clenched his jaw. 'Fucking artists' glue.' He didn't know for certain, but he now speculated that Adam could have used glue on his fingertips to level his prints and make them undetectable. It would have been easy to prepare. He knew Jack was coming because Greg had told him.

* * *

Ten minutes passed and Jack's mobile didn't ring. Frustration, humiliation and sheer bloody fury made him want to call the Killarney Garda back and demand to know what the hold-up was before he realised how unreasonable he was being. Jack headed back to the squad room to see if Ridley had finished watching the video for a second time.

As Jack headed for his desk, he could see that Ridley was now in the company of a thick-set man in a cheap grey suit, holding a brown paper bag. Jack glanced at Laura. 'He's a DCI from Hammersmith.

Been here a couple of times about Tania's suicide.' Laura drew quota-
tion marks in the air around the word 'suicide'. 'Did you read yesterday's paper?' Jack nodded as he eyed Ridley's office. Laura perched on
the edge of his desk again. 'Up. Her. Arse. Her own dad. He claimed
that he was trying to calm her down, unaware of what she'd already
taken. I mean . . .'

Jack's mobile rang, and Laura's dissection of the Wetlock case
faded into a low hum. The Killarney Garda Jack had spoken to earlier
was now calling him back. 'We've got no Adam Border connected
to any cannabis farm or artist's studio in Killarney. I sent a boy to
the only studio building you could have been referring to, but it was
empty. We do get artists using it as a retreat in the summer, but it
looked like there'd been no one there this year.'

Jack interrupted him, asking if there were any flowering plant
baskets hanging by the studio door.

'No, nothing hanging up, no plants, no property, no furniture,
no personal items. If you want the place to have a full going-over,
SOCO and all, make it official and I'll oversee it myself.'

Jack knew that if the cardboard tube didn't have Adam's prints
on it, then neither would anything else. He thanked the Garda for
his help and hung up.

Jack was gripping his mobile tightly in his fist to stop himself
from exhibiting any outward signs of the turmoil he was feeling
inside. when Ridley summoned him into his office.

Jack was surprised that Ridley was now alone. He must have
missed the departure of the Hammersmith DCI whilst he was
seething at being outsmarted by a bloody drug-smuggling art thief.

Ridley gestured for Jack to sit down. 'Well, that's one of the
worst things I've ever had to watch. But when it's played in court,
it'll turn the stomachs of the jury, too, and once we submit the

partial fingerprint, they'll associate it with Mahoney. So let me give you a quick catch-up on a few loose ends. We just found the Jaguar in Dave's garage in Leeds. It's being towed in by forensics, and he's asked for a solicitor. So he's not as stupid as he looks.'

'Well, no, he can't possibly be.' Jack's flippant remark was just what they both needed after the day they'd had so far.

'I reckon,' Ridley continued, 'with Mahoney being charged with Avril's murder, the Drug Squad have lost him. Their hope of striking a deal with him to name names, being a super grass . . . gone. He's getting life – no deals – so why cooperate? His men, however, who've been "no comment" throughout, especially those who feature on the video, will open the floodgates to save themselves.' Ridley rocked back in his seat. 'There's one more thing that needs discussing.'

Jack sat in silence assuming that, any second now, he'd have to explain how he traced Adam Border across forbidden Ireland and made the deal to give him 24 hours in exchange for the video.

Ridley unwrapped a clear mint, twisting the wrapper in his fingers before he continued.

'I've had a number of conversations with that DCI from Hammersmith over the past few weeks because he wanted my opinion on you – as a man, not as an officer – in relation to the death of Tania Wetlock.' Ridley's change of subject was a welcome surprise for Jack.

'I should have told him to get lost, but I went by the rules and put you on leave. Apologies.' Ridley put his hands in his lap. 'You had a meeting with their DC Lyle. He said that with your direction they brought in Elliot Wetlock for questioning. He subsequently admitted that he'd supplied his daughter with barbiturates, allegedly to help manage her anxiety. He also admitted that on the night of her death he administered rectal diazepam, having given it before for insomnia. His defence is that he had no knowledge of what she'd taken earlier that day, so he had no way of knowing that it would become a lethal cocktail. They'll go for manslaughter. Until you pointed Lyle in the right direction, they were going for suicide.'

Ridley leant sideways and reached down for a brown paper bag. He took out a bottle of Jameson's and pushed it across the desk towards Jack. 'They're cheapskates over there, but the sentiment is the same.'

'Shall we?' Jack took the bottle, then amended his question. '*Can you?*' Ridley said that while Jack was in Ireland he'd been told that his cancer was in remission. 'That's the best news I've heard all day, sir. Congratulations.'

'Thank you. I have to say, facing Mahoney really got the adrenaline going! I've missed that.' Ridley glanced at Jack's laptop. 'This is going to be one of the most horrific evidence disclosures I've ever done. And, tomorrow, I'll have to bring in Steve's team to explain how we got it. I plan to say that it was delivered anonymously.' Ridley looked directly at Jack and waited for a response, but he remained silent. 'I want you in my office at eight for a full and frank disclosure of what went on between you and Adam Border. I want to know everything, Jack. Then, together, we'll decide what leaves this room.' Ridley nodded to the bottle of in Jack's hand. 'Just the one, for now. Then let's go and charge Mahoney and get him locked up.'

As Jack poured two whiskies, he thought of Adam, and remembered talking to Julia – her astute words now meant more than they had at the time.

'*We got out Jack, me and you. But it leaves scars. My scars draw me to kids like these . . . your scars draw you to people like your missing man. We know them because we're seconds away from being them.'*

Jack knew he would have to think very carefully about what he was going to tell Ridley and what, for self-preservation, he would never tell a soul.

CHAPTER 44

The observation room was full of those allowed to witness their suspect being charged. Michael Mahoney was still in the interview room with a half-eaten ham sandwich and a plastic cup of cold tea in front of him, looking furious. The two male officers remained at the ready.

Ridley was waiting outside the interview room with Barker who was demanding to know why they'd been kept waiting for so long. 'Apologies for the delay,' Ridley said calmly, 'but further evidence has come to our attention, namely video footage recovered from inside the victim's property. It implicates him directly in her murder.' Barker demanded to see the footage before anything else was allowed to happen, but Ridley refused. 'The first thing that's going to happen, Mr Barker, is that your client is going to be charged with murder.'

In the observation room, as they waited for Ridley and Barker to enter, Jack leant against the glass. He'd been so impressed by Ridley today and couldn't wait for his defining moment. His interrogation had been perfect, he was in remission from his cancer and he was about to charge their suspect. Ridley hadn't lost his touch at all, he'd just been knocked off kilter for a while by one of the worst enemies anyone can face. But now he was back.

Ridley stood in front of Mahoney. He gave a nod to the officers to stand either side of the prisoner, and then tapped his right wrist to indicate he wanted the cuffs ready. 'Michael Mahoney, I'm charging you with the murder of Avril Jenkins . . .'

In a flash, Mahoney's rage exploded. He kicked his chair across the room and reached over the table in an attempt to lash out at

Ridley. The two guards acted fast, grabbing Mahoney's head and ramming his face down onto the table, while his arms were pulled behind him and the cuffs put on. Ridley calmly finished charging Mahoney, as he was hauled to his feet. Mahoney screamed and struggled, swearing at his terrified lawyer.

Jack took a long, deep breath. What must have been going through Avril's mind as she faced this monster? They could all hear him screaming awful threats as he was taken to the cells – that he would kill their children and families, then he'd kill every one of them.

Jack did not wait to congratulate Ridley – he just wanted to get home. He was exhausted. It had been a very long, hard day to deal with, and he needed to be with his family.

* * *

Jack sat on the sofa watching Hannah charge round and round him. Each time she came into view and saw her daddy, she screamed with excitement and each time she disappeared round the back she panted with the sheer anticipation of seeing him again. It was a far more interesting game for Hannah than it was for Jack so, on one lap of the sofa, as soon as she'd run out of view, he jumped up and hid behind an armchair. When Hannah emerged, the sight of an empty seat threw her into an instant panic, and she burst into tears.

Jack quickly crawled out of his hiding place and scooped her into his arms. 'It's OK, lovely girl, Daddy's here.' She settled quickly but didn't want to play the game again. Jack realised how fragile Hannah's little world was and how important his place in it.

* * *

Much later that evening, when all of the Warr ladies were in bed, Jack sat in his office, too wired to go to sleep. Instead, to take his mind off what had gone down at the station, he googled Giacometti. He was a Swiss artist who was born in 1901 and died in 1966. It seemed that for much of his life he lived in squalor, whilst working at fever pitch to create. In 1932, a bronze sculpture entitled *Woman with her Throat Cut* received notoriety for its explicitly horrific connotations. It reminded Jack of the hideous crime scene photographs showing Avril Jenkins with her head almost severed.

So much of what he was reading about brought back the emotion of everything that had surrounded Jack in recent weeks. *Hands Holding the Void . . . Invisible Object.* In one interview, Giacometti had been asked by someone called Genet why he treated men and women so differently. He'd said, 'Women seemed naturally more distant.' Even this quote made Jack recall how Adam had described his own mother as being unloving towards him and choosing fleeting partners above a son who could have truly loved her if she'd let him. Instead, she chose to deny his very existence.

An hour into his quiet research, Jack came across an article relating to a major fraud connected to Giacometti. A court case had been brought against a German gang accused of knowingly attempting to put a forged sculpture onto the market. In 2009, a Swiss auction house tried to sell it for $5.5 million, but this was brought to an abrupt end when an expert exposed it as a forgery. The subsequent court case was compared to an earlier one surrounding a master art forger, Wolfgang Beltracchi. Jack recalled that Adam had casually mentioned that name when he sarcastically scrolled through a list of men who could possibly have been his father. So, Adam must have known Beltracchi after his release from prison. Making him the first of two accomplished art forgers to play a role in Adam's life.

With three-quarters of a bottle of Jameson's to keep him company, Jack searched for the painting Adam had given him. He scrolled through page after page of Giacometti's work, until he found the painting that was currently unrolled on the desk next to him. This particular painting was of Giacometti's brother. They were known for their similarities – not necessarily in appearance, but in character. On the canvas, with their souls on display beneath dark, hooded eyes, they were clearly connected.

The painting was dark and ugly and moody . . . and Jack loved it. He wondered why Adam had chosen this particular painting as his gift.

Jack heard his bedroom door open and assumed that Maggie was on her way to the bathroom. Instead, she opened his office door and was about to ask when he planned on coming to bed, when she saw the painting. 'Good God, Jack, that's awful. Did you buy it in Ireland?' Maggie rubbed her tired eyes. 'Looks like you, if you'd spent twenty years living rough.'

'What if I told you it could be worth a lot of money?'

'I wouldn't believe you.' Maggie leant over Jack's shoulder and kept looking at the painting to see if it might get a little easier on the eye. 'You chose a lovely hotel, though.'

Jack explained that he would have liked to take her back to St Lucia but, seeing as that was beyond their budget right now, he wanted to find something nice closer to home.

'I don't care about fancy holidays, really,' Maggie said. 'Hannah's going to need a playroom and a big girl's bed soon, so I think we should just be careful for a while. Unless that monstrosity really is worth a lot of money. Then St Lucia would be lovely.' Maggie gently kissed Jack on the neck. Her lips made him tingle. 'Don't be long.' Maggie paused just inside the door to Jack's office. 'By the way, did you ever track down that man you were looking for? Adam something.'

Jack shrugged as if he had all the time in the world. 'Not yet.'

Maggie kissed him again, yawned and headed back to bed.

He gazed down at the painting. What Jack felt now was that Adam wasn't his nemesis, as he'd assumed for the past several weeks – he was a warning. He was the man Jack could have been if his birth mother had lived longer. And Jack was the man Adam could have been if his birth mother had died sooner.

Jack felt in his soul that the Giacometti in front of him was not a copy, but the original. Because that's exactly the sort of thing that Adam would do. He would give a painting by a brother, for a brother – both dark and troubled men, bound by an inexplicable loyalty.

He knew that in the morning when Ridley expected a full and detailed explanation of exactly what had taken place in Ireland, the painting would remain a secret.

He also knew – though he could never admit it – that he was looking forward to the day that he and Adam would meet again.

Acknowledgements

I would like to thank all the staff at my publisher, Bonnier Books, with special thanks to Kate Parkin, Bill Massey, Ben Willis, Ciara Corrigan, Nikki Mander, Blake Brooks, Nick Stearn and Ruth Logan. You all do such incredible work publishing my books, I'm so pleased to be part of the Bonnier family.

Thank you to my team at La Plante Global, Nigel Stoneman, Tory MacDonald and Cass Sutherland. Special thanks to Debbie Owen for all her help with her excellent research and advice.

In Australia and New Zealand, my thanks go to the team at Allen and Unwin, and in South Africa, to all the staff at Jonathan Ball. I do hope to be able to visit you soon.

In Ireland, many thanks to Simon Hess and Declan Heeney for all their hard work in selling and publicising my books. I've missed coming to Ireland, and I'm looking forward to having a drink with you all at The Shelbourne very soon.

To all the booksellers and retailers, reviewers and bloggers who stock, read, review and promote my books, thank you again for your support, time and words. You are all amazing, and I'm very grateful.

Thank you to my readers, who keep in touch via my social media and who I have met on Facebook Live in the past two years. I can't believe technology has enabled me to reach out to you, I have enjoyed it immensely and hope you have too.

ENTER THE WORLD OF

Lynda La Plante

ALL THE LATEST NEWS FROM
THE QUEEN OF CRIME DRAMA

DISCOVER THE THRILLING TRUE
STORIES BEHIND THE BOOKS

ENJOY EXCLUSIVE CONTENT
AND OPPORTUNITIES

JOIN THE READERS' CLUB TODAY AT
WWW.LYNDALAPLANTE.COM

Dear Reader,

Thank you very much for picking up *Vanished*, the third book in the DC Jack Warr series. I hope you enjoyed reading the book as much as I enjoyed writing it.

In *Vanished*, Jack must try and solve his most complex case to date, involving a double homicide, an international drugs operation, and art theft. But what happens when the prime suspect – and the person who appears to tie these crimes together – seems to have disappeared without a trace? As Jack becomes ever more desperate to find the elusive Adam Border, he must decide how far he is willing to go, and what lines he is willing to cross, to find answers. I find Jack a fascinating character to explore, as he navigates his duty as a policeman to operate within the law, and his burning desire to do whatever it takes to ensure justice is done.

If you enjoyed *Vanished*, then please do keep an eye out for news about the next book in the series, which will be coming soon. And in the meantime, later this year sees the publication of the next book in my Jane Tennison series, which I am very excited to share more news about soon.

If you want to catch up on Jack Warr's story so far, the first two books in the series, *Buried* and *Judas Horse*, are available now. And if you would like to delve into the Tennison series, the first seven novels – *Tennison, Hidden Killers, Good Friday, Murder Mile, The Dirty Dozen, Blunt Force* and *Unholy Murder* – are all available to buy in paperback, ebook and audio. I've been so pleased by the response I've had from the many readers who have been curious about the beginnings of Jane's police career. It's been great fun for me to explore how she became the woman we know in middle and later life from the *Prime Suspect* series.

If you would like more information on what I'm working on, about the Jane Tennison thriller series or the new series featuring

Jack Warr, you can visit **www.bit.ly/LyndaLaPlanteClub** where you can join my Readers' Club. It only takes a few moments to sign up, there are no catches or costs, and new members will automatically receive an exclusive message from me. Bonnier Books UK will keep your data private and confidential, and it will never be passed on to a third party. We won't spam you with loads of emails, just get in touch now and again with news about my books, and you can unsubscribe any time you want. And if you would like to get involved in a wider conversation about my books, please do review *Vanished* on Amazon, on Goodreads, on any other e-store, on your own blog and social media accounts, or talk about it with friends, family or reader groups! Sharing your thoughts helps other readers, and I always enjoy hearing about what people experience from my writing.

With many thanks again for reading *Vanished*, and I hope you'll return for the next in the series.

With my very best wishes,

Lynda

TENNISON
from the very beginning

TENNISON

HIDDEN KILLERS

GOOD FRIDAY

MURDER MILE

THE DIRTY DOZEN

BLUNT FORCE

and

UNHOLY MURDER

THE THRILLING NEW SERIES FROM THE QUEEN OF CRIME DRAMA

Lynda La Plante

IT'S TIME TO MEET DETECTIVE JACK WARR . . .
OUT NOW